SWEET HOPE

MARY BUCCI BUSH

SWEET HOPE

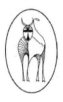

GUERNICA

TORONTO • BUFFALO • BERKELEY• LANCASTER (U.K.)
2011

Michael Mirolla, general editor
Lindsay Brown, editor
David Moratto, interior book design
Guernica Editions Inc.
P.O. Box 117, Station P, Toronto (ON), Canada M5S 2S6
2250 Military Road, Tonawanda, N.Y. 14150-6000 U.S.A.

Distributors:
University of Toronto Press Distribution,
5201 Dufferin Street, Toronto (ON), Canada M3H 5T8
Gazelle Book Services, White Cross Mills, High Town,
Lancaster LA1 4XS U.K.
Small Press Distribution, 1341 Seventh St., Berkeley, CA 94710-1409 U.S.A.

First edition.
Printed in Canada.

Legal Deposit – Fourth Quarter
Library of Congress Catalog Card Number: 2011925125
Library and Archives Canada Cataloguing in Publication
Bush, Mary Bucci
Sweet hope / Mary Bucci Bush.
(Prose series ; 91)
ISBN 978-1-55071-342-8
I. Title.
PS3552.U8215S84 2011 813'.6 C2011-902156-0

To my grandmother, Pasquina Fratini Galavotti.
You gave me the stories.

My great–grandparents Nazzareno and Maddalena (Spaccarelli)
Fratini and their four children: Marietta (Aunt Mary),
Pasquina (Granny), Giuliana (Aunt Julia),
and Guerino (Uncle Germany).

And all the inhabitants of Sunnyside Plantation, Italian and
African American, whose voices were never heard
and whose stories were never told.

PROLOGUE

ITALY was a dried–up fig, all leather and seed, hard and bitter on your tongue.

No. Italy is a wall of stone, they told each other, and everywhere you turn you walk into stone, hit your head against a rock, knock yourself out.

Impossible to make a living anymore. You fish to put food on your table, but who buys the fish? If you have wood to build a cart, who has money to buy the cart? The tobacco factory is sending people away. The fishery, practically closed down. And things only getting worse. The children have no life to look forward to if they can't even get a decent meal, a dry roof, a suit of clothes to wear.

But we're not starving, some said. Not like in the south. And even if we're lean, we're not dying from hunger. Not yet.

But what about the Antonellis? Didn't they lose everything, and two of them dead besides?

What about the Gregantis losing their land? Their fishing boat? Sending a child here, another there to live?

They said many things. They had many ways of saying the same thing, but all the ways came back to a single meaning: the children.

It was for the children that they left Italy and came to this place.

CHAPTER 1

Saving Tobe

October 1901

THE wagon rattled along the rutted dirt road, churning clouds of yellow dust behind it. Serafin drove, with his friend Lazzaro beside him and their families hunched in back amidst rakes and pitchforks and baling wire and jugs of drinking water.

"You're doing good," Lazzaro told him. He'd rented the wagon and was letting Serafin get a feel for driving.

They passed a family of Italians close to the road, several adults and a brood of children, their faces gaunt and sallow.

"You kids be careful when you drink the water," Serafin called to his children. "Amalia, make sure you run the water through the cloth first before you drink it."

The cloth turned brown when they strained the water.

The two women and the children looked at the jugs of water sloshing next to them, silty-brown, something you would throw out if you were back home — on your tomato plants or chard maybe, or against a tree. Fiorenza's old mother, La Vecchia, hummed to herself as she reached out to touch the cloud of dust trailing the wagon. Serafin's youngest daughter Isola watched the cloud and the old lady's hand and the space between the two that never grew smaller.

"If we had a damn barrel, we could haul water from the lake," Lazzaro said. "The lake water's not so bad."

It was a horseshoe lake, west of the river and a mile from their homes, whose southern tip curved back toward the river and dwindled into a little bayou not far from the company store and office. There was water everywhere, water you never saw. In the day the air smelled of dust, or the pungent, drying cotton plants and the stink of mule hides and dung. But at night the river and lake and swamps rose into the air, filling it with the smell of the ancient river mud and the swamp bottoms and the lush wet plants that grew tangled at the edge of the lapping lake.

They reached a crossroads, the levee rising ahead of them. On one corner stood a row of managers' houses with a big garden and a barn and fence for the mules and horses. They could hear the clanging of the gin mill near the two tall oak trees, and smell the wood burning for the boiler. Smoke puffed above the trees, mixing with the dust and the floating cotton lint stirred up by wagons on their way to the gin and back. Men shouted to each other above the noise of machines and mules and horses. Dozens of people worked here, the ragged black people and a few Italians, and now and then a pale clerk or ruddy overseer, well–fed and healthy and dressed in unsoiled clothes.

Lazzaro directed Serafin down the road that ran alongside the levee, past the mule yard and pigpen, beyond the hay barn and the lumber mill that was now silent. They passed the building that rumor said would be turned into a church for them — if the company ever sent for the Italian priest they had promised. So far the Italians had to settle for the *bianco americano* who came to say Sunday Mass from the village across the lake — that is, when he wasn't late or didn't forget altogether.

A dozen dairy and beef cows mingled in the tall lush grass along the levee. Some stood on the dirt road atop the levee while others paused on the banks, chewing with bored expressions or nuzzling through the grass that grew up to their shoulders. All livestock for the company; not for tenants or sharecroppers.

Serafin steered them into a field of mowed grass between the road and levee where the Halls and another black family were raking hay into bundles.

The Pascala children stared at the Americans: two of the Hall children and a brood of scrawny *neri* children who looked like weather-beaten fence posts, the same as their parents. Fancy Hall wore a faded sack dress that hung below her knees. Her head was tied up in a rag that might have been blue at one time. They all wore wide brimmed hats against the sun.

Step Hall motioned for the Italians to get down, and the others cast sideways glances, looking them over without much interest. He hoped he wasn't making a mistake giving them work. The two men were all right — and the young one's wife and her old mother. They'd arrived early summer, too late to make a crop, but they worked hard.

Serafin's wife was another matter. She'd arrived on her own with the three children just a week before, and when Step dropped them off at their cabin, she screamed at Step to come back and get her, and at her husband to take her home. At least he figured that's what she was saying. The next day she dressed herself and the kids in their Sunday clothes and took them out in the middle of a dusty cotton field like that, refusing to pick, cursing her husband, humiliating him. And the man stood there with dog eyes, taking it. The children stupefied and frightened. The oldest girl, pretty and dressed in a flower-brimmed hat and spit-shined shoes, fell to the ground and wet herself when Horton and his sidekick rode by shooting their rifles at ducks. He'd seen a lot of things, but he'd never seen anything like the Pascala family. At least they'd finally put away their Sunday clothes.

Step showed Serafin and Lazzaro how to rake the hay into bundles so the cut ends all faced one direction, and then how to tie them together. Then he pointed out the bales that were ready for loading on the wagon.

Fancy cast Step a look, as if to say, "This the one you told me about?" She handed Amalia a rake, and the woman stood there holding it.

Dry as it was, the hay was not as brittle and cutting as straw. Osvaldo swept a pile into his arms. "I wish my mattress had this," he said. "I could sleep good on this."

"You'd turn into a mule overnight," Isola teased him. "But taste it. It's good."

He gave his sister a questioning look, then put a blade of hay into his mouth and chewed.

"It tastes like grass," he told her.

"*Asino*," she brayed. He spit the hay out and ran complaining to his father.

Tobe Hall peered from behind his mother at Osvaldo's foolishness: a boy eating hay. The grown-ups were right. The Italians *were* crazy.

Serafin tied the bales while Lazzaro swung them into the back of the wagon. The women used long-handled rakes to make piles, and the children held them while Serafin looped twine underneath, pulled tight, and tied them off. La Vecchia went from one pile of hay to another, straightening the ends.

The dried grass soon gouged their hands, and the wire and twine cut them. Gloves would help, but Serafin had not seen a single pair of work gloves in his four months at Sweet Hope. Maybe Step Hall would have a rag he could wrap around his hands, he thought, like they did when they were cutting trees in the woods. The only good thing was that, with all of them working from sun up to sun down six-and-a-half days a week, they would pay off their transportation debt in no time. Then maybe they could start paying off the rest of their contract and go find work elsewhere, or go back to Italy sooner than planned, admitting their mistake in coming here.

Serafin stayed behind while Lazzaro took the full wagon to the barn to unload. His hands were starting to bleed, hands that had been toughened from working with ropes and nets and cold salt water but were no match for the tough dry stalks and hard earth. He would have to change places with Lazzaro before long. Maybe if they switched off they could make it through the day.

Finally Step called for them to stop. One of the black men unhitched the mules and they all trekked up and over the levee to the stand of trees, to eat their meals in the shade. A scrawny old man led the mules to the river for water. The others stomped through the grass to scare away snakes before settling in the shade to eat and rest.

Amalia unwrapped the loaf of bread from its cloth and tore off chunks that she passed around to her family, along with shoots of wild onion she'd found in a field they'd worked the day before. The food made her anger rise, a reminder of all they had given up, how they had been duped, what a fool she had for a husband, how she hated him. Eating like wild animals. When she saw the prices at the company store, she nearly fainted. Everything was canned or dried-up besides. Serafin had already wasted too much of their money in his few months here. So they searched the ground for anything edible while they worked.

Fancy raised an eyebrow at the raw onion, said nothing. When Amalia caught her looking, Fancy smiled weakly. "Sweet 'tata?" she said, offering a taste. Amalia stared at the food without answering.

"You're not going to be crazy enough to refuse food, are you?" Fiorenza chided her.

"*Grazie*," Amalia told Fancy. "Good." She used Serafin's fishing knife to cut the potato into several pieces that the children quickly devoured.

"*Pane*?" she offered Fancy in return, but Fancy politely refused the bread and onions.

Serafin gazed down at the flies hovering over his bloody hands, too tired to shoo them away.

"You work too fast," Amalia told Serafin. "You're wearing yourself out for nothing."

Some of the American people talked quietly as they ate; others dozed on the grass with their hats over their faces. Step's son Tobe rose from the ground like water slipping over smooth rock. His liquid hand reached for a piece of sweet potato, drew back. His body moved among the adults like a quiet trickling stream until he slipped away completely, into the woods where the man with the mules had gone.

Osvaldo watched the boy go. He rolled onto his stomach, pretending to play with twigs on the ground, all the while keeping his eyes on the path into the woods and digging his toes into the soft earth to push his body forward, away from his family, trying to make himself into the same smooth, flowing stream. Amalia was cutting strips of cloth for Serafin to wrap around his hands. The girls were staring at the bloody rags their father and Lazzaro had thrown down, already buzzing with flies.

Osvaldo stood and walked into the trees. He followed barefoot Tobe to the river where the man was watering the mules. The river was wide and flat, with rippling currents. Osvaldo sucked in his breath at the sight of its expansive brownness, just as he had the day they crossed over on the ferry. He knew the Adriatic sea, but he had never seen a river.

Osvaldo watched as Tobe picked up a stone and threw it to a narrow sandbar not far from the shore.

They were standing near a wide clump of water willow, just out of sight of the man. Osvaldo peeked toward the mules stepping daintily in the edge of the river as they drank. It was a relief to be away from the hot, dusty work and the watchful eyes of all those adults and his mother who had turned so strange and frightened him. Maybe Sweet Hope wouldn't be so bad if you had a boy like Tobe to play with along this big river.

He picked up a stone and threw toward the sandbar, too. It fell short. Tobe Hall glanced over his shoulder and grinned. He studied Osvaldo's clothes: the dirty new trousers and shoes, a faded white shirt tucked into his waistband; not like Tobe's ragged pants held up with a piece of rope, or his thin shirt flapping about his arms like a tattered flag. He made ready to throw another stone when the man turned the mules back from the river. The boys ducked behind the bushes and watched as the man shuffled close to them, leading the skinny mules whose sides heaved from exhaustion and satisfaction.

When the sound of the mules' hooves cutting the stones near the river faded and they plodded at last into the woods, Tobe scooped up a handful of rocks, stretched himself to his full four-foot height.

"Nobody throw far as me," he bragged. "Not Rupert nor Tallboy nor JoeJack — and he a growed man work at the lumber mill, muscles big as a ox. Betcha next year I be throwin clear 'cross the Mis'sippi."

Osvaldo studied the boy's bright face. Tobe's curious voice seemed to sing at times, lilting high, then low, running the words together, then slowing down.

Osvaldo knew what Tobe was telling him, although he could not understand a word he was saying. "*Allora, sono il piú forte*," he boasted in return. "'*So tirare la pietra attraverso.*"

Tobe motioned for Osvaldo to follow him closer to the river's edge. Sand ripples showed underneath the water until, a yard from shore, the bottom disappeared into murkiness.

The sandbar was five feet wide and nearly fifteen feet long, an easy target. Tobe's stones hit the edge of the bar, but Osvaldo's always splashed short. Soon they were panting from the exertion. Tobe poked his toes into the water. Osvaldo took off his shoes and stood beside Tobe, the cool water tickling his feet.

Tobe told Osvaldo how a whole steamship with hundreds of people on board was sitting at the river bottom right there where he was pointing. He repeated words for Osvaldo to say: "river," "gold," "pirates."

The river flowed steadfastly past them. Ocean waves pushed a shell or a clump of weeds onto the shore, then sucked it out, then threw it back on shore again. But whatever this river took did not come back.

"Go on," Tobe encouraged him, knowing the dangers of playing in the forbidden river. "Go swim." He pointed to the sandbar. "Swim on out to the sandbar." He motioned to his waist, assuring Osvaldo that the water was only that deep. Tobe found a stick, then poked it into the water as far in front of him as he could reach. "See? Ain't even deep," he said.

They were standing in the shallow water to their ankles, whipping the stick in the water and stirring up the muddy bottom while the woods behind them thrummed with insects and birdsong. "Big ol' giant fish live out in the deep middle," Tobe said. "He jump up one time, swallow a whole river boat, all one gulp." He squatted down, so low that water lapped at his rear end.

Then they were both sitting in the water. Tobe flung off his ragged shirt. They leaned back on their elbows and let their legs float, the current swaying them toward the landing.

Osvaldo heard a sound, like branches moving or someone walking, coming from the woods behind them, above the sound of the river. He touched Tobe's arm, and motioned for him to listen. But no parents emerged, no sisters. It gave Osvaldo a creepy feeling, as if the woods were alive and had eyes.

A great white bird rose up from the grassy shore nearby and flapped across the water, pulling its long dark legs in close to its body, its bulky wings almost dipping into the water as it skimmed the surface. And then the bird rose higher, stretched its crooked neck, made a graceful swooping turn and landed farther down near the shore.

Osvaldo asked Tobe if he'd seen the bird, but Tobe merely flopped onto his stomach and rested his chin in his hands, his legs floating behind him. Water licked at his face and he laughed and raised his chin. He had done this only once before, alone, but now with another boy beside him it was as if he had always played in the river.

Then a turtle floated by, and the boys waded in water to their knees to retrieve it.

Now that Tobe was in the water and his feet were still touching bottom, all the warnings he had heard about playing in the river vanished. It wasn't until his foot slipped and he felt his leg dropping, and then his body following, that something woke in him. He thrashed his arms and screamed for help.

Osvaldo took a step toward him, and then stopped. Tobe churned his arms toward shore as the current pulled him slowly in the opposite direction. His mouth opened and shut as he tried to cry out for help while spitting to keep the water from choking him.

Osvaldo turned toward the trees. "*Aiuto!*" he shouted. "*Aiuto!*" He turned back and shouted in Italian for Tobe to

swim, and he tried to reach an arm out to him. Finally he
ran for the stick the boy had been playing with and called
for Tobe to grab it, but the stick was ridiculously short. All
the while Tobe's panicked eyes stayed on Osvaldo. His face
bobbed farther out in the water, so that he looked like a flower,
a dark floating blossom. Osvaldo stared mutely at the bob-
bing flower, then took off running for the trees.

***

THEIR dinner break was nearly over when Fancy Hall and
Amalia Pascala each looked up, their noses raised as if catching something in the air. Their eyes moved slowly over the
children and adults sprawled around them, and their ears
listened, although neither of them knew in those moments
what they were listening for. Their eyes met briefly as they
rose to their feet. By the time they were standing, what their
bodies had unknowingly sensed turned to sudden conscious-
ness. Within seconds the entire group was running into the
woods, calling for the boys.

They broke through the trees onto the sandy clearing at
the same time Osvaldo leaped from the sand into the scrub
oaks, shouting incoherently. Step Hall reached out as if to
steady himself and caught the boy by the arm. For a moment
Osvaldo dangled in mid–air while a dozen pairs of startled
eyes watched his churning feet, the great river flowing behind him. Then Step dropped the boy and they ran for the
river.

Fancy screamed when she saw her son slapping at the
water, a dull, exhausted look on his face. He had already been
carried another twenty feet downstream and farther away
from shore.

Step splashed into the water while his wife followed, her
arms stretched toward the boy. The others grabbed her skirt

to keep her from throwing herself into the river. Step's foot slipped at a drop–off, and he plunged into water to his waist. He struggled against the current to keep his footing. Someone called for a rope, and the scrawny old man ran back to the wagons. Another man cursed himself for not bringing a rope when they had first run into the woods. Where else would young boys be, after all, than in the river where they weren't supposed to be?

As if on cue, the black Americans joined hands, making a chain of their bodies that allowed Step to venture farther into the water. The Italians added their own bodies as links in the chain. But the water became too deep and the current too strong. "Daddy," Tobe gasped as the river tugged at him. The distance widened between them.

Amalia pulled Osvaldo close and called the girls to her side. "Pray for the little boy," she told them.

Serafin waded into the water, holding onto the outstretched arms until he reached Step Hall, the shouting and crying close in his ears. He grabbed Step's arm and leaned over the river, reaching for Tobe as if beckoning him from the water. The motion jarred him: once again he was touching his brother Valerio's hand. He held the fingers for a moment, and then Valerio disappeared.

He let go of Step Hall. His feet touched bottom for just a moment before the current lifted him and he started swimming.

"Fool, Serafin!" Amalia shrieked. "Come back."

Osvaldo watched in horror as his father was carried away. "Daddy," he cried out. "Where are you going?" He knew he was the cause of this. "*Mi scusa,*" Osvaldo cried.

Serafin had seen foolish young men who thought they could fight the sea and win — a dangerous attitude for a fisherman to have. He never thought of himself as such a man, but now he felt his anger against the river rising, and he tried to calm it. It was the anger that killed you.

It was easy to reach the boy, as he knew it would be. Returning would be another matter. Tobe turned his eyes to Serafin like a baby waking from sleep. "*Stai bene*," Serafin told him. "You're going to be okay." He slipped his arm under Tobe's, lifting him in the water so that he could breathe. Tobe whimpered.

The water cradled Serafin and the boy as they held each other. Then Serafin turned his head sharply, to see how far he had drifted from shore, and the sight shocked him. I may as well be in the middle of the ocean, he thought.

The water felt surprisingly cold now. It tugged at his legs, and for a moment he kicked out violently, thinking he had become snagged in something, but it was only the current playing tricks on him. He plowed the water with his right arm while he fought to keep the boy above water with the other. He heard nothing from shore, but he saw the tense, frightened faces watching him, the way he had watched twice from his boat. The cold water made his legs feel heavy and sluggish. The boy was weightless beside him, an empty burlap sack. "Stai bene?" he called out, his lips brushing the boy's cheek like a kiss. There was no answer, just a slight movement, perhaps the splash of a hand.

His arm ached. He wondered how such a small child had been able to swim against the current for so long. He told himself to try not to think about the pain and the distance between himself and shore. It would have been hard enough to swim with both arms, but this way, holding onto the boy, it seemed impossible. Just one more stroke. One more and then another and then another.

Lazzaro waved his arms at Serafin as the group followed him slowly downstream. "Be strong," Lazzaro shouted. "Don't give up." Suddenly Serafin was afraid. It was as if the river had stopped for a moment and he could see everything clearly. It had not crossed his mind when he stepped into the water that he might not come out alive. Now he saw the terrified looks on his wife and children and best friend.

"Don't give up, hold on," Lazzaro called, and Serafin was stunned to realize he was drowning. What would happen to his wife and children? How could he leave them alone in the hell he had brought them to, with the pain of his death to further burden them? Visiting him at Hyner cemetery, where the rest of the godforsaken Italians lay.

A black man waded into the water, extending a rope to Serafin, then letting it drop when he saw that a rope was useless. "Come on," Lazzaro shouted. "Just a little more." Serafin blinked his eyes hard, trying to clear the water from them, and he was surprised a second time to realize he had actually inched himself closer to shore, even though the current carried him downstream. Just his fate, he thought, to die like this, not a mule's length from being saved.

The group formed a human chain again and eased into deeper water. Serafin found himself looking into the face of Step Hall, who held the rope. They were shouting at him and at each other, but a rushing sound filled his ears, and he could not make out their words. Step leaned into the river while the others held him. His face tensed, the eyes narrowed as he studied Serafin's face with the look of someone backed into a corner and gauging his last desperate move. Then Step Hall tossed the loop of rope with his one free hand. Serafin watched its slow flight in the air; it seemed to hang suspended in front of his eyes before plopping gently in the water a few feet in front of him. Several times Step pulled in the noose, then tossed it out again. Finally he stopped and cursed himself, fretting over the rope as if searching for the flaw in it. Then he leaned forward once more, set a steady gaze on Serafin's face and let go the rope. It sailed before Serafin's eyes for a moment — a fleeting shadow, a leaf blowing in the wind — before floating down over his head. Step let out a quick, triumphant shout, then pulled, and Serafin felt the pressure against the back of his neck. He raised his head in the water and arched his neck to keep the rope from slipping off. And then Step reached out, snagged Serafin's hand and pulled him in.

Step and Fancy Hall snatched their son from Serafin as he collapsed on his knees ashore. He felt the air heave around him, like a gust blowing in and out of a room. It was his family gathering at his side. And then there came a barely discernible touch, Amalia's hand on his arm, removing the rope from his neck.

Serafin noticed in the same hazy way the commotion a short distance from him, Fancy Hall crying and rocking her son as the others pried the boy out of her hands and laid him on the grass. Step slapped at his son and shook him saying, "Come on boy, come on boy" through gritted teeth until finally the boy coughed and vomited. Fancy touched Tobe's face, his chest, his arms. "Did you ever think?" she cried. "Oh Lord, did you ever think?"

Amalia slapped Serafin across the face with such force that he fell sideways.

"What the hell did you think you were doing going out there, leaving us?" she screamed at him. "I know your men die in water!"

"*Dio santo*," Fiorenza said, pulling her away. Amalia cursed Serafin, beating at his face while Fiorenza struggled to hold her back. Lazzaro pinned Amalia's arms to her sides until they went still and she began sobbing.

Serafin righted himself on his knees, taking his children's hands for support. "It's okay," he tried to say, but what came out sounded like he was attempting to clear his throat. He knelt for a minute, catching his breath, waiting for the feeling in his arm to return.

"You okay?" Lazzaro asked.

His wife and children stared at him mutely, their silence more painful than anything his muscles had felt in the water.

"Let me breathe," Serafin told them.

And Tobe was a newborn calf a few yards away, trembling and skinny and slick with water. His father helped him to his feet, but the boy's legs gave way and he sprawled on the ground, looking up at them with bewildered eyes.

Step put his hand on the boy's head. "Lay still now," he told him. "Let your strength come back." One of the men took off his shirt and laid it over Tobe's chest.

Serafin felt his hands stinging now, from the water drying in the cuts he had gotten from baling hay. Pale, bloated lines crisscrossed his palms, the whitened edges of the cuts like the mouths of dead fish.

He was there, all over again, four years ago, looking into Valerio's white, stone face as he lay dripping in the bottom of the boat. That awful understanding: his brother was dead. It was final; there was no changing it. If they had pulled him out of the water two minutes sooner, one minute, who knows?

Serafin had left in the dark morning as usual, taking Valerio along as he sometimes did. They had slipped out into deep water with Valerio talking about a girl he had met on the *via Villanova*, how he had walked with her all the way down to the sea and had gotten up the courage to kiss her just when she bent over to pick up a piece of driftwood. "I was kissing the air," he laughed. Talking, talking, always talking. They had gone out in his boat with Valerio talking and returned three hours later with Valerio dead. There was no way to explain the anguish. Valerio was no more.

Serafin knelt at the riverbank clutching his stomach, sobbing.

And yet the boy, Tobe Hall, was saved. Wonder mingled with grief, astonishment as heavy as grief, and painful, too, an astonishing, beautiful pain impossible to comprehend.

Valerio, after four years dead, you have come back to us?

The others watched uneasily. Step Hall's jaw tightened as he waited to see what would happen.

"It's okay," Lazzaro told Serafin. He tried to take the man by his shoulders, raise him to his feet, but Serafin could not be moved. "Everything's all right now, my friend," he told Serafin in a gentle, coaxing voice.

Lazzaro and Fiorenza exchanged glances with Amalia. It had been a while since they had seen Serafin like this. Amalia had been on the verge of telling Fiorenza of her plan to take the children and leave Serafin, even though such a thing was *infamante*. But then Serafin started to talk about America, and his old self came back, so she stayed with him and never mentioned the secret that she carried in her heart.

Serafin glanced over at Osvaldo, at his bare feet, the wet clothes. "What the devil were you doing in that river?" he said. His voice was weak, but the words made sense now. Osvaldo stepped closer to his mother, keeping his eyes alert.

"It's okay," Lazzaro told him. "*Grazie a Dio*, nobody got hurt."

"Hurt?" Serafin shook his head, as if he did not understand the meaning of the word.

"Go get your shoes," Amalia scolded Osvaldo, the fear trembling beneath her words. Osvaldo trudged away, searching the riverbank for his shoes.

Serafin's own shoes were on his feet. He thought of this now, how if he had taken them off first it might have been easier to swim. He could have drowned because of a pair of shoes.

Step Hall was standing before him. He grasped Serafin's hand with a powerful grip and pulled him to his feet. Step squinted into Serafin's eyes, as if straining to see something. Serafin smiled uneasily, tried to move his hand away. But Step Hall squeezed the hand tighter in his. Serafin flinched from the pain.

"*Niente*, it's nothing," he told Step. "I did nothing." He looked around helplessly. "You — you saved us both."

Lazzaro laid a hand on Step's shoulder. Finally the man let go of Serafin. They stood awkwardly, like drunken men, unable to speak, not even knowing what it was they wanted to say.

Step looked out at the river, then over at his wife and boy a long time. His feet were lead. For all his dreams, he was useless after all. He turned and called gruffly for the group to move along. He lifted his son and laid him against his shoulder like a baby, and when he started walking his family and friends followed.

The Italians fell in behind them, Osvaldo barefoot and carrying his shoes in his hands while his father stumbled forward, steering the boy with one hand laid across his neck. Serafin squinted ahead at the dark shape resting in his father's arms: the boy who was not Valerio. Behind them Amalia and the girls trailed, subdued and silent, and Lazzaro and his wife and the old lady, back to the hay field below the levee, back to the sweet grass and the grazing cows and the acres of flat, silent, dusty land, away from the beautiful, merciless river.

CHAPTER 2

Gratitude

October 1901

FANCY dangled the dead chicken by its bound legs over the side of the wagon, to drain the blood during the short ride. "Shoulda caught a couple rabbits, or some fish," she told Step. "Killin a good hen." She moved her leg against Tobe's, to feel his squirming, living body against hers.

"Wish't I had more'n a hen to give 'em," Step said.

"Corn too." She hated her pettiness, her complaining words that rang hollow inside her. She would give everything she owned, and then some, to save her child.

Tobe glanced with embarrassment back at Calvin and Birdie where they sat with a sack of their last sweet corn. "Don't see why I gotta go," Calvin had complained. Birdie was happy to go, though she didn't let on. She'd never been inside an Italian's house.

"We all goin," Step had told them. "That's what's proper, and that's what we doin."

All the families were stretched thin now, in the days before selling their cotton. The Halls had a small farm with a vegetable garden, more than any of the new tenants had, and more than many of the sharecroppers, too, something they were well aware of. Still, it had been a hard decision to kill one of their hens.

"You never done nothin like this before," Fancy told him. She glanced quickly down at Tobe as she spoke.

"Never had reason to before."

It had been two days now since the river. He had been brooding over the incident since it happened, trying to put together the picture that always left him standing on shore.

"You pulled 'em both out," Fancy reminded her husband now.

"At the end," Step answered through gritted teeth. "Boy was already saved."

Tobe fidgeted, kicking his leg against the footboard as he listened to them talk about him like he really had gone under the water and turned into a ghost.

✳✳✳

THE Pascalas came outside when they heard the wagon.

Tobe hung his head and wished he were anywhere but there, while the Pascalas crowded on their tree stump steps to watch.

Calvin peered at the family he had heard so much about. They looked like any of the other Italians, though not as raggedy — yet. Hanging back behind the rest of them, half inside the house, was the oldest girl, almost his age.

"Ho," Step called, raising his hand in the air.

"Ho," Serafin answered.

It startled him to see the boy sitting there in the flesh. Even Osvaldo sighed in relief.

"Come t' thank you proper for savin my boy," Step said as he walked toward Serafin. He noticed a pile of rocks at the side of the house.

Serafin took his hand. "*Niente. Prego.*"

Step called his family down and they stood awkwardly near the wagon, the dead chicken hanging limply at Fancy's side.

Angelina moved forward as well, and Calvin saw her clearly now. Her dark, shiny hair was pulled back, but a few curls escaped. Her eyes were large and dark, and her skin was smooth and the color of a pecan shell. As she moved outside the door, she placed a hat on her head, a straw–colored dress–up hat with a cluster of paper flowers attached to the brim. She flashed her dark eyes at him, and he swallowed hard and looked away. She was the prettiest girl he had ever seen in his entire life.

Serafin forced a smile at Tobe. "You good? No more the river, you."

Tobe hung his head in shyness.

"Git over here," Step told his son. "What I tell you?"

Tobe shuffled across the yard, head down, hands deep in his holey pockets. "Thank ya', Mister," he finally mumbled.

Serafin touched the boy's head, making Tobe look up. Serafin's throat tightened, his eyes stung. He forced a laugh, tousled the boy's hair. "Strong. Good boy. *Buon ragazzo*," he said. He looked at the bare feet of the Hall children, then at their ragged clothes.

Step saw the glistening eyes, and sucked in his breath. "Fancy, give 'em the hen," he called, to break the spell.

Fancy raised the dead chicken to them, but no one came forward.

Step had to take the bird out of his wife's hand and place it in Serafin's. Another mistake. It looked like the man would start bawling over a dead bird. But finally Amalia took the chicken and moved away quickly. The Pascala eyes were hungry, grateful, wary.

"Bring that sack a' corn," Step called to Calvin, and the boy came to attention. He walked self–consciously, all eyes on him now in the silence.

"This my oldest boy, Calvin," Step said, as if they could understand. Calvin straightened up, gloating. It was about time his father noticed how grown up he was. He could feel the girl with the hat watching him, but he dared not look her way again.

She stared at the odd way he carried the sack: pinched between his fingers and thumb, as if carrying something he disdained. The rest of him moved in a jumble: awkward, smooth, defiant.

When Step pulled out an ear of corn to show Serafin, he cocked his head quizzically. "*Perché*? For what?"

"What is it, daddy?" Isola asked.

"Corn," Serafin said, baffled.

"Maybe he'll give us a pig to go with it," Amalia said sarcastically.

Serafin swept his arm toward the surrounding land. "*Ma non abbiamo l'animali*." And then he was off explaining in Italian: It was just the five of them living there, as Step well knew. They had no cow or pig, no animals.

"What in the name of the saints do they want?" Amalia asked Serafin.

He shook his head.

Step shrugged at Fancy. Then he stripped back the husk, and squeezed a few kernels with his thumb to show Serafin the milky freshness.

Serafin held his hands out. "But no understand."

"Eat," Step told them.

"Eat?" Serafin asked, surprised. "*Mangia*?"

Step nodded, dug out a few kernels with his thumb and popped them into his mouth, then chewed in an exaggerated way. The Pascala children burst out laughing.

Isola made grunting pig sounds, but Amalia grabbed her by the shoulder and she stopped.

"Well I'll be danged," Fancy said. "Don't you peoples know 'bout eatin sweet corn?" Birdie grinned and made a face at Isola, before her mother could see.

With gestures and few words, Fancy asked for a big boiling pot and had Calvin fill it at the pump. Amalia and her children stood back and watched in surprise as the black woman took charge. Fancy kept Tobe by her side as she marched them all inside the house, indignant yet pleased, the Pascalas following.

The kitchen was nearly empty, save for the table and one makeshift chair, and a few shelves and a cupboard near the stove, unlike the Hall house that was cluttered with years of living.

Step went to stoke the fire and saw a few more rocks lying on the floor near the stove. "What the 'tarnation?" he said.

When the Pascalas first arrived, the shack had mortified them, but they were slowly turning it into a home. Now with the Halls inside, the shack was an embarrassment again, unfit for even a mule's shelter.

Angelina hung the chicken over a nail on the wall. Amalia took the hat from her daughter's head with a quick, disapproving look, and hung it on a nail near the chicken. Quickly, she brushed crumbs from the table, away from the statue of the Blessed Virgin Mary that stood on a crocheted doily, her broken arms extended. A stub of burned–out candle sat in front of her. It had been her grandmother's statue, one the old woman had wrapped in a woolen sweater herself for the family's journey. Amalia carried it like a baby once they left their ship in New Orleans and began the last leg of their grueling journey. It was across the river, as that horrible agent Rosconi prodded them over the cobblestones to the waiting ferry to Sweet Hope, that a frantic family jostled Amalia, and the bundle fell to the stones. Devastated, she refused to unwrap the statue to learn the truth she already knew until long after Step had dropped them off at the sweltering shack that would be their home.

Birdie reached for the statue. "Look, mama, a doll."

Fancy slapped the girl's hand away before Amalia had time to react. "Don't touch!" she scolded. "Ain't no doll. That their religion."

They left the door open while the stove heated. Serafin moved the rocks away from the stove, trying to explain about the *forno*, the need for a good oven, how he had brought some of the rocks inside to see if there was any way he could adapt their stove, make it bigger. "*Per pane*," Serafin told Step. "Bread. Eat."

Calvin stole a glance at Angelina, and she glared back at him so boldly that for a moment he couldn't swallow.

Fancy snatched Calvin by the back of his shirt and sent him and Birdie outside to shuck the corn. "Tobe, you stay right here where I can watch you." She spoke abruptly, looked about brusquely, as if everything annoyed her. "You got any salt?" she asked, and when Amalia did not answer, Fancy searched through the cooking items until she found a newly opened box. Amalia moved forward, clutching the front of her skirt as Fancy found a platter and fork and knife and set them on the table.

"Serafin, make her stop," Amalia said, but he only shrugged helplessly.

Tobe and Osvaldo crouched under the table grinning at each other, their ordeal at the river dissolved into the humid air.

The other two Hall children came in and dropped the shucked corn into the boiling water. Birdie made another face at Isola as if to say she owned the place, and marched right past her with her three short pigtails bouncing.

"Hey, *sporca*," Isola said. "*Sacco di stracci*."

"You kids g'on outside," Fancy ordered. "This house ain't big enough." She caught Tobe by the collar as he scampered from beneath the table. "Cep' you. You ain't goin nowheres."

"Aw, Ma," he said. He threw himself miserably at the table, leaning over it as if in pain.

"Won't take but a few minutes," Step tried to tell them, "once the water boil."

Serafin took him by the arm and motioned him proudly to the one chair at the table. It looked to be made of crudely woven grape vines and small tree limbs, still green. He would not sit down, so Serafin sat to show him how sturdy the chair was, then stood again. When Step still would not sit, Serafin tried to get Fancy into the chair, to no avail.

"From the big woods," he told them.

"Serafin, they don't care about your chair," Amalia told him.

She took a cloth–covered plate down from a shelf and brought it to the table along with a knife. She pulled back the cloth to reveal the end of an old loaf of bread. Both Step and Fancy raised their hands in polite refusal. Amalia left the bread uncovered.

Fancy stood near the table with her arms folded across her chest, as if willing the water to boil. She scanned the room, noticing little oddities: a large, round, flat sieve hanging on the wall; a wilted bundle of wild onions hanging to dry from the low ceiling, alongside another bundle of dried leaves she couldn't make out. The shelves were sparse, just a few dishes, bowls, tins and boxes of provisions. On one nearly empty shelf sat a strange white bowl, lacy and squat with fluted edges. She gave Amalia a questioning look and moved closer to see the bowl. The minute her hand went out to touch it, Amalia was at her side.

"*Attento!*" she warned.

Fancy drew her hand back. "Ain't hurtin nothin," she said.

Amalia picked up the bowl, and Fancy saw it was as lacy as the doily beneath the statue. "What the 'tarnation that?" she asked.

Amalia held the bowl up to show how the light passed through the crocheted designs. Then she let Fancy touch. It was stiff and hard as a thin board, but made of cloth. "Step, lookit this thing," she said. To Amalia, she asked, "How you do it?"

Amalia shrugged, waiting for Serafin to help out.

"Good, good, pretty, no?" was all he could say to their guests.

"Pretty," Step and Fancy both said, and Serafin smiled proudly.

"They like it," Angelina told her mother.

"*Vedi*?" Serafin told Amalia. "*É bello.*"

She had brought a few of her doilies and her sewing materials with her, but when she saw the mule barn they had to live in, she couldn't bring herself to touch them. It was Angelina who insisted that Amalia starch one of the doilies, as they did back home — soak it in starch water, then lay it over a bowl until it dried — to make something nice to brighten up the room.

Amalia put the bowl back on the shelf, trying not to show how pleased she was.

Step touched the back of the chair lightly with his fingers. This was the longest he'd been inside one of the foreigner's shacks. He stared at the white cloth bowl, then glanced over at the chunk of hard bread Amalia had offered them. Serafin smiled, and it sent a pang through Step.

"It's done," Fancy announced. She took the bread cloth from the table and gathered her skirt in the other hand to lift the pot from the stove. She stood outside the door and carefully dumped most of the water alongside the house, then called the children inside. The girls were running around outside, shrieking with laughter, while Calvin stood hunched at the stoop, pretending not to watch them.

She speared ears of corn and piled them on the plate, then motioned for the Pascalas to eat.

Fancy sprinkled the corn with salt, and handed it over to Amalia while the Hall children looked on hungrily.

"They want us to eat pig food," she told Serafin.

"What's wrong with 'em?" Birdie asked. "All that jabbering. How come they don't wanna eat?"

Step snatched the corn from his wife, took a bite, and chewed.

The Pascala children watched, a little frightened now. "Good 'n' sweet," he told them, smiling as he chewed. Finally Serafin took the ear of corn, sniffed, and took a bite. He chewed slowly, cautiously. Then he swallowed and licked his lips. "It's good," he proclaimed to his family. "*Strano.*" He took another bite.

"Let me try," Isola said.

"Me too," said Osvaldo.

Each one of them tasted. Each pair of Pascala eyes widened in surprise.

"Is that why the pigs get so fat here?" Serafin said.

"American corn," Amalia said. "Do you think all this time we could have been eating our own corn back home?" She reached out and wiped Osvaldo's mouth.

Serafin thought a moment. "No, it's too hard. This is soft."

The children scrambled outside to eat and play. "Ain't you comin?" Calvin dared to ask Angelina. Again that defiant face, looking him straight in the eye.

"You leave that girl 'lone," Fancy told him.

Angelina hung back a few moments, then followed.

Once the children were outside, Fancy asked Step, "Think they know what to do with a chicken?" She was already reaching for the bird.

Amalia stopped her. "No," she called out. She would have no strange woman cooking anything more in her house.

"Leave her be," Step said. "Everybody know how to cook chicken."

"You ain't gonna eat the feathers, too, is you?" Fancy said to her.

Amalia blocked the bird with her body. "Serafin, do something," she said, suddenly fearing they meant to take the gift bird back.

But Fancy was already moving away, shaking her head with a snort.

"Hope we didn't kill a good hen for nothin'," she said.

Step cleared his throat, looked at his wife. "Mr. Serafin," he said. "Time for us to go. You come work wi' me t'morrow, okay?"

"Work?" Serafin answered.

Step raised his hand in the air to slow the man down. "Not now. Tomorrow."

"Work, yes," Serafin told him.

"How you gonna get anywhere with these people?" Fancy asked.

Step gestured as if he were sleeping, then waking up. Birdie laughed. "T'morrow," he said. "I come for you, we work."

Serafin nodded, "Come work."

"T'morrow."

"Da marrah. *E anche Lazzaro? Mi amico*?" Serafin asked. "My friend, work too?"

"What 'bout Calvin was s'pose t' help you," Fancy said. "What 'bout Fred's son?"

"There's lots 'a work," Step said. To Serafin he shrugged, nodded. "Y' friend too."

The smile spread across Serafin's face as he took Step's hand and shook it vigorously. Fancy held her tongue.

Once the Halls left, the sounds of their talking, the odors of the food they had brought, and the space that their bodies had taken up lingered in the room. Serafin stood at the window, trying to understand. "You see?" he told his family. "We've got American friends already. And they've got a big farm, food, animals. Mr. Step, the boss of Sweet Hope."

"They dress in rags," Amalia told him. "Just like all the farmers here. Their children go barefoot."

Serafin looked at his own children, considering her words.

"All the Americans go barefoot when it's warm out — it's the custom here."

Amalia ordered Angelina to boil some water so they could pluck the bird. She was already planning what to do with the feathers: she would begin saving them to add to the mattress to soften the crackling cornhusks and leaves. Eventually they would add duck feathers, maybe even another chicken someday if the Halls continued their generosity. To Serafin she said, "She shouldn't have thrown out the corn water. Now I have to start over."

He shrugged. "They're going to help us, Amalia. Mr. Step will give me extra work, you heard him. We're going to be all right. To hell with the stories we keep hearing."

"We'll see," she said, fighting the flutter of hope that rose inside her.

"You kids pay attention," Serafin told the children. "Learn English fast so we can talk to the Americans."

"H'lo. G'bye. Ugly," Isola said, and then she laughed.

"That's good," Serafin told her. "See how fast you learn?"

He touched the back of the chair he had built from practically nothing and sat down, feeling the woven branches press the backs of his thighs. "Thank God that boy is okay," he said.

"*Grazie a Dio,*" Amalia answered. What seemed at first a curse — a near–death, maybe two — might actually have been a sign that things would turn out all right after all.

And Serafin's own thoughts raced. Sweet Hope only appeared to be a vast and desolate *purgatorio.* But nearby were the woods and lake and river, teeming with fish and game, wild berries, bee hives full of honey, all kinds of food, timber, anything they needed — even though the company tried to keep you on your own land, worked you to the bone so you could barely grab an hour to try to hunt or fish. But there was always a way around any obstacle. He looked at the table strewn with cobs, picked one up. He held it out to his wife as proof. "See?" he said, his face bright.

Mais.

Hands trembling, he turned to the statue of Mary on the table. "With the sweat of my own brow," he said to her. Neither she nor God had answered his cries for help that day years ago. So be it. Tonight they would eat chicken. Tomorrow their real life began. *Valerio, I'll make you proud. For you, this new life on land.*

The Blessed Virgin gazed back at him, her handless arms extended.

CHAPTER 3

Step Hall

November 1901

STEP Hall carried a secret life inside him. It existed just beyond the pale, like the Sweet Hope that exposed itself to him when mist rose from the lake or curled away from the great river, slowly climbed the yellow banks and crested the levee. Most of the time he carried that life the way he might carry a pouch of tobacco in his pocket, oblivious to its weight until something made him pause and dip into it.

Like now, heading to the company office to see about the new load of tenants coming in. There was no denying what was plain to see: planter Harlan Gates was engaged in a new form of human "investment" with his Italian colony experiment. And Step was right there in the middle of it.

Gates putting him halfway in charge, as if it meant anything. And making him work with the white manager Lee Horton, even giving him one up on Horton in some ways.

"You dreamin if you think Mr. Gates think you somebody," Fancy would tell him. "You just another black face to him. When he don't need you no more, won't even remember your name."

"Might be so," he'd tell her. But somewhere deep inside, a part of him hoped she might be wrong.

***

LEE Horton was sitting in the company office, looking out of place behind a desk. Most of the time he could be found riding the fields on the company's roan, rifle jutting from a sling. He tapped a pencil on the desk and sat up when Step entered. "What'd you do, come here by way of Alabama?"

"No sir," Step answered. "Come here the road of man and mule. Same as one you took." He had almost said "jackass" instead of "mule," but thought better of it.

Horton peered up at him, the strain it took for him to endure working with a black man showing in his face.

"I ain't got all day, you know," he said.

"No sir, Mr. Horton."

Horton spread a map on the table and pointed to the southern portion. "Mr. Gates got another load comin this March," he said. "He wants to put 'em here at Fish Bayou."

Step scowled at the map. Everybody knew that section of Fish Bayou was about the worst place to farm, all swamp and mosquitoes. "Mr. Gates say that?" Step shook his head. "I don't know." He pointed farther north on the map, near the middle section of the plantation where a grove of water oaks grew around two small ponds. "We should be settlin this part, never mind Fish Bayou." He sucked in his breath, still not comfortable being so direct with a white man. Even if the white man was a fool.

"Now why the hell you think we been bustin our backs, clearin trees and puttin in drainage ditches at Fish Bayou for?" Horton said. "If we ain't putting tenants on it?"

Step let his gaze fall just short of the man's eyes. *We?* he wanted to say. *I don't see you bustin your back while men's bones break for real, from twistin their arms off tryin to get them stumps out.*

"The malaria, Mr. Horton," Step answered in an even, patient voice. "Got to clear the swamp land to cut down on the malaria. What you clean out down here at the bayou... " He tapped his finger at the bottom of the map. "It pay out on what you get up here where it's dry." He tapped his finger back in the center of the map. "Peoples can't make cotton if they half dead."

Horton stared at him, as if daring Step to say more. For Horton, everything was a matter of getting away with doing as little work as possible. Since the bottomland was already being cleared, he'd just as soon put the new houses there as prepare a new section of farmable land for the incoming tenants. Never mind that such an action would cut into Gates' profits — and probably kill a few Italians along the way.

"I already told Gates we was puttin the new farmers down there," Horton insisted.

Step blinked at him. "What Mr. Gates say to that?"

Horton was getting agitated. He glanced away a minute, then turned back to gather up the map. It was killing him to treat a black man like his ideas actually counted. He started searching through his satchel, pulled out a tobacco tin, then scrounged through his coat pocket for papers.

"What you think Mr. Gates goin say to that?" Horton growled. "Now what the hell you think a planter's gonna do with his land that he just spent good labor workin up if he ain't puttin farms on it?"

Step turned away to conceal the smile he felt creeping across his face. It was mutually understood that they both knew perfectly well what Harlan Gates had said: "I think you had better go have a talk with Step Hall about that."

Step picked up the iron poker from beside the stove, opened the door, and moved the wood coals around. He laid another log on the fire and replaced the poker. He could hear Horton folding his cigarette paper and licking it.

Step picked up the coffee pot and sloshed it around to check how much was left, then put it back on the stove. "Coffee's hot," he said. "How's about a cup, Mr. Horton?" He had succeeded in erasing the smile from his face.

"Don't want no coffee," Horton said.

"You want I should get started on buildin those cabins?" Step asked. He moved away from the stove and pretended to busy himself studying the county map on the wall as he waited for Horton to answer. Horton struck a match and a smell of sulfur rose, then dispersed.

"We've gotta have houses for them, don't we?" Horton said. "We've got to put those Dagoes somewhere when they get here."

"Yes sir, that's what I'm sayin. But I do have to know where I'll be buildin."

Horton snatched up the map, rattled it open, and bent over to scrutinize it once again. He straightened up and threw his arm out, as if he had just made a discovery. "There's hardly any cabins up there at the Modena section," he growled. "What the hell you been doin? You hold off buildin at Fish Bayou till we get those others up."

Step's expression did not change. His demeanor said that he was merely taking orders, as he had been raised to. Inside he was shaking his head over the fool standing in front of him.

Horton stomped across the room and opened the door. "Jorland, where the hell you at?" he shouted. "You gonna get me those seed prices or what?" He waited for an answer, then slammed the door.

He turned back and glared at Step Hall. "What you waitin for?"

"Want to be sure where I'm buildin them houses, that's all. Modena section, 'stead of Fish Bayou? I got that right?"

"Get the hell out of here," Horton said.

✳✳✳

STEP Hall was born a slave in 1857 on Ezekiel Harrington's plantation, the very same plantation he now lived and worked on and that, after changing hands a number of times, came to be known as Sweet Hope. Back when the threat of Stark County turning into a prime Civil War battlefield site was becoming real, the Colonel moved his slaves and livestock to Texas where they waited out the devastation in relative peace. His mulatto son and daughter stayed behind to take charge of the plantation. Malek Hall, the man Step had always thought of as his grandfather, and Auntie T, the woman who raised him and his sister after their mother's death, were his family in Texas, as were Auntie T's own children whom he called cousins. Fred Titus was the only one of them living back on Sweet Hope now.

The only memorable events for Step during the Texas years were seeing an armadillo waddling along the side of a ditch and finding a cactus growing on a sandy trail near a dry streambed. The armadillo's rounded, horned back stopped the boy cold, sending goose bumps up his arms. The animal reminded him of something that had crawled out of the earth up from the depths of hell. He saw it just once, but he used to go to the ditch whenever he could, and crouch beside a scrub willow bush in the hope — and fear — of seeing another.

The cactus he stumbled upon was small, not six inches high, with long sharp spines sticking out all over. He liked to lie on his stomach and look at it, and liked to touch the tip of a finger to the spine points to test their sharpness and his bravery. The cactus, too, put him in mind of something that might grow in the underworld. Spread over everything was a washed–out sky that would fill occasionally with flocks of black birds cawing and screeching so fiercely that they sent him running from his hiding places back into the work fields. Once he became so terrified of the birds that he ran straight into Auntie T's arms. It was one of the few times he remembered being held by her, and then only briefly. "Gonna be worse things in life than blackbirds to scare you," she told him. Her arms felt to him like rough fence posts. But she was kind, and loved him in her way, and his Uncle Malek was good to him, too. He didn't remember his mother at all.

Step pulled his jacket closed and did up the middle three buttons against the brisk day. There was a hint of rain. He was driving the wagon toward the lumber mill north of the landing, trying to shake the bad feeling from having spent more than two minutes in the presence of Lee Horton. The fields were empty and quiet under the gray sky. Far in the west the clouds had thinned out and the air was light, blowing slightly his way.

He heard the whine of the saws as he neared the lumber mill. A pile of old sawdust the size of two wagons stood near the corner of the building. The side yard was filled with stacks of plank lumber, some fresh and yellow, others cured and pale. Two boys carried a long plank from the far end of the mill. They stopped alongside one of the stacks and swung the board onto the pile, then trudged back into the mill.

Step pulled the wagon near the open door where the smell of newly cut wood hung in the air. "Freddy, you here?" he called. He waited a minute, then eased himself down and poked his head inside.

The open doors on either end of the mill let in light, as did the long rows of windows. The building smelled of warm machinery, damp sawdust, and that peculiar odor of trees heated by steel teeth churning into their flesh. Fred stood at the far end of the room, waiting for a plank to fall into the hands of the waiting men. When it came free, he put both his hands on what was left of the log, waited for the man on the other end to stop the one blade and start the other, and guided the log back from where it had come.

Sant'Angelo the Sicilian and an older man from the Bolognesi section worked together setting up the logs, a hard job calling for strength and nerve. Then there was Pietro, who used to be a shoemaker. They worked methodically, with little talk. Fred's son JoeJack and Step's oldest son Calvin carried the cut planks outside to stack. Step squinted down the way at Calvin, uneasy as always to see him working in such a rough place. They'd argued over it, Calvin insisting he was old enough for the sawmill now that he'd turned twelve, Fancy pointing out that there was plenty of work in the fields or mule barn.

"You still a boy," Step told him. "Sawmill's a man's job."

"JoeJack — "

JoeJack was fifteen.

Fred saw no problem with Calvin working there; his own boy had started at a younger age. He needed the help, and Calvin was familiar with the workings of the mill. Step had held Fred to the one condition: make sure his boy stayed off the machinery.

"Pa," Calvin said, and Step raised his chin in salutation.

Fred motioned for the log–setters to hold up, then wiped his hands down the sides of his pants. "How's the day goin?" he asked Step.

"Just came from seein Horton."

Fred gave a knowing snort. "He givin you any trouble?"

"Nothin I ain't already seen."

Fred looked down at the sawdust accumulating near his feet and went for the shovel.

"You got me lumber for five or six more cabins up to the Modena section?" Step asked.

Fred dug the shovel into the sawdust and flung it into the barrow. "I got enough lumber to build a town, you want to build a town."

"Can you start haulin it up there?" Step asked. "We can start buildin next week, I get a crew together from the woods."

"You want a couple more, I got 'em here," Fred said, flinging another shovelful.

"I was thinkin to take Calvin," Step told him. "Can take JoeJack too if you can spare him."

"Hmmph," Fred said. "Have to see 'bout that." He stabbed the shovel into the pile, gripped the wheelbarrow handles, and headed for the door. "We'll start haulin tomorrow, day after."

When they reached one of the sawdust piles, Fred tipped the barrow. "Thought fifty families be 'nough by now," he said. "Thought Mr. Gates woulda stopped bringin 'em."

He straightened, drove the shovel into the ground and gazed out at the fields across from the mill. They'd talked about it a number of times, how ten years ago there were nothing but Negroes on the land. And now, just a handful left while Mr. Gates had them clear land and build cabins, and he shipped in more and more foreigners from somewhere across the ocean.

"Fancy keep sayin Mr. Gates fixin to get rid of us bye an' bye," Step told him.

"I'll tell you this: if I was just a farmer plantin cotton, I'd be gone by now."

Step could understand that. He and Fancy had talked about leaving, too, when they saw so many of the other sharecroppers heading out. But it was different for people like him and Fred, in charge of settling the new Italians or running the lumber mill, on top of running their farms.

"Don't make sense, Mr. Gates makin 'em sign a contract to work here, whilst he keepin all a' us on sharecroppin," Step said. "We got two Sweet Hopes right on top a' each other."

"Day the boss tells me sign a contract, that's the day I'm gone," Fred told him. He squinted at Step. "Why you care 'bout those Italians all a sudden anyway?"

All he could do was shake his head. "Ain't right. They don't even know what they's signing up for."

"We all come out the same in the end," Fred told him. "Ain't got but a nickel in our pockets."

"Nickel?" Step said. "You tellin me you gettin that much?"

***

HE drove out to the Modena section for another look. The last two years they'd had good crops; the market had been recovering, bringing six–and–a–half cents a pound and then last year over seven cents. Seven cents again would make him happy, and eight cents was something to dream for. Of course, the Italians would get less, Mr. Gates taking his interest out of their crop, and making them sell wherever he decided was best for his pocket. The new Modena section was good land, though, and should do all right. But that Fish Bayou bottomland would have brought in half of any other farm, and probably would have made the tenants sick, if it didn't kill them. Should put Horton's farm down there near the swamp if he's so keen on the land being farmed, Step thought. Put him down there with the cottonmouths and mosquito swarms and Lally Mo and her hoodoo, see how long he'd last.

While he thought about cotton prices and Lee Horton, he ticked off the condition of each farm he passed. He knew them by section and by number: 1 through 20, north of the landing, Ancona; 21 through 30, Senigallia; 31 through 40, Vicenza. And so forth. He noticed the weeds that grew or didn't grow. He knew which lands had been pulled and burned, and which had had their dry cotton stalks plowed under. He ticked off the fields of the sick, where the stalks still rattled in the wind, some with small, dirty balls of cotton still clinging to them. He could tell if a farmer had grown too sick to work halfway through harvesting his crop, and he could tell which farmers had died. Even more, the fields said something about the workers' personalities, about their hopes and their pride. All that from a dry, barren field in the middle of November. He noticed it all, and the information registered, but then he was thinking about other things.

He was thinking of how he was going to rise up on Sweet Hope. He'd seen it in those glory years, as young as he was then after the war, when Blacks pretty much ran the county. It didn't last long, but it had happened, and he didn't forget it. These would be different glory years. Mr. Gates was already helping him, but would give him more authority on Sweet Hope, raise his pay. Might even have him manage the entire plantation. Then someday he'd take that pay and leave Sweet Hope, buy his own plantation, hire his own workers. They'd have a real house, in town, and his children would go to a real school, and they wouldn't have to work like dogs in the fields.

He thought of Birdie sitting down at the supper table the other night and saying *mangia*, let's *mangia*. "Where you get that from?" he'd asked her, and she'd shrugged, and Tobe had covered his mouth to keep from laughing. He knew they'd picked up some language from the Italians, even as they made fun of them. Already he'd seen them running with those two of Serafin's, no matter what had just nearly happened. "You goin near that river again?" he'd asked Tobe harshly, a cold shiver passing through his body. Fancy watched the boy with her own worried eyes. "No sir," Tobe answered, so serious that Step knew he was telling the truth. "Better see you keep it that way, too," he'd said.

And then he thought of the sawmill again, and how dangerous a place it was for a boy to work: Fred's grown boy JoeJack, and his own Calvin who was straining to grow older. Not Tobe, though. He didn't want Tobe anywhere around machines, nor water either. That left only the dirt fields for him, which was fine with Step. He tried to convince himself, once again, that Calvin was big enough to take care of himself.

"Except 'round girls," Fancy would say. "You see the way that Italian girl looked him over? An' him turnin it right back on her."

"Ain't nothin," he'd told Fancy. Just the same, he'd had a few words with Calvin: "Be careful who you lookin in the eye."

"Aw, Pa, why you an' Ma always thinkin somethin bad?" the boy had answered. "They just the same as we is."

The boy had half a point. The Italians weren't white, but they weren't black either. He wasn't sure what they were.

He pulled the mule up into the Modena lots. The land was lumpy, from where tree stumps had recently been pulled. There were already half a dozen farms in the section. The land was good, rich. The stand of trees meant the farmers would not have to go far for firewood, or to get out of the heat of the sun in the summer. He'd have to build a couple of storehouses here for the new tenants, for holding their cotton, and he wondered if the company was going to raise the Modena rents to cover the cost of a few planks of wood. He started planning his crew: Calvin and JoeJack, Serafin, and maybe his friend Lazzaro. The boy down on farm 38 whose father had just died, he'd give that boy some work.

He turned the mule back toward his own farm. If Sweet Hope were his, he'd do things differently. It would be a better plantation, more productive. Get rid of Horton, and the others like him, that would be one of the first things. Put some of the Italians in charge, but not the traitors like Rosconi. Dig more wells, put in filters. Get rid of the interest charges, and let them gin and sell their cotton where they wanted. Treat them fair, like human beings.

Yes, he knew all about it. But the plantation was not his.

CHAPTER 4

Ceravone's Visit

November 1901

CERAVONE was the oldest Italian farmer on Sweet Hope and a member of the first colony, the one that had disbanded before Harlan Gates bought the property. He was happy to go to Lazzaro and Fiorenza's house to talk. People usually didn't invite him. Who would think to invite an old man when the company had eyes and ears that seemed to float in the very air they breathed?

Lazzaro had come right out and asked him. To hell with what people said, to hell with rumors. He wanted to get to the bottom of things. He'd been assigned as a day laborer on Ceravone's farm, since he'd come too late to make his own crop. Most of the Italians came too late to start a crop. That was another thing they either learned or figured out on their own: the company deliberately brought them in too late. That way they could charge rent for the houses and land, charge outrageous prices for food and staples over the fall and winter and all the next year until the Italians made a crop. They would already be in debt before half a year was out. There'd be no way they could pay off their contract. They'd be stuck at Sweet Hope indefinitely in a never–ending cycle of debt. And with no letters allowed out, and travel off the plantation forbidden for Italians, it seemed they were doomed.

A truce, Serafin had begged of Amalia that first night. He had tried to get word out to her, to stop her from coming with the children, to no avail. She was enraged when she realized that the shack she'd been taken to with the children after their long journey to America was their new home.

She had made him sleep on the floor. The children tried to make room for him in their bed across the room, but it was too cramped. He vowed to build another bed, so that the girls would not have to sleep with Osvaldo — and so that he would have a place to sleep as well if she did not relent. Finally after several nights of hard boards and splinters, he ventured in beside her like a thief in the night. She let him stay. They had signed a contract to come to Sweet Hope, after all.

Now, before going to Lazzaro's house, they sat on their floor around a board of polenta, sharing the three spoons from which they ate. Serafin's bare feet stuck out from the bottom of his pant legs. His feet were finally starting to feel normal again. His shoes and socks were propped on logs in front of the stove. Amalia had insisted on drying them for him, soaked as they were from working in the swamp all day. He could smell the stinking mud even though he'd washed himself outside, and she had taken the shoes and socks out to rinse as well.

Osvaldo poked the spoon in, then trailed a lump of polenta across the board toward himself. Angelina took the spoon from his hand. "We'll eat yours if you're not hungry. Right, mama?"

The boy grabbed the spoon back. "After we talk to the man tonight," he said, "can we go live in the nice village?"

"We're living in it, *scemo*," Isola berated him.

When his lower lip quivered, Isola laughed, and Amalia gave her a warning squint.

"Someday," Serafin told them, "we'll live in a beautiful village." He tousled Osvaldo's hair. "Don't you worry about that."

From where they sat they could see through the open doorway into the long, withered fields. The gin mill clanged, and it was like hammers banging against their chests, so that at times they found themselves breathing to the rhythm of the gin mill without even thinking of it.

***

ONCE it was dark, they gathered at Lazzaro's house, making sure the windows were covered in case one of the company managers came snooping around. The men had been working for day wages anywhere they could on the plantation. The last couple days they'd been sent to the swamps to cut firewood for the gin mill and to clear stumps. Even the women and children worked, cutting the smaller branches or carrying wood. And the damn company made them rent the tools they used and charged them interest on top of it.

The children sat on the floor while the adults, even Fiorenza's old mother La Vecchia, gathered around the table. Fiorenza had pinned up the old lady's gray hair to keep it from falling in her face. She wore a baggy knitted sweater and kept winding a stray length of yarn from one of the sleeves around a knitting needle.

Lazzaro owned two chairs and a stool, and had brought in a stump of log that he stood on end, and Serafin had carried the chair from their house. Lazzaro sat on the big spaghetti pot that he had turned upside down. His shoulders barely reached the tabletop, and he leaned forward, arms folded on the table.

Serafin could feel his damp shoes through the dry socks he'd put on, and he smelled the swamp mud wafting up now and then. He wasn't sure if it was coming from him or from Lazzaro. At least they were done with the swamps for a while. Tomorrow they'd be picking cotton again with Step Hall, the last of the crop on a sick family's farm. When Lazzaro caught Serafin's eye he winked as if to say, "Now you'll see. Now we'll get somewhere."

Ceravone sat among them, a thin, white-haired old man with sagging cheeks and youthful eyes, from *Le Marche* region like so many of them. Lazzaro had helped out on his farm a few times and learned that the old man knew more than anyone about the workings of Sweet Hope — and was always happy to voice his opinions. Fiorenza poured the man a short glass half-full of pale red wine, the wine Lazzaro had pressed from wild grapes they'd gathered near the swamp. "See? Only a few months here, and already I've built a great wine press!" he told them, pointing to rocks and a board and an old washtub.

Ceravone smiled into his glass. He leaned back in his chair, tapping the side of the glass with his forefinger, as if he were accustomed to being the center of attention.

They watched him drink the wine, and they waited patiently for him to talk because he was old and because he was one of the first Italians to settle at Sweet Hope.

"Well," he said at last. "I suppose you want to hear something, eh?"

Only three families remained of the first immigrants, Ceravone told them. "Dead from malaria or starvation. Not like you hear, I know, they say there are dozens of us, rich, living like kings. Pah."

Lazzaro and Serafin eyed each other. It was hard for them to admit how they'd jumped at those stories of an America, *il Paradiso*, that awaited them with open arms. But it wasn't just them, they had to keep reminding themselves. Lots of people were leaving for America.

There'd been other Italians, Ceravone told them. Some said a priest led them north to the hilly land to grow grapes. Others said it was a prince from Italy who came on a white horse, led them across the whole state of Arkansas to those vineyards.

"But they could leave?" Serafin asked. "How was that possible?"

"Our big–shot owner Harlan Gates — you know he's one of the biggest planters in the Delta?" Ceravone said. "He let them go, who knows why — things were different then. There wasn't a stitch of cotton up there, not a single plant, and no malaria either. But they found worse nightmares: gunshots in the night, peoples' homes burned out from underneath them — some *brutti Americani* trying to force them out."

These were the things Ceravone had heard, he told them. He didn't know for sure. There were hills there, three hundred miles away from Sweet Hope, but there was no prince living among the people, that he knew for a fact.

"Eh, I stayed only because my family died of malaria," Ceravone told them. "Every last one of them. I didn't care to walk across the state of Arkansas right then. What did it matter to me if I died here alone from starvation or wild animals or swamp fever?"

La Vecchia laughed, and Fiorenza took the needle away and started unwinding the yarn from it. "There's yarn on the bed, mama. Don't unravel your sweater."

"Think of a fairy tale," Ceravone told them, "and then you will begin to understand. Everything that is real here is fantastic. Fantastic like Dante's hell that you hear about. Hell is something we can all understand. But the Garden of Eden — who has seen that place? Even God forgot where he put it."

Eventually, Ceravone's only remaining relatives, a grandson and his family, came from Italy to live with him and work the farm. "A big mistake," he told them. "Hundreds of us imported to the Italian colonies in America, herded in with lies to work like animals."

"That doesn't explain — " Serafin ventured. He paused. They hadn't called for this meeting to hear Ceravone's long family history. "Listen, here's what we want to know: about our contracts. What have we gotten ourselves into? We can't even step off the place to dig greens for a meal or they threaten to shoot us."

"Oh, that," Ceravone said, waving one bony hand through the air as if it were nothing. "Too bad you came to Sweet Hope. Any other place in America, you might have been better off."

"The contract," Serafin insisted. "What do we have to do to get out of here?"

"Everything they told you was false, a lie."

"Then we're not really under contract?" Lazzaro asked.

Ceravone laughed. "No, not that. The contract's the one thing that's real."

They stared at him, waiting for more.

"Those agents, Rosconi, people like him?" Ceravone said. "Eh, the company pays them for each one of us they bring over. Of course they're going to tell us anything we want to hear. *Come to Paradiso.* Not until we die, my friends, and even then — well, who knows? Those contracts you signed?" Ceravone laughed lightly. "The company owns you. Owns every last one of us."

"*Merda,*" Serafin said. "That's not true."

Lazzaro agreed. "If what you're saying is true, someone would have found out, put a stop to it by now."

"Yes, every once in a while some Italians here call for an uprising," Ceravone told them. "You know, like the work strikes back home. Always the same thing here, though — big talk, nothing happens. They want an Italian priest to save them, they want to get word out to the Italian government to save them, the American government. Eh, priests, governments." He spat on the floor, right there in their house.

They stared at the spittle on the floor.

"But why would the Americans want to do such a thing?" Serafin asked. "Treating us like *schiavi*, slaves."

"Slaves, that's right," Ceravone said. "Now you see." He leaned closer and lowered his voice, as if to tell a secret. The children cocked their heads to hear. "You see all the dark Americans around here?" Ceravone shook his head. "What a thing. Worse than what happened to some of those poor Sicilians back home. There are rumors — you'll hear them — and some of them are true." He looked over at the children, as if considering whether he should continue. "This is a bad story. Long ago the *bianchi*, the white Americans, went to their country, stole them, put them in cages and sold them like animals. Branded their skin with hot irons. I've seen a man with the marks right here on his arm." He pointed to a spot near his shoulder, paused to let his words sink in. "Who knows? But there's another story."

The children watched, wide-eyed.

Serafin didn't believe a word of it. "Look at Step Hall," he said. "Better off than us, in charge of half the workers."

"That's right," Lazzaro agreed.

"You'll see," Ceravone told them.

Serafin was losing his patience. "What are you trying to say, *vecchio*? These stories of yours don't explain anything."

Lazzaro raised a cautioning hand to his friend.

"He's not telling us anything," Serafin complained.

"You came here to work?" Ceravone said. "You'll work. *Schiavi*. That's a good way to put it." He rubbed his thumb across his fingers. "Money, eh, isn't that what it's all about? You've been bought, my friends."

They looked around the table at each other. Already they'd been shocked by the high prices at the company store. And then there were the stories from the other tenants about debt, hunger, sickness...

"Well then," Serafin said. "So you have been telling us a story."

"Not exactly," Ceravone answered. "But that's how it is."

Fiorenza rose to pour more wine, which Ceravone politely refused. She did not bother to add to the thimble–full sitting in the bottom of Lazzaro and Serafin's cups. It was a courtesy, the wine, for their visitor, between him and the two oldest men. At home you never had to think about being stingy with your wine. Here, everything had to be weighed and measured, even your words, even your thoughts. Except if you were Ceravone. He talked as if it were the most natural thing in the world to reveal his life to strangers. And then it turned out — he had as much as admitted it — that what he was telling them might not be true, either.

"We keep hearing about the first immigrants," Lazzaro told Ceravone, "just like you say, how rich they are, lackeys for the Americans, working against us. No wonder we never see these big farms of theirs. They don't exist."

Ceravone nodded gravely. "Now you understand."

Serafin felt his insides collapsing on him. All of Amalia's fears, all her accusations — true? "But our contracts," Serafin insisted. "Are you telling us nobody gets ahead here? Nobody owns his farm?"

"Just the *bianchi*," Ceravone answered.

Serafin was drowning, sinking into deep water right there in his seat. Why was it that Lazzaro didn't seem devastated by this news? Nor the women? He raised his hands, as if to struggle to the surface, but they felt like lead.

"There're plenty Italians working against you, my friends," Ceravone told them. "They don't care a rat's ass if you live or die, as long as they get paid."

"Anybody else around here is afraid to open their mouths," Serafin said. His voice was accusatory, distrustful.

"Look at me," Ceravone said. "I'll be dead pretty soon, thank God. What do I care what I say anymore?"

"History, that's all he's told us," Lazzaro said to Serafin. "What's the problem with that?" But his voice was trembling.

"You're right," Serafin told Lazzaro. "There's no problem with telling history." What he was thinking, though, was how terrible it must be to get so old that you don't care anymore what you're saying. To not care because all your family is dead and you are at the end of your life.

Fiorenza rose and went to the stove. Only a few sticks of firewood lay on the floor, and she debated whether she should light a fire. She glanced at the children sitting on the floor. A clear line of snot ran from Osvaldo's nose, but otherwise they gave no indication that they felt the cold. She listened at the doorway where her mother sat on the bed arranging her balls of yarn. Fiorenza caught Amalia's eye, pulled her sweater close about her and raised her eyebrows to ask if she felt chilly. Amalia shook her head, no. She was fine.

"Can I offer you a piece of bread?" Fiorenza asked Ceravone. "I'm sorry we don't have anything more right now." She glanced at Lazzaro as she said this.

"Oh no, thank you," Ceravone said. "I'm full. Too fat as it is. I couldn't eat a piece of bread if you forced it down me."

They looked at his bony frame, smiled and nodded.

"Ah, you know what I really miss, most of all?" Ceravone said. "The mountains. All this flat land will end up making you crazy."

"You can still go up there where the grape growers are," Lazzaro told him. He sympathized with the man, working with him just these few weeks. "Why don't you go?"

After all he'd learned, he talked this way about going here and there as if they were back home, as if it were perfectly natural for someone to have the freedom to travel about where he wished whenever he wished.

Ceravone shook his head wistfully. "Go? My grandson's with me now, and all his children. It would kill them if I went." He looked up at the black window a moment. "Besides, a mountain is nothing," he said, "if your family is not there with you."

Lazzaro nodded.

"Well, surely your grandson and those great–grandchildren of yours must give you some comfort," Fiorenza told the man, wondering when he would leave. She looked over at Amalia's huddled, miserable children. "It's good to have children around. They make us forget our troubles."

Ceravone turned to her. "Children?" He said it quietly, as if it was something new to him that he would have to think about. "My children are all up at Hyner. I go there sometimes to look at the graves."

Fiorenza went to the stove again, touched the cold iron and held her fingers there a moment. Amalia folded her hands on the table. From where she sat she could see the tops of her children's heads. Something cold went through her.

"Ah, well," Ceravone said. "What's the use to think about all that now?" And then he was quiet.

Serafin raised his eyes to the dark corner near the ceiling, and there, suddenly, was Valerio, drifting through the dark empty space above their heads, near the ceiling. He blinked his eyes, shocked at the sight. Twice they had lost men at sea. Twice he had been there to help pull them in too late. One of them his own brother Valerio, barely twenty. Serafin had leaned over the boat to grab the flailing arm, but there was no saving him.

His throat tightened, and for a moment he felt as though he himself were floating up toward the ceiling.

Fiorenza clanged the stove shut, and Valerio was gone again.

Amalia was staring at Serafin, as if she could see his thoughts written across his face. Those narrowed eyes, daring him to speak his brother's name. "After all the hell you've put us through," he could imagine her saying. "Because of Valerio?"

He knew it had been bad, what he'd been like that first year after Valerio's death, him crying all the time, never knowing what would set it off: the way the sky looked on a certain day, the flap of a bird's wing.

"It's like living with a crazy man," Amalia would complain. "I can't bear it anymore. Your children need you. I need you."

But it hadn't been because of Valerio that he had wanted to come to America, not really. To get away from the dreams of him, the bad thoughts? Not entirely. Lots of people were coming to America — and wasn't Lazzaro the one who had told him of the agents in the first place?

"You too," he'd told Amalia when she railed at him after she arrived at Sweet Hope. "You wanted to come to America too. Don't blame it all on me."

"Maybe I did," she'd answered. "For different reasons."

Lazzaro cleared his throat. "Ah well," he said, trying to get the old man moving. "Let's hope we have good weather again tomorrow."

The others agreed. Yes, at least you weren't suffocating anymore while you worked.

"You'll want to bring in more wood, though," Ceravone told Lazzaro. "You need to keep your firewood stocked up, the weather turns so fast. Keep it under your house so it'll stay dry. And start a big pile behind your house, too."

"Yes, I'll do that," Lazzaro said.

Serafin looked at the dark window. There was always that feeling that they were doing something they should not be doing, and that *l'americani* would find out and make trouble for them. They were always riding around with guns, treating them like criminals. They could put you on a chain gang, throw you into a jail you never returned from, your family abandoned and still having to pay off their debt. So the rumors said.

Ceravone didn't seem worried, though. He was old, and soon he would be dead, thank God. "What do I care about the Americans, about anything they could do to me?"

Anyway, it was getting late. Ceravone needed to get back. "No need to walk me to my place," he told them. "I know every inch of Sweet Hope. I could walk it in the dark with my eyes closed. But don't you try it."

"Good riddance," Serafin said after the man had left.

They remained at the table, their faces clouded with worry.

"We wanted some answers," Amalia said miserably. "There's our answers."

"He's just a bag of hot air, a crazy old man," Serafin said. "Listen, if we can find a way out, we'll get out. Meanwhile, we'll work hard, we'll show this damn company." Already he was thinking ahead, scheming.

"Yes," Fiorenza said. "I think he was just making things up, talking to hear the sound of his own voice."

"Still," Lazzaro said. "I don't know. There has to be some truth to it. *Schiavi*. Isn't that what it's like for us, after all?"

"You'd think the Italian government would know what was going on and put a stop to it," Serafin said.

"We never heard anything bad back home," Lazzaro said.

"You didn't ask Ceravone if anyone got out of here alive," Amalia said. "Have any Italians paid off their contracts and gone back home?"

The one important question, and no one had thought to ask.

"Let's just forget that old man," Serafin told them. "He doesn't know what he's saying. We'll work hard, and we'll get ahead. That's all it takes."

"I don't see anybody making it here," Lazzaro answered.

"Tomorrow," Serafin told him. "I'll figure something out, you'll see."

"Mama, I'm hungry," Isola said. "Can we have some bread and wine now that that old man's gone?" The other children approached the table at the mention of food.

"Don't be impolite," Amalia told them.

"It's all right," Fiorenza said, gathering what crumbs were left, and pouring a little wine into Ceravone's empty glass. "Here," she told the children. "Everybody gets a little taste. When it's gone, it's gone."

***

THE sun was growing warm as Serafin and Lazzaro worked beside Step on the sick family's farm. The croker sacks that dragged behind them became heavier with each passing minute. Their fingers cracked and bled, but when Serafin caught Lazzaro's eyes he winked.

He tried to calculate how much they'd come to Sweet Hope with: what amounted to twenty American dollars. They'd have to repay their passage, whatever that added up to, and then with two dollars a day here, a dollar there, Ceravone be damned... He stopped himself, uncertain how much day labor he could count on over the winter.

When the noon dinner break was called, he took Lazzaro aside. "Listen, *amico*, come with me, and I'll show you how we're going to make it."

"What?"

Serafin pulled him along without answering.

Step gave them puzzled looks as they left. "Back, be back," Serafin told him. "To see a man."

They walked swiftly, chewing on their dinner of hard bread and cheese as they took long strides along the road. In his pocket, Serafin had wrapped the *lire* equivalent of three American dollars.

"What are you up to?" Lazzaro asked.

"You'll find out soon enough," Serafin answered.

"I need to take a rest."

"Tonight you can rest. In your bed, while you sleep."

When Lazzaro threatened to turn around, Serafin took him by the elbow. "I'm going to make some money. You too."

The store was crammed with bins and counters and shelves full of everything anyone would need to live at Sweet Hope: food, clothes, tools, cooking supplies, wagon parts, buckets and tubs and mule harnesses. Only a few people were shopping, Italian women with children and a black man buying a new mule harness. The clerk looked up at them as they walked down one of the aisles.

They passed Barretto the translator's table, where the man sat digging a knife blade into a belt to make another hole, and made their way to the axes and saws. Serafin fingered the money in his pocket. Even when you asked the price of something it seemed the money never added up to what you thought it should. He should start keeping his own records like some of the others were doing, he told himself. But who had the paper to write on and the pen or pencil? And what could you do, anyway, when your numbers came out different from the company's?

They stopped in the back of the store.

"Saws?" Lazzaro asked.

Serafin picked up one to test its weight and the flex of the blade, then laid it down and tried the other one. "What do you think? This one's a little better, eh?" Neither of the two seemed as good as the ones the company rented.

"You want to buy a saw?" Lazzaro asked. "What for?" They kept their voices down, glancing around occasionally to see if anyone was watching.

"I'm going to rent tools to the tenants, like the company does, only cheaper. The farmers will come to us for their tools, and we'll turn a little profit. Before you know it, we'll have our own business."

Lazzaro's eyes widened as the idea sank in. His wife, her mother, maybe he'd be able to give them a better home to live in, better food, keep the old lady from going downhill the way she had in just the few months since they'd arrived. He fingered a saw. "But look at this piece of shit," he said. "Won't we need something better than this? It'll break in two in no time."

Serafin shrugged. "It'll just take a little longer to start making a profit, that's all. We've got to stay one step ahead of these crooks. Let's see which one is cheaper."

He carried the saws to the American clerk, his heart racing now that the deed was almost done. The clerk watched as the two men approached and Serafin laid the saws on the counter. The clerk looked down at them, then up at Serafin.

"What do you want?" he asked.

What did the clerk think he wanted? "To buy," Serafin said. He held out his hand. "*Quanto?*"

"You want to buy two saws?" the man said, holding up two fingers as he said it. "What are you, nuts?"

Serafin smiled in relief. Not as high as he thought. "Two *dollari?*"

He nodded to the man, pointed to the saw that seemed to have the stronger blade, and pulled the lire from his pocket, separating out two thirds of the money. Lazzaro hung back, impressed with the way his friend was conducting business with the American.

"What the hell are you doing?" the clerk said, pushing the money back into Serafin's hand. "Get out of here."

"No?" Serafin said.

The man took the saw away from him, then pointed to Barretto across the room. "Go ask Barretto," he said. "If you can't understand English you have Barretto to help you. God Almighty."

"English," Serafin said. "Me talk l'English. Me buy."

"No buy," the man said. "Never mind buy. Not for sale. No sell, understand? No sell to Italian." He pointed again to Barretto. "Go talk to him."

"No *Italiano*?" Serafin said. He reached for the saw, while trying to give the money to the clerk again, but the clerk pulled back and started cursing him. "Barretto," the clerk called out. "Barretto, get the hell over here."

Barretto looked up from his table. "What's the problem?"

People were starting to whisper among themselves.

"Come get this stupid Dago," the clerk called to him.

Barretto rose from his table with a disgusted shake of his head.

"What's going on?" Serafin asked. Now Lazzaro bowed his head, fidgeting with his hat in his hands.

Barretto marched over to the counter. He eyed Serafin, then Lazzaro. "What the hell are you two trying to do?" he asked in Italian. "Why aren't you working?"

"I'm trying to buy the saw. He tells me two dollars, I give him two dollars, then he takes the saw away and says no."

Barretto and the clerk exchanged words in English, pointing to the saws, then to Serafin with rising voices. The few women moved closer, pretending to shop while they strained to hear what was going on.

Finally Barretto turned to Serafin. "He didn't tell you the saw was two dollars, he was asking what's wrong with you that you think you're going to buy two saws."

"No, just one," Serafin said. "That one there." He reached for his money again, but Barretto stopped him.

"You can't buy a saw. Those are for the Americans to buy."

"What are you talking about?"

Barretto looked at the clerk, then back at Serafin. For once he didn't seem like he was so happy about being such a big shot at the company store. "Italians have to rent the tools," he told the two men. "You can't buy them, only the *americani* can."

"What? Why not?" Serafin insisted. "I've got the money. Look." He pulled all his money from his pocket again and held it cupped in his two hands to show the men.

"They won't take your *lire* anyway," Barretto told him. "You have to exchange it for lead scrip."

"Then I can buy?"

"Put your money away," Barretto told him quietly.

"I want to buy a saw," Serafin insisted. "I've got the money right here."

Barretto talked to the clerk again for a minute while the onlookers whispered to each other.

Barretto turned back to Serafin. "He says the saw costs fifteen dollars."

Serafin stared at him, speechless. "I can buy a whole damn farm for that," he shouted.

"Not at Sweet Hope," Barretto told him.

"My money's no good for you now?" Serafin shouted to the clerk who understood none of what he was saying. "It's only good to buy supplies that disappear — a sack of moldy flour or rancid oats that you charge ten times the price for? Here's to your rotten store, you thieves." He threw his money to the floor and stalked away while Lazzaro stared in fear.

Barretto reached out to stop Serafin. Of course the man had a right to be angry, but he couldn't just throw his money on the ground. He had a family, a farm to run, debts to pay. "Wait, *amico*, be sensible," he said.

Finally Lazzaro was able to move. He followed his friend quickly, afraid of leaving the money behind, but more afraid of staying there alone.

"Don't sell to Italians," Serafin kept saying, shaking his head. "What the hell kind of place is this? What the hell did they bring us here for if they don't want to do business with us?" He brushed past the embarrassed women pulling their children aside.

Barretto picked up the money and went after Serafin. When he refused it again, Barretto pushed it into Lazzaro's hands. "He has to think of his family at least," Barretto said.

"Treating us like animals," Serafin said bitterly. He hurried out of the store with Lazzaro clutching the money.

"You better get used to it," Barretto said. Then more softly he called to them: "Look, don't make trouble. We all have to get by here."

They walked in silence back to the cotton field. Tears, mingled with dust, stung Serafin's eyes.

Lazzaro put his hat back on. He walked in a daze. His wife, her old mother drifted for a moment before his eyes. "Maybe we can try again some other time, when someone else is working at the store."

Serafin said nothing.

"They can't all be bastards," Lazzaro said.

Serafin spat at the side of the road in response.

They reached the field and passed Step's inquiring eyes. "Where you been at?" Step asked.

Serafin laughed. "Eh, *niente*. Everything good."

They picked up their croker sacks, hooked them over their shoulders, then turned quickly to hide their humiliated faces.

CHAPTER 5

First Christmas

December 1901

Across the land came the occasional cry of birds in the bordering trees, and now and then the honk of geese or ducks flying toward the lake. Clusters of Italians came from every direction, their lanterns winking in the dark, all heading for the little storage building near the lumber mill that served as a church. Some families were dressed in rags — it was obvious even in the dark. Some walked slowly, stumbling along the dirt road, some leaning on a stick or on another's arm. Sick from the fever or from months or years of having too little to eat or sick from drinking the silty water that smelled as bad as it looked.

Buona sera, they called out to each other. *Buon natale.*

Now and then music and laughter wafted across the fields in little waves; and then the waves were gone. Serafin raised his head to catch the sound. "*I neri*," he proclaimed, the blacks off in their shacks, celebrating Christmas Eve.

The building was crowded with so many people that they had to stand outside. Some of the farmers had turned their lanterns down, to save kerosene. A couple of lamps burned in the windows of the church, giving off a faint, eerie light.

Angelina had had dreams about the river, ever since the day her father almost drowned going after Tobe Hall. She would see the water creeping up the bank to the landing and spilling across the land, and then in one big wave crashing into their house and taking them all. It had long watery arms, like octopus tentacles, and it grabbed each one of them by the throat and held them under cold water as they kicked and flapped their arms until she finally woke up gasping for air.

The nights were so black that even with her eyes wide open she could see nothing. Nothing at all in the world, and she was alone in all that black nothing. She would pull out the small holy medal from beneath her blouse and finger its triangular edges — the *Madonna di Loreto* — and wonder if the Blessed Mother could see them there now, in the dark, so far from home. Then she would hear the crackling of a mattress behind her, or one of the children sighing in sleep, or her father's gentle snoring, or sometimes her mother crying softly.

In Montignano at *natale*, the inside of their small stone church would flicker with burning candles that reflected off the altar and stone floor and walls, so that the air itself was breathing, pulsing white light. Evergreen boughs lay heaped at the altar, tied with faded red ribbons and scenting the air with balsam that mixed with the smell of incense and hot wax.

Father Molina would say Mass and read the story of the Christ child's birth, and after Mass he would kiss all the children and give them each a few almonds or chestnuts. Then people would walk home through the streets together, singing, stopping to visit their friends and relatives to have a coffee or a nip of *grappa* or maybe a bite of *pasticcino* — if they had any coffee or *grappa* or Christmas cake. Even among the poor the sound of singing voices and moaning bagpipes would continue through the night.

Here, instead of bagpipes or singing came the murmuring complaints of people waiting outside the plantation building that served as a makeshift church, stamping their feet to keep warm and wondering out loud where the American priest was. One of the men went down to the company store to see if anybody knew anything even though people told him the store was closed.

But where is that damn priest, they asked each other? Did he get lost? Did he forget us?

Serafin caught sight of Ceravone's grandson and family, but the old man was not with them. Some women inside the church started saying the rosary, and soon the people outside joined in. An old man standing near the side of the church took off his hat and held it in his gnarled hands. He bowed his head and moved his lips, mumbling along with the women.

Not everybody prayed. Some people talked, as they often did, about the money they owed the company. Some talked about the chances of getting an Italian priest to come to Sweet Hope, and how he would speak up for them, put an end to the injustices. Others talked about getting word of their plight to the Italian government, so they could pressure the Americans to let them go. Maybe someone could get to New Orleans and go through the Italian Consulate there. And some cursed the plantation owner.

Eh, you think that son–of–a–bitch Gates cares anything about his workers? Wring as much money from our blood and sweat as he can, that's what he cares about.

Take a man's balls in his hands and squeeze till all that's left is a little black olive pit.

And he'd sell that, too.

Half of us sick or dead now — malaria, fever. If the work doesn't kill us, disease will.

We're filling the cemetery faster than a dog will piss on a tree.

The man who had gone to the store returned breathless and shouted the news: The store's all closed up. The managers' houses all dark, too.

What did he expect? Who would stay here on Christmas if he could get out?

But is it true? No overseers, no Americans? We can leave, right now — let's pack up and get the hell out of here.

Silence. Then a jumble of voices. Let's go. No, it's a trick. They've posted men outside Sweet Hope.

Through the woods, then.

They'll come with dogs, throw us in jail, shoot us.

Where the hell would we go, anyway? Into the river? The swamps? We don't even know where we are.

We're in hell, that's where we are.

I'm going, is anyone coming with me?

Will you carry your wife and your kids on your back?

And so they bantered, debated, searched the black fields in the black night with their hopeful, desperate eyes.

A man called out that it was over an hour past the time the priest was supposed to be there. But maybe they'd heard the time wrong.

No, no, too many people had heard: the overseers had told them — Step Hall himself had told them — the company was sending the American priest from the village to say midnight Mass. We wouldn't all have heard it wrong, would we?

Another lie, somebody said. Another lie to shut us up, keep us pacified.

"What if the priest doesn't come?" Angelina asked her mother. "If we don't go to church for Christmas, aren't we sinning?"

Amalia said nothing. But inside she was trembling over this latest insult. Was it possible that even the American God was against them? She put her hand on Angelina's shoulder to reassure her.

Do you think they'll let us go to the village in the morning for Mass? somebody said.

Are you crazy with swamp fever? a man answered. The company isn't going to let a hundred of us leave when they won't let even one man step foot over the boundary.

"Mama, I'm cold," Osvaldo said. "Can we go home now?"

"See?" Fiorenza said. "This kind of thing would never happen if we had an Italian priest."

Two men began arguing. "We're sheep, blind sheep," one of them yelled. "To hell with you," the other shouted. "I'm already in hell," the man shot back.

People were starting to leave. They murmured among themselves or hung their heads and walked in silence.

Angelina adjusted her flowered hat that no one could see in the darkness. She pressed her hand to the velvet yoke of her dress, holding back the tears.

"Come," their father said.

"But papa," Angelina begged, "what if the priest comes and no one's here?"

"Then he'll have to go back home without our money in his pocket," Serafin said, spitting.

"We can pray at home," Amalia told the children.

They walked behind Lazzaro's family under the cold starry night. Angelina wiped her cheeks. She kept her eyes on the hem of La Vecchia's coat as they walked. The cold air stung her wet eyes and face.

Suddenly, across the field a shape loomed. Amalia took Serafin's arm.

They stopped and stared into the blackness at a giant animal with long tusks. A bull? they wondered, afraid it would come after them. A stag? But it wasn't the right size or shape for either.

They started walking slowly, keeping their eyes on the animal. Every now and then it seemed to take a step or sway.

"Is it moving?" Amalia asked. "Is it coming after us?"

"Could it be dead on its feet?" Fiorenza whispered.

They passed the animal. Amalia looked back at the shape in the field, under the glittering stars. The beast took a step toward them. She put her hand on Osvaldo's shoulder. "Walk quickly, everybody," she told them. "Before it charges."

They hurried along until they heard La Vecchia screech. She had stopped behind them and was laughing her shrill laugh. "*Aratro*," she sang.

They stopped and strained to see the beast through the darkness. Finally they were able to see what the old woman saw: someone had left a plow standing in the field overnight. It was a plow, all right, the handles like long tusks.

"God in heaven," Serafin murmured. The children laughed nervously.

La Vecchia began to sing under her breath. *Tu scendi dalle stelle*, she sang in her high thin voice. *Tu scendi dalle stelle, O Re del Cielo*. You come down from the stars, Oh King of Heaven.

***

NEXT morning, Amalia rose early, scrounged some ingredients, and baked a batch of *torcetti* which she drizzled with the last of the honey from the beehive Serafin had knocked down in the woods. She cut each child a small chunk of bread, and poured a cup of coffee for them to share.

Osvaldo ran to check on the *presepio* he'd made from a cypress branch and pebbles and came back crying that there was no baby Jesus.

Serafin drank his coffee standing at the window. He looked at the table, at the empty egg bowl. "He's hiding on you," he told Osvaldo. "Maybe you'll find him digging ditches in the swamps or shoveling manure in the company barn."

At the last minute Amalia snatched the starched doily bowl from the shelf before going out.

They trudged the half–mile to the Hall farm. Amalia still could not get over the strange sensation of opening their door and stepping out into acres of barren, ragged fields. Walking to visit a neighbor left her hollow inside, for the neighbors might as well be in another country with all this flat land between them.

Angelina carried the bowl, careful not to crush it or get it dirty. "Can we make another one for ourselves, mama?" she asked. "I want to crochet the doily this time."

"We'll see," Amalia answered.

She was thinking of her old mother at home; this was their first time apart. She saw the woman in her chair by the window where she sat every afternoon. Sometimes the yellow cat would jump onto her lap and sleep with her and Amalia would stop and look at them, the way she was looking at them now. Inside her a knot kept twisting this way and that, so that she barely knew what she felt anymore, one minute to the next.

"Maybe Father Molina can come from home to live with us," Isola said.

"It'd kill him," Angelina put in, talking the way the old ladies did. "That's all we need."

Amalia gave a little grunt that Serafin could not interpret.

Osvaldo scuffed his shoes through the dirt, humming a tune he had learned from Tobe when they worked together, although Osvaldo did not know many of the words. He was thinking of slingshots and rabbit snares and how he would like to hunt rabbits with Tobe Hall and his father. If he had a slingshot he might even be able to kill a goose while it was flying, or a duck on the water, who knew, maybe even a turkey, except you could catch a turkey by running after it and throwing your jacket over its head.

Angelina stepped carefully, so as not to dirty her shoes. "I wonder if the Halls have a *presepio*," she said.

Isola began telling Osvaldo about American Christmas, how Americans must give you a penny when they saw you.

"You're just making that up," Angelina said. "All you ever do is make up stories."

"Birdie told me, you fat head."

Osvaldo asked if each one of the Halls would give him a penny. If so, he might be able to buy a slingshot.

"Only people you meet on the street."

Dejected, he hung his head, since they had met no one on the dusty Sweet Hope roads. But then he brightened. "You go in their house first, and tell them to come out and meet me."

In the distance, a small shack jutted from the pale earth. The sky was streaked with thin fingers of white clouds. Ducks and geese honked across the sky. A hawk ignored two smaller, screeching birds swooping at it. But the land was quiet. No one was out walking or driving a wagon, and the gin mill was silent. All the shacks of Sweet Hope were closed up, the people separate, apart. You would never know it was Christmas.

"I should have made something else to bring," Amalia said. "If you'd caught more fish... "

"It's enough," Serafin said. "They told us not to bring anything." But he felt the awkwardness of the situation.

"You can't go to someone's house empty-handed," she said, and she checked the bowl Angelina carried, to make sure it had not been harmed.

The Halls came out to meet them, the Titus family behind.

"*Buon natale!*" the Pascalas called.

"Happy Christmas, Merry Christmas," the families called to each other.

Fancy motioned them inside.

The Halls' house was bigger than theirs, though crowded now with everybody inside: Step and Fancy with their three children, Fred and Lud Titus with their nearly grown boy JoeJack and girl Lecie, a little older than Angelina. The table

was laden with bowls of strange food, the house full of unfamiliar cooking smells.

Amalia handed the basket of biscotti over to Fancy who
made a polite fuss, showing off the contents to the curious
children.

"What is they twisted things?" Birdie asked her mother.

"Some kinda bread?" Fancy said, glancing quickly at
Amalia.

"Sweet, good," Serafin told them, urging them to taste.
Calvin took the opportunity to stumble forward, his face
bright with expectation, not for the *biscotti*, but for Angelina.
She refused to look at him.

"Gonna eat dinner first," Fancy said. "Lud? We 'bout ready,
ain't we?"

Amalia nudged Angelina forward, and the girl held out
the bowl and lowered her head to a surprised Fancy Hall.

"You brung your cloth bowl?" she said, inspecting it, the
others gathering to admire it. "See, Lud, this what I was telling you 'bout. Made outta doily cloth." She held it up for Lud
to see.

"How they make it stand up stiff like that?" Lud placed a
bowl of greens on the table, wiped her hands on her apron,
then inspected the bowl.

Serafin tried to explain, but didn't know the word for
"starch." He opened and closed his hand, then made like he
was stirring water with his hand. Then he laughed and
shrugged.

"Tol' you they do hoodoo," Birdie said.

"That's craftsman's work, not hoodoo," Calvin said, and
Birdie punched him in the arm and taunted him: "*Craftsman's
work*"!

Fancy put the crocheted bowl on the table. When Amalia
protested that it would get wet, Fancy moved it to a shelf.

She directed the adults to the four chairs around the table where they had set out the plates of food. At Fred and Step's places stood upturned peach boxes. Serafin cursed himself for not carrying their own chairs to the house. He looked in wonder at the food that crowded the small table, then at Amalia who was surveying each dish with a critical eye.

Birdie showed the children to their place: a cloth on the floor near the stove. Isola plopped down on the cloth, but Birdie pulled her to her feet, pointing to her father and the others. They were standing around the table, holding each other's hands, their heads bowed, waiting for the children and Pascalas to join them.

"What?" Amalia asked Serafin.

He shrugged.

Step cleared his throat, looked up toward the ceiling, and began: "We thank y' Lord for your bountiful food — "

"*Preghan*," Amalia said. She crossed herself and fell to her knees, motioning the children down beside her. The others looked at them in surprise, Birdie stifling a giggle. "What the — ?" Lud said. The Pascala children knelt on the floor with bowed heads, Serafin reluctantly following.

Step looked cautiously around at the group, then continued: "And thank you Lord for our fam'ly, and for these friends who come share a table with us." He paused a moment. "And we ask y' look over everybody here at Sweet Hope. Amen."

The Pascalas stood up, and Lud and Fancy dished out the food while Step carved slices of meat. Lud raised her eyebrows to Fancy, but said nothing. She was slightly plump, with an oval face, no teeth, and a nearly bald head that made her look older than she was. Fred was just a little taller than his wife, thin and loose-boned, with dusky skin. The Titus children squatted on the floor with the smaller ones. Like her mother, Lecie tended toward the round side, although unlike her

mother she was quiet and shy. Her brother JoeJack took up
a big chunk of floor space. He was the biggest man in both
families, although he wasn't yet a man.

The food was simple, yet extravagant for Sweet Hope: the
small wild pig Step and Fred had trapped and smoked, a few
roast rabbits Step had snared, a pot of greens, biscuits, and
the two potato pies for which Fancy and Lud had managed
to gather enough sweet potatoes. They'd been cutting back
on sugar all month for them.

Fancy fixed Tobe a plate and motioned him closer to the
table. He and Birdie rolled their eyes at their mother, but
Tobe inched closer just the same. The Pascala children looked
in surprise at the plates of food Fancy placed before them.
In their family, the children — and often the entire family — ate
from the same dish or bowl.

"Go on, eat up," Step told the Pascalas.

The Tituses shot meaningful glances at each other. Those
looks said: "You see 'bout Step and Fancy? Goin down some
kinda funny road bringin these Italians in they house. Lookit
how they eatin, like they ain't never seen no ham bone before."

Serafin pointed to the pig. "You? Gun?" He made the
gesture of aiming and firing a gun.

Step laughed. "No sir. Hunt 'em with snare. You know
snare?" He made a loop with his hands, nodded his head
forward, then slipped the loop over his head and neck.

Serafin shook his head no, as he swallowed and felt the
loop of rope fall around his own neck again, and the river
churn beneath him.

"Rabbits, too, hunt 'em with snares. Tobe help me." Tobe
and Osvaldo had raised up on their knees to watch, Tobe
grinning the whole time.

Tobe made a snare with his hands and grabbed Osvaldo's
foot, knocking him off balance.

"Tobe Hall, I swear," Fancy scolded.

"I'm just showin him how to hunt, mama. He don't know nothin, less I show him."

Serafin told Step: "My papa in Italy, grow this." He pointed to the rabbits. "*Conigli.*"

"Grow 'em?" Step asked.

Serafin nodded happily.

"That's rabbit," Step told him. "Rabbit."

The Pascalas had eaten rabbit cooked in stew, and they'd had greens, but not this kind. Theirs were cooked in oil with a little garlic, not simmered in water with chunks of fat and meat. The pig was different, too, smoked and then glazed with a crust of molasses and sliced apples. The crumbly biscuits were nothing like the chewy bread they were accustomed to eating with greens.

"*É buono,*" Osvaldo said from the floor, and the other children laughed as he heaped more greens on his biscuit, and it fell apart before reaching his mouth, some of the mess sticking to his chin.

"*Vacca,*" Isola said, and Birdie grinned, even though she did not know the word for cow.

Now every time Isola put a bite of food in her mouth, Birdie did the same, exaggerating the way Isola chewed, so that the boys laughed. Angelina flushed. "Stop giving the farmers something to make fun of," she said in Italian.

Calvin was wilting in the girl's presence. When Angelina daintily picked up a piece of rabbit with her fingers, he jumped to hand her his fork. She put the meat back on her plate.

"I ain't makin fun," he told her, flushing miserably. "I was just tryin to help out."

"You a big help," Birdie jeered, and she picked up a slab of ham with her fingers and gnawed at it just to spite her brother. "These Italians don't know nothin," she said between chews.

Lecie Titus sat with a plate of food on her lap, eyeing the spectacle. JoeJack stayed as far away from the children as possible. He was a man, and should have been sitting with the adults. As soon as he could get away he was going to slip over to see his girl.

Birdie threw a biscuit and hit Isola in the face. The other children howled. Isola took only a moment to recover, and was ready to lunge at Birdie when Fancy lifted her daughter nearly off the floor by the back of her dress. She set Birdie down alone on the opposite side of the room.

Step held up his hand to stop Serafin from going after Isola. "My girl always trouble. Jes set down an' eat."

Once again, Lud and Fred exchanged knowing looks.

The food was the best the Pascalas had tasted since leaving home. Amalia discreetly nodded approval at Serafin. "Good," he told the others.

"Ain't nothin," Fancy said, pleased. "Just plain food."

"*Molto* good," Serafin said, and they laughed.

The children scattered about the room. Tobe and Osvaldo hunched in one corner, sneaking cranks on the coffee grinder Tobe had taken down from a shelf. Lecie and JoeJack drifted toward the table, to listen to the adults talking. Angelina, too, drifted closer to her mother while Calvin harangued the two younger boys with his superior knowledge of the workings of machines. Birdie crept across the room toward the stove, found a piece of charred wood and a flat board from the side of a salt box, and made a show of drawing pictures while Isola watched with curiosity. Soon the girls were sitting side by side, taking turns drawing for each other. Isola wrote "ABC," telling Birdie in Italian how she had learned to write some letters in Italy. Birdie gave her a disdainful look, snatched the charcoal, and also wrote "ABC." Then she wrote "CAT."

"I can write better'n you," she told Isola. "I gone to school here. Miss Betty come teach us four times a'ready. You can't even spell nothin."

Isola stared at the wooden slate, barely understanding half of what Birdie had said.

Birdie pointed to the word. "See? 'Cat'." She made a mewing sound.

Isola shrugged. She looked over at the table of adults struggling for conversation, pretending she was no longer interested in Birdie.

"I'll show you somethin," Birdie said. "Mama, how you write 'girl'? Mama?"

Fancy turned from setting down one of the pies. "What you say?"

"I say how you spell 'girl'?"

"Why you askin such foolishness? You know I don't know no writin business."

Birdie bit her lip. "Oh," she said. Then she bent over the slate and scrawled a few letters: C–D–R–A. "See?" she told Isola. "I can write, but you can't."

A loud metallic sound stopped them all. "What in God's name?" Fancy called out, catching sight of Tobe and Osvaldo huddled in the corner. Step was already upon them, taking the coffee grinder out of their hands, and pulling a fork from the hopper.

"You crazy?" Step shouted at his son. He rattled the coffee grinder and turned the crank to make sure nothing was broken.

"Tobe, I told you stay 'way from that boy," Fancy yelled. She shot a glance at her guests to see if the adults understood, but they appeared not to. "Did they break it, Step?"

"No, looks a' right."

"I can't stay 'way if he's in our house," Tobe answered.

"Don't you sass me. You git right over here."

Fancy went back to cutting the pie.

Serafin wolfed down the pie. "You like it?" Fancy asked, struggling to keep the smile from her face.

"Good," Serafin told them. "Like, we all like."

Amalia eyed her untouched little basket of biscotti near the stove. When she caught Serafin's attention, he raised his finger and nodded slightly. *Say nothing*, he was telling her.

Fred left the table and came back with a small, well-used concertina. He took his time sitting back down, placing the instrument in his lap, and running his right hand gently over one wooden end, as if it were a good child he was going to reward with a story. He unbuttoned a latch and let the instrument breathe open with a moan — then laughed at the Pascalas' expressions. The children moved closer.

"It sounds like a bagpipe," Osvaldo said.

"*Fisarmonica*," Angelina said.

"Is that what it is, papa?" Osvaldo asked.

"*C'é un* — how call, Mr. Fred?"

"Squeezebox," Fred told them. "Ain't you ever seen no squeezebox?"

He pushed and pulled the sides, to the children's delight.

"Skwee-bahk," Serafin told them.

Osvaldo reached for it. "*Voglio suonarlo*."

"Hey," Fred said, pulling back. "Hold on there, tadpole."

Serafin admonished his son: "You listen, that's all."

Fred played them a short, lively tune, smiling at the children as he pushed the sides of the squeezebox in and out and nimbly pressed a few buttons on one end. Then he played a slower tune and started singing in a gravelly voice. The Halls sang along with him, while Lud only nodded her bald head.

When Fred finished the song, he held the concertina out to Serafin. "You play?"

Serafin shook his head, surprised. "No, no, me no play — nothing."

"No? How 'bout you sing?" He brushed his hand from his mouth into the air and sang the word "sing."

Serafin laughed. "No sing."

"Sometimes you sing," Osvaldo said. "Doesn't he, mama?"

"Hey, don't tell my bad secrets," Serafin said. He paused, then smiled shyly and began:

Nanna-ó, Nanna-ó,
il bambino, a chi lo dó?
e lo dó all'omo nero
che lo tenga un anno intero

The children giggled to hear his wavering, unmelodic voice, and even Amalia smiled. "You have to sing that? A baby's lullaby?" she said. "Not even a Christmas song?"

For answer, he became louder, exaggerating his bad voice with comic gestures, and nodding to encourage the children to join in. Fred tried to squeeze out a few chords to the singing, but was having trouble following the tune. Osvaldo stood and sang along in the last few lines, about the baby being given away to Befana, and then to the bronze man and then the brass man so that he could pay his rent.

They applauded when the song ended. Amalia, however, kept her hands folded in her lap as she gazed at her crocheted bowl sitting on the Hall's kitchen shelf.

Birdie wrinkled her face. "That's a funny song. Don't make no sense."

"How you think our songs sound to them?" Step said.

Tobe shrugged. "Good?"

Fred tried to get them to sing another, but Serafin refused, embarrassed now that he had been so bold.

"You sure?" Fred asked. He shrugged, took up the instrument again.

The Halls sang along. Fancy brought out a jar of whiskey that the men passed among themselves, Serafin accepting a cup. Fancy and Lud took small sips, while Amalia refused.

She glanced at the window. "It's getting late," she tried to whisper to Serafin. "Fiorenza and Lazzaro will wonder what happened to us."

He too looked at the window while Fred launched into a slow song. It was a strange tune, with Fred repeating some of the unintelligible lines in a mournful way. The *fisarmonica* reminded him of sad bagpipes filling the air at Christmas, or at a funeral.

Amalia looked at the same window and saw her old mother across the sea, all the relatives gathered perhaps at that very moment, perhaps talking about them, or wondering about them, or praying for them. Serafin saw his fishing boat bob feebly once more on the Adriatic while he headed for shore with Valerio's still body. The years were passing. How was it possible that he was living in America of all places?

The song came to an end. Fred laid the concertina in his lap. Serafin sighed. He touched the cup of whiskey in front of him, turned it this way and that. The jar was nearly empty.

"In *Italia*, we live, *il mare*. I have big boat." He spread his arms wide to show them. He rolled his hands to make waves. "*Il mare.*"

"Water?" Step asked. "A lake?"

"The big," Serafin answered, spreading his arms wider. "Most big water."

"The ocean?"

Serafin nodded. "*L'oceano* we live. Me, big boat, fish, big fish." He showed them how he cast out his nets and pulled in fish. "Lotta fish come, big, little."

"You was fishin on the ocean?" Step asked. He had never seen an ocean, though he'd seen the Gulf of New Orleans that led out to the ocean.

"*Sí, sí,*" Serafin answered, smiling. His children watched, amazed that their father was speaking English so easily now, telling the Americans about their life in Italy.

"*Il mio fratello*, brother, he fish with me."

"Serafin, no," Amalia warned him.

"No good," Serafin told them. He didn't know why he was saying it, but he couldn't stop. "In the water he gone. *Morto.*"

"Please, not today," Amalia told him. "Really, we have to go."

"My brother." He tapped his chest. "Dead."

The Halls and Tituses shifted uncomfortably in their seats. Fred buttoned the concertina shut and laid his bony hand on top of it.

The children waited for the silence to end while Serafin sat quietly, staring at the picture that floated before him: Valerio, his boat, the sea.

"I never seen no ocean," Step finally said.

Fred shook his head. "Cain't say I ever seen it neither."

Fancy offered her company a little more of the potato pie, a little more wine or whiskey. "Ain't you gon' play us 'nother tune, Fred?" she asked. But Fred didn't move his hand from the concertina in his lap.

Step rose and went to the stove, all eyes on him as he chose a log. The log was warm, from the heat of the stove. It had never crossed his mind what the Italians had left in coming here. He'd just never thought about it one way or another. They simply got off the ferry as if that was the very moment they sprang into existence, all pretty much the same: incomprehensible, woefully ignorant, and a little pigheaded. Now shadows of the lives they had lived before Sweet Hope loomed inside him, strange and haunting.

"Well... 'nother Christmas come an' gone," was the only thing he could think to say.

He laid the log inside the stove and watched until an edge of bark caught and a tiny flame began to burn.

CHAPTER 6

Plowing

March 1902

SERAFIN took the reins from Step and ran his hands along the leather as he had been shown, from the mule's knotty neck back to the plow handles, to make sure the reins lay flat. The mule shook its head and tried to pull away. Serafin quieted the animal, then checked the position of the blades. Step nodded, and Serafin slapped the reins. "Gee," he called, the way Step had taught him, and the mule lurched forward, straining against the weight of the plow until it moved. They had weathered their first winter at Sweet Hope, and finally could begin working the fifteen acres they had been renting since last July.

The plow tipped to one side, and Serafin struggled to straighten it. "Keep your weight down on the handles," Step called to him.

Pale dirt spilled open in front of him. He walked unsteadily in the narrow furrow, one foot in front of the other, the hills of dirt like parting waves on either side of him. A sharp smell of freshly turned earth rose up.

"That's the way," Step called. "Hold on, keep it straight."

Serafin held tight in concentration; then his serious expression eased for a moment, and he managed to smile. Finally, he was plowing their own land, their own farm.

Amalia held the children back from the furrows as they watched the rows of clean earth open behind Serafin. His face was alert and determined as the blade bit into the earth, uncovering what had been buried. Then he moved on, oblivious to what he laid bare.

Sometimes, after Valerio died, he would go out in his boat to fish at night, but return in the morning empty-handed. She imagined him sitting there under the stars, never putting his nets out, weeping for Valerio. Three hungry children and that was how he acted. Osvaldo had been born just a year before the death, and Serafin would carry him through the house, sobbing until Osvaldo screeched and she had to pry the child out of his own father's hands. That was the father Osvaldo knew, a man who sat in his boat all night while his fishing nets lay rotting at his feet — a father who cried at the sound of a chirping cricket or sight of an apple tree at sunset and felt no shame over it.

He had improved in the last two years, at least he threw his nets in the water, but he was still bad. They blamed their problems on the hard times in Italy, but in her heart she told herself he was the cause. America would be his answer to everything. Well all right, then, America, she had said. Let him dream, let him cry. Let him blow like a leaf with the wind. She would give him one last chance. He knew nothing of what she carried in her heart.

Serafin made another pass with the plow, taking his hand from the handle for a moment to wave at them. He took the hat from his head and wiped his face with the back of his arm. The plow tilted to the side again, and he pulled it straight.

"Osvaldo," Amalia called, "hurry, take the jug to papa." Reluctantly, the boy left off throwing clumps of dirt on the flies that swarmed above a pile of mule droppings in one of the rows. "Osvaldo," she called again sharply.

He went for the jug of water and ran with it to his father, his small bare feet flying over the soft dirt, the water sloshing in the jug as he ran.

"Look, a flower," Angelina cried, and she jumped across the furrow her father had dug. She bent to retrieve a small white flower that dangled over the edge. "I'll plant it at home." She held the flower out for her mother to see.

"It'll die before we get home."

Angelina packed a small ball of dirt around the roots and cupped the plant in her hands. "What kind do you think it is?"

"It's just a little weed," Amalia told her.

"Probably a stink flower," Isola said.

Once Serafin seemed confident in his plowing, Amalia and the children left him to join the others working in the woods. The fields were full of men plowing. A few women and children followed behind them, collecting roots or stones or sticks and carrying them in buckets to the side of the road. Now and then someone returned from the company store carrying a special purchase: axle grease, leather straps to repair a harness, a sack of flour or cottonseed, quinine pills. Some people were already starting their planting.

When they had almost reached the woods, Fiorenza and her mother caught up with them. The old lady wore a black sweater that hung like two loose sacks at her elbows; a large round comb jutted from the top of her gray hair. She walked in a trembling way, as if the earth were unsteady under her feet. The children eyed her.

"At least it's not cold or raining anymore," Amalia said. "At least now we can plow our field." She was bothered by what Fiorenza had told her yesterday: she was going to have a baby. It had given Amalia a cold feeling, to think of knowingly bringing a child into this place.

"Yes," Fiorenza answered cautiously. "But already it's too warm for me. Hot and cold, that's all we get here." She walked with her saw slung over her shoulder.

Winter had surprised them, with its cold wind rattling through the chinks in their walls. They'd stuffed the cracks with rags and mud. Twice there'd been a dusting of snow. There was even an ice storm that had splintered dozens of trees with the weight of the ice that hung from the branches like extravagant jewels. She had to admit — the destruction was beautiful.

Isola followed behind La Vecchia, imitating her walk. When Amalia caught sight of what she was doing, she grabbed her arm and shook her. "What's gotten into you, for god's sake?" Osvaldo covered his mouth and laughed.

Fiorenza said nothing. Isola and Osvaldo ran ahead, while Angelina walked with the ladies, cupping the flower she had rescued from her father's plow.

"Well, soon we'll be done in the woods," Fiorenza said. "Then we'll have to worry about the sun scorching our heads all summer." She looked up at the sky. *"Marzo marzaccio..."*

"I'll be glad to get out of the woods," Amalia answered bitterly. "Snakes, everywhere you put your hand, snakes and bugs. And my back's ready to break in two."

"At least you don't see many snakes in the cotton, that's the only good thing," Fiorenza said.

La Vecchia started repeating "snakes in the cotton," as if she were singing a song.

Fiorenza took her mother's arm, letting her sing.

Amalia glanced at the two women. She had tried so hard to convince her own mother to come with them. Now, as much as she missed her, thank God the woman had refused to budge. And then there were the other relatives she'd left behind, and friends, the town itself. It was odd, how she missed it all, even the barren, twisted olive tree that grew behind their house; even the old shed that was ready to fall down.

She looked out at the sunken fields of Sweet Hope, a dilapidated shack poking up here and there, a few old mules straining to pull a plow while worn-out men struggled behind. "We'd be better off if we'd gone to Sicily instead of here," she told Fiorenza.

Fiorenza smiled at the thought. "At least we might have a tomato to eat."

The company store sold canned tomatoes, but they didn't taste right, and the prices were steep, as usual.

"Fresh tomatoes, real tomatoes," Fiorenza said. "*Allora.*"

"It's our land," Amalia complained. "We pay to rent it, we should be able to plant what we want." She nudged Osvaldo away from the mule droppings he was poking at with his shoe. "Well," Fiorenza said, watching Osvaldo run to catch up with Isola. "They say if we get our priest, things will be different. The Italian government and the church together — they won't put up with this nonsense. They'll make the Americans treat us right or let us go back home."

"Have you heard any more about it?"

Fiorenza shrugged. "What we all hear, the same thing. Rumors. Nothing. And who can you trust?"

"Not that bastard Rosconi, that's for sure," Amalia said. "Nor any of these damn *Americani. Merda cani.*" Dog shit.

Fiorenza raised her eyebrows. "You seem to be doing all right with these damn Americans." As soon as she said it, she bit her lip.

"What's that supposed to mean?"

Fiorenza steered her mother away from another pile of mule droppings in the road. "Nothing," she said, waving her free arm through the air. "Just, you know, Step Hall, helping you out. You'd think your two families are related sometimes."

"Helping us out?" Her face flushed with anger. "Why do you think you're cutting wood today? I knew you were mad because we go there sometimes on Sundays. And Christmas — we came to your house too." But it had been late when they'd finally gotten there, and they only stayed a short while. "Shame on you."

The children were listening. The old lady was laughing softly.

"I didn't mean anything by it," Fiorenza said. "Forget I ever brought it up."

"*Ma certo*. Certainly. Just like that I'll forget about it."

They walked in silence. Amalia shifted the saw to her other shoulder. She felt her throat tightening. Fiorenza against them, too, she thought, and for all the help they'd given besides.

✳✳✳

THE woods loomed before them, and Amalia tensed. The children, too, looked warily about. You never knew where you'd find a snake. They slithered through the swamp and the water, but they liked the logs and branches as well. Often she would see snakes sunning themselves on the stacked wood and logs, or draped over piles of branches, especially after a rain. She called for the children to watch where they walked, to look before they touched anything.

And yet Amalia could not help noticing the flowering trees, too, the redbud and dogwood that showed here and there among the oaks and locusts and evergreens. She thought of the scraggly lemon trees at home, the sweet fragrance of their blossoms.

"Look, mama," Angelina said, pointing, "aren't they pretty?"

Amalia looked about, inhaling, nodding. Her throat tightened. "We're here to work, not to look at the flowers," she reminded her daughter.

But when she passed a wild chicory plant she swooped and pried it up by the roots, then tucked it into her dress pocket. It wasn't beautiful, but it was food, and her eyes stayed sharp now for other plants they could eat.

Few men were out today. The sounds of their chopping and sawing carried from deeper in the woods. Once in a while they called out to each other in tinny, echoing voices. In another couple of weeks they would stop entirely to devote all their time to plowing and preparing their cotton fields. All along this stretch, between the road and the woods, were numerous clearings half an acre wide where the men hauled the branches and left them for the women and children to trim and cut. Other clearings had been formed deeper in the woods, and eventually the clearings became larger until they finally met and several new acres of farmland were created. Sometimes the men had to dig ditches, as wide and deep as small canals, to drain the marshy land. A wide path went into the woods, so that the horses could drag out the felled tree trunks to the lumber mill.

As the women set their tools out and decided which pile to start on first, three men entered the clearing from the plantation: Fred Titus and his son JoeJack leading two big harnessed work horses, and Calvin Hall carrying a loop of extra trace straps over one shoulder. Fred tipped his hat to them as Calvin straightened himself and walked tall. "Mornin, Misses," Fred called, and the women nodded in return. They watched Fred and the boys take the path into the woods. "Don't let the 'squitoes eat ya up," Fred called.

Calvin looked over his shoulder, found Angelina, and did the one thing he had been planning since he first laid eyes on the beautiful girl: he smiled at her.

She did not return his smile, but she watched until the group disappeared into the woods. Then she bent over and scooped damp earth from beside a clump of ferns, and packed it around her flower's roots. Her face was burning from his gaze.

Hand on her hip, Amalia waited for her daughter to finish. Finally, Angelina took the saw Amalia held out for her and went to work on a branch while Amalia hacked at another and Isola and Osvaldo piled the leafy twigs to dry for kindling, taking the bigger pieces to the firewood stacks. From where the women worked, they had a view of the dirt road and the fields across it. The land was not as fertile as much of the rest of Sweet Hope, but the company put up new shacks there anyway, and brought in new families, charging the same rent as for anywhere else. Two of the fields were being plowed right then.

An uneasy feeling crept into her again. She thought of the woman whose cotton they had picked last fall, her sick children, their girl who died on Christmas Eve. Only the mother and an older boy left now, but who knew for how long? If Amalia had known, she would have refused to work that farm. Why chance bringing a curse upon themselves? But of course, even if they had known they were picking the cotton of the dead and dying, what could they have done, really?

She glanced at her children, suddenly aware of how lean they had become. Her mind raced with thoughts of tonics she might brew, soups she could cook. Once again she scanned the surrounding area for greens or herbs to dig.

***

They looked up as an American steered his horse into their clearing. It was Lee Horton, the big red-haired man, his hat pulled down over his eyes. He scowled at them as he reined in his horse amid their stacks of wood. "What you all doin out here, havin a party? Get to work," he growled.

When he caught sight of Angelina working a distance from the others, he steered his horse closer and stopped to watch her. She tensed and remained hunched over the branches she was sawing. The longer he sat there watching, the hotter her face flushed.

"You workin up a sweat, little filly. Like to see you workin like that for me."

She had no idea what he was saying. She kept her head lowered as she sawed.

"Wouldn't you like to come show me what you can do for me?" he said.

Moving only her eyes, she searched for her mother. Amalia and Fiorenza had stopped working and were watching.

He nudged the horse closer, making it prance over branches and the sticks of wood Angelina had stacked. She backed away from the horse's hooves, still afraid to raise her head.

In a flash, Amalia was there, pulling the girl away. "*Diavolo*," she yelled at Horton, pushing Angelina behind her. "What the hell's wrong with you, you bastard?" She shook her fist at him. "Get out, get out."

Horton laughed at her frenzy. He turned his horse in a sharp circle through the ferns, knocking into a stack of logs while Fiorenza held the other children out of harm's way. The animal reared up, then pawed into the scattered pile until Horton regained control. He grinned at the mess, then trotted down the path into the woods where the men were cutting trees. "Damn crazy Dagoes," he cursed.

"What does he want?" Angelina finally asked, unable to hide the trembling in her voice.

Amalia brushed the hair from Angelina's eyes, trying to conceal her own worry and contempt. "Back to work," she told the children. "Let's go."

"My flower," Angelina said. She searched for it, but there was no trace of it among the trampled woodpile.

"Angelina," Amalia called, "Let it be!"

She went back to swinging the hatchet at the branches. For the *bastardo* to come around intimidating the girl... she'd known from the first time she'd set eyes on him that he was the son of the devil. From now on she vowed to keep a closer eye on that one.

CHAPTER 7

First Planting

April 1902

THE new shipment of Italians came from Modena in late spring while most of the tenants and sharecroppers were planting. Step made several trips driving them from the landing to their new cabins. With each trip, Italians looked up from their plowing or planting with angry, knowing eyes, the Pascalas among them. And with each family he left off at their new shack, Step had to endure the confused or angry or disbelieving cries and questions in a language he did not understand that assaulted him as he drove away. He cringed as he drove the new families through the fields. He flinched as he unloaded them and drove off. The cabins Fred and his men had built were good by Sweet Hope standards. But they were shacks, nonetheless, especially to people who thought they were going to a prosperous American city to work. At least fifty Italian families now, maybe sixty. He tried to assure himself that Mr. Gates knew what he was doing, that Mr. Gates would make things right in the end, that he'd take care of his workers. But what he'd seen the last few years worried at him.

Yet, he had a job to do, he told himself. And if not him — he who had some sense and compassion and treated human beings like human beings — no telling what kind of abuses the Italians would suffer. He thought of them under the hand of Lee Horton, and the thought confirmed that he was doing right to stay on at Sweet Hope.

After he left off the last screaming woman and her brood of frightened children, he wearily turned his wagon toward the Senigallia section before heading to his own farm. Two days of rain had battered the new cotton. Some portions of the bottomland had almost washed out completely, though most farms were safe. The land was already drying out.

Fancy had been after him to let the Pascalas be. But something kept drawing him back to the family, even if they did have some funny ideas and ways of behaving. None of the Italians knew the first thing about working cotton. They had to be shown everything. He shook his head over what Serafin had told them all at Christmas, about his brother drowning in Italy. You'd think the man would never set foot in water after that. And there it was, again, the picture he could not escape: Tobe floating down the river, a shake of a tail away from going under. And the Italian plunging into the river, barely able to bring his boy back, both of them almost lost. And Step, standing there on shore watching. It seemed like hardly a day went by without that vision playing in his head.

He saw the hunched figure in the distance and knew it was Serafin — digging through his newly planted seed. He stopped on the edge of the Pascala property, then walked gingerly down the lane. Serafin straightened when he saw Step.

"Go home," Step called to him. "You gonna ruin your crop, diggin around, trompin the rows like this after that rain."

Serafin held his hands out and shrugged, to indicate he did not understand. "*Non capisco.*"

Step pointed to Serafin's house. "Go home. Git outta here. No good for you to be here."

"No good?" Serafin answered. "Why no good?"

"Let your crop grow. Won't grow if you keep troublin it."

"She no grow," Serafin answered. "Seeds all dead in the rain."

"Dead?" Step said. "Seeds ain't dead."

"Drown in the rain."

"You sure somethin," Step told him. He squatted a few feet away and gently moved the earth aside, then held up a seed to show Serafin. It had swollen, and was just beginning to sprout a white root.

Serafin smiled sheepishly. "No dead, eh?"

Step took him by the elbow and led him to the edge of the property. He positioned Serafin at the right angle and pointed out to the land. It took Serafin a minute to see the slight haze of green just visible near the middle of the field. "Couple days, the whole crop gonna be bustin up," Step told him.

Serafin smiled. And then he laughed. "I got the cotton. She's growin. Make a good crop." He flung an arm around Step, making the man stumble. "Good man. Thank you, *mille grazie*."

Step pulled away, laughing in spite of himself. He'd never seen anybody so happy about his cotton sprouting.

"I tell Amalia, the kids," Serafin said. "They gonna see."

"Hold it there," Step said, catching Serafin's sleeve. "You all stay the heck outta this field, hear? Don't go walkin in the field, and don't go diggin, hear me?" He pointed to the lane. "You look from there. No walkin in the field."

"Yes, yes, yes," Serafin told him, and he was off.

***

LATER, the Pascala family stood at the edge of the field, Serafin pointing the way Step had, and they all saw. Seeds that had washed out the day before had now burrowed miniature roots into the soil. Those that had sprouted and had lain on their sides were growing straight. It was as if the warm, humid air itself somehow fed the seeds and plants. They thrived under the soil and on top of it. They seemed to grow before their eyes.

"Do you believe it?" Serafin murmured.

"It's a miracle," Amalia answered. She, too, had feared the rain had ruined their crop.

"Daddy, are we growing cotton?" Isola asked. "We're going to make money?"

He drew the girl close while they huddled at the edge of their field. The sun was casting long bands of light across the land as the warm, humid air surrounded them, holding them still and quiet and peaceful. For a moment they remembered the stories they had heard about this lush paradise. For a moment they believed some of the stories might be true.

CHAPTER 8

Lightning

July 1902

IT was true for the people as much as for the land. What you saw on the outside did not necessarily match the life inside. It was that life inside that kept Step awake some nights, wondering where everything was leading. Wondering who the hell he was, why he was still here when he could have just as easily packed his family up and left a dozen times over. Fancy had it; they all had it, the inside life. It led to another one of their "tussles," as he called them, when he asked her to help the Pascala woman out. With their pump on the outs, it was one more burden for the family. "Just take her to the lake to do her washin. Give her a little push to get by." Even as he said the words, he couldn't understand why he cared.

"You done paid your dues," she'd told him. She winced inside at how ungrateful the words sounded. She'd always be thankful for Tobe being saved. But there were a hundred Italians on Sweet Hope, and just a handful of Blacks left, and everybody could stand a little extra help, themselves included.

"Not talkin 'bout no dues. Can you just do it?"

She felt sorry for the Italians at times, though she didn't let on to Step. It was pitiful the way they tried to get by with all they didn't know, like that one bringing those cookies at Christmas, barely a taste of honey on the outside, no sugar at all inside — her, the one she and Lud were going for now, the one Step had said might be "tetched in the head" at the same time he asked Fancy to help her. Not crazy like the old lady who sat in back of the wagon with Fiorenza, but not all right either.

Like at Christmas, waving her hands all over the front of her body and kneeling down right there on the floor while everybody else was standing. Making the kids get down there with her. It gave her a crawly feeling. "Take her friend, too," Step had said. "See if you can teach 'em a thing or two."

Which got her thinking about the one less chicken in their yard and the black, scuffed, eyelet shoes pinching her son Calvin's feet whenever he emerged from cutting trees in the swamp. Of all the darn things — that Italian coming to their house with a pair of his oldest daughter's good shoes, wanting to trade them for a chicken. Not to eat, but to raise. Trying to make a farm. And Step saying yes.

And now this, Step telling her drive a load of Italian women to the lake for washday.

"Who gonna help us?" she had asked him. No answer, as she well knew.

***

Amalia stepped out the door with her bundles of clothes, clutching Osvaldo's wrist, and peering nervously at the wagon. She'd kept him home because of his fever, though he didn't act very sick. Her face showed relief when she caught sight of Fiorenza and La Vecchia in back. She nodded politely to Lud and Fancy and to Lud's twelve-year-old Lecie who sat between them.

Fiorenza got out to help lift the two bundles of laundry into the back. "We'll walk behind, you, me, and the boy. There's no room in there for all of us." Her rounded belly strained against her dress. "*Va bene*," Amalia answered.

Okay, all right, Fancy understood that much. Everything was *va bene* with them, even when nothing was.

The two women fussed over Osvaldo, feeling his forehead while he tried to pull away. He looked well enough to Fancy. He should have been out hoeing weeds with the rest of them, at least he could do that much. Too small to help with washing, and he'd only get in the way.

"You want a pinch?" Lud asked her.

"Nuh–uh." Fancy glanced sideways at Lud as she pulled the dip pouch from between her breasts, took a pinch, and handed the pouch to Lecie. Lecie scooped out a pinch and sat contentedly with it inside her lip.

"Ya'll ready to move?" Fancy called to the Italians.

In one quick motion, Fiorenza swooped the boy up and sat him in the back of the wagon.

"Let me go," he cried.

Fancy caught the boy's eye. "You stop that triflin now," she called sharply, and he started, went still. She turned back and slapped the mule reins, and the wagon creaked forward. A smile worked at the corners of her mouth at the look on the boy's face.

"Comin to blossom," Lud said of the cotton.

"Be open 'fore we want 'em to be," Fancy said.

And then long silence again, the creaking of the wagon, the occasional chattering of the Italian women walking behind. Complaining, as usual, for sure. Or else scheming how to get out of Sweet Hope, break their contracts.

"They all right back there?" Fancy asked.

Lud glanced behind, then shook her head disdainfully at Fancy.

"Told you, was Step's idea," Fancy said.

"They gon' expect this every time we go now?" Lud asked

"Won't do 'em no good if they do."

"Thought the gov'ment didn't let no crazy people in," Lud said.

"Ain't no other kind comin to the Delta."

***

When they reached the lake, Fancy and Lud began unloading the bundles of clothes, expecting the Italians to follow their lead. Instead, they gazed out across the pale brown water toward the barely visible village along the distant shore as if looking at some holy vision. Willow branches dangled on this side, into the shallow edge. Nearby, bulging cypress trunks rose out of the water, a few ducks paddling among them. It was a pretty lake, one that could make you almost forget you were on Harlan Gates' Sweet Hope plantation.

Osvaldo took off running for the shore, and Fancy narrowed her eyes, wondering why Amalia didn't get after him. It was him, after all, who had gotten her boy nearly drowned.

At last Amalia called him away from the water. When he didn't move fast enough, she called again, holding up a piece of bread to coax him.

"See how she treat that boy?" Lud said.

At the word "boy," Amalia looked over at them, then back at Osvaldo dipping his bare feet in the water.

"Osvaldo," she called. "You stay in the shade here, near the hanging down trees, while I wash."

Fancy clucked her tongue. Lud nodded in agreement.

They got to work setting up the washtubs. Lecie helped drag the tubs down to the water, and then helped the Italians carry their bundles of clothes. Within moments, La Vecchia was heading for the water. "Miz 'Malia," Fancy yelled. When Amalia didn't answer, she told Lud, "Ain't I got 'nough to do without tendin one a' theirs?"

"She gonna drown herself," Lud said, "don't somebody watch out for her."

Finally Fiorenza noticed and went after her mother. "We're at the lake to wash, mama. You stay here with us."

Worse than the boy, Fancy thought. What they gonna do once the cotton comes?

She picked up the scrub board. "You know how to use a scrub board, don't you?" she asked. And then, because of their smiling, blank faces, she placed the board in the tub, took up a wad of wet trousers, rubbed in a sliver of soap, and worked the trousers up and down on the board. "Now where your soap at?" They shook their heads, not understanding. "Soap," she repeated, holding out a piece. "You got soap, ain't you?"

Finally she cut chunks of soap from her own bar and handed them around. And so she left them, to figure out the washing on their own, while she went back to the trouble working inside her.

Not just the one less chicken — two if she counted the one they gave last fall — and not just the pinching shoes on Calvin's feet, but what those things meant — and the look in Calvin's eyes.

"You dreamin," Step had told her.

"That's all we need, that kinda trouble," she told him. "You better keep a watch on that boy."

"Heck, she just a little bit of a thing," Step told her. "Ten, eleven year old at the most."

"She big as Lud's girl Lecie. Dressin up in the cotton fields, touchin her hair."

"He ain't hardly ever laid eyes on that girl."

"Somethin bit that boy," Fancy told him. "Puttin a white girl's shoes on his feet."

He snorted. "They ain't hardly white people."

"Whatever they is."

Which brought her to another thing between her and Step: what the company was really up to. They'd heard about other plantations and mills in the south bringing in Italian labor. "They gettin rid of us," she'd told Step.

"Naw. They need us," he'd answered.

"For how long?"

She let her eyes drift towards the Italian ladies. The two crowded together to share a wash tub, Amalia's face a hard stone, all mixed up with pain and fear and arrogance. It made Fancy weary just to look at them.

"How'm I s'pose to teach her anything when she don't even talk English? 'Least her husband tries, I'll give him that."

"You hear 'bout they gonna have a church meetin Saturday night? You goin?"

"Y'mean Miss Betty wantin to start up a regular school house here on Sweet Hope? Preacher wife ain't got 'nough to do."

"Well, I think I'm goin to hear, jus' the same."

"School," Fancy said. "Got farms to run, that's what we got." Still, she looked out across the fields, wondering how a school might make any difference.

Lud wiped her chin. "Somebody say Lally Mo comin out the woods to do a healin."

"There's another one," Fancy said.

"Mm–hmm. But she do fix people."

Osvaldo was down near the cypress trees now, splashing in the water with a long stick. Amalia yelled at him to get out of the water and stay out.

He dragged the stick as he jumped away from the lake and began walking in the grass. "I'm not in the water," he told her.

"Come sit down near us while I'm washing."

He started walking away from her.

She called again, but he kept walking.

She charged at him, so quickly that she was inches away before he saw her and tried to run. But she grabbed his arm, spun him around, and slapped him hard on the backside. A few more swats, and he was wailing. She dragged him by the arm back to the washtubs. "You stay put or there's more where that came from."

The others stared. Fiorenza kept a worried eye on her friend while the boy sat crying.

"Worried he's sick, then she go thrashin him," Lud said.

"Tell Step go talk to her himself if he wanna talk," Fancy said.

"Oughta send Lally Mo to work on her."

Osvaldo had flung himself on the grass. He lay on his stomach, scowling while La Vecchia dusted the stump she was sitting on.

"You okay?" Fiorenza asked her friend.

Amalia waved her aside.

Osvaldo was watching Lecie. She had carried a pile of washed clothes up from the water and was laying them out to dry on the grassy shore near the trees. She was bent over, her back to the trees, when her body tensed. Osvaldo got to his knees to watch. She straightened herself slowly, and inched forward, away from the trees. He looked past her at the leaves twitching in the breeze. Birds whistled and sang to each other, and then went silent. He pouted out his lower lip and chewed it. A little flock of brown birds rose from the trees and flew away.

"Lud, bring us some a' that sweet water," Fancy called out. "We gonna faint w' this heat."

The Italians wouldn't drink it.

"Ain't lake water," Fancy told them, stifling an exasperated sigh. "It's good, it's sweet. Look here." She put the jug to her lips and took a drink to show them.

"Our soaped up clothes gonna be dry before we get a chance to rinse them," Lud said.

Osvaldo was creeping closer to his mother's knee, his face defiant, yet cautious.

Finally Amalia tasted. "*Dolce*," she murmured, embarrassed at her behavior.

Fancy steadied the jug for Osvaldo as he tilted his head back and drank, all the while keeping his eyes on her. She was surprised at how dark his skin was, that close, darker than some of her own relatives. The eyes were dark, too, oddly innocent, the face delicate.

"You want to sit a little more?" Fiorenza asked her friend.

Amalia knew the black women didn't like them, yet here they were, trying to be kind. "I want to wash my clothes," she answered.

With that, she walked like a hoodoo ghost to the washtub, all eyes on her, even La Vecchia pausing from her stump cleaning. Amalia held the side of the tub. Then she plunged her raw knuckles into the water.

Fancy and Lud fell into a rhythm, scrubbing their clothes in one tub, rinsing in another, with Lecie spreading them out in the grass at the lake's edge. The clothes would be dry in an hour with the heat, in full sun. They'd brought along a few clothes to mend and a fishing line for filling the last hour, though they'd be slowed down anyway with helping the Italians. "They work faster than us in the field," Fancy said. "Don't know why a washtub slow 'em down so."

"Seem the water make 'em crazy," Lud answered, indicating the lake.

"Actin like it's the Pearly Gates 'cross in the village," Fancy said.

The mules rattled their harnesses and the wagon creaked with their movement. "See that?" Lud said, nodding toward the sky. Thick clouds were moving toward the lake from the west. The Italians were spreading their washed bedding on the grass alongside Fancy and Lud's clothes where moments before the sun had shown.

"Might still blow over," Fancy said. She watched the dark clouds churning across the sky. Sometimes what looked like certain rain would pass over without a drop. Other times the sun blazed through a downpour. A breeze gusted, and some of the dry garments billowed and folded over on themselves.

Fiorenza looked up at the sky. "*Piove?*" she said. She held her arm out, checking for drops of rain. Amalia, too, looked at the sky. "Osvaldo," she called. Thunder sounded in the distance.

"Told you," Lud said. "Washin clothes, course it gonna rain." She hurried to gather the shirts and dresses from the grass as the sky darkened. Lecie was already bundling them.

"Always something," Fancy complained. She moved fast, plucking her clothes from the grass, calling for the Italians to pack up, get moving. "Rain comin," she called to them. "Throw your clothes together, hurry up." She waved them toward the wagon while large drops pattered down on them.

Lud snatched up clothes as she ran. "Git movin." She and Fancy threw clothes into the wagon — wet and dry, clean and dirty together — while urging the others to get in. But La Vecchia was down at the water's edge sweeping the lapping water with a long switch while the wind whipped at her dress and hair.

"Mama," Fiorenza called.

In an instant the air turned cool and the dark sky seemed to split open with thunder. Rain battered down and lightning flashed. Fiorenza ran toward the lake, shouting for her mother. Her wash lay tangled and splattered with mud.

"Osvaldo, run for the wagon," Amalia shouted. They were all running, crying out, while Fancy and Lud tried to calm them. When the mules started to move away, Fiorenza screamed.

"No, no, no," Fancy told them. She shushed her finger over her mouth to make them stop yelling, while she tried to hold the mules still with one hand. But in a minute the animals broke loose and lumbered blindly through the sheets of rain.

"We're going to die," Amalia cried.

Fancy motioned them to the trees. "Git under the trees." Trees and lightning were a bad combination, she knew, but standing out in the open was worse.

A flash hit the ground near Amalia, but she kept running. Her clothes were plastered to her skin, and she could barely move against the wind. "Osvaldo," she cried. "Where are you?" Rain pelted her skin.

"Miz 'Malia," Fancy shouted. She, too, had lost sight of the boy. "Miz 'Malia, come back."

Lud and Lecie went for the old lady, down near the lake.

That was when Fancy saw Osvaldo through the sheets of rain, standing forlorn and drenched near the stump where his mother had been using the washtubs. She sprinted toward the boy. In almost the same instant, Amalia saw her son, too, called out his name, and ran to him.

"Mama," he cried, too frightened to move.

He was standing with his arms stretched toward her when the flash hit, a forked flash, with one big fork cracking the tree stump, the smaller one appearing to touch the back of his head — the flick of a serpent's tongue. For a moment Fancy thought she could see right through the boy's skin, to the veins running like cobwebs across his head. But maybe the light came from outside, the flash lighting up everything around it. In that long, stretched-out moment, Amalia reached for her boy and stiffened as she grabbed his arm. Fancy stood riveted only a few yards away. Never in all her life had she seen such a thing. Death, in front of my own two eyes, she thought.

Finally, Amalia's hand fell away. Her nostrils flared, as if she had just awakened to an unfamiliar smell.

"Osvaldo," she screamed. She shook him so hard that his head flopped back and forth. "Osvaldo."

Fancy tried to pull her up, but Amalia clutched her son tighter and would not budge. *After all the bad feelings I had for her,* she thought, sorry, ashamed, under the eyes of God. *Another burying coming.*

"Miz 'Malia."

Osvaldo struggled against his mother's arms. "I can't breathe," he whimpered. "Mama!"

Fancy jumped back in fright.

At last Amalia let the boy go. He stood blinking at her.

"Are you hurt?" Amalia cried, running her hands up and down his arms. "Are you all right? Did it burn you?" She reached out to touch his face, then drew her hand back.

Osvaldo rubbed the back of his head. "Why did you keep pushing me?" His voice quavered, and it seemed that he would cry. "Why were you pushing on my head?"

"No, I didn't," she tried to explain.

Fancy's disbelieving hand went out to touch the boy, then stopped. She didn't know if it was God or the Devil showing off the boy's powers.

He was looking past them at the lake. "My horse!" he said, and he tottered off unsteadily to retrieve the stick that now lay in the mud. He picked it up and shook it free of mud and rain. "My horse got caught in the storm," he told his mother. "He ran away from me."

Amalia stared at her walking, talking son as she knelt there in the mud. If Fancy had not been frozen in place, she would have fallen to her knees alongside the woman.

The boy smiled at them through the rain, then winced. Amalia looked up at Fancy. "*L'hai visto?*" she said. She pointed to her eyes, then to the boy who was rubbing the back of his head again. "You saw?" Then she clutched her breasts.

Fancy felt her mouth working, but she could not answer. Maybe it had all been just a trick of their eyes in the storm. She helped Amalia to her feet, and they stood in silence while Osvaldo galloped about on his stick horse.

"Miz 'Malia," was all Fancy could manage, shaking her head. No one else had seen.

As quickly as it had begun, the storm was easing up. La Vecchia wandered out from under the trees and stood in the drizzle, touching her hair that fell like strings of soggy yarn across her face. Her long dress stuck to her skinny body. Fiorenza, still holding a soaked dress over her head, took long strides across the spongy grass to reach her. Their clothes lay tangled and muddy on the lakeshore. One bucket was turned on its side and a washtub had blown against a tree trunk. Lecie stood by the stricken tree stump, calmly gazing out at the women.

Don't that 'bout seal it? Fancy thought, as she stared at the light–head boy.

Lud walked down the road calling "Hy–iee, hy–iee" to the mules. Far away, a mule brayed in response. Fancy moved like a sleepwalker, righting a tub, throwing their clothes in while she waited for Lud to bring the wagon back.

A short distance away, Amalia talked haltingly to her friend, trying to explain what had happened. She kept glancing anxiously at Fancy.

Fiorenza only shook her head. No, Amalia was obviously mistaken, upset, seeing things.

"I felt it too," Amalia told her. She motioned with one hand from the tips of her fingers to her breasts.

"But he's okay," Fiorenza said, looking at the boy, then back at Amalia in an odd way. She moved her hands over her belly.

Fancy Hall watched and thought: *With these eyes, Lord. I knew there was somethin strange 'bout that boy.* She shivered.

"Tell her, Osvaldo," Amalia insisted.

"My horse ran away," he said without looking up.

Amalia examined Osvaldo's head, parting the hair as he tried to pull away. "Nothing, there's nothing there," she murmured. Those eyes of hers, looking, searching out Fancy, a kind of pleading in them.

Osvaldo galloped a few feet away, lowered the stick to the ground and told his horse to eat some grass.

"Maybe you saw something else," Fiorenza said. "Things look funny here, who can tell?"

And there was La Vecchia, a wad of burdock leaves in her hand, trying to wipe the raindrops off a tree trunk. And quiet, obedient Lecie gazing curiously at the boy too.

Like a dream, Fancy thought. But one you cannot speak because it is closed up inside you, with no words to let it out, and no way for others to understand those words even if they would come.

Lud was leading the mules back.

Hmmph, she'd say, if Fancy tried to tell her, and maybe spit her tobacco juice, and maybe shake her head, her own closed up way of saying *That Miz 'Malia ain't the only one lost something in the haystack.*

Fiorenza picked through the clothes, trying to sort out the ones that hadn't been splattered and stained with mud. Amalia watched, silent now.

The sun burned bright. Heat rose up out of the earth, and the air was steamy and hot. Green leaves lay scattered across the grass where they had been torn from their branches. But the lake was smooth again, though muddied, and the sky was clear. Except for the wet trees and the torn leaves on the grass and the steamy air it would be impossible to know there had just been a violent storm.

"Clothes worse now than when we come," Lud said. She motioned for the Italians to start loading their belongings. "What wrong with you?" she asked Fancy.

"Some storm," Fancy said.

"Guess we comin back tomorrow to wash," Lud said.

But Fancy did not answer. She was watching Osvaldo tug at his mother's skirt, asking her something. He covered his ears, then pulled the hands away. Amalia tilted her head as if to listen. She shook her head, no. But he persisted, until she dropped to her knees in front of him and took him by the arms.

He looked scared, tried to wriggle free while she hugged him closer. And then that look again on her face, like she was smelling something. She let the boy go. Fiorenza called Amalia's name, tried to pull her to her feet.

Lud made a clucking. "Ain't they something?"

"Mm–hmm," Fancy said. Meaning *I know.* But why you do such a thing, God? Ain't I got troubles 'nough?

Amalia would not let up. She kept trying to convince her friend, though she herself looked baffled and disbelieving.

So that Fancy wondered if she, too, had only imagined what she saw; and so looked around at the lake, the tattered leaves and muddied clothes now loaded in the wagon, La Vecchia waiting in the wagon with her damp tangled hair, the boy tending to the stick that was his horse. Her eyes rested on Lecie, and Lecie looked away.

"We goin or what?" Lud said.

Amalia with that pleading look, Fiorenza not saying it, but showing it just the same: Crazy, my friend is crazy.

Didn't Step warn me she was tetched? Fancy thought. But sent me here, too.

Amalia turned her pleading face to Fancy: Tell her what you saw.

Fancy waved at them. "Git in the wagon."

Then she stepped toward the boy who looked up, startled, went still. Fancy lifted him into the back. He was weightless, almost, light as air. Yet warm flesh in human clothing. And with a faint smell, pungent, like wet leaves. She pulled her trembling hands away from him.

"You comin?" Lud called from the driver's seat.

Osvaldo swung his legs off the back of the wagon, watching Fancy. And then, before she had a chance to move away, his face broke into a smile.

Fancy climbed into the seat beside Lud, took the reins, trying to erase the boy's face from her mind. "Gee up," she called, and the mules strained forward.

CHAPTER 9

Debt

Autumn 1902

As far as Serafin had been concerned, he could get by without fixing the water pump on his farm if it meant not adding another penny of debt to his company credit. If he kept working at the pace he was going, he was sure to get his crop in early, pay off his debt, and buy what he needed for the next year free and clear. He'd been hauling water in buckets from the neighboring farms for two weeks, a burden for all of them.

But now Angelina had come down with a fever. She lay in bed sweating and breathing in little pants, looking like a suffering angel. Amalia had done her best to treat her, but nothing was cutting the fever. He'd heard the company store was selling quinine pills without charging tenants for a doctor's visit.

"If you're going to the store after work," Lazzaro told him, "I'll come with you." He touched the brim of his hat with one finger. Most of it had separated from the rest of the hat and it hung precariously, allowing a band of light to shine across his face. Fiorenza had sewn the two pieces together several times, but every time he took the hat off to wipe the sweat away or swat at flies or mosquitoes, the thread gave way. "I have to break down and get another hat."

"After supper then." Serafin balanced on the edge of the wagon and shook the last of the cotton from the croker sack over the wire mesh sides. He couldn't get the picture of

Angelina out of his head, and a little worry began to play at him. People here died from fever.

"A hell of time to be spending money," Lazzaro said.

"I'm not going for the pump," Serafin told him. "Angelina –" He had to choke back the words.

"What?"

"She's in bed. Sick. The fever." He shook his head hard, to get a grip on himself.

"Jesus, *amico*." After a minute, he added, "Don't worry, she'll be all right. Make her eat something, that's all. Not just weeds from the fields."

"Eh, maybe." Now that his crop was nearly in, he'd be able to get to the lake, catch a few fish. They'd all been working too hard, with too little food.

"Anyway, how's Fiorenza?" he asked, to change the subject. He felt sorry for his friend, the wife so big she could barely move right when she was most needed in the fields, and then the crazy old lady to look after besides. The baby would be just one more mouth to feed. "Any day now, eh?" Serafin asked.

"Another month to go," Lazzaro answered. "But she's like a house already. Maybe the baby will come out big enough to work in the fields." He took off his hat and wiped the sweat from his brow. "Jesus, I keep forgetting," he said, looking at the hat.

Osvaldo came trudging up the row and handed over his sack. Serafin frowned at the boy when he felt how light it was. "I thought you said you've been picking."

"I have been."

"You'd better straighten up," Serafin said, dumping the cotton.

"My head hurts," Osvaldo complained, squinting up at his father.

"Where's your hat?"

"You leave it laying around, you'll end up like me," Lazzaro put in.

Osvaldo felt the top of his head for the lost hat. "It's gone," he said.

"Gone?" Serafin said, shaking his hand in the air to show Osvaldo that he'd be in trouble if he kept up this way. But inside, Serafin was concerned. He still didn't know if he believed what Amalia had told him. "You just don't get hit by lightning, then get up and walk away," he'd told her. But Osvaldo had started getting headaches, and then dreams that woke him in the night.

"What kind of dreams?" Serafin had asked.

"A big boy wanted to play with me."

"*Un malo?*"

"I don't remember."

"Maybe if you did your work like you're supposed to you wouldn't have bad dreams."

Osvaldo hoped his father wouldn't ask any more questions about his missing hat or why he'd picked so little cotton. He'd sneaked away with Tobe to follow a dead mule a couple of men were hauling from the Sant'Angelo property to the swamp. The boys had hidden in the brush, and when the men left the mule, the biggety chicks, the vultures, swooped down onto the animal and began ripping their sharp beaks and claws into its eyes and flesh. It was horrible but they couldn't stop watching.

He wasn't afraid of the swamp, even though his father said it could swallow you up. Sometimes in the night when his family was out walking they saw the *fiammata*, the little lights flickering deep in the swamp. "See?" his papa would say. "*Il gobbo* is getting ready to cook his supper. Don't let him catch you or you might end up in his pot."

Sometimes at night Osvaldo thought about *il gobbo* catching him and trying to boil him in a pot, but he would run so fast that the hunchback would never be able to catch him. Or he thought of sinking slowly into the muck, with no one there to pull him out and being sucked down so he couldn't move his arms or legs and it came up to his chest and then his neck and chin and then his nose and he breathed in mud, water, snakes, and it suffocated him and he was dead. And then he would wake up crying. But in the daylight it was different. The men had dragged the mule there, and nothing bad happened to them, even though they had to wear bandannas over their noses because of the stinking swamp gas. And Tobe was there with him and he was not afraid to be there in the swamp.

Now a man rode up in a cotton wagon with two mules tied in back. He nodded to Serafin and Lazzaro. "Good crop this year," he said.

"Big cotton," Serafin answered. "Good crop."

The man hitched the fresh mules to the wagon loaded with cotton. "Yes sir, good crop so far," he said.

He drove the load off to the scales at the cotton pen, leaving the empty wagon behind. It was hard to believe they'd picked so much. And more, two other wagons. They'd picked every single fluff of cotton with their own bare hands.

"See?" Serafin said.

"Eh," Lazzaro answered, knocking the dust from his pants.

"Go find your hat," Serafin told Osvaldo.

***

AFTER supper, Lazzaro met up with Serafin and Osvaldo. "Did you hear the news?" he asked as they walked toward the landing.

"Now what?" Serafin asked, his mind on his problems.

"We're getting our Italian priest, for sure. Boss man Gates thinks it'll make us work harder." He snorted.

"Where'd you hear that?" Serafin asked.

"Fiorenza. Some of the ladies got it from Ceravone."

"Where else?" Serafin said. "We've been hearing that story since we got here." He glanced at Lazzaro. The broken hat made him look like a clown. "Why don't you take that damn thing off?"

"Maybe we should go talk to Ceravone ourselves tonight," Lazzaro said, removing the hat.

"To hell with that *chiacchieron*," Serafin answered. "Besides, I'm beat."

The noise of the gin mill became louder as they neared the store. A wagon passed them on its way to the gin with its load of cotton.

"Another one done picking?" Lazzaro said. "Am I the last one?"

A skinny, yellow-faced old man went into the doctor's office behind the store. "Is that Sant'Angelo?" Serafin asked. "Jesus."

"He looks bad," Lazzaro answered.

Serafin drew his son closer. "Watch where you're walking," he told Osvaldo. "Don't breathe all that dust the wagons kick up."

Osvaldo stared, wide-eyed. The dead mule had come from Sant'Angelo's farm, and now Mr. Sant'Angelo was yellow and sick.

But he was just another one with the fever — like so many of them, not bad enough to kill him, but bad enough to make him sick all the time. The company doctor gave out useless pills for which he charged dearly. If you were an American, he could cure you. If you were Italian, you paid to stay sick.

"Well, he can kiss his money goodbye," Lazzaro said.

They went around to the front of the store, and nearly walked into Step Hall's wagon. Fancy, Birdie, and Tobe were in back, loading several oat barrels that Step passed up to them.

"Ho," Serafin called, surprised to see the Halls there at the same time. Step nodded. "How do," Fancy said out of politeness. Birdie and Tobe grinned at Osvaldo.

He flapped his arms at Tobe, a signal of what they had seen earlier in the swamp. "We goin the store," he told the Hall children.

Fancy looked them over, her face wary of the "light–head boy."

"My girl sick," Serafin explained as he took Osvaldo by the arm. "And the pump no good. I get paid my crop."

"Gotta wait till pickin's over," Step told him.

"No, for my wife and kids, better now," he said. "Almost done pick."

Step's face clouded over. "Told you, pick your crop first. Don't go askin for nothin now."

"I go see the medicine," Serafin said. Then he turned and climbed the steps.

A couple of people nodded hello to them, a man picking up supplies, and one Italian couple they had seen but didn't know. They stopped to let a woman pass by with her children in tow.

"Let's see how much the bastards are going to overcharge me this time," Serafin said. Just as he said it, the company office door opened and an Italian tenant from the Veneto section came out, manager Wade behind him. The Veneto turned, and he and Wade shook hands before Wade went back inside. Wade almost had a smile on his face.

Serafin poked Lazzaro, but he'd already seen: it was the first time they'd witnessed such a friendly gesture between a manager and an Italian.

When the Veneto passed them he nodded a sign of encouragement and patted his pocket.

"What?" Serafin asked him. "What happened?"

"I finally made some money," the man said as he hurried down the steps.

"What's he talking about?" Serafin asked. "You think he got paid?"

Lazzaro shrugged. "Ah well," he said. He opened the screen door to the commissary. Serafin took Osvaldo's hand. "Don't touch anything," he told the boy, and he brushed past Lazzaro and headed for the office instead of the store.

"Hey, *pad'ine*, what the hell you doing?" Lazzaro called. He let the commissary door slam shut and followed Serafin.

Tom Wade sat behind his desk. He glanced up at them, a look of bewilderment on his face. The room seemed small with all of them in there. There was a stove and two chairs and walls filled with maps and shelves of books and ledgers. An arc of brown stains mottled the floor around a spittoon near the desk. On a wall near the desk hung a big, ornately carved brown clock that ticked loudly. Osvaldo stared at the clock.

"What?" Wade finally said.

Serafin cleared his throat and stepped closer to the desk. He took off his hat and clenched it in his hand. He didn't know what had possessed him to come into the office.

"*Signore*, me done pick, come see money."

There, the words were out. Serafin and Lazzaro exchanged nervous looks.

The man's face was hard and unfriendly.

Outside the office window a figure passed, Step Hall. He stopped at the railing and turned sideways so that he could have been looking out at the road as easily as into the office at them.

"Mr. Wade, my girl sick, pump broke," Serafin said. "I got only this much flour left to eat." He held his hands out in front of himself to show two handfuls.

"What're you looking for, an advance?" He glanced at Osvaldo, making the boy blush.

"No, I want to get paid." The boldness of his words surprised him as much as they did the others.

"Paid?" the man said, so loud it made Osvaldo jump. "Paid for what?"

"The cotton, she picked," Serafin told him.

"We don't tally up till you're baled and wrapped and shipped. You have to get your cotton sold first. What're you talking about, paid?"

"Maybe if you see how big a lot I pick, you pay some now," Serafin said, speaking slowly, trying to get the words right. "I pick a lot, I telling you."

The man eyed them a long time.

"What's your name?" Wade asked.

"Pascala, Serafin Pascala," he said, his hopes rising. "Me big crop, good cotton." Lazzaro gave him an encouraging nod.

Wade grunted as he flipped through the pages. Above him the clock whirred and ticked. Then its door opened and out came two little men with axes facing a small carved tree. Frightened, Osvaldo ducked behind his father, then peeked out at the clock. The miniature men took turns swinging their axes at the tree, a chime ringing out with each swing. Seven times. Osvaldo stared at the box in disbelief as the men and tree slid back inside.

Mr. Wade stopped turning pages. "Pascala," he said. "Fifteen acres, lot twenty-three." He looked up at him. "Were you rich before you came here?" he said. "You've only had two advances from us."

Serafin smiled at the man, not grasping the meaning of the words.

On the porch, Step Hall moved to the window, dropped his hand back against the glass so that they all looked up at the sound. Again his hand fell, but he was turned away from the window. He could have been tapping time to a tune.

"What the hell's wrong with that nigger?" Wade said. "Get away," he shouted. "Get away from that window."

Finally Step moved forward and the man laid his big red hand on the page of his book. "When your cotton is sold," he told Serafin, "then you'll get paid. I can advance a month's supplies."

"He don't want to owe no more," Lazzaro said. "The interest bad, too much."

"He should have thought of that before he came to Sweet Hope."

"Why you pay that other man, you no pay me?" Serafin asked, indignant now.

"What other man?"

"*Il Veneto.*"

Wade thought a minute, baffled. "Parelli? Just in here a minute ago?"

"*Sí*, yes."

Wade shook his head at Serafin, then pointed to a shelf with stacks of books and papers. "He made us a cabinet for the ledgers." He motioned to the wall, the cabinet. "Took a few dollars off his debt."

Serafin sucked in his breath.

"*Carpentiere,*" Lazzaro murmured.

But they were there, they were inside the office. "Please, *Signor* Wade," Serafin said. "I pick three big wagon full. How much bale you think that make? You put in the book now, no? To make no interest for me."

Wade looked at Serafin in a hard way. Then he slammed the book shut. Osvaldo jumped. "Three wagons, five wagons," Wade said. "You people all think you're going to get rich, don't you?"

"No, no, we work hard, no get rich, just to eat, live," Serafin insisted. "We good people."

"Even if you picked eight wagons you'd still be in trouble," the man said.

"Trouble?" Serafin asked.

"You're in debt. What do you think? You're going to stay in debt this year. Understand? *Debt*."

Serafin's face turned ashen and he seemed to stagger right there where he stood.

"Debt?" Serafin whispered.

"*Papá*," Osvaldo said. The American words were getting all jumbled up inside him. Had the man said *dead*?

"Get out of here," Wade told them, fanning the air in front of his nose. "You stink to heaven, all of you."

"*Signore*," Serafin pleaded, his voice shaking. "Me work hard, do good, good crop." He hated the way he sounded, like a child, begging.

The man waved his hand in the air at them.

"Go," Wade said. "Get out. Don't bother me any more."

Serafin stared at Wade in disbelief as the rage built inside him. Finally it boiled over. "I go to the village. I leave this shit hole."

Wade laughed at him. "You ain't goin nowhere except back to work."

"Hell to you!" Serafin shouted, sweeping his arm across the desk and sending Wade's ledger, pens, and pocket watch flying to the floor. He turned on his heels and stormed out of the office. It wasn't until he stumbled against Osvaldo that he remembered the boy was with him. He grabbed Osvaldo's arm and pulled the terrified boy out the door, Lazzaro following in his own fear.

The sun, though low in the sky, made Serafin squint, nearly bringing tears to his eyes. The humidity fell on them like a heavy, damp blanket.

Step was standing near his wagon and looked at them in a curious way. "Mr. Serafin," he said, but Serafin hurried past him. Step started to follow, as Lazzaro shrugged and turned his palms skyward. "He say he going to the village."

"What the hell you two do in there?" Step asked, just as Wade come out onto the porch. "Pascala," he shouted, "you son–of–a–bitch. You set one foot off this plantation, you gonna get shot."

Serafin kept walking.

"Jorland, go get Horton," Wade called to the stocky bearded man who was leaning back in a chair, his boots on the railing, smoking a small cigar.

"Dago says he's leaving," Wade said, pointing to Serafin who had made it to the road leading to Fish Bayou, the only road out of Sweet Hope.

Jorland jumped to attention. "You want me to go after him?"

"I said get Horton, goddamnit."

Jorland took off on his horse.

Fancy waited in the wagon with Birdie and Tobe, the three of them tense with watchfulness. Serafin was growing smaller as he neared the bayou road. In the distance came the sound of two galloping horses. Step climbed in the wagon and urged the mule toward the bayou.

"Step, no!" Fancy cried.

"Can't let the fool get himself killed."

"You'll get *us* killed."

He urged the mule into an awkward trot.

"Let us out!" Fancy cried, but he kept going.

Osvaldo walked beside the two men, keeping his worried eyes on his father.

"*Ladri*," Serafin hissed at Lazzaro. "They think we're going to put up with another year of this shit?"

"Think about what you're doing," Lazzaro told him. He nervously looked behind them and saw Step's wagon heading their way. He should never have agreed to go with Serafin. Surely the company would spew its wrath on both of them now. He thought of grabbing Osvaldo and ducking into the nearly bare fields, just run for it with the boy; at least save him. But Serafin still had a grip on Osvaldo's arm.

"We'll figure something out," Lazzaro told Serafin.

"We worked like dogs," Serafin said. "It's all a dream. A nightmare."

Step pulled his wagon alongside them. "Get in the wagon," he told them brusquely. "You gonna get us all killed."

Serafin looked at the family, enraged, humiliated. "All lies here, big lying hell," he told them bitterly. "I leave this hell. Shoot if they want to."

"Mr. Serafin, you gotta think of your boy, your family."

Horton was galloping toward them, Jorland beside him.

"Step, turn the wagon around," Fancy said.

Horton pulled in front of Serafin, blocking the road to the bayou. "Where the hell you think you goin?"

Serafin threw his shoulders back. "I go out. I go find job, feed my family. Medicine for my sick girl."

It was ridiculous; it would be sunset in two hours.

Horton drew his rifle from its sling and aimed it at Serafin's face.

"God in heaven," Lazzaro cried. "We're going back. We're going back now." He took Serafin by the arm and tried to pull him along, but he would not go.

"You shoot me why?" Serafin demanded. "I do nothing wrong. I walk on this road, I go look for a job."

"You got a job, you goddamned Dago. Nobody under contract leaves Sweet Hope until you've paid off your contract. Get back to your shanty before I put a hole in your head."

"Mr. Serafin, come on, I give you a ride," Step said, his voice softer now, and cautious.

"I go where I want," Serafin said, and he started toward the bayou again, dragging the whimpering Osvaldo with him.

Horton's gun exploded, and the Italians froze.

"The next one goes in your head," Horton said.

"For god's sake," Lazzaro cried, "let's go back. Look what you're doing to your boy."

Osvaldo was whimpering, his pants wet, his nose running with snot.

Serafin stared at the boy as if he didn't recognize him. Then he cleaned the boy's nose with the back of his hand, almost gently. "You want to go back?" he asked Osvaldo.

Osvaldo looked at him with trembling lips, his eyes welling. "Yes."

Without a word, Serafin turned and started walking back toward the landing.

Horton watched for a moment. "You better keep your Dagoes in line, Hall," he said. "That ice is getting mighty thin under your shoes."

He and Jorland trotted back to the landing, kicking their horses into a gallop and sending up a whirl of dust as they passed the Italians.

Fancy said nothing as Step turned the wagon around and started back home. He was riled now, more than he had been. He planned to drive right past the Italians, but as he did, Serafin called out to him: "Nothing but shit here, *merda*, and my boy gotta see this. What kind American company you got here? Shoot me, kill me? No money, no food. We just a worm to them. Eat the dirt. *Mangiaterra*."

"Hey, *pad'ine*," Lazzaro said.

"We work hard, all the time work, work the best, the best clean, the best crop," Serafin yelled.

"You think other people ain't workin?" Step yelled back at him. He stopped the wagon. "Sweet Hope fulla people workin 'emselves to death. You ain't no different. You just one more drop in th' bucket."

Osvaldo was chewing his lower lip, as if he would start crying again. Lazzaro put his hand on the boy's shoulder.

"Osvaldo, straighten up," Serafin shouted. "Wipe that look off your face or I'll give you something to cry about."

"Hey, *amico*, he's scared enough as it is."

"I'm not scared," Osvaldo answered in a quavering voice, his eyes on Tobe Hall as he spoke.

"You see us?" Step shouted at Serafin. "Open your eyes. We been here more'n two hun'red years. We still here. We still workin. You been here one year and you cryin."

"You got farm, chicken, everything good," Serafin shouted back. "You a boss."

Fancy let out a snort. "Lightnin tetch him too."

"Boss?" Step spat. "Boss? Where you get that from?"

"You in charge, give us work, good farm."

"Boss?" Step said bitterly. "I ain't no boss."

The words hung in the air while Serafin tried to comprehend.

"No," Serafin said. "You boss, you help me, help my children."

"Only thing I got over you is a little bit a' sense," Step answered.

"I thought you my friend," Serafin said.

The word caught Step off guard. His voice softened a notch. "Look here, forget 'bout Italy, forget 'bout home. You just one more damn fool body." He was trembling, the words surprising him with a truth he had not wanted to look in the eye. Fancy turned her gaze across the fields, as she willed her insides go hard and empty.

"This your wake–up time," he told Serafin. "You wanna get by? When you home, inside your shanty — inside that head a' yours — you can be whoever or whatever you wanna be. But when you out here on Sweet Hope plantation, you nothin. You belong t' the company."

Serafin stared about the fields, the awful words sinking in. Finally, he raised his fist to Step. "You go to hell!"

Step flushed. He teetered on the edge of lashing back at the man. Instead, he lashed at the mule and drove the wagon forward.

The Italians stood a moment in the dust before trudging ahead again. Lazzaro dared not speak a word. Osvaldo lagged behind the men, also afraid to make a sound.

A couple hundred yards down the road the wagon stopped.

When they caught up to it, Step turned without fully looking at them. "Get the hell inside," he said.

The Italians climbed in. Serafin sat clutching his hands and staring at the darkening cotton fields as the wagon creaked forward.

CHAPTER 10

Baptism

Two years later August 1904

FATHER Odetti rose from his table and went to the window. He unbuttoned his shirt at the collar, took a handkerchief from his trouser pocket, and wiped his face and neck. The heat was relentless. He had been at Sweet Hope a week. Already he had said the Mass for the Dead three times and tomorrow would make the fourth. All of them had had malaria. But they were malnourished as well, so who could say what they really died of?

He looked out at the green cotton plants that stretched as far as he could see. Here and there a narrow dirt road cut through the fields, or a small shack rose from the sea of green — or far in the distance a stand of trees that hid the lake finally broke the monotonous fields. Flat, flat land that went on forever, like nothing he had seen before, so flat it seemed sunken, lost. In some of the fields people walked, inspecting the bolls that were beginning to open. Because of the distance and the similar straw hats and tattered clothes, he couldn't tell if the people were black or Italian. The Italians were unrecognizable to him, dressed in rags and covered in filth, and living like animals in cramped, dingy sheds. They had gone wild, almost heathen one might say, in their prolonged exposure to the elements and the absence of God. For them, one day was the same as the next — Sundays or holy days, what did it matter? In fact, after that morning's

Mass, most of the Italians left for their fields or the swamps where they were hauling wood and digging drainage ditches. Others were going to the lake to wash clothes, or to carry water to their homes.

In Italy there would be no work today. Even among the poor, there would be dinners — regardless how meager — and families and friends visiting back and forth, talking over a game of *scopa* or *briscola*. Here, wraiths shuffled into the little building that served as a church, or else they stood clustered outside its doors while he said Mass in the sweltering interior with no altar, no pews or chairs, only a few rough-hewn benches reserved for the sick and elderly. Once he said the *Ite, Missa est*, they shuffled back out, dispersing along the dusty roads to their farms, their work, and their misery.

He was afraid of them. There was something sub-human about them, the women and children especially, the way they lived in the dirt without seeming to notice it. The Italians' very language was changed. It had become both more high-pitched and guttural, rising and dropping in volume like a strange music. The longer a family had been here, the more pronounced their language distortion seemed, so that at times he had trouble recognizing their speech as Italian. And the few who spoke English, the children in particular, sounded not like the Americans he had met from New York, nor even like the Southern plantation owners and managers, but rather like the black ones whose English rose and fell in that same unusual cadence.

He went to the table and poured himself a glass of wine — he could not drink the yellow water — then looked at the letter he had begun writing to the bishop shortly after his arrival. At least it had begun as a letter, but had turned into a dialogue with himself. He would never be able to send it home. How could he begin to express the impossibility of ministering to such a people in such a place? When he arrived they had descended upon him, a ragged, stinking mob fighting each other to have their complaints heard, as if he had the power to do a single thing about any of it. The water, the mosquitoes, the inflated company charges and interest, the crooked Italian agents working against their own people, the intimidations, the injustices, the sickness, the death. There was no end to it. His heart sank; an odd, hollow sensation swept through him. He wanted to go home. He was only twenty–three.

He decided he must word his letter to the bishop in such a way as to suggest his leaving as an inevitable and obvious conclusion, his coming here an unfortunate mistake.

He wandered back to the window, glass in hand. Would he be able to lie outright, say that these people for all their complaining and agitating had refused him, insisted he be sent back? No, he would tell the truth, the simple awful hopelessness of the place, plead inexperience and youth, insist on help or better yet, a replacement, someone older and experienced in mission work. He glanced out the window, debating his wording when he was startled by the sight of a small, bent woman walking along the dirt road toward his home. A mangy brown dog trailed her.

Please, let her walk on by, let her not be coming here, he prayed, and was immediately overcome with shame. He went to the table and stood waiting, as if removing himself from the window would encourage the woman to keep going.

He gripped the rough table edge, waiting. When he heard the knock he looked down at his whitened knuckles. Bloodless, he thought, and not just his fingers. She had to knock a second time before he moved to open the door.

She stood imploring him with her eyes, a skinny dirty woman dressed in rags, a dark kerchief tied under her chin.

She could have been in her fifties as easily as in her twenties. Her skin was drawn and wrinkled and brown from the sun, but with a yellowish tint, too, from the fever. The dog sat in the dirt, halfway down the lane.

"Can you baptize my baby?" she asked.

Sicilian. He recognized her as one of the many who had swarmed him when he arrived, wanting her baby baptized right then. But so many other needs pressed for his attention.

"Now?" he said. "Sunday afternoon?" He heard the irritation in his voice, and it surprised him that he would talk to a woman in such a way.

"He's sick," she said. "If he dies, like this... " He could barely make out what she was saying, what with her dialect and peasant accent, even though he had studied a number of Italian languages. She made a feeble motion with her hand as she gazed into his eyes. "He won't get into heaven," she said. She was emotionless. She could just as easily have been talking about someone getting a ride across the river on a ferry as about her dying baby.

He had to make an effort to soften his voice. "It's probably just the colic," he told her. He spoke slowly and loudly, in case she had trouble understanding him. "What makes you think he's dying?"

"They all die," she said.

He didn't know if she meant all the babies on the plantation or all of her own babies.

"Well," he said, not knowing what else to say. "Did you call the doctor? You should call the doctor."

She looked at him a long time with her large, sunken eyes. Then she opened her palm to him. "No money," she told him. "They die with the doctor anyway. At least if he could get into heaven I wouldn't feel so bad."

Her clothes were dirty, and he could smell the sweat and dirt. She had no money, but she would be charged for his visit, he knew that much. The owner, Harlan Gates, had explained everything to him: The tenants would be charged a small monthly fee to help pay for his room and board on the plantation. In addition, there would be burial and baptismal and wedding charges — minimal, of course, and all of which the tenants could well afford, Gates assured him, sweeping his arm to indicate the lushness of the Delta. Father Odetti was to keep records of all the visits he made and of all his priestly activities and hand them in to the office manager who would then put the charges down in the family's record.

"There is a baptismal charge," Father Odetti told the woman, and she looked at him wide-eyed and silent.

Finally she told him: "If you say there is."

Her words and her gaze settled like ice inside him. Mr. Gates had seemed likeable enough when they met in his fine house in Greenville — friendly, courteous, concerned for the welfare of his tenants. He had offered Father Odetti a glass of whiskey and a cigar, then apologized, saying he did not know what had gotten into him, offering such vices to a man of the cloth. Gates hesitated, taking the cigar back and opening the desk drawer from which he had removed it. Then he winked at Father Odetti and laughed good-naturedly as he held the cigar out to him again and offered a light. Father Odetti had laughed too. He liked the man, his easy-going manner, and his handsome, robust looks. It was the first cigar he had ever smoked.

Reluctantly Father Odetti went for his baptismal articles. He also took down the crucifix and candles and holy oil, in case the baby really was dying. He buttoned his collar and slipped into his jacket and they left.

The felt hat offered little protection against the blistering sun, and his dark clothes soaked up the heat. He would have to get lighter clothes, he thought, and a different hat — that is, if he stayed. If he was forced to stay. Since his house was at the edge of the plantation, at least there were a couple of trees behind it. But where they walked now there were no trees, only the endless cotton fields.

The woman shuffled silently beside him, and the mangy dog followed at a distance. He felt terribly awkward. He thought he should say something, but what could he say? "It's hot," he finally announced. The woman plodded along, saying nothing.

✳✳✳

SERAFIN and Step were nailing a tin roof to one of the new houses when they saw the priest walking with Mrs. Sant'Angelo toward the bayou shacks, a scruffy dog following a few yards behind. Taking the priest to a house down there meant only one thing: bad news. Even from the distance the priest seemed to be wilting from the heat.

Serafin sat back on his heels, balancing on the roof's slope, trying to let the air move through his sweaty shirt for a moment. On the outside he was more quiet and accepting than he'd been that first year, but inside he calculated and planned. One way or another they would escape from Sweet Hope, and when they did, there'd be hell for the Americans to pay for what they'd put them through. *Just bide your time*, he'd tell himself. *Until the time is ripe.* But now this. He had thought Amalia and Fiorenza would cry when they first laid eyes on *il prete* a week ago. "What's the *maledetta* company up to now?" was all Amalia could say. He'd wondered that himself. Why, for all the company's harshness, would they concede to bringing in an Italian priest?

He had tried to keep Amalia from getting too upset over it: "You know, some of the saints, the martyrs, were young, only children. The Blessed Virgin herself — "

The expression on her face had stopped him instantly. He didn't believe all those stories himself anyway. And, as for her, although she still made the children join her in daily prayer, the prayers had grown shorter while a fine layer of yellow dust collected on the statue of Mary. Now this — a boy priest.

The dog was from the fall litter at the hay barn, one of several mongrels the managers had forced upon some tenants on the off chance there might be a decent birder among them — in which case, they'd simply confiscate the grown dog. "Can't even feed themselves, and now they got to feed a dog," Step said.

Only a few families lived down in the bayou shacks, along the stagnant marsh. Rotting planks had been laid over a shallow ditch to gain access to the houses, the worst on all of Sweet Hope. Great swaths of their land lay submerged when it rained, or were too mucky to grow anything. The company had tried to drain the land and thought they had succeeded, but after the winter rain the swamp reclaimed its place. The tenants weren't allowed to move, despite Step's protests, and despite the few vacant houses in the better areas. The cursed of the cursed, the other Italians called the ones down there.

"Why you no tell Mr. Gates move that family out?" Serafin asked Step. The whole family was underfed and sickly, and their new baby had been sick since it was born.

Step paused in his work, removed his hat, and fanned himself. "Whatever I got to say fall on deaf ears," he said. He motioned to his ears. "They don't listen. Don't care what I got to say 'bout the ones down there."

"The ones down there" were mostly the sick and dying, the women without men, or the families whose men had tried to leave Sweet Hope. Sant'Angelo had tried more than once.

Serafin couldn't understand how the company refused to listen to Step's pleas. As far as he could see, Step was some kind of plantation boss, no matter what he said to the contrary.

"I don't know if the Sant'Angelos gonna make it," he told Step. It bothered him, more than he could say. Forcing them to live down there seemed crueler than anything he had endured.

"*Debole*," Amalia would call him. Weakling, softy.

"Is it wrong to care about your neighbor?" he would counter. "To be compassionate?"

Her raised chin said "Worry about your own family." End of conversation.

He was smart enough to know he didn't trust Gates finally bringing in an Italian priest. Throw the dog a scrap so he won't see that the dish is empty?

Step put his hat on and went back to work. His suspicion was that Gates didn't even know about the family being sick. It was the managers who decided more and more where a family was settled and what became of them afterward, as Gates moved deeper into politics, with an eye to becoming senator. And it was the managers who would just as soon let a family die if the cost of saving them threatened to cut into their profits. After all, there were plenty of fresh, unsuspecting bodies ready to take the place of those who fell.

Which was exactly what was weighing on Step's mind under the blistering sun and humidity in the glare of the new tin roof. Not just the sick family but also a nagging concern over his part in the Italian colony experiment. And with Gates gone so much now, he felt whatever slight hold he once had on the reins slipping from him.

Almost no Italians were seeing a profit. Yet most had resigned themselves to their plight, working diligently, and still believing that somehow their hard work — or God — would eventually pull them out of their misery. Like Serafin here, after he recovered from the shock of finding out that all that his first year of hard work had amounted to was putting him in debt.

Step helped when he could, like now, with this roofing job that would amount to two dollars lead scrip for Serafin. Even Fancy had softened a little, though she still kept her distance. No matter how hard she tried to appear indifferent, her eye had been caught by Amalia's handiwork. Step had even talked Fancy into selling one of Amalia's dresses in town, which he hoped wouldn't turn out to be a bad move. "Don't think I'm makin a habit a' carryin that woman's clothes every time I go to town now," Fancy had told him.

✳✳✳

"In d' swamp live d' swamp rat man. Big as a mule. Man's head w' rat ears, a rat tail an' long claws — an' what he like best to eat is chil'ren. That why you don' ever wanna go near d' swamp — 'specially at night. If a chil' go on by wi' no protection, he git call'd into d' swamp. Once he git call'd, he got to go. Once he go, he don' never come back."

Uncle Blue was sitting in his cane chair under his music tree while the children sat on the ground listening: Birdie, Tobe, Osvaldo and Isola. Above them the chimes in the music tree began to tinkle as a breeze stirred the pieces of hanging junk: rusted forks, dented tin plates, shards of pottery, a scuffle hoe tine.

Blue was one of the longest-standing Sweet Hope residents, having been there since slave times. Harlan Gates let him stay in his old shack at the edge of the woods and raise a little patch of cotton, even though the man brought in virtually no revenue for the plantation. But Gates could always hold Blue up as proof of his benevolence.

He cleared his throat, a low rumbling sound that went on a long time. His old dog lay near the man's feet, flattened out in the grass and so still he could have been dead.

"People's tried to catch 'im," Blue said. "Big, strong mens try t' catch that swamp rat man."

He leaned forward, his cloud of white hair moving with him, and lowered his voice. "But not one a' them mens ever come back. Swamp rat man got ever last one."

"I thought you said he ate children," Isola said.

"Hmmph," Uncle Blue said. "You!" All eyes turned to Isola. "Swamp rat man eat whatever he wants. What's wrong w' you?"

"She got the hoodoo," Tobe said, grinning.

"You shut up, Tobe Hall."

"Who say hoodoo?" Uncle Blue said.

"Lally Mo's got the hoodoo, not me," Isola said.

"Lally Mo? I declare," Blue said. "Be careful don' say that name too loud."

The children closed their mouths and looked at each other. Lally Mo had power, everybody knew that. The Italians called her a witch. The blacks called her a hoodoo lady and said you couldn't walk by her house at night. But people sent for Lally Mo if somebody was sick or dying. Sometimes she came.

The Italians had the hoodoo too, Isola thought, though they didn't call it that. Old lady Turine could take the *malocchio* off you. People were careful around her, watching what they said and did, and they didn't want their children going near her. But if somebody was sick or dying or in trouble, they sent for old lady Turine.

He shook his head, making a rumbling sound in his throat. "Y'all better git now," he told them. "Gwan', now." He bent forward and clutched his knee. "Ohh, somethin in the air," he said. "My bone crackin, tellin me watch out." He looked at Isola as he spoke, holding his knee with one gnarled hand.

The children rose slowly, keeping their wary eyes on Uncle Blue, then tore off for the bayou. A cottontail bounded from the grass and stopped in front of them. It moved toward the bayou water, then stopped again and sat up. Tobe motioned for them to be quiet. Suddenly the rabbit sprang into the bushes and was gone. A moment later, Lecie Titus came upon them, carrying a small burlap sack.

She ducked her head and raised her hand halfway in greeting.

"What you doin out here, Lecie?" Birdie asked.

Lecie shrugged. People said she was born shy. You'd never know she belonged to Lud and Fred Titus, the way she kept so quiet.

"Diggin roots?"

"Uh-huh."

"Wish't you could find a root to get rid a' cotton weeds," Tobe said. It took Lecie a moment before she grinned at the idea.

"Ain't you got nothin for headache?" Isola asked. They knew she meant for Osvaldo.

"She just learnin," Birdie chimed in. Then, almost in a whisper, she added: "From Lally Mo."

The children widened their eyes at the name she had dared to speak.

"*Testa dura*," Isola called her, but nobody laughed.

Lecie was squatting near the water's edge. The others watched her take out a short broken-handled knife and dig at a plant with it.

"What you find?" Birdie called.

Lecie inspected the plant. "Nuthin." She placed it in her sack.

"Let us know, you find somethin good t' eat," Birdie said, but Lecie moved ahead without answering.

"Come on," Tobe said. "I know a place where they's blackberries big as a hickory nut."

The children hesitated.

"We been gone too long," Isola reminded them. "We better go back to work or we'll get in trouble."

"Scairdies," Tobe said. "It's on the way home, anyways."

Osvaldo took Lecie by the hand, and she blushed and pulled back. But then she went with them as they followed Tobe in the shade along the woods.

They'd gone only a short distance when Osvaldo stopped them.

"Hear that?" he said.

"I don't hear nothin," Birdie said.

"Somethin in the woods," Osvaldo whispered.

"He's always hearin things," Isola told them.

"You hear it, don't you, Lecie?" Osvaldo asked.

She lowered her head and shrugged her shoulders.

The children looked around at the still trees, the wilting leaves.

"Somethin watchin us," Osvaldo said.

"Why you always talkin somethin crazy?" Tobe asked him. But the children spoke in whispers as they looked about at the trees. Here and there a leaf twitched ominously.

"Think it's the swamp rat man?" Osvaldo whispered.

A twig snapped, and Birdie shrieked. Like a flock of startled birds, the children took off running. Osvaldo grabbed Lecie's hand and pulled her along. They didn't stop until they reached the crossroads at the Senigallia section.

***

SERAFIN hunkered down into the rhythm of hammering, trying to ignore the sun's heat while he thought about money. Two dollars for today, against this year's eighty–six–dollar store debt. Maybe more roofing tomorrow. Four dollars in one week would be good — all lead scrip, but money just the same. If they could just get by the rest of the summer gathering what grew wild, catching fish, stretching their flour and lard... And maybe Amalia could sell a couple more dresses, and get paid in real American money. He looked over at Step, wondering if he dared ask for another favor so soon. Step shook his head to fling the sweat from his eyes, disturbing the mosquitoes that buzzed at his face. Not yet.

From their vantage point on the roof, the plantation was lush and green all about them, with the narrow yellow roads cutting through here and there. The cotton looked good, the bolls abundant and well–formed. So far, no drought, no excess rain, no insects or disease. They prayed the usual farmer's prayer: that the weather held and the market was good. Maybe this would be the year, finally, that they saw a profit.

In the distance near the northern end of the lake woods, Serafin was surprised to see his two youngest children hurrying toward home. "What they doin way over there?" he said.

Step craned to see. "My two with 'em? Better not a' sneaked off to swim in the lake."

"I'll give them the lake, when I get home. They supposed to be helping their mother."

But he couldn't keep an eye on Isola and Osvaldo every minute, and they were running wild lately, one worse than the other, so that he and Amalia sometimes forgot their worry over the boy's condition. Amalia would be angry when she discovered they'd sneaked away again, if she hadn't already discovered it. Serafin had left them with plenty to do: a sack of dried tubers to grind into make–do flour, and then a two–foot deep drainage trench to dig out along the southern border of their property. Then, tonight, Lazzaro and his family were coming to visit. He would make the two stay inside the house while the others played *bocce*, no visiting for them.

A white heron rose from the edge of the woods and floated over the children, startling them, so that they started at a trot for home. The bird curved slowly away and dropped behind the trees. Serafin hammered another sheet of tin in place, not stopping to wipe the sweat from his face.

"You come my house after supper?" he asked Step. "We play the *bocce* tonight. Lazzaro come too, everybody."

"*Bocce*," Step said.

"Bring all you family. Everybody like that game."

"How you gonna play *bocce* after cookin up here in the sun all day?" Step asked.

"That's okay. I forget you an old man. You go home, better rest if you too tired."

He went back to nailing the edge of the tin, trying to hide his smile.

Step played right along. "We'll see," he said gruffly. "Maybe I can play sittin in a chair."

As they inched their way to the ladder, they caught sight of the priest returning from the bayou. He was alone this time, dressed in his white shirtsleeves now and carrying a bundle.

It took the two men a minute to see what he carried: the brown dog lay wrapped in the priest's black jacket, its head and front paws protruding.

"Don't tell me he got the Sant'Angelo's dog," Serafin said.

"Can't even walk on its own four feet?" Step said.

The animal moved its head from side to side like a contented baby. "Gettin a dog from the bayou," Step said.

They watched for a few moments as the priest clumsily made his way toward home. Then they climbed down the ladder, shaking their heads yet again over the boy–man.

CHAPTER 11

Bocce

August 1904

AMALIA sat on the front step with her sewing in her lap. Green plants rose up around her, blocking any view of the other shacks in the distance. For much of the year she felt dropped in the middle of an endless, flat expanse of land. When the crops were high, she felt trapped in a cage and hidden from sight. Either way, planting or harvest time, she didn't exist. None of them did.

Not far from the house was a spot of bare earth and the chicken shed they'd built from scraps to accommodate their three hens, with hopes of more. The Halls' mule and cart stood next to the shed, and not far from the shed stood the *forno* Serafin had built by carrying sand and mud from the river to make a mortar to hold the rocks he'd gathered. Now they could bake several loaves of bread at once, and without heating up the house in the summer. It left her hollow: all these signs of making a permanent home here.

"*Ho vinto,*" Osvaldo shouted, and she looked down the yellow path strewn with watermelon rinds where the men and children laughed and argued over the *bocce* game.

"Game's not over yet, squash head," Isola told him.

"I knocked your ball out."

"Hey," Serafin told him. "Go find it now."

Fancy sat a few yards away on an upturned bucket, laboring over a doily she was crocheting. Now and then she glanced up at the game without interest.

"Put down flat," Amalia told her. "No pull tight."

Fancy bristled. Even though she was just learning to crochet, didn't she know enough not to pull a stitch too tight?

Fiorenza's boy Getulio tottered after one of the wayward balls, and she scooped him up. "Mama, you're supposed to watch him," she told La Vecchia, as if the old lady really could look after a child. "Let me go," the boy demanded, and she finally set him down again.

The narrow path was choked with bodies — Lazzaro's family with his cousin Claudio, their own family, the Halls. They should have gone down into the road to play, where there would be more room, and where they would not have to search through the cotton for a stray ball. But no, always everybody on top of each other. She and Serafin had ordered Osvaldo and Isola to stay inside for running off to the lake, but with visitors there, they had relented. When Angelina heard that the Halls were coming, she drew a bucket of fresh water and hurried to the wash basin inside where she scrubbed her face, then brushed her hair and patted her damp hands up and down her dress to clean it, ignoring her sister's taunts.

And that was one more thing: Calvin clopping around in those shoes, his eyes sliding this way and that as Angelina turned away from him in a way that showed how much she was turning toward him. Even Fancy's eyes flared each time she saw the shoes flapping in the dust.

Fiorenza sat down on the step beside Amalia, holding her struggling boy. "*Hai finito*?" she asked.

Amalia moved her hand on top of the sewing. She glanced at Fancy who labored to pull even stitches. "Miss Fancy," she called. "No good?"

Fancy held up the doily. A design of triangles and circles was beginning to take shape.

"You make good," Amalia told her.

"We should have known better," Fiorenza said. "What did we expect?"

She was talking about the new priest, of course.

"You saw the way he ran out after Mass this morning?" Fiorenza said. "He couldn't get away from us fast enough."

It hurt too much to even think about it. Why bother trying to say anything?

Osvaldo let out a shout and ran to measure the distance and pronounce whose ball was closer to the *pallino,* and Fancy looked up at him — Osvaldo, the light-head boy. He carried a small stick in which he had cut notches. Always making something, doing something strange. And Tobe was right there alongside him, but Fancy could not say anything to him with the others around. Step wouldn't listen. She had told him that day she'd seen the lightning hit him, and Step had cocked his head and asked her, "Now how you s'pose such a thing can be?" in a way that let her know he thought she'd been dreaming. So she'd let it be. Nobody knew, but she knew. The Italian boy had been marked.

Getulio laughed and scampered on his hands and knees into the cotton plants. La Vecchia tried to follow, but Fiorenza pulled her back. The old woman was thin and frail, all gray hair and bones holding up a loose sack of a dress. Fancy looked at the sky, calculating how much longer they'd be there.

Calvin positioned his toe at the line in the dirt, narrowed his eyes, leaned forward carefully, and gently released the ball in imitation of the way the Italians threw: palm down, then flick the wrist up and let the ball go in a slow arc. It landed a good foot away from the others. Angelina gave a haughty laugh, and he looked at her with hope. She brushed at a spot on her dress.

Fiorenza gave a knowing nod to Amalia. Fancy clucked her tongue.

The girls were leaning against the watering trough now, watching twigs float. Birdie pulled off a few cotton leaves and laid them on the water, then put tiny twigs on top. "My ferry boat loaded with cotton," she said. Isola followed suit, making her own boat. Birdie stirred the water, then splashed it until the leaves sank. "Big storm comin," she called out. "Shipwreck. Too bad, you lost all your cotton."

"You too," Isola said, splashing the water as well.

"I got money, I can plant me some more," Birdie told her. "But you in big trouble. You owe the company lots a' money."

"Do not."

"Yeah, 'cause you lost all your cotton and jumped contract," Birdie told her. "I'm puttin you on the chain gang."

Fancy stood abruptly. "Birdie, get over here," she called. "What you think you doin?"

"Playin," Birdie said.

"Now," Fancy said, pointing sternly to a spot beside her as the other two women watched.

Birdie plopped down heavily beside her mother.

"Don't let me hear you talkin that foolishness no more," Fancy scolded

"Jus' make–believe, mama."

"*E tu,*" Amalia scolded Isola. "*Lasciala stare.*"

"I didn't do anything," the girl answered.

"You want the *sculaccia*?" she said, motioning with her hand. She smiled weakly at Fancy, then tugged at the dress she was sewing, straightening the hem. She knew it had not been Fancy's idea to take that other dress to the village to sell for her, as much as Fancy seemed to admire her sewing. But Amalia had accepted the help, and the dollar went into a rusted tobacco tin that she and Serafin stashed inside the bottom corner of their corn husk mattress, separate from their provisions money. Not even the children knew about it.

Fiorenza told Amalia: "Maybe if we put your tomatoes and ours together we'd have enough for one pot of *sugo*. I'll go crazy if I don't get some soon."

"We talk tomatoes," Amalia told Fancy. Fancy glanced over at the few plants growing near the stoop.

"You still have your *asciugapomodoro*?" Fiorenza asked her friend. "For the tomato paste," she told Fancy.

"*Ma certo*. But who's got anything to put on it?"

"You can buy bushels a' tomatoes in the village," Birdie said. "They sell 'em at th' store there — an' all th' farmers sell 'em too. Cheaper'n here."

"That ain't no business a' theirs," Fancy told Birdie. "Jus' hush now."

"Tomato in village?" Amalia asked. "Miss Fancy," she said, seeing her opportunity. "I make two new dress. Maybe sell."

Fancy adjusted her shoulders slightly. She gave her daughter a disapproving look, then slid her eyes over at Step. He was deep in the game. Ever since Step had talked her into selling Amalia's dress, she'd been waiting for the Pascalas to ask her to sell more.

"I go 'cross," Amalia said. "Me. I go village, sell dress. You tell me how."

"You?" Fancy fairly shrieked.

"Shh," Fiorenza whispered. "Amalia, don't — "

They instinctively looked around, as if one of the Americans might be lurking in the cotton plants, listening. There was only Osvaldo and Tobe playing with a bucket and piece of rope.

"Miz 'Malia," Fancy said, lowering her voice, "you know you can't go over there."

"Maybe if I go, company see no problem, then we all go."

"I don't hear anything you're saying," Fiorenza said, shocked at Amalia's suggestion.

"I'll go with you, mama," Isola said.

"Me too," Birdie said. "I wanna go too."

Fancy stopped her daughter with a wave of the hand. "Ain't nobody goin nowhere."

"Nobody ever try," Amalia insisted. "If we try..."

"Don't go gettin y'self in no trouble," Fancy cautioned. "Your men tried plenty a' times. You know what happen to 'em."

"Men don't do nothing," Amalia said bitterly.

They looked over at the game, the men weary but happy, at least for these last few hours of the day. "Ain't much they can do," Fancy told her.

"Bet we could sneak 'cross th' lake in your priest's rowboat," Birdie said.

"Birdie Hall, what got into you?" Fancy exclaimed. "Don't give 'em no ideas."

Amalia gazed across the field. The company had given the priest a rowboat, to take himself to the village. Sometimes he shopped, or met with the American priest there, over church business. "Buying whiskey and cigars, that's his church business," Lazzaro had scoffed.

"Mama, how come the 'talians over to Three Point can go where they want?" Birdie asked.

It was the plantation halfway between Sweet Hope and the village. The company used day labor from Three Point when they needed, always black workers. Amalia turned to Fancy. "Is true, isn't it?"

"Mr. Gates got his ways."

"You take me," Amalia said. "I say I'm from Three Point."

"No, no," Fiorenza said, covering her ears.

"Go sit over there, if you don't like what I'm saying," Amalia told her, pointing to the water trough.

"You know I can't take you," Fancy said, although part of her wondered why no one else had thought of the idea.

Amalia smoothed her hand over her sewing and looked staunchly across the fields. "Maybe I go myself. Isola, you come with me. We sell the dress, buy the tomato." She glanced at Serafin, wondering how he'd react if he found out. Better not to let him find out.

"We can take the mule cart," Isola said. "If you won't take the boat."

"Ain't nobody gonna let you outta here in no mule cart," Fancy told them, feeling herself getting sucked into the scheme in spite of her resolve.

"We can take 'em in ours," Birdie said. "Didn't you say you was gonna go — "

Fancy raised a warning hand at her daughter. "Your daddy have a conniption fit, he find out we talkin like this. You just shush up." She looked at the two women. "All a' yous, you don't say a word 'bout this, hear?"

Amalia smiled, ever so slightly. "So you take us, yes?"

One game ended, and the other children wandered off. "Haven't you had enough?" Fiorenza called to Lazzaro.

He waved at her. "Let me win one lousy game before we go."

She turned to Amalia. "Tomorrow they'll complain about how tired they are."

Step and Serafin took sides against Lazzaro and Claudio, but the boy only played half-heartedly. He'd come to Sweet Hope to join his cousin Lazzaro, and when he found out they were practically slaves to the company, he was all fired up, full of ideas, talking insurrection and uprising. By the end of his first month he'd become as resigned as the rest of them. Every now and then he eyed Angelina as she picked up watermelon rinds and flung them daintily into the cotton while Calvin pretended not to watch. Finally Claudio told his cousin, "She don't like Italian boys, eh?"

"Why're you asking?" Lazzaro said, glancing over at the women.

"*Eh.*"

Fiorenza nudged Amalia.

"A fool doesn't recognize himself," Amalia answered.

"Well, she's a pretty girl. And growing up fast, what do you expect?"

The mule let out a piercing cry, followed by a shout from Osvaldo. The boys struggled to hold the mule still while it brayed and tried to pull away. Tobe yanked on the halter and yelled at Osvaldo to get the rope free while the mule kicked and complained and Osvaldo darted in and out between its legs, struggling to calm the animal.

Everyone came running. "Now what the hell you boys done?" Step called as he rushed to free them. The mule stumbled against him, its front right leg caught in a tangle of rope and a broken switch.

"Was Osvaldo's idea," Tobe insisted.

Serafin and Lazzaro held the mule while Step bent over and untangled the foot, mindful not to get kicked in the head while Amalia shouted for the men to be careful and the children to get out of the way.

"What is this? What happened?" Serafin called to his son.

"A snare," Osvaldo said.

"Snare? You gonna break this mule's leg," Step said angrily. He pulled Tobe by the collar and gave him a slap on his backside. "All I need's a dead mule. Where you get such a crazy fool idea?"

"Seein if we can catch a big animal with a snare," Osvaldo said.

Serafin shook Osvaldo by the arm as he scolded him for endangering the mule.

The men ran their hands up and down the mule's legs and along its back while the others stood back watching. Claudio held the halter as he shushed the animal.

"He think he gonna catch the swamp rat man," Tobe said, rubbing his behind.

"Swamp rat man?" Step said.

Isola taunted her brother: "*Scemo, pazzo*. That's a fairy tale."

"No, he's real," Osvaldo countered. "He lives in the swamp. We see his fires."

Serafin looped the rope between his elbow and hand. "Where'd you find this good rope?"

Osvaldo hung his head. "In the wagon."

Lazzaro pulled the boy to his side. "Hey, *sfrenato*. Don't you know not to touch things that aren't yours?"

But Step was lighting into Tobe again, blaming him for going along with such a fool idea while Fancy glared at the scene, her arms folded across her chest.

Claudio stood with his hands in his pockets. "I guess that's the end of our game, eh?" he said.

Lazzaro patted the mule's side. "Good thing she didn't get hurt. Catch a mule by the feet, I never heard of that before."

"Many sorry," Amalia said to Fancy, but Fancy was staring at Osvaldo, shaking her head.

"I told you stay by my side if you're not playing *bocce* with your father," Amalia scolded Osvaldo. "Acting up twice in one day! Get over here." It dawned on her, suddenly, that the boy's mind had been injured after all by the lightning strike. She drew Osvaldo to her, feeling his head, looking into his eyes. A little boy causing trouble was one thing. But as he grew older — a grown man — his behavior would not be tolerated. "*O Signore*," she cried out, cradling the struggling boy.

Serafin tossed the rope back in Step's wagon, then turned to Osvaldo. "You don't touch, hear?" he said sternly. "Don't touch anything that's not yours." He was trembling over the near–disaster. "I sorry, Mr. Step. The mule's okay, no?" To buy a mule, now, when they were already in the hole. To buy a mule at Sweet Hope prices.

Step shrugged, trying to hold his anger down as he tightened his grip on the mule's halter. They should put a halter on that boy, that's what they needed to do.

"Remember that mule dragging Pietro," Lazzaro reminded them, "when we were cutting trees. Broke the harness, broke the man in pieces, but not a scratch on that mule. They're tough."

"Eh," Serafin said.

"Strong as a mule," Lazzaro said. "Isn't that the saying?"

The men tried to laugh now. They talked with relief and fear of the stubbornness of mules, and the troubles they'd seen from mules. But they no longer spoke of this mule, Step Hall's mule.

Fancy caught Step's eye with a look that said *See what I been tryin to tell you?*

But Amalia intervened. "We okay now, yes?" she asked them. "Mr. Step, Miss Fancy?"

Fancy shook her head at Amalia meaning no, forget the tomatoes, forget the village.

"Yes, yes, we go," Amalia said. "Everything okay." Step thought she was merely talking her broken English about the boys and the mule. But Fancy knew what she really meant.

"You wearin me thin," she told Amalia.

***

ANGELINA stood apart from her family, staring at the animal in forced concentration as Calvin circled closer. And he was choking, uncertain what to say, how to say it. The mule had turned into a jumble of words; it was floating up into the sky. He was beside her, flushed with heat, and now vaguely aware that his mother was gathering their things to leave.

"Time to get on home," Step said, and Serafin sent Osvaldo and Isola to collect the *bocce* balls.

"Why me?" Isola complained. "I didn't do anything."

Calvin shoved his hands in his pockets, cleared his throat. Angelina glanced his way, acting surprised to see him standing beside her. She put her hands on the edge of the water trough, as if to steady herself.

"Like my shoes?" he blurted. He couldn't believe that was the one stupid thing he could think to say.

Reluctantly, she looked down. The feet were big and dirty, the toes of her barely recognizable shoes cut off to accommodate the large feet, the shoes tied together with baling twine. Something awful turned over in her stomach. She wanted to cry.

"Beautiful," she said coolly.

He laughed, moved in front of her, did two steps of a dance for her, he didn't know why.

"Made 'em myself," he heard himself saying.

She was trembling inside, trying to force herself to act aloof. But he smiled so brightly, looked at her so brightly.

"If you think you going to be a shoemaker, better find another job," she told him.

He inhaled quickly, barely able to breathe. "You said it," he answered, his feet no longer touching the dust of the earth.

***

ONCE the visitors trailed off, Serafin left Amalia to finish her sewing in the failing light, and followed the children to the bedroom. He sat on the small bed he'd made for Osvaldo as the girls climbed into theirs.

"You better not scratch and jump around all night," Angelina told her sister.

"Why? So you can think about your boyfriend?"

Serafin patted the bed, motioning Osvaldo closer, and the boy scooted over. "What am I going to do with you?" Serafin asked, his voice full of worry.

"You should ship him off to somebody else's farm to work, papa," Isola piped up from across the room.

"Better to ship you off," Angelina answered.

"Close your eyes and sleep," Serafin told them. He ran his hand through Osvaldo's thick hair, then rested it on the boy's head, as if he would be able to learn something from mere touch. Finally Osvaldo moved his father's hand away.

"Papa, did you ever hear of the Swamp Rat Man?" he whispered softly so that his sisters wouldn't hear.

"What? What nonsense are you talking about?"

He motioned his father closer, and when Serafin leaned down, the boy cupped his hands to Serafin's ear. "I think it's *il gobbo*, and he lives in the swamp woods. He keeps his pot of gold there."

Serafin sat up. "You stay away from the swamp woods, you hear me?"

"Shh," Osvaldo told him.

"Isola, Angelina, have you kids been going to the swamp woods?" Serafin asked. "I want you to stay away from there."

"He's cuckoo, that's all, Daddy," Isola said.

Serafin sat looking down at the boy. Finally, he pulled the mosquito netting over the children's beds. "Sleep," he told them. "And no more talk of the swamp."

He joined Amalia on the stoop, and they sat in silence, looking down the path to the road as they swatted mosquitoes from their arms.

"Do you know how much it would set us back if we had to buy them a mule?" Amalia said at last.

"From now on, he works with me," Serafin told her. "I don't let him out of my sight."

"He was right under your nose tonight," she reminded him.

"*Allora*," he answered. There was always something, always some commotion. They had already said the words too many times: wild animals. Not just their own, but all the children of Sweet Hope.

"Serafin..." she said. "Do you think there's something... you see how he acts. I think his mind was hurt."

"That again. I told you, it never happened."

"I know what I saw."

"He's a boy, that's all. Full of the devil. That's how boys are."

"Maybe."

They could see straight down their lane to the dirt road. A man and boy walked past in the setting sun, balancing several short planks of scrap lumber on their shoulders, the man walking with great effort: Sant'Angelo and his oldest son.

In the next minute they were gone, obscured again by the tall cotton plants. "Jesus," Serafin said to Amalia, remembering the priest going with the woman earlier that day. "Their baby?" He started to tell Amalia about seeing the priest and Mrs. Sant'Angelo, with the dog trotting after them. He shook his head. No. It had been a good day, in spite of Osvaldo acting up with the mule. What did they have to complain about?

"I think they're making a coffin," he told her.

They stared down the lane at the spot the man and boy had crossed. Only green cotton plants were visible now, and a yellow road, and a sky streaked with pink and orange.

CHAPTER 12

Stealing The Priest's Rowboat

August 1904

THE women eyed each other across the sack Amalia clutched on her lap. Their two girls giggled behind as Fancy leaned into the oars.

If they got caught, Fancy would say she and Birdie had gone to the village to see their friend William at the livery stable, discovered the Italians, and were bringing them back to Sweet Hope. If it weren't for the prospect of finding Calvin a job, she wouldn't be sitting in the rowboat now, she told herself, although she could have easily taken their mule cart to the village. Without the Italians.

Amalia had some nerve to keep pressing her, after that light–head boy of hers nearly killed their mule. Ask and ye shall receive? Fancy had her own asking to do. She was going to see if William could spare some work for Calvin, get him out of the lumber mill. William had a small farm outside Sweet Hope, and Calvin could walk there, then ride into the village with him.

Amalia stared nervously at the receding bank, then lowered the kerchief over her face.

"Miz 'Malia, set easy," Fancy told her. "Ain't nobody lookin after you." She quickly scanned the shore, hoping she was right.

Amalia smiled weakly, then rested her hands on the sack holding the two dresses she had worked so hard on. The boat wobbled beneath her. It had been years since she'd been in a boat, and the movement and the wide lake suddenly filled her with sadness.

She was brought back around when Fancy ran the boat onto the shore.

A soft grassy bank rose above them, and a large oak tree spread its branches over the water's edge. They could see the tops of buildings and hear people and wagons as they hurried out of the boat. A couple of men dressed in city clothes stood under the tree above the dock, eating peanuts from a paper sack and tossing the shells on the ground as they watched them disembark. Amalia turned her face away, imagining that the men could somehow tell that she'd sneaked away from Sweet Hope.

"Jes' keep quiet," Fancy told them. "Nobody bother you if you don't go actin up." She looked hard at the girls when she said this.

They scrambled up the bank, and Isola gasped at the sight. Rows of clean shops fronted by wooden walking paths lay before them. Leafy green trees grew alongside the roads. Even the horses and mules looked clean. "Mama," she murmured. "It's beautiful."

Amalia, too, looked about with hungry eyes. "So this it." They had lived in the dust for so long.

She pulled Isola to her side as they followed Fancy toward the center of town. A few people were out, mostly American men going into the gin company building. Some of the men looked at them strangely. A black man driving a wagon down the street tipped his hat at them.

They paused under a window awning outside one of the gin companies. When the men they'd seen down near the water approached, talking in low voices, Amalia held her breath, waiting for the worst. One man crumpled the paper sack he'd been eating from and dropped it on the ground as he talked about a railroad expansion. Birdie snatched up the bag just as the men disappeared into the telegraph office. Amalia breathed a sigh of relief.

Fancy tried to slap the bag out of her daughter's hand, but Birdie pulled away. She uncrumpled the bag and sifted through the few broken shells inside, then popped a piece of peanut in her mouth. A carriage clattered by, the passenger dressed in a bright yellow dress and a flowery hat, and Fancy pulled the girls away from the street. "*Santo cielo*," Amalia whispered. "Do you see what she wearing?"

"Prob'ly from Greenville," Birdie said. "Bet she come from all the way 'cross the river."

"For why?" Amalia asked. The village streets looked drab and dusty now that the beautiful carriage was on them.

"Rich lady," Birdie said. "Probably own some plantation over here. Or her husbin do. Comin to show off."

The carriage turned a corner ahead of them. The horse's tail swayed jauntily behind its sleek haunches.

Fancy led them past the hotel whose tall white pillars reached up to a second floor balcony. Two white wicker chairs stood on the front porch near the door, as if waiting for someone to sit in them. When they reached a dry goods store, Fancy stopped. "This th' place. You girls wait outside while me an' Miz 'Malia do business."

"I wanna see the dresses," Birdie complained.

"I don't want no trouble from you," Fancy said. "You stay where I tell you, hear? An' don't talk t' nobody."

They left the pouting girls and entered the store. It was full of bolts of cloth and stacks of thread, with bright men's and women's clothing hanging along the walls. The room smelled of new fabric mingled with a hint of lavender and oiled floorboards. Amalia held the sack close to her. "Maybe bad idea," she whispered to Fancy.

The proprietress took a long time approaching them, even though no one else was in the store. "Did you need something?" she finally asked, as if she had never seen Fancy before.

Fancy took the sack from Amalia and extracted the two dresses. She shook them out and laid them gently on the counter.

"My," the woman said.

Both dresses were made of the best solid colors Amalia could find at the company store: one blue, the other a pale rose. She had stitched white yokes and collars on both, with embroidered flowers along the edges. The skirts were gathered, then cinched at the waist with a simple cloth band and decorated off–center with a rose made of cloth and netting. They would be prefect Sunday dresses for some little American girl. The woman ran her hand along the yoke of one dress and Amalia stared at her slender, pale fingers and pink fingernails.

"Miz 'Malia make these dresses," Fancy said. "We lookin to sell them. They's lot fancier than the last one I brought you." Amalia smiled without raising her eyes to the woman. She sucked in her breath and kept her hands at her side. She felt dirty, and was suddenly aware of how bad she must smell. But Fancy seemed confident and right at home.

The woman picked up the blue dress.

"You live here in town?" she asked, a slight edge to her voice.

"Come from Three Point," Fancy lied to her.

The woman looked around the store, as if debating. "I already have a passel of dresses in stock. Middle of summer is a bad time to sell a pretty thing like this." She gave Fancy and Amalia an apologetic smile. "Maybe in the fall or winter, for the holidays..."

"These dresses sure gon' catch somebody eye," Fancy insisted. "Make some little girl mighty happy." She picked one up and admired it, then set it back down. "We gon' sell 'em

today. If you don't want 'em, I know a lady over to the hotel..."
She started gathering the dresses.

"Now let me think," the woman said wearily. She touched
the dresses, then held one up to examine it again. "I suppose
I could give you seventy–five cents apiece."

"Seventy–five cents?" Fancy almost hollered it in disbelief. She'd been hoping for two dollars each. One–fifty at
the least. Amalia gave her a questioning look. Again, Fancy
made to gather the dresses up.

"I can go as high as one dollar," the woman said.

Fancy put the dresses down. "Cost nearly that much to
make 'em."

The woman cast a suspicious eye at Amalia, as if to ask,
"Where'd you get the money to make them?" They turned
at the sound of a customer coming in, a tiny elderly woman
who stopped in her tracks when she saw them. "It's all right,
Miss Lillian," the proprietress said, waving her in. To Fancy
and Amalia she repeated her offer: "One dollar each."

They watched her count out the money.

Once outside, Fancy and Amalia hurried the girls down
the street.

"Did you make a lot of money, mama?" Isola asked.

They stopped at the corner to catch their breath.

"That old butter bean think we was gonna hand over your
dresses for nothin?" Fancy said. She put her hands on her
hips and rocked her head from side to side as she spoke in
a high–pitched voice: "I s'pose I can give you seventy–five
cents." Then she lowered her voice. "I s'pose I could give her
somethin."

A few passersby looked their way.

"She give you money, though," Amalia said. "Me, she
wanna give nothing."

"You gotta stand up t' these people," Fancy told her. "Don't
let 'em go walkin all over you."

Amalia pulled the money out of her pocket and looked at it. "Two American dollars. That's much."

Isola touched the money in her mother's palm. "American money," she said.

Fancy led them to the small fruit and vegetable store on the Negro side of town where prices would be more reasonable. On the way to get the tomatoes, she planned to stop at the livery and talk with William. She gazed up the village street; another couple was eyeing them. "You girls better go wait f' us down the lake. We cuttin a parade through town, th' four a' us, middle a' the day."

"No! My girl stay with me," Amalia said.

"Birdie know her way 'round here. Thought you jes' said I know how to do things?"

Amalia looked in the direction of the lake, only a few blocks away.

"It's okay, mama," Isola told her. "I go all over Sweet Hope by myself."

"*Allora*. But you girls stay under the big tree where we come. Stay in the *ombra*, wait for us." She touched Isola's face. "No mischief, hear?"

As she and Fancy headed toward the other side of town, she cast one last look over her shoulder. Isola waved happily.

"Why you live Sweet Hope?" Amalia asked Fancy. "Why you no live here where it's pretty?"

"Pretty?" Fancy said. "You got some funny notion 'a what pretty is." She looked around the narrowing street.

"Mr. Step no like?" Amalia asked.

Fancy snorted. "Yeah, I reckon Mr. Step no like."

✳✳✳

As Birdie and Isola neared a church with a statue of the Blessed Virgin Mary out front, Birdie pointed. "That where your priest go sometime."

Isola kept glancing at the church as they walked past. "I bet we could wash the floor in the church to make some money. Or clean something for the priest."

"Nuh–uh," Birdie said. "Bad spell, goin inside that place. They do hoodoo in there."

"That ain't true," Isola said.

"Sure is. Blood an' burnin sticks. Make you go on your knees an' eat they potion."

"That's the kind of church I go to," Isola said. "*Catolico* church. Ain't no hoodoo." But she wondered if the Mass was different here in the village, or if it was different all over in America. When the American priest used to come to Sweet Hope, he'd say the shortest Mass she'd ever heard and then leave, no hoodoo or potion. But maybe when you all spoke the same language there was more to it. Maybe there was something she really didn't know.

"What kind of potion they make you eat?" she asked Birdie.

"They kill a goat, or a pig," Birdie told her. "Sometimes they even kill a baby. Make you drink the blood an' eat the raw meat right off the bone. Then they hang a chain 'round your neck and say some hoodoo words. You got to say 'em back right or else they pound nails in your feet and throw you in a fire."

They hurried to Main Street. More people were on the street, ladies as well as men now, coming out of stores, walking together and talking. When they reached the big general store, Birdie tugged on Isola's arm. "Wanna see somethin?" she asked.

"We better not."

"Come on, scairdy." Birdie pulled her into the store.

There were only a few people inside, and the girls ducked quickly behind a pickle barrel, out of the clerk's line of vision. Everything looked bright and new, nothing like at the company store where the plantation dust covered everything.

Two ladies were talking about a trip one of them had taken to Jackson, and a man was paying for a tin of sardines and sack of meal.

The girls leaned over the edge of the barrel and peered down into the dark briny water. Isola took a deep breath. "Smells like the ocean," she told Birdie. She dangled her arm into the barrel and touched the top of a floating pickle so that it sank under water, then bobbed up again. "I could eat a pickle and a loaf of bread."

"An' I could eat that an' a tin a sardines an' a bushel a apples an' a sugar cake," Birdie said.

Isola smelled smoke, and at almost the same instant a hand was on the back of her neck, pulling her away from the barrel. She gazed up at him, a big American with a mustache, his sleeves rolled above his elbows, an apron tied around his waist and a fat cigar in his mouth. He held Birdie with one hand and herself with the other.

"What you girls doing here?"

It took Birdie a moment to answer: "Shopping."

The man squinted at them through the cigar smoke. "If you got money to buy something," he said, "then buy it. If not, get out." He let them go with a shake.

Isola's legs wouldn't move. She kept her eyes on the man's hands, unable to tell if there was a gun tucked into his waistband under the apron.

"What plantation you from?" the man growled.

"Birdie," Isola pleaded, but Birdie was already scrambling away.

The man took a step toward Isola. She saw Birdie running for the door. "Get my mama," Isola cried to her. "Mama," she shouted, and then, because she couldn't see Birdie anymore and because she couldn't move, she started to cry.

Several Americans had gathered around and were looking at her and whispering while the man yelled, asking her what was wrong, why was she was crying, what was she doing there? When he reached his hand out toward her she dropped to the floor as if he had shot her and rolled under a counter. She pulled herself as far back under the shelf as she could, where it was dark and cool and dusty and all she could see were the shoes of people standing there calling for her to come out. Nobody was barefoot like her and Birdie. If she pushed herself back far enough against the wall, maybe the people would forget about her and go away. Then she could sneak out and find Birdie and they could go home.

She saw a pair of shiny black lady's button–up shoes and heard a woman's voice asking the man what he had done to the little girl.

"I didn't touch the beggars," he said. "Coming in here straight off the plantation mauling over the goods with their filthy hands. Who's going to buy anything after they muck it up?"

People murmured agreement: "Niggers getting bolder every day. Filthy Dagoes, worse'n the niggers. Should keep them all out."

The woman bent down, and her yellow skirt billowed around her black shoes, blocking Isola's view of everyone's feet.

"Honey, come on out now," she coaxed Isola. "Nobody's going to hurt you. I'll help you find your mama."

Isola stopped crying to listen to the woman's voice. It was sweet and soft, like music, and her skirt smelled like honey-suckle flowers when the sun beat down on them.

The woman felt under the shelf until she touched Isola's arm. "Don't be afraid, honey. Miss Irene is your friend. We're going to find your mama, I promise."

Isola let the woman keep her hand on her arm, and then, before she knew what was happening, the woman was helping her out from under the counter and standing her up and brushing her off. Isola blinked at the yellow print dress and straw hat rimmed with flowers: the woman they had seen in the carriage. She brushed the hair from Isola's sweaty face.

"It's one of them Dagoes," somebody said. "Must be from Three Point. Was in here with a nigger girl."

The woman hushed the bystanders and led Isola by the hand past the crowd and straight out the door. Isola's hand felt hot and dirty inside the woman's soft white perfumed hand. But the woman would not let go. They walked into the hot sun and across the road while the man from the store stood in the doorway watching them. "If they stole anything, you're paying for it, Miss Irene," he called after the woman. "I wish you'd get your charity cases somewhere else."

Isola searched up and down the street, but Birdie was nowhere in sight. No mother, no Fancy Hall. For a minute, she wondered if they had taken the rowboat and gone back home without her. "I have to go," she said.

"But don't you want something cool to drink?" the woman asked. "Don't you want to find your mama?"

Isola was afraid to say anything that would get her mother in trouble. "I lost my friend Birdie," she answered.

"The little nigger girl? Why what kind of friend is it that runs away when you need her?"

It suddenly occurred to Isola that she was standing in an American village talking to a rich American lady, and she was hardly even afraid anymore. "She wasn't running away," Isola said. "She was going to get help."

"Just listen to you, what a darling little foreign accent you have," the woman said.

Isola wasn't sure if she liked the American lady or not, but then the lady stopped walking and looked up and down the street. "Birdie," she called. "Oh, Birdie, your friend is looking for you."

Isola stared at the woman as she called in her high, funny voice. A few people on the street glanced at them, then shook their heads at each other. But Birdie didn't answer.

"Maybe they put her in jail," Isola said.

"In jail," the woman screeched. "Who put her in jail? Why?"

"The Americans," Isola said.

The woman knelt down on the floor of the hotel porch and clutched Isola's arms. Isola looked around to see if anyone was watching. "Honey, honey," the woman said. "We don't put little girls in jail, nigger or otherwise."

Isola felt herself blush at the way the woman was talking: loud and down on her knees in front of everybody, holding onto Isola's arms.

Miss Irene stood up, took Isola's hand, and led her to the hotel entrance.

"I have to go home," Isola blurted, trying to pull away. "My mama's looking for me."

"I insist you have a glass of lemonade before you take another step anywhere," Miss Irene said, adjusting her large flowered hat. Isola gave one more glance behind her before following the woman inside.

The hotel was big and cool, a ceiling fan turning in lazy circles above their heads, moving the air like a little breeze blowing inside. Along one wall were several large stuffed chairs and across from them a long counter with little boxes and hanging keys behind it. A wide door opened to a dining room and stairway. The man behind the counter nodded. "How do, Miss Irene."

"I simply must get this poor lost child a glass of lemonade," she said as she steered Isola into the dining room. "Or she'll drop in a faint on me."

"Yes ma'am," the man said in a tired way.

A man sat at one of the dining room tables swiping a piece of bread across his plate. A young black woman cleaned off one of the other tables with a rag.

"Oh, Miss Annie," the lady called to the black woman, "bring us some lemonade, would you?"

The woman glanced up while moving her hand in slow circles across the table, first at the American lady, then at Isola. "We's done servin dinner, Miss Irene," she said.

"Just a teensy cool drink, couldn't you? Just two nice glasses of lemonade?" She gave a hard, sweet smile until Miss Annie lowered her eyes and turned away. Miss Irene took an embroidered handkerchief out of her pocketbook and patted her face with it.

"Wouldn't you like to have a seat, honey?" she asked Isola, and she motioned to a table and sat down.

Isola followed her. The chair was big and heavy, and her feet dangled in the air. She had never sat in such a room before, at such a big table with a white cloth over it. She put her arms on the white tablecloth, but when she saw how dirty they were against the white cloth she put them in her lap.

"As soon as my heart stops fluttering, we'll go looking for your friend," Miss Irene said. She patted her face again. "My goodness, who would have thought when I got up this morning that I'd get caught in such an adventure!"

Isola looked around the dining room. "Is this where you live?" she asked.

Miss Irene tilted her head back and laughed in a soft trilling way, like someone trying to imitate a yellow warbler. "Heavens, of course I don't live here," she said. "The idea." Then she leaned over the table and peered at Isola. "Is it true you Italians live together with the pickaninnies?"

"I live with my mama and papa," Isola told her.

Miss Irene sat back, disappointed. "And now you've lost them? How sad!"

"I lost Birdie," Isola told her. "Mama's..." She bit her lip before she revealed too much.

"Was it your little friend Birdie who brought you all the way here to the village?" the woman asked.

Isola stared at her, afraid now that maybe the woman was working with the American men, helping them hunt for Birdie.

"I came by myself," Isola said. "To look for a job."

This time when Miss Irene threw her head back and laughed she sounded more like a grackle than a warbler. "A job," she laughed. "I declare."

Isola watched her wipe the tears from her eyes with the handkerchief. When the woman came and put two glasses of lemonade down on the table, she was still laughing. "Did you hear that, Annie," she said. "The little girl says she came all the way from Three Point to look for a job. Is that where you said you were from, honey?"

Isola bit her lower lip and waited.

"Now why would a sweet young girl like you be needing a job?" Miss Irene asked.

Isola fidgeted with a piece of the tablecloth in her lap. "My mama and papa need some money," she told the lady.

"Oh!" Miss Irene exclaimed, so that Isola jumped. The woman was peering closely at Isola. "My goodness," she said. "It just came to me. This is the very first conversation I have had with a foreign child!"

Isola saw the black woman across the room, standing near the doorway with her eyes on them. After a moment, she went through the door out of sight.

Isola looked down at the glass of lemonade in front of her. She touched the beads of sweat dripping down its side, but didn't dare drink, as thirsty as she was, until the lady said it was all right.

Miss Irene lowered her voice. "You know, some people don't like you foreigners," she said. "Just like they don't like the Negroes. But I say where would we be without the Negroes?" She looked over at the doorway where the woman had been standing and smiled, like she was thinking of something nice. "Some people don't even like me, can you imagine that? It's because I'm too nice. Because I care about the downtrodden. Don't you like your lemonade?" she said. "Why, you haven't even touched it!" She lifted her own glass to her lips and took a dainty sip, then patted her mouth with her handkerchief and smiled at Isola.

Isola picked up her glass. She smelled the sugar and sweet lemons, and it reminded her of home, their house above the sea. And then there was the strange coolness of the glass on her fingers. She took a sip and it made her shudder.

"Is it too sour for you?" the lady asked her.

Isola shook her head no while she held the glass near her mouth. She wanted to tip the glass and drink the lemonade all in one long gulp. She wanted more — two glasses, three, a whole pitcher–full.

"It's good," she managed to tell the lady, and she thought of Birdie, crouched somewhere in the heat, swatting mosquitoes, wondering what the Americans had done to Isola. She tilted the glass and drank.

"What's your name?" Miss Irene asked her.

"Isola," she gasped.

"Isola!" the woman shrieked. "What a name. I declare, it sounds like a niggra name."

"They call me Issy, too," Isola told her, putting the empty glass down on the table.

"Issy, Issy," the lady said. "That's definitely niggra. Does your daddy have him a niggra lady on the side who named you?"

Isola wasn't sure what the woman meant. "No."

Miss Irene looked at her suspiciously. "Why, of course — why would you know about such things?" She peered intently at Isola, then reached out and touched Isola's hair, smiled strangely, and drew her hand back. "Do you people really stomp around barefoot in tubs of grapes to make your wine?"

Isola glanced at the woman, puzzled. Maybe Miss Irene was like La Vecchia, not right in her head. Isola shrugged. "I don't know."

"That's all right," Miss Irene said, patting Isola's hand. "It's nothing to be ashamed of. Anyway, I think it's wonderful the way you all work so hard, and right alongside the Negroes. It's... beautiful." She gazed across the room and smiled.

"I work good," Isola said. "I sweep and wash floors. I can sew clothes." She glanced at the door the black woman had disappeared through. "I cook." All the work she hated, but that's what grownups thought girls should do.

Miss Irene laughed. "Aren't you precious?" she said.

Isola waited for her to offer a job, but the lady said nothing more. Isola gathered her courage. "Can I wash your clothes?" she blurted. "For pay?"

Isola watched Miss Irene's powdered face crinkle up in laughter and her big teeth flash in the light. Isola's throat tightened, and she was afraid she might cry. Suddenly Miss Irene turned serious and leaned across the table again. "Miss Issy, I already have a girl who washes and cooks for me. And a yard boy."

Isola tried to think of an excuse she could give her mother and Fancy once they found her. She could say Birdie ran away and she got lost, but Birdie would tell them the truth then. She could just say that a strange American lady had snatched her off the street, but wouldn't they ask her why Birdie didn't come yelling for help?

"I have to go," she said, standing up. "I have to find Birdie."

Annie came out to take their empty glasses away. "Isn't she darling?" Miss Irene told her. "She's worried about her little pickaninny friend."

"Yes, ma'am," Annie said, carrying the glasses away.

"Wouldn't you love to stay here in the village and be my little friend?" the lady asked, and she laughed. "I wish I had a little friend like you."

Isola leaned back, ready to bolt, afraid the woman was going to grab her and make her stay in the village, or maybe lock her up in jail. But then Miss Irene patted her face again with her handkerchief, opened her pocketbook, folded the handkerchief inside, and took out a change purse.

"I want to give you something to remember me by," she told Isola, and she handed her two coins. "That one's for you," she said, pointing to the larger gray piece in the palm of Isola's hand. "And that one's for your little friend, if you ever find her." She pointed to the smaller brown piece. "Remember: the white one for you, the brown one for her," Miss Irene said, breaking into another warbler laugh.

Isola closed her fist over the coins, wondering if it was enough money to help her parents out of debt. She moved away from the table, worried that the lady would follow her outside and keep her from ever finding Birdie. "Goodbye," Isola said. And then to be polite about the money she added, "Thank you."

"Wait," Miss Irene cried, dropping her hands from the flowery hat she was adjusting. "Before you go, you have to tell me in Italian. Tell me thank you in Italian."

Isola flushed. She looked around, grateful no one else was in the room. "*Grazie, Signora*," she whispered.

"*Grazi*," Irene repeated. "That's precious! Oh, honey, don't forget your friend Miss Irene. Don't forget that I love you foreigners, no matter what anybody else says about you."

Isola ran out of the room, then on through the lobby and out the door while Miss Irene called out, "Annie, Annie, didn't Mr. Walker come by asking for me today?"

Birdie was nowhere in sight. Isola headed down the street to the lake, afraid the rowboat would be gone and she would be stranded in the village. But would her mother really leave without her? The boat was there where they'd left it. She started running down the embankment, clutching the two coins in her sweating hand.

She leaned against the rowboat catching her breath, looking up and down the shore for signs of her mother and Fancy and Birdie. Two old men stood apart from each other fishing from the bank. Down in the other direction a couple of American boys waded in the water, turning over stones.

The lake looked wider than ever. She couldn't even see Sweet Hope from here, just the trees at the edge, and part of the roof of a storage shed. She wished the American lady, Miss Irene, had offered her some food to go with the lemonade. She dipped one hand in the lake and drank. Then she opened her other hand and studied the strange American coins with pictures and writing on them.

"Ha!" Birdie yelled, grabbing Isola's arm and making her jump. She closed her hand so the coins wouldn't fall.

"I thought you was lost," Isola yelled at her. "I thought the Americans caught you and put you in jail."

"I thought you was lost," Birdie said. "I thought that white lady done somethin to you."

"Where's our mamas?" Isola asked.

"Not here yet, lucky for you. What they done to you?"

Isola tried to tell Birdie about going into the hotel and drinking lemonade, and the funny way the lady laughed. "But why'd you run away?" she asked.

"I come hid in the lake bush when the white man started hollerin. Why you had to cry like that in the store, makin trouble?"

"I wasn't crying," Isola said. "I wasn't makin trouble."

"Was too," Birdie said. "You a fool scairdy cat."

They saw their mothers walking with difficulty toward the lake, each lugging a bushel basket heaped with ripe tomatoes, and they ran out to meet them.

"Mama, you got them," Isola said, plucking one up and breathing deeply of the fruit.

"Help me carry this," Amalia said.

The girls each took a handle from their mothers, and they slipped down the embankment.

"You been good?" Fancy asked in a tone that implied she expected the worst.

"Yes ma'am," Birdie answered.

They heaved the baskets into the boat. Fancy watched Amalia retrieve a fallen tomato, then quickly rearrange the others so they would not fall from the baskets. "Hope nobody missin us," she said impatiently.

Amalia straightened. They had been gone a long time.

"Did you get a good price, mama?" Isola asked. Red juice was running down her chin, and she reached for another tomato.

"Good enough," she said tersely. "Don't eat all these tomatoes."

This time Amalia sat next to Fancy and they each held an oar. The girls sat on the boat bottom, leaning against the two bushels. It took the women a few minutes to find their rhythm and get the boat to go straight.

"Mmm, smells good," Isola said.

Amalia felt a little sad now that the dresses she had worked so hard on were gone. She had almost bought more tomatoes with the money, but instead decided to put the American dollar in the tin with the other one. Two American dollars. Just thinking of it made her feel better, as if the money could multiply on its own.

"Next time, maybe somebody pay more for my dress," she told Fancy.

"Next time?" Fancy said. She'd already spent half her day, all for nothing. "No work," William had said. "Maybe in th' winter. For sure in th' spring." That's my life, she thought, staring at the flat water in front of her.

"Maybe you find him some better work for your boy someplace," Amalia said. "You see."

"Mm-hmm," Fancy said, keeping her eyes straight ahead.

Isola waited until they were a distance from shore before leaning into Birdie. "Look what I got," she whispered. She glanced behind her to make sure their mothers couldn't hear. "The American lady gave me this."

Birdie stopped sucking juice from a tomato. "Money," she said.

"Some of it's for you," Isola told her. "The lady said this white one's mine." She handed Birdie the smaller one. "Brown one's for you." The minute she laid the brown coin in Birdie's hand she saw what Miss Irene had meant, how clever she had been.

Birdie narrowed her eyes at Isola. "Brown one's mine?" Birdie said. "How come you get the nickel and I only get a penny?"

"That's what the lady told me," she told Birdie, faltering now.

"I don't want no stinkin penny from you," Birdie said, her voice rising. "What you think I am, a hobo?"

"What goin on there?" Fancy called to them.

"Nothin." Birdie handed the money back while the boat drifted in a slow arc.

"Better be nothin," Fancy said. The boat straightened.

Isola stared at Birdie, trying to understand what was wrong. "But the American lady said give you the brown one."

Birdie scowled. "You never listened to white folks before, what makin you start now? Anyways, you the one always cryin 'bout you need money," Birdie said. "Keep it. Go buy yourself another tomato."

"But Miss Irene..."

"You a white girl, that's what you is," Birdie told her.

Isola turned back around and stared at the water. She held the two coins pressed in one hand as tears stung her eyes.

She wouldn't tell anybody about the money. She wouldn't even tell them that for a minute she thought she would be able to buy a farm for her father, and get them all out of debt.

She squeezed her hand around the coins until she felt them cutting into her flesh. American money, she thought. Crazy like Miss Irene. Crazy like Birdie and all the Americans. And then she opened her hand and let the coins plunk into the water, first the brown one, then the white.

CHAPTER 13

Visiting The Priest

November 1904

Serafin pulled his jacket tighter around himself and shoved his hands into his pockets. The day before there had been a light dusting of frost on the fields, though by noon they were working in their shirtsleeves. Almost all the crops were in. Their small gardens were finished, the cotton was being ginned, and the clanging of the gin mill filled the air day and night. Some of the farmers worked at the mill now, or at the storehouses loading cotton to take to the mill, or over at the landing, sending the baled cotton across the river to be sold. The rest of them were out clearing land.

The news was eating at him. Word had reached Sweet Hope that Cesare Sant'Angelo and the Sicilian friend he'd left with had been caught and put in prison in Alabama, and nobody knew what was going to happen to the men or their families. Their crime: looking for work off the plantation to pay their debts while their families ran the farms. Sant'Angelo had the hardest head Serafin had ever seen. His wife and children sick with malaria and he himself half–dead from it, their baby recently lost to it, and didn't he go and jump contract as soon as most of his crop was picked? The children would never be able to finish the work in their condition. Something about that pitiful family kept gnawing at him. He couldn't shake the sight of the baby's coffin from his mind.

He started walking and was almost at the priest's house before he realized he'd been planning this visit all along. He wouldn't have gone for himself. They could still stand on their own two feet, thank God for that, as bad as things looked. But Mrs. Sant'Angelo...

Serafin was relieved but nervous to see a light on at the priest's house. He had talked to Father Odetti only a few times since his arrival, barely more than a hello after church or at the company store. The man had been quiet, almost shy when he first came, but then he began spending time with the Americans because he could speak their language — or at least the tenants thought that was the reason. He laughed with the managers and even had a glass of wine with them, and now — after his few short months here — the farmers spoke openly of the priest being a lackey for the Americans.

He took a deep breath and knocked on the door. Inside, a dog yapped, and Serafin heard it trotting through the house. Then Father Odetti opened the door and peered out. Serafin removed his hat.

"Father, excuse me, I'm sorry..." What the hell was he doing? His own family needed help with their debts and problems. He thought of making some weak excuse, turning and leaving, but Father Odetti opened the door wider.

"You're — "

"Serafin Pascala," he answered.

When there was no response, Serafin added: "Down near the bend, near Mr. Step."

Father Odetti nodded and motioned him in, and the dog sniffed at Serafin's pant leg. "Get away," the priest told the dog, swatting at him, and the motion seemed to sweep Serafin into the house.

The priest was dressed in his usual dark pants and white shirt, open now at the neck, his suspenders sagging. His hair was cut close to his head, and he wore round silver–rimmed eyeglasses that made him look like a schoolboy, not a priest in the middle of a swamp.

"Is something wrong?" Father Odetti asked. Behind him, a lamp burned low in the room, and Serafin realized the man may have been going to bed.

"I've come to talk to you for a lady," he stammered. "She's got trouble, bad trouble." He fidgeted with the hat in his hand.

"Is she ill?" the priest asked him.

Even though he was from Ancona province, he spoke Italian like a *gentiluomo*, not like the *Marchigiani* fishermen and bricklayers and carpenters who farmed the plantation.

"Well, yes, she's sick, but it's not that — "

The priest motioned him into the room. He turned up the lamp, then put two glasses on the table, took a jug of wine down from the shelf and poured a little into each glass.

Serafin sat awkwardly at the priest's table, aware of his worn clothes and ragged hands. He glanced around: a long sideboard, an ornate mirror on the wall; four chairs, a table big enough for a large family, new screens covering the windows. They looked out of place in the shanty. But of course. The company had forced out the Luccesi family, then given their house over to the priest. Only God knew where such furniture had come from.

Father Odetti motioned with his glass toward Serafin, in good health — *salute* — and took a drink. Serafin nodded self–consciously and returned the gesture.

The dog leaned against Serafin's feet under the table. He tried to move the animal away, but it would not budge. If it were his own, he would make it go outside, and it annoyed him that the priest allowed his mangy animal to flop on top of a visitor. Fat son of a bitch, he thought, though he knew the animal was not to blame. When the dog leaned more heavily on him, he moved his chair, as if he were moving closer to the priest to talk.

Serafin put his glass down and cleared his throat. "It's about Mrs. Sant'Angelo. You know what I mean?"

Father Odetti's face turned solemn. "I know the woman." He moved his head slightly, as if to look for the dog under the table, and said no more.

For a moment it occurred to Serafin that maybe the priest was involved in what had happened to Sant'Angelo and his friend. After all, who knew how far a man would go for money, comfort? He gazed again at the ornate mirror.

Father Odetti sat stiffly as Serafin surveyed the room.

"They put Sant'Angelo in jail, you know, Father."

"I heard," the priest answered cautiously.

"Father, they keep us here like animals. You know those papers they had us sign don't say what they told us they said. The way they got us here, we'll stay in debt till we die."

"Well, that's yet to be seen," the priest stammered.

Serafin had never imagined it possible that he would challenge a priest to his face, confront him with doubts or disapproval. It was never a good idea to let someone of position know how you really felt — even if the position was in the church. "Excuse me, Father, but some of us waited a long time to bring you here from Italy. That's why you came, to help us, no?"

"*Esatto* — but of course," the priest said. But then he shook his head and said no more.

"How much does the church know of what goes on here? Or the government? Can you get them to help us?"

Father Odetti stifled a sound of surprise. He leaned forward uncomfortably. "They know of the Italian colonies, certainly. We've heard that some people are unhappy. I don't believe it's gone beyond that."

Serafin waited for more, but there was no more.

"That's it? Then tell me, what are we going to do? Stay here like animals until we die? There's no way people can pay their debts unless they get work somewhere else. The company throws us a scrap here and there to shut us up — yes, now we can have a small garden, a couple chickens. But the prices stay the same, the interest, the debt, the filth — the threats, sickness, death." He stopped, checked himself for rambling. The faces of his own family floated before him. "Mrs. Sant'Angelo. She's sick half a year now. How can those children of hers run a farm by themselves? And you see that piece of swamp the company put them on. Why not move them to better land where the air won't kill them?"

The priest shook his head again, then answered meekly, so at first it seemed that he was agreeing with Serafin: "That Sant'Angelo has been a troublemaker from the start, costing the company money. Maybe he should have thought of the consequences before he ran off."

Serafin dropped his hands so heavily that the table shook. "Troublemaker? Ran off?" So it was true. The priest was nothing more than a crook, another Rosconi paid by the Americans to betray his own people. "They stick him in a swamp to live and you call him a troublemaker?"

The two of them stared at each other for a long, awkward moment.

"I'm doing the best I can, believe me," the priest finally said. "You don't understand the complicated details behind such a large operation. The company has a business to run."

"*Business*?" Serafin said, his voice rising. "That's what you call our lives?" Almost instantly, he lowered his voice. "Father, what do you think God would say about all this?"

Father Odetti took a white handkerchief from his trouser pocket and wiped his face. "It's not as simple as it seems to you," he said.

"Tell that to Sant'Angelo. You tell his wife and children. Tell all the dead ones buried out at Hyner."

Father Odetti poured another glass of wine for himself. He lifted the bottle to Serafin's glass, then thought better of it, and set the jug back on the table.

Serafin moved the jug aside. "It seems to me, Father, if you came here to work for the Italian people, you should work for your people. If you came to lick the boots of Mr. Gates, then I've got something to tell you." He was shocked at the words coming out of his mouth. Sweet Hope makes you crazy, he thought, turns you into somebody else. But he could not stop. "We've learned some bad things down here, you know?" He nodded for emphasis. "Father, we're going to stay alive any way we can."

Serafin was mortified with himself. Had he just threatened a priest? But he was powerless, what could he do to anyone?

He wasn't entirely sure how the words had affected the man. For a minute it seemed that Father Odetti was going to break down in remorse. But then he composed himself. "What do you want me to do?" he asked.

Serafin wiped his brow. "Help us. Tell Gates to let Sant'-Angelo and his *paesano* out of jail. Move his family away from the bayou before they all die of swamp fever. And tell him to let us go off the plantation to work so we can pay our debts. Or pay us fair prices here. You tell him."

The priest flinched. "Me tell Mr. Gates how to run his plantation?" he murmured.

"What are you afraid he'll do to you?" Serafin said. "Take away your nice furniture? Or maybe send you out in the fields to work with the rest of us?"

"I'm not afraid to work," the priest said, sounding like a defiant child. "And I'm not afraid of anything Mr. Gates might do to me."

"No?" Serafin said. "That's good. I'm happy to hear that. Because you know, some of these families have been here four, five, six years. That could be you, eh? Stuck in a filthy shack with mosquitoes eating you alive, your bones sticking out of your skin."

Father Odetti shook his head in a gesture of helplessness.

"You make your boss let us sell our cotton across the river," Serafin continued. "Let us do business off the plantation where we can get a fair price, maybe make a little profit, at least get out of debt."

"*Basta*. Enough," Odetti said.

"You see any rich Italian farmers? How many fine horses, fancy clothes?"

Father Odetti raised his hand to make Serafin stop.

"Maybe instead you can tell me how many Italians you've buried since you came here, how many babies."

"I know it's bad," the priest said. "I'm not saying it's not bad."

"You think we're asking Gates to let us sit under a tree stuffing ourselves with sausages and cakes while the money falls out of the sky and fills our pockets? We're asking for one thing, that's all. To get out of here alive."

"Yes, of course," the priest said. He took his eyeglasses off and wiped them on the handkerchief. "I know that. I'm sorry."

The priest pushed away from the table.

And that was that. A dismissal? The end of talking.

Serafin stood up.

Father Odetti fumbled to rise from his chair. He gripped the handkerchief in his hand as he walked Serafin to the door. The dog trotted after them.

"I'll talk to Mr. Gates," the priest said. "I'll try to talk to him."

The dog sat in front of the door, its fat belly protruding.

Serafin glanced at the dog, then back at Father Odetti. "Thank you for the wine," he said, and he stepped over the dog and out the door.

***

His face burned in the cold night air. He walked fast, his whole body on fire at the things he had said. If Father Odetti whispered a word to the company — Serafin couldn't bear to imagine what would happen to him or his family. Already he felt like a drunken man who would wake the next morning aghast at what he had done.

It was late, but he was too disturbed to go home. He turned down the lane before his house and slowed, breathing deeply of the cold sharp air. The glittering stars and sliver of moon lit the road and fields. Everything looked ghostly, now that the crops were almost all in. The flat fields stretched out around him in the pale night, and the air was filled with the muffled croaks and cries of animals and in the distance the incessant clanging of the gin mill that seemed to match his own labored breathing.

The land itself made him think of a cotton gin, the way it creaked and chirped like a machine that never stopped, day or night. Underneath the night chirpings he heard music, probably a *fisarmonica* coming from the Titus house. They'd just sold their cotton, probably hadn't made a penny, but their field work was over. Step and his family were probably there, visiting with Fred Titus and his wife, as they often did on Saturday nights. The children would be up playing, chasing each other around the kitchen table. To play music in this place, to make a party — he'd done it himself, even while in debt, but it all seemed ridiculous to him now.

He found himself heading for the Titus house, all the while thinking that Amalia would be wondering what was keeping him so long, and that he should go to bed and sleep because of all the work to do in the morning. He still needed to finish clearing his land of the dried cotton stalks, then help Lazzaro fix his mule cart, Sunday or not.

The Titus house was lit up. Behind the music he could hear people talking, children and women, and every now and then Step Hall's deep, low chuckle.

Serafin knocked at the door. When no one answered, he rapped again, louder, and soon heard shuffling footsteps before the door opened. Lud Titus, her bald head wrapped in a bandanna and wearing a sagging dress, let out a sound of surprise.

"Lordy, Mr. Serafin," she said. "You look like you just seen a hent."

"Sorry, too late night," he told her.

She held the door open and motioned him inside. "You okay?"

Serafin smiled sheepishly. "*Scusi*," he said as he entered. "Too late night."

"Mr. Serafin? Come on in," Fred Titus told him, resting his hand on the top of his concertina a moment. He nodded toward the bottle of whiskey on the table.

Step cocked his head at Serafin.

Arms and hands descended on him, steering him past the children to the table, putting him into a chair as if he were a blind man who was a guest of honor. Children were everywhere, crouched on the floor or chasing each other around the room, or leaning against walls or against their mothers. The room was hot and smelled of warm bodies, wood smoke, fried bread, whiskey. After the cool night air, and after the shock of his talk with the priest, he felt almost dizzy. Someone put a cup in his hand and he inhaled the sweet dizzying smell of the whiskey and then he drank and it burned smoothly down his throat. They smiled at him as he drank, and when he was done he put the cup down on the table and smiled back. "Good," he told them. "Good whiskey." And they laughed.

A deck of cards lay scattered on the table. JoeJack sat among the adults, hunched over and studying the cards, a drop of whiskey in his glass.

Calvin left the group of children and moved over to the table, eyeing Serafin shyly. He tried to pull a chair up to the table.

"Boy, what you think you doin?" Fancy said, and he shrugged, pushed the chair back near the wall, but hovered near the table.

"What take you out this time a' night?" Step asked him. "You ain't been out workin by the moonlight?" They all laughed at this, and Step took a drink from his cup. They were feeling good; their crops were in and soon they would be paid.

Serafin looked pleadingly at Step Hall, the one man on the plantation besides his friend Lazzaro whom he could trust. "Mr. Step, I been to see the priest," he blurted.

Step's face turned serious. "Trouble?" he asked.

"Is for Mrs. Sant'Angelo I go," Serafin told him. "You know."

Step blanched. "Now why you go an' do that?"

"Can't your priest do nothin to help that woman?" Fancy asked. Step shot her a look, and she countered right back: "Well? You know Rev'rin Monroe an' Miss Betty do what they can to help us."

"He say he can't do nothing," Serafin told them. "He say he gonna think, gonna see. I know what that mean."

"When white folks tell me they gonna see 'bout somethin," Lud Titus said, "they means they hopes I forgit I ever asked."

"Just what you tell that priest?" Step asked him.

"Tell him talk to Mr. Gates' men, help *la famiglia* Sant'Angelo, move them out the swamp. That we got to pay the debts. Don't put us in jail for work someplace else to pay the debt."

Step looked around at the others, then back at Serafin. "What he say?"

"What I tell you, he gonna see."

"You shouldna' gone," Step told him. "Whyn't you talk to me first?"

"What you gonna do? He our priest."

"Damn it," Step answered.

Fred raised his eyebrows at Step. Then he laid his concertina on the table. He took a drink, put the glass down and patted his mouth with his bony fingers. "Ain't worth gettin hot over," he told Step. "What's done's done."

"Least he was tryin to help one a' his own," Fancy said. She turned her eyes away from her husband before he had a chance to reply.

"You took her 'cross, to the village?" he'd said. "An' th' girl too?"

"Don't go gettin riled." It was his idea, after all, that she help the Pascala family.

"An the boat? Anybody find out, they jail you f' stealin."

"Ain't nobody gonna find out," she told him, shooting a warning look at Birdie. Not even the Tituses knew. And as far as Serafin was concerned, Fancy had gone alone to sell the dresses, and bought the tomatoes with the money.

Step stared at the back of her head now, but she refused to look at him.

"Don't know why that fella had to run all the way t' Alabama," Fred said. "They got Italians workin near Pine Bluff. Up all around Memphis, lots of 'em up there. They doin all right in them places, too, better 'n here for sure."

"Yes?" Serafin asked. "Is true?" He had heard about Italians working cotton in the surrounding areas, under better conditions. Wasn't that why Sant'Angelo had left, after all?

Calvin inched closer to the table. He sat on the floor, listening intently. "Company track 'im down in Memphis fast as in Alabama," he said. "Should go north, Detroit, Chicago, that's what JoeJack say, right?"

JoeJack looked up from the cards he was laying down. "What I say?"

"Boy, this ain't your business," Step admonished Calvin, and Calvin shrugged and looked away.

"Pa, I'm just saying..."

"JoeJack all talk," Lud said. "He don't know nothin 'bout no place."

A baby started crying, and Lud went and lifted it from a basket of clothes in the corner and laid it on her shoulder. The baby whimpered, then quieted as Lud paced, bouncing it on her shoulder. When she passed Serafin she touched him on the back. "Mr. Serafin, you always worryin 'bout folks. Here, lemme pour you 'nother cup."

He raised his hands and shook his head. "No, no, too much drink. Got to go home, sleep. Sleep, work, no?"

"Mr. Gates don't know the half a' what goes on here," Step was explaining to the others. "That's the problem right there. Cain't run a Delta plantation from Washington, D.C."

"Don't know, huh?" Fred answered. "Money goes in his pocket, sure he knows."

"Why you always standin up for that man?" Fancy asked Step.

"I ain't standin up," Step said. "I'm sayin he should keep a better eye on what his managers doin."

"Think the mouth don't know the hand feedin it?" Fred said. "Only gonna get worse, now, with all his politickin."

"What pol–tickin?" Serafin asked.

They tried to explain: "You know, like a mayor?" Step said. He did not know the word. "Guv'nor? Boss–man, but bigger, like a president?"

"*Presidente*?" Serafin asked.

"Not like the president," Fred said.

"Boss–man for big place, boss of the village, boss lots a' villages."

"Big boss? *Politica*?" Serafin asked.

"That's right, *politica*," Step answered.

When Serafin thought of politics, he thought of *l'anarchia*. Anarchy, a word he'd heard plenty of times in Italy: the people, the workers, standing up for their rights, trying to overthrow a government that treated them like swine.

"If trouble, we stand up, we fight. We not afraid no more." But he knew that wasn't true. Everybody was afraid, himself included. And all he had done, after all, was talk to the damn priest.

Calvin was nodding in agreement. "Tha's right. Stand up and fight," he said. "Ever'body too tolerable here, that's why we don't get nowhere."

Fancy shot him a look that made him scoot back a few feet, but Serafin smiled at the boy. "See? You think good. That's how my own papa talk."

"Jus' hold on a minute," Step said. "Ain't nobody fightin nobody." He sounded weary, uncertain.

"Maybe should fight long time ago," Serafin said, the whiskey working on him. "Maybe we all not in hell then. Why you no fight? Why you no all stand up together?"

The others fell silent. Lud Titus made a tsking sound.

"You don't know what you talkin 'bout," Step told him.

The looks on their faces surprised him. "*Amici*," he stammered. What he was trying to say was, "I thought you were my friends," but the words caught in his throat. "What I say wrong?"

"That's all right," Lud finally told him. "Don't pay it no mind. There's a wide river 'tween here an' there, best we don't go in it now."

The one truth Serafin knew was that there was no understanding the Americans and their big cotton business. Maybe they'd all be better off if they were like the priest, he thought. Let the company use you any way they wanted, so long as they gave you food, a good place to live. No matter that they turned you into something that was no longer a man. A priest, he thought. Maybe they weren't men to begin with.

The men sat at the table, silent. Fred busied himself tinkering with a loose button on his concertina. Step turned the whiskey bottle in his hand, contemplating something that seemed infinitely important in the glass. Serafin wondered if the priest really was working for the company after all. A priest who is not really a priest, he thought. And my friends?

Serafin stood. His legs felt numb, as if they had fallen asleep on him. "Too late," he said. "Must go home."

He moved toward the door, stumbling over Calvin's big bare feet before the boy had a chance to pull them in. Lud took Serafin's arm, telling him how he should work less and eat more and not worry so much.

"G'night," he told them at the door. Step made his way through the children to the door. He took Serafin's arm from Lud and led him outside. Alone now, he seemed more troubled than ever. His fingers gripped Serafin's arm a moment before he let go.

They stood in the cold night air. The stars glittered in the black sky and the land chirped and rustled and the gin mill clanged.

Finally Step told him: "We gonna start clearin more swamp in a couple days. Cuttin the trees out near Fish Bayou."

Serafin shook his head. "No good, the swamp."

"You want work?" Step asked. His words came out harsher than he'd intended.

"*Sí*," Serafin answered meekly.

"Aw'right, then. You got work."

CHAPTER 14

Retaliation

November 1904

LEE Horton rode up in a cloud of dust while Step and his family pulled and burned the last of their dried cotton stalks.

"Meet me at the company office in half an hour," Horton said. "And bring that Dago friend of yours."

Fancy stiffened at the orders. They knew exactly who he meant by "Dago friend."

Step glanced at his children working a distance away, then strode past his wife without a word.

First he went to the house to clean up, then he hitched the mule cart. He found Serafin, as he'd expected, clearing out stalks in his own field. "Got some feed barrels down at the mule yard I need help movin," Step told him. "Can you help?"

Once they were on the road, Serafin asked: "Is nobody else at mule yard to help?"

"We ain't goin there. We got called to the company office." He held the reins loosely as he sat forward, elbows on knees. His tense body gave lie to the relaxed reins.

"For why?" Serafin finally dared ask.

Step didn't answer. He slapped the reins lightly to keep the mule moving.

Serafin stared straight ahead, afraid to ask more. His mind raced over the past few days, his crop, his debts, his children, his wife — even Lazzaro and his cousin Claudio — while he kept the one thing he should have been worried about safely at bay.

"Jus' keep quiet and let me do the talkin," Step told him, and at these words Serafin knew he was in deep trouble.

Horton was sitting behind the main desk smoking a small cigar, while the new man, Garlock, rummaged through a stack of maps and ledgers on a shelf near the wall. The shiny wooden clock ticked loudly behind the desk.

Step and Serafin removed their hats and waited while Lee Horton drew on his cigar, then let the smoke out. He looked the men up and down, a pleased expression on his face. "Garlock, you find that ledger yet?" he asked without taking his eyes from the men.

Garlock carried a heavy ledger over and dropped it on the desk in front of Horton.

"How you feelin?" Horton asked Serafin.

"Good," he answered warily.

"You're not sick?"

"No, no sick." He glanced at Step, and laughed nervously.

"Glad to hear that," Horton said. "Lotta sickness goin 'round—swamp fever, malaria. Your friends the Sant'Angelos got hit hard with sickness."

Serafin clutched his hat, the blood draining from his face.

"What this about, Mr. Horton?" Step asked, although he knew exactly what it was about.

"I'm just havin a friendly conversation with your Dago friend here," Horton replied. Garlock hooked his elbows on the map shelf behind him and leaned back to watch.

"Thought Mr. Pascala would want to know the Sant'Angelos are doin lots better. Gettin all kinds of help now," Horton said. "Since his talk with the priest."

"No make trouble," Serafin said, shocked that the company had found out so quickly about his visit with the priest;

barely a day and a half had passed. For a fleeting moment he wondered if Step had told them.

"What you tryin to say, Mr. Horton?" Step asked.

"I'm sayin Pascala was right, the Sant'Angelos needed help. So we got them help. Doctor saw them this mornin, treated the whole family, mother 'n three kids."

Step shook his head slowly in disbelief.

"And we hired on day labor to help them get the rest of their second picking in, if it ain't ruined by now — been standin out there on wet land."

Step and Serafin stood rigidly while Garlock smiled at them from across the room.

"What you getting at?" Step asked.

"Just business as usual," Horton said, smiling pleasantly. He opened the ledger, thumbed through some pages. "Let's see, Pascala: doctor's visit, that's a three dollar charge. Medicine, another three dollars." He wrote carefully in the book, then looked up at the men. "Visiting the priest, two dollars."

"What — you chargin Mr. Serafin?" Step said, his voice rising.

"Somebody's gotta pay. He's the one asked for the help, not the Sant'Angelos. Now the day labor, that's gonna add up for him. Three men, a dollar a day each, what's left a' pickin, then clearin the field. Have to see how many days it takes 'em." He wrote in the ledger again, then let out a low whistle. "Lotta money. But generous of you to take on their debts."

Serafin felt his legs go weak. "No," he said. He gave Step an imploring look.

"You can't do that," Step said. "What you tryin to do?"

Serafin shook his fist at Horton. "You somabitch. You no good — " he shouted.

Step grabbed his arm just as Garlock pushed away from the wall, ready to intervene. But Horton waved him aside. He had things under control.

"I told you before, Hall," Horton said to Step, "you're slippin up on your job. Your Dagoes are gettin too high–minded." His mock–friendly voice had turned hard. He glared at the enraged Serafin. "Somebody's gotta rein 'em in, or the plantation's goin to hell."

"He was just tryin to help that woman," Step said. "If Mr. Gates knew 'bout how bad — "

Horton closed the ledger abruptly. "Ain't you heard? I got promoted." Garlock grinned and nodded.

"Mr. Gates made me general plantation manager." He paused, waiting for the news to sink in. "That means you better straighten up, old man, or it'll be more'n these Dagoes cryin about the mess they're in."

Step looked at each man, trying to catch the lie.

"Don't believe me? Go ask Mr. Gates y'self."

Garlock chuckled. "If you can find him."

"You answer to me now," Horton said, his face hard. "You pull another stunt like this, Hall... I'll have you thrown on a chain gang."

Step held his tongue. He wasn't sure if Horton could have him put on a chain gang if he wasn't already a convicted criminal. But there were other things Horton could do, and he didn't want to find out what they were.

"We're only chargin' you three dollars," Horton told Step. "For all the trouble you and your Italian caused. Everything else is charged to him." His eyes were cold. "Lettin you off easy this time, since Mr. Gates thinks so highly of you." The last words came out as a sneer.

Step's insides turned over, but he held steady. He'd had plenty of unpleasant interactions with Horton, but this put things on a whole different level. Part of him suspected Horton was lying about being in charge, but he couldn't be sure. The other part of him said to be careful.

"Whatever you say, Mr. Horton," Step said evenly. "You're the boss now." It was killing him.

Horton smiled his crooked smile.

"If I was you, I'd give your Dago a talkin to," Horton said. "A good thrashin might knock some sense in him."

Garlock laughed. "I'd like to see that. Darkie whippin a Dago."

Horton shot Garlock a look to quiet him. Then he ordered the two men back to the fields.

Step nudged Serafin ahead of him and out the door. They walked stiffly along the porch and back to the mule cart. Serafin sat with his fists clenched, unable to get any words out as they pulled away from the landing.

The silence hung heavy between them as the harness creaked and the wheels turned softly in the dirt.

Serafin waited until they were well away from the store and office. "You tell Mr. Gates what happen. You fix, he fix, yes?"

"You go 'round muckin things up, then 'spect me to jump in and fix 'em for you?" Step fumed. "Why'd you have to go talk to that priest?"

Both men knew no answer was expected. Just the same, Serafin said, "I just try to help."

"Cain't nobody help nobody here," Step answered. "When you gonna get that in your thick head?"

"If Mr. Gates — If the boss man knew –"

"I can't tell Mr. Gates nothin. He's gone half the time. Never know when he's around no more." The truth was, he had talked face to face with Harlan Gates only three or four times in his life. When Gates had first taken over the plantation, Step had been surprised — and honored — that such a man wanted to entrust part of his plantation to him. And Gates was there almost every day, riding the land, keeping an eye on how things were run. Step still held onto that time as if it was something current and real. But in the last couple years he couldn't recall talking with Gates at all. The managers had become the go-betweens, men Step thought he could trust to do the owner's bidding even though he wouldn't trust them for anything else.

"You don't tell nobody, okay?" Serafin asked him. "Don't tell Amalia."

"Don't you think she gonna find out?"

His question was met with silence.

"Okay," Step told him. "But why you gotta go stick your neck out for some fam'ly you hardly know?" Step said.

Serafin shook his head, glanced sideways at Step. "You helping me."

Step snorted.

"Our priest," Serafin murmured. "I like to get my hands on him."

"You ain't got no priest. That's a company priest, don't matter he come from Italy or Timbuktu. You still ain't learned?" He felt like he was talking about himself. "Now — you think you can git through the rest a' the year without muckin up anything else?"

***

WHEN Serafin entered his yard, he found Osvaldo struggling with a small stone, trying to pound a loose board into place on a peach crate. The house was closed, a thin curl of smoke drifting from the chimney. It was suppertime.

The rag tied around Osvaldo's head dangled in one eye.

"How's your head?" Serafin asked.

"Okay."

"No headache?"

"No."

He peered at his boy, the face smudged with dirt and darkened from the sun and weather. He was getting big, almost nine years old. Serafin touched the rag, but Osvaldo pulled away.

"No. It's my protection."

"Protection," Serafin said. He shook his head in dismay. "Come over to the water trough, and wash your face. What have you been doing, rubbing your head inside the stove?"

Below the trough a few white and yellow daisies bloomed. *Margheritine.* He'd barely noticed them before. Now he stood at the trough and examined the flowers, delicate yet sturdy, swaying in the slight breeze. Other flowers grew against the side of the chicken shed, he noted with surprise, and even alongside the house — yellow mustard, a small clump of blue *cicoria*. And all he had ever seen was the cotton and weeds and acres of farmland. He looked out across his field where the dried stalks had been pulled. He could see as far as Lazzaro's farm, and beyond it, little shacks barely visible here and there, dotting the flat land. What he would have given in Italy for this much land.

Osvaldo had found a scrap of rope and was tying one end to a short stick he propped under the crate. He backed up, holding the rope. "*Guarda, papá*, if I put some food under the box, I can catch a quail or turkey."

"It would have to be a blind and deaf bird," Serafin told him.

"Well, if I had longer rope I could hide from it."

"You're a good hunter." His insides ached.

"I can hunt with snares, too. I'm going to make us rich."

"You think so?"

"If I could make a snare big enough."

"You leave Mr. Hall's mule alone, I told you."

"I am."

The sun would be setting soon, and the air was turning cool. He felt like a hollow drum inside. "Do you think your mother would like these flowers?" Serafin asked, pointing to them.

The boy shrugged. "She'd rather have some olive oil and tomato paste." He pulled on the rope so the box fell, and smiled at his genius.

Serafin leaned against the edge of the water trough and watched swallows and killdeer swoop over their field while Osvaldo played with the crate. He would have to find extra work, anything he could, to try to cover the Sant'Angelo charges. Just hope Step keeps hiring me on, mad as he is, he thought. He chastised himself for not doing more to help his own family. What had he been thinking, to stick his nose into someone else's business when they themselves were wanting? But that old lady Sant'Angelo, bent over and determined as she was, with two children dead, her husband beaten down. The husband and his boy carrying scraps of lumber to make a dead baby's coffin — why did he have to see that? He patted his heart with his open palm.

"What're you doing?" Osvaldo asked.

"Nothing."

"Are you praying?"

Serafin looked at the house, tears stinging his eyes. If only he could pray, he thought, a real prayer, one backed by real belief instead of despair and fear. He felt the small hand on his knee.

"*Coraggio, papá.*"

He almost laughed at the boy's words.

"You're like your uncle," Serafin told Osvaldo. "I wish you could have known him." His throat tightened. It was the first time in years he'd spoken aloud of his brother.

"I do," Osvaldo said.

Serafin raised a questioning eyebrow.

"The boy I play with in my dreams. He said his name is *Zio.*"

"*Zio*, eh?" Serafin said. "Listen, come here." He pulled the boy in front of him, holding him by the shoulders. "What do you see when I hold up my hand like this?" He raised his hand before Osvaldo's eyes, spreading the fingers wide.

Osvaldo squinted suspiciously at him, then shrugged. "A hand, papa, what do you think?"

"Oh hell," Serafin said. "Forget it." He didn't know what he was trying to do. *Pazzo.* Maybe he was the crazy one, not the boy.

"What's your mother cooking for supper?" he asked his son. Osvaldo crinkled his nose. "Tubers again."

They dug them up in the woods and the swamp, as the Halls had shown them, and fried them in lard. Like potatoes, but not potatoes.

"Eh, what the hell," Serafin muttered. "Come on, give me a hand," he told the boy.

They picked a small handful of the daisies and went in the house.

CHAPTER 15

Flood

June 1905

"You do things too late," Fiorenza told Serafin, and then her face flushed at having spoken out of line. Fancy Hall raised an eyebrow to her, then resumed feeding Amalia mashed chicken liver from the soup. She'd been coming for several days, first with herbs and tea for Amalia and greens and corn bread for Serafin and the children.

"She needed you before, too, that's all I'm saying," Fiorenza stammered. "Now she's getting well."

"It's never too late," Serafin answered in a thin voice.

Of course Fiorenza was right. He looked around the bedroom cluttered with people, bedclothes, the pot of tea, bowls and cups, then out the window at the pounding rain. His fault, that's all he could think — her fainting in the field, the blood, the sickness.

Now she was sitting up in bed, her hair brushed back, taking a few swallows of Fancy Hall's soup. "You look better," he said, dismayed at her sunken face. She blinked her eyes once, slowly. They had not mentioned the baby that was not to be.

"Go rest," Fiorenza told him. "There's nothing for you to do here."

"I'll have plenty of time to rest when I'm dead," Serafin answered.

He went to the window, sorry as soon as the words escaped his mouth. He knew how foolish he was, fretting like an old lady when in fact he'd been doing nothing to help — absolutely nothing but sitting in the room day and night — while the two women tended his wife. He brushed aside the buzzing mosquitoes and flies that hovered at the glass while outside the rain poured down.

It had come all winter and spring, stopping long enough for the land to dry out for planting, and giving the crops a week of sun here and there. Then it would start in again, and the cotton struggled to grow in all that wetness. The river crept up steadily until the water was just a few yards below the top of the levee.

Along with the bad weather, their debts piled up. In spring they lived on greens from the fields and woods: dandelion and chicory and the low, trailing purslane. He had never told Amalia about his visit to the priest, and Horton's charges afterwards. "I'm growing roots from eating this food," Serafin had said more than once. "My skin will turn green." At first he said it jokingly, then despairingly. The water was too high and roiled for catching fish; and he had little luck using snares.

Thunder cracked above the sound of rain, and white streaks of lightning split the sky. The Pascala children set out more pans and bowls to collect the steady streams of water pouring through unseen holes in the roof while the adults whispered and Serafin worried about their crops, their debts, their health. He touched his face, refusing to believe that he, too, had a fever.

It was exhausting, this fretting, this doing nothing but listening for a sound, a word, a request, and waiting for time to pass. Exhausting to stay in one room day and night, with the two women changing bedclothes, washing Amalia, feeding her, helping her onto a commode and then cleaning her, seeing to every move, every bodily function while he watched and waited and time hung like the thick humid air that would not stir.

The cotton shimmered green across the fields as far as he could see, so that his vision blurred and he was looking at green air — a peaceful and softly humming green air.

Just to see the sea one more time — what he wouldn't give for that. To breathe the fresh salt air, feel the waves lapping against the side of his boat, feel the weight of his nets as he flung them, the heaviness as he pulled them in. And most of all, to see the rolling hills as he sat in his boat. He would climb those hills when he was done fishing, feel the familiar pull in his calves as he strode upwards, home, through the olive groves, the fields of grape vines. He always paused at the top to turn and look below again at the sea, blue or green, depending on the sky. How could he have been such a fool to leave?

He felt a hand on his shoulder.

"You'll get 'et up standin in that window, Mr. Serafin," Fancy told him.

She led him to Osvaldo's bed across from Amalia and sat him down. He was aware of the gentle pressure of her fingers pushing against his chest, and then his body falling back. "Why'nt you lay down a spell?"

He closed his eyes, saw the turquoise sea below, the emerald hills above. The net was heavy in his hands.

***

Step came pounding on their door early in the morning, a slicker over his head to protect the lantern he gripped with his other hand. Behind him stood Calvin and Fred Titus with his grown son JoeJack; Lazzaro and Claudio and a couple other men he knew only by sight waited in the mud.

"River risin. Kin you help sandbag?"

Serafin shot a look back at his family as they peered past him at the group outside. "I want to come too," Osvaldo said. "I'm big enough."

"Don't any of you leave this house for anything," he told them. "You kids watch after your mother."

Amalia stood shakily in the kitchen, as if the rain had broken the spell of illness. "Go back to bed," he told her, but she did not move.

"No time to waste," Step said.

Serafin looked out at the soaked men, their legs and feet clumped with mud. "I'm coming," he told them.

Amalia handed him his hat and a jacket. He was already down the stoop, starting to follow the others when she called him back. "To eat," she shouted over the pounding rain. She tossed a small bundle at him: half a loaf of bread that Angelina had made while she lay ill. He tucked it inside his shirt.

They trudged through the slashing rain, sinking to their ankles in places. Lazzaro gripped Serafin by the elbow to steady himself. "Jesus in heaven," he said.

"How bad is it?" Serafin called to Step.

"Bad," Step answered. Then he shouted to them over the rain: "Mr. Gates come back to see to the sandbaggin."

"Boss man?" Serafin said. It surprised him that Gates was there, and worried him, too, that the threat of flooding was that serious.

Fred shouted back: "Figure he better try to save Sweet Hope — look good if he want be some guv'ment big shot." He hunched his shoulders and let the rain pour off his hat brim. "Complainin it's a hell of a time for a flood," he hollered. "Ain't never no good time for a flood."

Through the dim morning grayness a new ghost land slowly appeared: fields under water, ruined crops. "The cotton," Serafin said, meaning with that one word everything: food for his family, clothes, their health, their hope of escaping debt. In the distance they saw strange, lumbering animals, their silhouettes bending and heaving against the muddy sky.

As they neared the levee they saw that the strange animals were merely other men like themselves, some shoveling dirt and sand into bags, others dropping the bags in place to form a barrier against the rising river, others lugging already–filled sandbags up the incline of the levee to heave into place.

Horton rode his skittish horse along the bottom of the levee, shouting directions to the men below. But when they saw Step and the others approaching, they broke and descended on him.

"Mr. Step, no good. What we do?" one of the men called.

"Our family, have to get out."

"You take us out here," another pleaded.

"It's okay," Step tried to tell them. "Levee's still holdin."

Horton brought his horse around, shouting over the rain. "I got this under control, Hall. Go make yourself useful. The rest of you, get moving."

They waited for Step's direction.

"Spread out, fill in where you're needed," Step called to them. Once he started up the levee, the others followed. Horton fumed behind them.

"He's a bastard, even in a deluge," Lazzaro said.

Serafin climbed heavily toward a break in the sandbags. He felt sick. Too many sleepless, fitful nights, and his head not right. But wasn't that the case with most of them? Just keep working, no matter, he told himself. His legs were heavy with mud. The levee trembled under his feet from the force of the swollen river pounding against it. One of the managers — between the rain and the slicker covering the man, he could not tell who — was screaming at the line of men to move faster, pile the sandbags. A nervous buckskin horse pranced towards Serafin, the tall rider draped in a long slicker calling for more men.

Someone shouted from below: "Mr. Gates, can't ride your horse up there. No room, too dangerous."

Gates shouted back, "Wade, get to Three Point and round up as many men as you can find. Bring them in chains if you have to."

Harlan Gates' horse bumped against Serafin, pitching him onto the sandbags, and he clawed at wet burlap and held on. Just yards below, a torrent of dark, muddy water roiled by, spreading half a mile east toward the other side, and disappearing into the gray air and slashing rain. Whole shrubs, tree trunks, barrels, and a shed atop which a stunned goat splayed its legs to steady itself rushed past him down the swollen river.

Another few inches and he would have been thrown into the river. No one seemed to notice. The horseman was gone.

He rose clumsily and peered out where the levee should have sloped down to the landing. The road, the ramp, the stairs — all of it was gone. It was clear now that if the river crested the levee it would flood all of the farmland and sweep everything downstream. His first thought was to run for his family, get them out to higher ground — impossible, he knew. Where the hell was higher ground? His second thought was of his crop, and how everything was lost.

"Hey, you," a man shouted, and heaved a full sandbag toward Serafin. He caught the bag and slapped it in the mud at his feet, next to the others. The men had formed a brigade and were heaving sandbags his direction, with Lazzaro just a few men down. Another man came in to close the gap in the line. It was Father Odetti, with his wide–brimmed hat bending under the weight of the rain. He bowed his head to the work and said nothing. *So, you too?* Serafin thought. He could strangle the man for the hell he had caused. *Just another body slogging through mud now.* Above them all, the sound of the rain, the shouts of men, and now and then the frantic yelling of the managers.

Hardly a day had gone by all spring without someone commenting on the rising water. But as long as the rain held off, they said, as long as the weather stayed steady until harvest time. The Negroes, and others too who had been in the Delta a long time, had tried to tell the Italians about the dangers of rain in places they couldn't see, rain 500, even 1,000 miles away, high lakes and rivers in other states — not that anyone could have done anything about it. "Been nothin but rain since March up north, all through the middle states. Pretty soon gonna take its toll on us."

Serafin sloshed sandbags into the yellow mud of the trembling levee and thought of Harlan Gates out there somewhere, riding among them, called back from his political campaigning to try to save Sweet Hope. Serafin thought of the man's horse pitching him toward the river as if he were nothing more than a fly being swatted by the horse's tail. And Gates moving on, uncaring. *A hell of a time for a flood,* he'd said? What had Father Odetti told him? *You don't understand. The company has a business to run.* It finally dawned on Serafin: it was the land itself, the cotton crop, they were trying to save, not the people.

The jacket had fallen from his shoulders and was gone. His left arm kept catching on something, slowing him down. He felt with his right hand the wet lumpiness of his shirt, then stuck his hand inside the shirt. What he pulled out was a soft, soggy ball that he held in his hands. Bread. It took him a few moments to understand how it had gotten there. But the bread was ruined. He threw it down into the mud, and as soon as he did he thought of the words he'd heard somewhere long ago, "Cast your bread upon the water." And then

what? he wondered. It will come back? He could not remember
what came next, did not even know what the words meant.

Suddenly, hot tears were running down his face, mixing
with the rain. He would never know if his child had been a
boy or a girl, never know its face, the sound of its voice. What
had he been thinking, touching Amalia that night, taking
the chance of bringing another innocent child into such a
hell? He lowered his head so the other men would not see
him crying — as if anyone could, with the rain.

Men shouted to each other, calling for more sandbags or
for help lugging the filled bags up the levee. Other men were
laying planks down the slope of the levee for men to walk
on. If they ventured up the levee bank itself they sank and
slid to the bottom. Horton went past on foot, leading a frantic
horse and cursing the men for being so slow. When he saw
Serafin, he narrowed his eyes and kept moving.

Serafin looked down at the insignificant sandbags at his
feet, then out at the river rushing past and a sudden jolt of
fear stabbed through him. It was a miracle that the levee held
at all. Their feeble work seemed ridiculous — why couldn't
the others see that? "We have to get out," he called to them,
stumbling as he tried to straighten himself. He felt weak,
lightheaded. "Get out before the whole levee collapses under
our feet. Get our families away from here!"

The man next to him looked up, mud and rain streaking
his face. "What? What did you say?" he shouted.

"We're pissing into the sea," Serafin yelled back. He gestured, shouted again, trying to make the man understand.

The man shook his head, fear in his eyes, and heaved
another sandbag into place. "Can't understand you."

Serafin looked around wildly for Step Hall, Lazzaro,
somebody who would understand. The other men were bent
on their work. Not one of them seemed to comprehend the

danger they were in, the futility of laying down puny sandbags when the entire fifteen–foot high berm of earth they stood on wasn't enough to hold back a mad river.

He felt a slight breeze, a cool salt breeze it seemed, and he lifted his eyes to the lapping water. A man was walking toward him, someone he vaguely recognized, and he wondered where the man was coming from and how he had kept himself so dry.

The man stopped, and the water lapped at his feet as he kept his eyes intently on Serafin. "What's wrong with you? Why are you crying?"

The question startled him. "What? Who the hell are you?"

"Why won't you bury me?" the man asked him.

Serafin stared at him a long minute before recognizing the familiar eyes and mouth, the thick hair falling across the forehead. "Valerio?"

The man only gazed steadfastly, saying nothing. Serafin glanced to his side, to see if Lazzaro or Claudio were witnessing what was happening. And then, just like that, the man seemed to be going away, backing up, or somehow turning into air. It was hard to see just what was happening.

"Wait," Serafin called out.

The river was moving, pushing south with its branches and debris. Around him, men slipped in the mud as they heaved sandbags into place. All had happened so quickly — yet seemed to have lasted a long time. He tried to recall the face, how the features were those of a stranger at first, and then became familiar. Almost Valerio's face, yet not quite. Was he losing his mind? And he didn't feel sad or afraid, not exactly, just tired, emptied. A jug filled with water, then emptied out.

He closed his eyes, tried to call up the face again. Bury him? he asked himself.

"Hey," Lazzaro shouted.

"What?" he answered, frightened.

"I said, pray the rain stops before we drown like rats."

∗∗∗

AMALIA'S face grew as dark as the roiled sky while she sat with a cup of weak coffee Angelina had made for her and listened to the rain pummel the house. After several days of not eating, the coffee turned her stomach. She pushed it away so she would not have to smell the sickening aroma and sat eyeing the statue of the Blessed Virgin that stood at one end of the table. The face was mild and impassive. Her children hovered over the pots, checking the level of rainwater. Each time one of them opened the door to empty a pan, the view revealed more of their crop flattened in the mud, and wider rivulets of water washing down the dirt path between the road and their house, and the widening ponds across the fields. "Don't look, mama," Angelina told her.

Amalia went into the bedroom to see how badly the roof was leaking. At the foot of her bed lay her old work dress folded on top of a sheet. She lifted the dress, wondering what it was doing there, until she saw the faded stains Fancy and Fiorenza must have tried to wash out. She remembered now her pain while working in the field, collapsing, the fever and fitful sleep and dreams. She knelt at the foot of the bed, fingering the dress, and the funny thought came to her that somewhere hidden in folds of the cloth she would find her baby. She drew her hand back, wondering what it meant that such a thing had happened. Was there something wrong with her that had killed the baby? The sinfulness inside her bringing a curse on her for the way she treated Serafin and the children as well — hot one minute, cold the next. Stealing the priest's boat and then lying about it, making her own daughter lie. And poor Osvaldo, failing to protect him, failing to get help for him. She crossed herself as she knelt, and began murmuring in earnest, "Oh my God, I am heartily sorry for having offended thee..." But as she prayed she thought she heard the faint sounds of a baby crying. She buried her face in the stained cloth, breathed deeply, and let the tears come.

At last she stood and gathered the dress and carried it to the door. She flung it out into the rain while the children silently watched. "Let the rain leach the stains, let the mud swallow my torment," she said. She turned back inside and took down two croker sacks from their pegs.

"What are you doing, mama?" her frightened children asked. "Where are you going?"

"You stay in the house, don't you dare move," she scolded. Then she softened: "I have to take care of the chickens. At least we'll have them if our cotton's ruined."

"Mama, let me go, you're too sick," Angelina said.

Amalia tucked one croker sack under her arm and put the other over her head. "Don't leave us," Osvaldo pleaded.

"I'm coming right back, silly," she said, touching his head.

"What a big crybaby," Isola sniffled, fighting the stinging in her eyes.

Amalia left them standing in the open door and stepped barefoot down into the mud.

"Close the door!" she shouted to them.

The children stood watching her struggle as the mud clutched at her feet.

The chicken shed was only twenty feet away, but it felt like a mile. Each time she put a foot down it sank in mud over her ankle.

When she yanked open the door of the flimsy shed, the musty stillness stopped her. She ducked inside and gasped at the heat and the acrid, moldy smell of wet straw and manure and feathers. The shed was dark. She could barely make out the chickens huddled against the back wall, staring at her with glittering eyes. Not dead after all, she sighed.

She slipped the wet croker sack from her head. The place was a shambles, most of the straw and dried grass ruined by rain, with part of the roof sagging in one corner and water streaming in. The earth was slick beneath her feet, a mixture of mud and manure. If I had waited another day, she thought, the shed would have collapsed, the birds scattered or drowned.

Her eyes moved quickly, calculating, planning. All four birds were there. The first hen — Old Shoe, they called her — then the second they'd bought the next summer, and the two pullets they'd hatched from their own after borrowing Step's rooster for a few days. She moved slowly, feeling the nesting ledge for dry straw. Whenever she touched a dry spot, she stuffed what she could scoop into the bottom of the croker sack. Next she lifted the wooden barrel top, weighted down with a rock, and reached in for the grain sack. It was only damp on one side. This too she dropped into the sack. And then she went for the chickens.

They backed away, clucking and flapping their wings, but they were too disoriented by the storm to put up much fight. They looked ridiculous, their wet feathers plastered to their scrawny bodies, dry tufts sticking out here and there. Grabbing the first two was easy — they huddled in their fear and stupidity against each other instead of scattering. She grabbed them by the legs and put them in the sack, holding the top closed after each one. The third chicken danced around the fourth, moved away toward the wall, then back as if it would make a break for the door. But the pouring rain sent the chicken back toward her and she nabbed it. The fourth one did not run. It paced back and forth along the ledge. When

Amalia got close it flapped its wings and took a small flying leap that landed it two feet from where it had started. Finally she took an empty wet feed sack from the ledge and flung it over the bird to subdue it, then lifted it into the sack.

She pulled a piece of twine from where it hung on the wall and knotted the top of the sack for good measure then took one last sweep of the shed, her hands feeling delicately through the straw. She found only two eggs. A third had been smashed. She put the wet sack back over her head, gently cradled the two good eggs against her breast with one hand, and lifted the loaded sack. A few pounds of feed and four birds made for a heavy load. The birds clucked and shifted in protest, then held still as she stepped again into the pounding rain. Her feet sank. She flung the sack over her shoulder and grunted and struggled with each step forward.

Halfway to the house she looked up to see the children standing in the doorway watching her. "Close the door," she shouted, "you'll flood the house." But her words were blown back into her mouth with the rain. She yanked her foot from the mud and lurched forward with her load. When she reached the step her children held out their hands, and she handed the heavy croker sack up to them, then the precious eggs. Then she heaved her own body up the steps and collapsed on her knees, dripping and streaked with mud.

"You look like a big crawfish," Osvaldo said.

Panting and flushed, she let the wet croker sack slip from her head. "Careful," she told Isola as the girl set the eggs in a dish.

Angelina knelt down and wiped Amalia's legs and feet with the wet croker sack. "*Buona ragazza*," Amalia told her.

"Mama, you have to get out of those wet clothes," the girl answered.

The chickens clucked softly and rustled against each other in the sack that lay where Amalia had dropped it. "The chickens," she cried, going for the sack.

"Are you going to cook them?" Osvaldo asked her.

"*Diavolo* no," she answered. She laid her hand against the sack, as if feeling for a heartbeat, then tore at the twine. "The wet sack, they can't breathe!" She opened the top, reached in and pulled out a soaked chicken. "Thank God," she said, cradling the bird to her breast. "We have to take care of them. They would have died in the shed."

And so they scattered some of the straw on the floor in one corner and set some grain out in a dish, and let the chickens wander freely through the house. There was no box, no wire, no way to make a cage.

"Why can't they go outside?" Osvaldo asked. "They won't run away."

"No, but they'll drown — or starve," she told him.

"What about daddy?" the boy asked. "Will he drown too?"

The children stared at their mother with worried expressions.

"He'll be all right," she said, the insincere words catching in her throat. They listened to the rain battering the roof. "Pray," she told them softly.

A chicken strutted near her and she tried to pick it up, but it flapped and screeched, sending out fluffs of down and feathers. She picked up a stray feather and pressed it against her cheek.

"Mama, please, take off your wet dress," Angelina told her. "You'll get sick again."

"All my clothes are wet," Amalia told Angelina, touching the sleeve of her dress, the front, the yoke. "Everything's wet."

"We're fish," Isola said, feeling her own wet clothes.

"Yes," Amalia answered. "Fish and chickens, living together in a floating barn."

The dark day turned darker. Amalia glanced at the statue of the Blessed Virgin Mary. How many times already she had asked Mary for help — and then begged forgiveness for only turning to her in times of despair?

She pinched the ash and wax from the cold candlewick and lit it, calling the children to the table. "Pray for your father and all of us," she told them. "And thank God and the Blessed Mother for making the rain let up."

"It didn't stop," Isola said.

"It will," Osvaldo said. "If you tell God you think it stopped, he'll believe you."

"What are you talking about?" Amalia said, aghast. "You think I'm telling you to trick God? The rain's letting up, that's all."

The boy shrugged, and Isola smirked at him. "Sometimes it works," he told his mother, and she pulled him by the ear closer to her side, but gently.

Angelina took the *Madonna di Loreto* medal from inside her blouse and clutched it, closing her eyes as her mother led them in prayer. But soon Angelina's thoughts wandered, as she added her own prayers for her poor father. She pictured him on the levee, drenched and worn out, working with the other men while the dangerous river swept past them. All those men she knew — Lazzaro and Claudio, and Pietro the crippled shoemaker, and all the other neighbors near them; and then Step Hall and Fred Titus with Calvin and JoeJack. Not Tobe, he was only as big as Osvaldo. She pictured Calvin's smiling face, saw those crazy shreds of shoes on his feet, the little dance steps he did to show off when they were playing *bocce*. Her throat tightened, and her eyes filled with tears as she imagined never seeing him again. "Please, dear God," she moaned aloud, so that the others looked at her. Amalia smiled faintly, pleased with the girl's devotion, yet pained to see the children so frightened.

Angelina bowed her flushed face. She could not believe what she had just discovered: that she liked Calvin Hall, and had liked him for a long time.

Finally, Amalia stood and made a small fire from what dry firewood was left in the house. She heated water for polenta. There was little else in the house, save some flour and beans, one loaf of bread and a cup of the soup Fancy Hall had brought yesterday. She stepped around the chickens as she prepared the meal, trying not to worry about Serafin. The men had been out since dawn without shelter or food. She didn't even know if they were alive. She set Fancy's soup on the back of the stove to warm, a way to ensure that Serafin was still with them. Then she waited.

When the water boiled she stirred in the cornmeal. The feeble heat of the stove barely touched her skin. She swallowed hard, trying to fight back the ache in her heart.

Even in the winter during the ice storms the house hadn't seemed like such a tomb. At least once the ice stopped falling from the sky you could walk outside and the air would be bright and full of the sounds of people building, repairing, shouting, striking a bell for work time. When you opened the door or window there was always someone going by down on the road, on foot or in a wagon. But now, nothing. Closed up in a tomb in the land of the dead, no way to reach those who were outside, no way to get word from them, no way to know whether or not they'd been swept away.

Osvaldo and Isola were trying to herd the chickens under the table, but the birds would not stay put. Angelina scoffed at the two, then went and took the spoon from Amalia's hand. "Sit down, mama."

"I'm too worried to sit," Amalia told her. But she sat just the same. Angelina stirred the pot while fingering her holy medal and gazing at the shuttered window.

When the door rattled open, Amalia jumped up. "Serafin?" she called.

But a stranger stood in the doorway, a bent man caked with mud from head to foot; even his hair was clumped with it. He held onto the door frame as if it were holding him up. Fear gripped her heart.

"The men?" she demanded.

The children held back, watching the stranger.

"Amalia," the man croaked. He held his hand out and stumbled into the room.

"Daddy?" Isola said.

"Serafin, is it you?" Amalia cried, rushing to help him to a chair.

"Mud, I'm all mud," he mumbled.

Angelina brought him water and the children stared as he gulped it.

"Are you hurt?" Amalia asked, feeling his arm, his face.

"All right," he answered.

"The levee?"

He leaned over the table and rested his head on his arm. "Holding," he sighed. Dried mud clung to his eyebrows.

"Bring the pans of water," she told the children. "We have to wash him."

"Here, mama?" Angelina asked. "We'll make a mess."

"It's already a mess," Amalia told her. "For now we live in the mud."

He lay on the floor, and they stripped the clothes from his body, and they washed him. Even his pubic hair and genitals were clumped with mud. "What were you doing, swimming in mud?"

"I was eating the dirt. A worm in the dirt. *Un' mangiaterra.*"

She instructed Angelina to pour pans of water on him while she combed through the mud with her fingers. Angelina was embarrassed at the way her mother ran her fingers through his private parts, lifting them gently as she poured the water. He lay still as they prodded and washed him. "I could go to sleep right here," he mumbled. Angelina stared at her father's naked body, thinking of Calvin and other boys she had noticed, self–conscious now, remembering how she had wondered what it would be like to see them naked, to be with them naked. She blinked and looked away, trying not to think of her mother and father in that way. Amalia prodded the girl to get more water as she scrubbed Serafin's arms and chest.

Slowly, the man they knew emerged, his skin ashen, his body still as a corpse. The face, the body, like that other Pascala whom Amalia had helped wash, though he had been brought to them clean, pulled dead from a clean sea. But no, you are not dead, she kept telling herself, you will not die.

"My arms," Serafin murmured, breaking the spell. "I can barely move them."

"Don't try," Amalia whispered.

They dressed him in the driest clothes they could find, helped him into the chair. "Even Gates came to the levee," he mumbled. "The king to his castle." Amalia tried to make him drink some of the soup, eat a few spoonfuls of mush. "Too tired," he told her.

"Sleep then," she said.

They helped him to bed, Amalia under one arm and Angelina under the other.

"But are we safe here tonight?" she asked as she laid him on the bed. "Will the levee hold?"

He turned his head away and groaned. "Why would you ask a man made of mud?" His arms and legs, his whole body, felt heavy. Then they felt weightless. Then he was asleep.

Amalia sent the children back into the kitchen. She stared hard at her husband, watching for the slow rise and fall of his chest. A stone face, weary, closed to her. She knelt beside the bed, her face inches from his.

"Damn you," she said through gritted teeth. "You're not leaving me now, you hear?"

The only answer was the pattering of the rain, and the rise and fall of his chest.

She lay beside him, clutching his unconscious body and biting her lip to keep silent. He smelled like no one she knew — like rain and mud and the river. But she knew if she held on long enough he would become familiar again.

CHAPTER 16

Drowning

June 1905

DAYS after the river began to recede at the landing, an occasional dead cow or mule floated by, half–rotted or half–eaten by vultures. Sometimes a floating carcass would snag in a bayou or find its way into one of the drainage ditches until the stench drove the tenants to search it out and either pry it back into the current or bury it in the muck. Many of the farmers, along with their children, stole away to the levee for a few minutes to watch the high water carry debris and the floating carcasses. It was with despair that they turned their eyes back upon the swamped fields of Sweet Hope.

A third of Serafin's crop was gone, half of Lazzaro's, a third of Step Hall's. Some people, those in the lower areas close to the lake or bayous or swamps, lost all. The rain washed away Uncle Blue's cotton. Ceravone lost only a third. "Good riddance," he said. The Sant'Angelos' fifteen acres was almost gone. Two–thirds of Pietro's crop wiped out. The Tituses lost half.

It was the first time in months that Serafin had pulled the tobacco tin out from under the corner of their mattress, but this time it felt different. He opened the lid and stared at the two American dollars. "Amalia?"

She blanched.

"Where?" he said. "How?"

"Fancy Hall," she stammered. She was thankful Isola was not in the house. "She sold another dress."

He studied her a moment. "I thought she bought us the tomatoes with that money."

Amalia nodded. "There was money left over." She snatched the tin from Serafin. "I was going to tell you once there was more."

"We'll need to spend it. No way we can last through the winter." He knew what she was thinking, though: Sweet Hope scrip could only be used on the plantation, but American money was good anywhere. She was saving for when they got out. *If* they got out.

"We'll eat greens," she said, clutching the tin to her breast. "We'll eat fish."

He eyed her a moment, wondering how much she knew of his own secrets: all those extra charges piled on them because he had tried to help the Sant'Angelos. "What will the mules eat?" he asked.

"I swear on the heads of our children," she said, "you're not touching this money. Not yet."

"We're just sinking deeper in debt, Amalia — "

"Everybody's in debt," she told him. "I spit on the Sweet Hope debt."

***

HARLAN Gates was relieved that, in spite of the heavy losses, the levee held and Sweet Hope survived the flood. He stayed long enough to ensure the plantation's stability before taking leave back to Jackson and then on to Washington where he had secured meetings with two legislators to discuss his immigrant labor model for the south. The meetings would also serve as an investment in his future bid for senator. Before he could depart, though, Lee Horton asked to speak with him. The tenants were causing trouble now that the water was receding and they saw how bad things were.

"Trouble? What kind of trouble?" He stood tall before Horton, his handsome face showing wear from the last few days.

"Just a lotta grumblin so far, but something's in the air." He'd been practicing his speech since the sandbagging, when the tenants he'd been giving orders ran like drowning rats away from him to Step Hall. "I think we better remove all firearms from Sweet Hope," he told Gates.

"The Italians are already denied firearms," Gates said.

"It's the blacks I'm worried about," Horton answered.

The words caught him short. "Now what?" Gates asked, an uneasiness settling into him. "What's been going on here?"

"Nothing so far. Like to keep it that way."

Gates narrowed his eyes, considering the man he had never much liked from the start. But Horton's sometimes ruthless behavior dampened the Italians' intractability. There was something to be said for intimidation when used against people too ignorant to understand the greater good. "Has something happened I should know about?"

Horton paused, to choose his words. "Let's just say insubordination. Leadin toward who–knows–what."

"If you've got a trouble maker on your hands —"

"Ain't nothin I can lay my finger on right now," Horton replied, feeling he was digging himself deeper into a lie.

"Mr. Horton, you're not telling me a damn thing. I have a train to catch."

"How about niggers sneaking firearms to Dagoes? They's planning something together, and I don't want to wait around to find out what it is."

Harlan Gates paused. He wondered if all his time away from Sweet Hope had loosened his grip on the largest business enterprise in the Delta. The Italians grumbled, but they worked hard and seemed fairly harmless. And the few remaining Negroes appeared to be trustworthy.

"Are you sure the Negroes aren't just sneaking firearms so the Italians can hunt game? They've become quite friendly with each other."

"No chance a' that," Horton answered. "Dagoes don't eat game."

The comment didn't ring true. "You can't take a gun away from a free man," he told Horton. "How are they going to hunt? Protect themselves?"

"Ain't nothing to protect themselves from on Sweet Hope," Horton countered. All he could think of was Step's posture and attitude toward him, acting like he ran the place. "They use snares and traps to hunt. They fish all the time. Hardly use those guns a'tall. Would be a mistake to sit on our hands waitin till somethin blows up."

Gates pulled out his watch, debating whether he had time to go speak to Step Hall himself. But the train would not wait for him. "You leave the Negroes' guns alone, you hear?" he told Horton. "Until you talk to Step Hall. If he determines there's a problem, have him talk to the other Negroes and let him handle it."

"Just hope he's not part a' the problem," Horton said.

"What's that?"

"Just sayin."

***

BY the time Gates was on a train to Jackson, Horton had taken it upon himself to reinterpret the man's words. He told Step Hall: "Mr. Gates says you niggers lost him half a' Sweet Hope crops with that flood. You don't shape up, he's gonna take all your guns away."

"That don't make no sense," Step said. "God made the rain come down, not us."

"See? Right there, you're steppin outta line. Just what I'm talkin about. Mr. Gates say if you spend half the time workin as you do cozyin up to the Dagoes, Sweet Hope wouldn't be in such a mess. You wanna keep your guns, better straighten up."

Angered, yet cautious, Step nodded and quickly removed himself from Lee Horton's presence.

His family and friends were working hard clearing dead plants and debris from their fields when he told them. Some of the land was still too wet to get to, and mosquitoes swarmed over the pools of standing water.

"First thing I get this crop in — if it ever grows to harvest — " Fred told them, "all you see is the back of my head goin down the road."

"'*Cozyin up*'?" Lud said. "Now what *that* s'pose to mean?"

"Why they wanna take our guns away?" Fancy said. "We never done nothin."

"We're losin ground," Fred said. "I tell you, we just keep losin ground." He kept his eyes from Step as he said this.

***

THE children listened, but put little stock in the adults' concerns. For them, the near–flood spelled adventure. Puddles formed in the woods, puddles big as ponds, and the "fish from nowhere" swam in the water. Even stepping on what looked like dry land became a risk. Put your foot on a grassy spot and you might find yourself in water over your ankles.

Amalia stopped Isola as she tried to leave the house. "Until our fields are dry enough to work, you've got sewing to do." She took the dress Isola had been working on and shook it out. "Look at this," she said. "What's going to happen to you when you try to get a husband and he sees you make a mess like this?"

"I don't want a husband," Isola answered.

Amalia made a sound like she was spitting coffee grounds. Then her thumb swooped across her breast as she crossed herself. "Dear God, what's going to happen to you?"

Isola scratched the ball of her foot against the rough floor. This mother who was as unpredictable as the Sweet Hope weather had tricked her again. The flood had turned her into a kind stranger, someone strong and sweet and loving. But now, as suddenly as a Sweet Hope rain, the old *strega* mother was back.

"Can I just go pee first?" Isola asked.

"*Piscia.* And then I better see a needle and thread flying between your fingers."

Osvaldo was out with Serafin, catching frogs or maybe a turtle for their supper. Even Angelina sat outside in the sun with her dreamy face, stringing tomatoes to dry from the small basketful they had salvaged before the rain could pound them. Isola stuck her tongue out as she jumped past Angelina and ran to the road. Step Hall was driving a mule and wagon down the road. He raised his hand wearily to her as he drove by.

Birdie followed behind him on foot, trailing a branch in the dirt. She stopped alongside Isola. "Whatcha doin?"

Isola looked at the swirls in the muddy dirt. "Nothin."

Step turned and called sternly to Birdie, "Don't you be dawdling here. Git back home and help your ma."

Birdie watched her father drive away. Then she told Isola, "Daddy say a man drowned in the lake. Say his boat got turned over."

"Drowned?" Isola said, wide-eyed. It was the one thing they had been afraid of during the raining days, but now that the rain had stopped it seemed odd that anyone would drown.

They hunkered behind a clump of cotton so Angelina wouldn't be able to see or hear them.

"Daddy spec' he tryin to cross the lake to see his gal," Birdie told her. "He goin to see now."

"He going to see a drowned man?" Isola said.

"Got to bring him back and bury him if he from here. I'm mad he won't take me."

Isola shivered as she remembered Tobe floating down the river that day long ago. But the lake. Everybody went fishing in the lake, and swimming sometimes too, and the priest and the company men crossed the lake to the village sometimes in their rowboats. She'd done it herself, with Birdie and their mothers.

"If we was in the woods," Birdie said, "we could see when Daddy brung him back."

"Mama told me I have to stay in the house and sew," Isola said forlornly. But even as she said the words she saw the swollen shape of a man being pulled from the lake and then him lying on the ground, his wet clothes plastered to his bloated body while she moved closer to get a look at his drowned face.

"Sew? So what?" Birdie grinned.

The girls took off and didn't slow down until they reached the bayou near the Sant'Angelo house. Isola had played with the oldest girl a few times, even though it was hard to understand her Sicilian language.

They inched closer to the plank laid over the bayou water, leading down to the few houses near the swamp. "Watch out for the snakes," Birdie said, grabbing Isola. They could see them, sunning themselves on branches hanging near the water.

Isola pulled her arms in. "You see her?" she whispered.

"I don't see nobody," Birdie said. They walked slowly, craning their necks. The house was closed up tight. A mud line ran along the house, a foot above the doorsill, showing how high the water had risen during the flood.

The Sant'Angelos' small vegetable garden lay flattened in pools of water. Sticks entangled with old twine stood upright, while tomato plants lay flattened in the sandy dirt. A few smashed tomatoes lay among them. Larger pools of water surrounded the house in what used to be their cotton field.

Mr. Sant'Angelo had been brought back to Sweet Hope from jail in Alabama, thin and beaten. A *criminal*, the company called him. But some of the Italians sneaked over and talked to him, to find out what the rest of America was like. "Nothing like here," he told them. "Real jobs, and they pay you. People out there got their suspicions about Sweet Hope. I tell you, if we keep at it, the smell of shit here will carry the truth out."

"We're criminals, too," she told Birdie in a whisper. "Maybe the company will put us in jail too for going to the village — if they find out."

"You the criminal, not me," Birdie said. "We can go wherever we want to." She made a face at Isola.

"My mother says we all have to watch out now," Isola told Birdie. "Maybe the Americans make more trouble for us if they see us playing with the Sant'Angelos." She lowered her voice. "If we play with Nina the Americans might shoot us."

Birdie took a step back. "Where you got such a crazy idea?"

"That's what Mr. Gates' men do," Isola said. "My papa told me."

Birdie put her hands on her hips. "You dumb or something? White folks don't shoot white folks." She walked faster, so that Isola had to trot to catch up with her.

"But we're not white," Isola told her. "We're Italian."

They reached the corner field where a few people were working their soggy fields, next to the Titus land. Workers tromped in the mud through the tall green plants checking for damage and hoeing weeds. Lud Titus called to Birdie to get home, her mama wanted her to work. Birdie waved back to Lud, and then she and Isola started running, not down the road that went to Birdie's house but straight ahead toward the woods.

The *bosco* was on the way to the lake. A road ran alongside the woods, and if a wagon came, especially a wagon carrying a drowned man, they'd be able to run out to see. A few fallen limbs, cracked from the storm, their white insides shining, dangled from the trees or lay strewn in the weeds and low grass. The girls ran to the big pond just inside the trees. The ground was spongy under their feet, and mud squeezed through their toes.

"I wonder if the fish is back," Birdie said. She splashed her feet at the edge of the pond. Isola followed, stepping into the cool water. She rubbed her feet along the grass under the water and watched the mud swirl up.

"See any?" Birdie said. She waded a little farther and bent over, letting her dress get wet.

"There's something," Isola said, pointing. She jumped, but then stood still again. She was afraid of snakes, ever since she'd felt for eggs in one of the chicken nests only to find a big snake slithering through her fingers.

The fish were small, only a few inches long; a pretty silver color. Isola's mother said the fish swam in the earth, in water underground, to get to the puddles in the *bosc'*. But her father said they came out of the river and walked across the land at night, jumping into whatever water they found. Isola wondered why she'd never seen any fish walking at night. Or why they never found dead fish on land, the ones that couldn't make it to water. And how did they walk, since they didn't have any legs? *Pesci di bosc'*, the old people called them, though they said there was nothing like them back home. They'd only seen such things here in this strange country.

"I'm gonna catch one," Birdie said. She crouched and moved cautiously through the water, ready to grab the first thing that moved.

Two fish darted past and Isola shot her arms into the water. The hem of her dress fell and was suddenly soaked halfway up her legs. The fish got away.

"You got to sneak up behind 'em," Birdie told her. "You git over here, stir 'em up, chase 'em my way."

"I'm gonna get one myself," Isola said, but she stirred the fish Birdie's way just the same. Birdie lunged for the fish, landing on her knees.

Isola knelt down in the cool water next to Birdie. They moved their brown arms through the water and watched the ripples travel slowly to the edge of the pond. Silver fish swam around them.

"How come your sister and Calvin's so sweet on each other?" Birdie said.

"Who told you that?" Isola asked, surprised. But it was true that Angelina was always anxiously looking up from her fieldwork if somebody happened by, and she hurried to clean herself if the Halls came to visit. Isola herself had teased Angelina over it.

"Don't take a hoot owl to know what's what. Mama's always yellin at him 'bout it."

"Why?" Isola asked.

Birdie turned her face away, as if talking to the trees in the woods. "Say mixin git you in trouble, 'specially now, the company fussing 'cause a' you people."

"Us?" Isola shouted. "Fussin 'bout what?"

"I ain't even 'spose to be playin wi' you, noways," Birdie said.

"Why not?" Isola demanded. Everybody always said the Pascalas were hard workers, clean, and good people. How could someone say to stay away from them, as if they were some dirty *barboni*?

Birdie shrugged. "Just 'cause."

A woman started singing, far off. Birdie cocked her ear. "See? They be looking for me soon enough."

Isola stood up, outraged. "Well, I don't wanna play with you neither!" Her dress was heavy, and water poured from the skirt. She looked down to see the cloth unfold and a silver fish tumble out. She grabbed it before it fell into the water. Birdie shrieked, then laughed. Isola splashed out of the pond with Birdie following and threw the fish on the grass.

"Did you know it was in there?" Birdie cried. "Didn't you feel it?" And she patted her own dress, as if a fish might be hidden inside her clothes too, ready to drop out and scare her.

"I didn't feel it," Isola said. "I didn't even know there was no fish near me."

Birdie placed a finger on the fish's side, then pulled back. "Slimy," she said. "Let's make a puddle for it."

They dug clumps of dirt and grass with sticks and started building a levee around the fish. Then they scooped water into the pool but most of it seeped into the ground. The fish flipped around and moved its mouth and stared up at the sky with its shiny eye. "A fish drowns in air," Birdie told Isola.

Isola watched the small mouth and gills opening and closing. She couldn't understand how breathing could kill a fish.

"A man drowns in water," Isola said. She laughed, then stopped.

Her father had told them about a man drowning once, when they lived in Montignano and he worked on a fishing boat over in Senigallia. Not her uncle Valerio, who he never talked about, but somebody else. They had to pull him in with a fishing net, and there were fish in the net with him. The fish they brought home and sold. The man they brought home and buried.

There was a noise just outside the woods, a man's voice, and a girl crying out. "Must be they found out who the man is," Isola said. They moved toward the edge of the woods near the road and the fields so they could hide and watch the wagon go by. The man shouted out, sounding angry, and the girls ducked behind a bush and waited.

It was Lee Horton. He was dragging a girl into the woods, a hand over her mouth. They could see the pistol tucked into his pants, the way the boss' men sometimes carried them. "Shut up," Horton yelled at the girl. He was pulling at her clothes as he dragged her.

She cried and slapped the air — a big girl, as big as Angelina. When she turned just so they saw that it was Lecie Titus. Birdie rose up on her knees, as if she would go help Lecie. But instead she put her hand on Isola's arm, and Isola looked at her. There was nothing they could do.

Horton pulled the pistol out of his pants. He tossed his hat and pistol on the grass and the gun shone there, silver. And then he pushed Lecie onto the ground and climbed on top of her. When she cried out he slapped her face, and then he kept his hand on her neck.

Isola stared, horrified. She knew what was happening, though no one had ever told her about such things. She felt Birdie's fingers digging into her arm. All she could think was if she had stayed home and done what her mother had told her maybe this wouldn't be happening to Lecie. She thought of sewing, how she hated it, but how she would learn to love it, and would help her mother take in sewing and they would make a lot of money and save it all and then go back to Italy like her father said they would.

Horton stood up and wiped his hand across his face. He picked up his hat and the pistol and pushed the pistol back into his pants. "Get to work," he told Lecie, "before your whole family catches hell." Lecie stood up, whimpering. "You breathe a word to anybody, I'll kill your mama and your daddy — and then I'll come after you." Lecie moved away from him, and then she turned and ran, the back of her ragged dress wet and covered with mud. Horton brushed at his knees and walked out of the woods.

Birdie and Isola stayed crouched behind the bushes, hardly daring to breathe. Birdie's eyes were bright with unshed tears. The girls stood slowly, keeping their eyes on the spot where it had happened. The woods were so quiet. The birds sang, the woods smelled rich and muddy and green, and everything was so peaceful. But as they moved closer to the pond, they saw the matted spot on the ground where Lecie had lain with Horton on top of her. And then near the pond was the little levee they had built, with the silver fish still in it, but the water had seeped out. The fish's mouth moved slowly, with long rests in between.

Isola picked up the fish. It felt dry, and pieces of grass and twigs stuck to it. She threw it back into the pond and it floated.

"Stupid," Birdie said, tears ringing in her voice, and she turned and ran out of the woods as fast as she could. "Stupid Dago."

CHAPTER 17

Ceravone's Death

December 1905

ON a cool, bright December morning, just a week past his ninetieth birthday, old Ceravone, who had been suffering from weakness and coughing spells that no one imagined were serious, surprised everyone by crossing the threshold and departing Sweet Hope forever.

People came in and out of Ceravone's house, offering condolences to his grieving grandson and family. The Halls and Tituses came out of respect, although their eyes were wary after Horton's threat about confiscating their firearms. Even people who didn't know Ceravone — though it was hard for anyone not to know him — felt a catch in their hearts at the news. He was, after all, the last of the first settlers.

The house breathed people, and each breath told a memory of Ceravone. Those who remembered nothing told what they had heard from others. The grandson embraced men and women he had barely met and listened with surprise. "I didn't know," he murmured. "I never heard about that."

To Osvaldo, Ceravone was a wooden coffee grinder. The boy had been warned twice already by his mother to keep his hands to himself in the house but again was reaching up to touch the coffee grinder on a table near the stove. Sticking out of the top of the box was a black metal crank, and when he turned it he felt the hidden gears move beneath his hand, and then the drawer in the brown box filled with ground coffee. The crank and gears and drawer put him in mind of the clock he had seen in the company office, and he wondered if the coffee grinder held some secret about the little men inside the clock.

"Whatcha doin?" Tobe Hall asked.

"We could use a crank and gears," Osvaldo said.

"For what?"

"Something, I bet."

Amalia yanked Osvaldo by the ear toward his sisters where he shoved his fidgeting hands into his torn pockets and sulked. He cast miserable glances at Tobe, then at his sisters. "I'd fly away from here if I could," Osvaldo complained to Tobe.

"Huh!" Fred Titus said to the boy. "Like them fellas over to North Carolina, built a flyin machine." But he wasn't his usual friendly self when he said it.

"What?" Osvaldo said, straightening up.

Fred shook his head over the boy.

"Flying machine?" Osvaldo asked Tobe.

Angelina stood with her arms folded across her chest, secretly trying to feel her small breasts as she watched Ceravone's oldest granddaughter cut pieces of *ciambalone* and cornbread for the visitors. Lecie Titus hovered in the shadows, as if she could hide her growing belly that people could not stop whispering about. Angelina stole a glance at Calvin Hall who stood tall and lanky and embarrassed with the rest of his family, his eyes fixed on the edge of the table in the center of the room as he tried not to smile. She, too, stared at the edge of the table.

Isola watched Angelina and Calvin not look at each other. Then she watched Angelina toss her hair behind her and nervously slide toward the door, pause in the open doorway as if to catch a breath of air, then slip outside, where Isola wanted to be. She looked to see if her mother had noticed.

She had not. When she looked at the door again, Calvin was disappearing into the light. Birdie grinned at her.

Serafin steered clear of the Sant'Angelos, the old man back on the plantation again, but for how long? There was work out there, he had told people, and they treated you halfway decent — if you dared leave this shit hole. Eh. But not one word to Serafin from either of the Sant'Angelos, not a thank you, not a sorry for the trouble we got you in. *Niente. Proprio niente.* Still, after all the man had been through, he had a restless, crazy look in his eyes — calculating, planning. But what did it matter if there were good places to work in America, Serafin thought. They were stuck here at Sweet Hope.

Amalia cast him an understanding, long-suffering look.

It had been a hell of a year. So many sick, his family included, so many dead, and every death was a reminder of what they had gotten themselves into. Think of poor Pietro, who'd paid the ultimate price, drowning during the rains. He sidled closer to his wife. "You know, we should all just up and leave," he said just loud enough for her to hear. "The company won't be able to come after all of us."

"What are you talking about?" she asked, startled to think he had found out about her sneaking away to the village.

"I've been thinking," he said. "Look..." He waved his hand around the room. "This is what it comes to for us."

Her eyes were on him, hard, uncertain. "Don't," she told him. "Not here. Not now."

He let his hand drop heavily to his side. "Eh, Ceravone, the poor bastard."

Fiorenza brushed the hair from her mother's face, the old lady gaunt and yellow-skinned and wheezing now sometimes when she breathed.

All the while old Ceravone lay silent in the room he had shared with his three grandsons, scrubbed and dressed in clean clothes and stretched out one last time on his lumpy bed, a crucifix and burning candles on a table next to him. The room was thick with the smell of hot wax and smoke. People shuffled in, knelt a moment in prayer, touched his face or folded hands, kissed his cheek, then wandered out again to talk with friends or go back to winter plowing or other work.

Hovering, hesitant shapes approached him, Sant'Angelo and his three children. Mrs. Sant'Angelo crossed herself — "poor man" — and knelt to murmur the *Salve, o Regina* and *L'eterno riposo*. Sant'Angelo shook his head at old Ceravone. The girl stood beside her father staring at the corpse while her two brothers hung back, hands in their pockets. No babies. No more babies for them. Sant'Angelo reached into the coffin. He opened one of Ceravone's stiff hands, inserted a coin, and folded the hand closed. Tucked a chunk of bread under Ceravone's other hand, against his stomach where it would not be disturbed when he was lifted into the coffin — and where Ceravone could snatch it up quickly to throw to the yapping dog. Bowed his head to Ceravone and left.

In the kitchen, Amalia suddenly realized her oldest girl was missing. Instinctively, she searched the room for Calvin Hall, then nearly lunged for the door, but stopped herself, lest people notice. It took all her strength to compose herself as she put an arm around Isola's shoulder and bent close to her. Her order was terse and urgent: "Go outside and bring your sister in. Immediately!"

To Serafin she said one word: "Angelina."

It took Serafin a moment to realize what she meant. "Hell," he said, and he started for the door. She stopped him with a nod toward Isola.

"When we get home," she said, and she drew her finger sharply through the air to indicate "the end," *finito*.

Birdie raised her eyebrows at Isola before she slipped out the door and down the two steps into the cool, bright day. Her feet took her past the *vicini* nailing the coffin together, and then along the side of the house. She stopped at the corner and peered around. Angelina was leaning against the back of the house, with Calvin next to her, shyly talking, although Isola could not hear what they said. She glanced up at the small window above them — the room where Ceravone lay? Calvin leaned closer to Angelina as if to whisper something, and she turned her face to him, and Isola could not believe what she was seeing: her sister — were they really? — kissing a boy!

She opened her mouth to yell, but no words came, and almost at the same instant she pulled back around the corner, out of sight. She stared out at the brown fields, breathless, seeing those two faces moving closer again, meeting.

Angelina thought she would die, those hot lips, that soft face. She peered up with one eye at the window above. It was hard for them to get away to see each other, and yet that was all she could think of since that day, that day they'd met in the woods and she'd told him how she'd prayed for him during the flood.

"Yeah?" he'd said, smiling broadly.

She pulled from her neck a thin tarnished chain. At the end hung a small triangular medal that she dangled before placing in his hand.

He peered closely. "Who this lady? This you?"

She laughed, delighted. "It's the *Madonna di Loreto*, from near where I come from. She watches over us." She thought to tell him it was a black *madonna*, but hesitated. "She's dark," she told him. "Like us."

He grinned. "A good luck charm?"

Angelina pointed to the sky. "The mother of God, in heaven." Then blushed at the thought of the *Madonna* witnessing their meeting.

"She's the one I prayed to for you during the flood."

"You talked to this lady 'bout me?"

"Yes, we had a long talk about you."

He cocked his head. "She tell you anything bad 'bout me?" He placed the medal up to his ear and listened, then shook his head. "She ain't talkin now." He slipped the chain around his neck, flicked the medal, let it fall against his chest, posed for her.

She laughed. "Pretty."

His face turned suddenly serious. "You the pretty one." He reached out and touched her hair, her face. "Angelina," he whispered.

She could barely breathe. "How come you like me?" she asked.

He looked surprised by the question. "You sweet," he told her. "Even if you try to act like you ain't sometimes."

She smiled, thinking of how badly she had treated him in the beginning.

"Why you like me?" he asked.

She thought of all the reasons, one tangled up with the rest, not one of them able to be separated out. She shrugged, smiled. "Must be somebody put a spell on me."

His face was against her neck, and his words were hot and sweet against her skin: "Yeah. I liked you the first time I set eyes on you."

"Me too," she whispered, amazed that it must have been true.

Suddenly, the river was moving inside her and inside him at the same time, she could see it in his face. Its enormity and power filled her with a strange, exhilarating fear. The fear said: Come closer; step into my waters. She stood shakily on the dangerous bank. "Put ya' hand here," he told her.

She pulled back. "I can't," she said. But her hand was moving anyway, inching that way, hot, wanting.

But they were not married; they were children; it was a sin; her mother would kill her; the *Madonna* was right there watching them; God would kill her; God who saw all and knew all would send her to hell to burn forever.

She reached up and tucked the medal inside his shirt.

"Jes' touch me, touch m' pants," he said, and he took her hand and she let him.

Quickly, she looked around at the lake, the woods. She was always hearing things, always afraid of being watched. "Somebody will see us."

He pulled her down into the hollow of a fallen tree. "That better?"

Heat surged through her body, a flash of lightning. A door she had never even noticed before flung itself wide open, the doorway flooded with blinding light, that rushing river somewhere behind it. She closed her eyes, sank into the heat of his strong arms as they wrapped around her. "Better," she murmured, as she walked through the door.

***

ISOLA cupped her hands to her mouth and shouted: "Angelina, mama wants you in the house right now!"

Angelina and Calvin bolted to attention, frantically looked around.

Isola ran back into the house. Her mother's eyes were locked on her, but she merely bowed her head and went near the stove, pretending to be interested in a missing button on

Osvaldo's shirt. Amalia waited for the flushed Angelina to appear, then gave her such a look that the girl felt she would shrivel up and die right there. Fancy Hall saw, Step Hall saw, their faces stern and unhappy. Could they tell? Did everybody know?

Angelina knew they were waiting for Calvin to appear now. No one else seemed to notice. Amalia gestured sharply, and Angelina went to her mother's side, yet as far away as possible. "Acting like this, in a dead man's house, before a burial," she hissed at the girl. To Serafin, she turned a face that spoke as loudly as words could have: see what a disgrace your children have become?

The table was full of meager gifts of food and drink for the family and visitors, and people sat or stood around it, filling the room, drinking a glass of wine, eating a piece of cornbread or a sliver of cheese. "He would have been happy about the food, that's for sure," the grandson said. "And the wine."

Calvin slipped in nonchalantly and stayed near the door, refusing to look at his parents who were shooting dagger eyes at him.

"Uh-huh," Lud Titus said to Fred, but she stopped herself. How could she say anything now, with Lecie's belly growing the way it was?

Amalia helped the women clean away dishes and cups and replace them with fresh ones, all the while running her eyes over Angelina. The mothers avoided looking at each other. But then their hands collided as they helped clear the table.

"*Scusi*," Amalia said.

"My boy workin too hard at William's blacksmith t' have time for triflin," Fancy said without looking at her. For she had finally gotten him the job.

"Triflin?" Amalia said. "He come after my girl."

"That what you call it?" Fancy said. They moved around the table, picking up a plate here, putting it down there, trying to keep their voices from rising. "After all I done t' help you, shoulda knowed better." A few people turned their heads to see what was going on. In a minute Step and Serafin moved in to separate their wives.

"White folks, always twistin things to suit them," Fancy told him.

"Wantin to take our guns away," Fred added.

"What's going on?" Lazzaro asked. "Serafin?"

"*Niente*," Serafin answered. "Everybody cool down."

Lazzaro eyed the Halls, then Amalia, then Angelina. "See?" he said to Serafin through clenched teeth. "That's why the Americans say watch out for the niggers."

Step pretended he hadn't heard. "Time to go," he said, nudging Fancy along. He mumbled apologies to Ceravone's family.

Amalia carried an empty coffee cup to a washtub near the stove. She stood there, brushing imaginary crumbs from her hands. Serafin nodded self-consciously to Step. "Tomorrow, we work, eh?"

Step eyed him a moment. "Right," he nodded.

At last, Fancy took Calvin by the arm, and he stumbled over his feet and out the door as the Halls and Tituses bid goodbye and left.

"Well," Fiorenza said.

"There, you see?" Lazzaro added.

Amalia's face told them to mind their own business, don't say a word. She turned to Ceravone's grandson, trying to regain her composure. "It's been a long day for you," she told him.

"Yes, a long day for everybody," he agreed.

The hammering stopped. The two men who had been building the coffin stood in the doorway.

"It doesn't seem right, not going for the priest," Fiorenza said.

"He always said no, no priest for him," the grandson told them, and the others nodded, for they all knew how Ceravone felt about priests.

Especially this one, with a spine like overcooked linguini. "When I die, throw me in the swamp or toss me in a hole in the ground, do what you will. Just don't let a damn priest anywhere near me. I didn't follow one when I was alive. Not about to follow one just because I'm dead."

They looked at the open door beyond which Ceravone lay. A white finger of candle smoke curled out of the door.

La Vecchia let out a shrill laugh and reached for Getulio as he ran past her.

One of the neighbor men cleared his throat nervously. "Well, you see, we've finished with the box. Do you think...?"

Suddenly they were all quiet.

"Oh, Jesus," the grandson murmured.

"The men will lift him into the coffin," Amalia assured him. She glanced at Serafin.

"I'll help," he said. He looked to the room. It was strange, this uneasiness he felt, as if he could hear things, feel things. Maybe it was just fatigue, the slight fever he could not shake.

"Are you ready?" he asked the grandson, who nodded and followed them into the stuffy room.

Just another dead man. Serafin, Lazzaro and Claudio lifted Ceravone into the box. They stepped back, giving the grandson and his family room.

"One last look," the grandson said. He laughed nervously, blinking back tears. "He took us in, you know, after my father died. Brought us here." One by one they bent to kiss Ceravone's cold cheek.

They lingered near the coffin until the neighbor cleared his throat again. His farm, work to do. A hell of a time for a man to die, right after Christmas, and so much work to do. God bless you, Ceravone, just the same.

The grandson nodded, the two men laid the cover on, nailed it shut. The young man stifled a sob.

"It just never feels right without a priest," Fiorenza whispered to Amalia, as they followed the casket out of the house. Amalia steered Angelina by the arm as they walked, pinching the flesh above her elbow and making the girl squirm in pain. "In front of everybody," she hissed at her daughter. "For everybody to see."

Serafin put a hand on his wife's arm, and she turned a distraught face to him. "It's okay," he told her. "It'll pass."

Fiorenza took her mother's sweaty hand when the old woman stumbled. "Be careful, mama."

Osvaldo looked up at the brilliant blue sky where a lone bird with outspread wings hovered against a cloud. Flying machine, he thought.

Maybe Ceravone was right anyway, Amalia thought. What could a priest do for him now?

One of the men reached for the shovel leaning against the side of the house and they filed down the dusty road toward the cemetery, the coffin hoisted onto their shoulders: the grandson and Claudio in front, Serafin and Lazzaro in back.

"An old man can't live forever," Lazzaro murmured. "Just the same..." He shook his head.

The coffin was light, as if old Ceravone had turned to dust already, disappeared into thin air. "Gone," Serafin murmured. He didn't know why he was saying it. The sunlight hurt his eyes.

A wagon was approaching. They guiltily averted their eyes when they realized the driver was Father Odetti. His mangy brown dog sat in the seat beside him like an apologetic schoolboy.

Father Odetti studied the procession. His first thought was that the group must be going to bury one of the Negroes, since he had not been informed of a death. But then he saw there were no Negroes in the group. He slowed the wagon, and the group shifted their eyes at each other and then at the ground. "*Diavolo!*" Serafin muttered.

"Good day," the priest said, confusion sounding in his voice.

"Good day, Father," all but Serafin answered grudgingly.

When Father Odetti saw Serafin, he averted his eyes. He knew full well the trouble he'd caused the family.

The brown dog gave a yap, then jumped from his seat to the ground and started sniffing after the group.

"Bruno!" the priest called. "Bruno, get back here."

Amalia raised her eyes knowingly to Serafin who responded in kind. They could not forgive the betrayal that had cost them so dearly. The other adults fidgeted with their own unspoken opinions: caring more for that mangy dog than for the Italians he'd been hired to help.

The dog was at Serafin's heels. His children bent down to pet him, calling him by name. Serafin kept one hand on the coffin while he shook his leg at the animal. The dog trotted happily along, wagging his tail and yapping now and then with the pure dog pleasure of barking on a cold, sunny day.

"Is there something I can do to help?" Father Odetti asked. He pulled the mule to a stop. The group of mourners, not knowing what else to do, stopped as well.

"Well, you see..." the grandson started.

"No thank you, Father," Serafin said stiffly. "We don't want to take you away from your company duties."

Father Odetti let the sting of the remark go. "Who —?" He stopped himself when he saw the expressions on their faces. It hit him, suddenly. Have I been so blind? he thought. Yet there was no turning back now.

"At least put the coffin in my wagon, let me carry it for you." As an afterthought he murmured: "No one is going to charge you anything."

He slapped the reins against the mule's haunches and turned the wagon in a wide circle, his head dizzy, his face burning, ashamed, mortified.

The mourners averted their gazes. They did not move.

Father Odetti turned in his seat, humiliated. "Slide the box in back; it won't take me a minute out of my way." He watched their reluctant, shuffling movements as they put the box in the wagon, Ceravone's family standing in front of the others, distraught, tight–lipped.

"So, it's Ceravone," Father Odetti said, surprised that the old man was finally gone.

They said nothing.

"I see," the priest murmured. "I understand." But he didn't, really. "Ceravone, God in heaven," he said as he urged the mule forward.

The others fell in behind the wagon, so surprised at the turn of events that several of them began sobbing. Father Odetti intoned the prayers for the dead to the clop of the mule's hooves and the yaps of the dancing dog.

He stopped the wagon on the little rise of land that was Hyner cemetery. Here and there fresh graves dotted the land. He stood apart, repentant, his eyes stinging, as they fell to digging the new hole. When they were finished, he said a final prayer, and they used ropes to lower the coffin into the ground.

"Grandfather," the grandson sobbed. "*Nonno.*"

La Vecchia swayed as she watched with her steely, knowing eyes.

CHAPTER 18

Love Across The Delta

Summer 1906

THERE was love at Sweet Hope, in spite of broken bones and tears and disease and death and hunger and suffering and betrayal and shame and jealousy and fear and despair and loneliness. In a hard place, at a hard time, there was love.

As there had always been.

***

ISOLA loved the glint of a fish's scales beneath the water's surface.

***

ANGELINA loved the glint of light in a certain boy's eyes.

***

OSVALDO loved the flight of birds, the sound of gears meshing, the turning of wheels.

***

TOBE loved the crush of sweet blackberry warm on his tongue; the slap of his bare feet in oozing crawfish mud.

***

Birdie loved her friend Isola, but loved even more a boy named Shake.

***

Amalia loved the clots of blood that would have become her fourth child, and loved as well the three flesh and bone children that emerged from her body whole; lived, and grew.

***

All of the children loved not working.

***

Lee Horton loved to watch Angelina Pascala, the long–haired, olive–skinned, stuck–up Dago beauty, loved to think just what he'd like to do to her if he could only get her alone somewhere.

***

Father Odetti loved God and his dog Bruno.

***

Fish loved the water; birds loved the air.

***

The river loved its bed, and loved to leave it, too. The flooding waters loved the low flat land.

***

Serafin Pascala loved his wife, sometimes in tears, sometimes in joy, sometimes in unabashed need, sometimes in passion tinged with wariness or hesitation because of the child that was lost and the suffering of the children that were living.

***

LAZZARO loved his wife Fiorenza, but no matter how much they loved each other they could not make another child; in sadness and gratitude they loved Getulio, their one and only.

***

La Vecchia loved the air.

***

STEP Hall turned his weary face to his wife Fancy lying by his side while their three children slept or pretended to sleep, and he waited for something to stir in both of them, something that would relieve and replenish them; then received her touch, her kiss, received her breath, her very life. He was feeling older each year, and this year, especially, was bad, wearing him down.

Fancy Hall loved to feel the breathing, living man beside her, loved his weariness and his strength, his raw–boned goodness, his clean–earth hands, his true love.

"Want me get up, rub your feet?" Fancy asked him.

"I'm all right." He lay a tired hand on her shoulder.

"Go soak your feet, and I'll rub 'em, an 'your legs too."

"You should be sleepin," he said.

She turned, put her hand to his neck, and began kneading the muscles there. He let out a sigh. "You gotta be careful, Step."

He knew she was referring to Horton.

"Don't worry 'bout me."

"I'm sayin for all a' us." Her fingers pressed into the knots on his shoulders, his neck, and he felt his body relaxing while his mind tensed at her words. "This farm work gettin too much," she said. "Maybe time to look for somethin else."

"Hmm," he said. What else was there in the Delta, after all these years? He'd missed his chance for leaving.

As if she could read his mind, she told him, "William got his blacksmith shop. People got stores. You good with numbers."

She was just dreaming. He was too old to go looking for a different kind of work.

"The children, if they went to a reg'lar school, all year," she said. "'Least Tobe an' Birdie get a chance for decent work when they grown, not sharecroppin."

"Gonna make 'em all take care 'a us. We won't have t' worry 'bout workin no more," he told her, half–joking. "Calvin already—"

"Calvin," she said. She stopped rubbing his shoulders. 'You better talk wi' that boy."

"I already talked."

"Well, it ain't took. You gotta do somethin."

He knew full well—as did Fancy—there was no talking anyone out of love.

"He's a grown boy, Fancy. How you gonna stop a stallion when he see a fine mare prancin in front a' him?"

"She ain't no fine mare. She just another poor fool workin in the dirt."

***

ALL across Sweet Hope, men and women loved each other, some of them planting seeds that were not cotton, seeds that would instead become new human flesh. Some of these men and women did not even think how those children would drive them deeper into debt and despair before they became old enough—if they lived—to help work the farm, though some of the lovers did think such thoughts even in the midst of their passion.

***

FIFTEEN–year old Angelina Pascala lay fitfully in her bed, haunted with aching and longing, waiting for the sound of her family's quiet, even breathing; then she gently lifted the mosquito netting so as not to disturb her sister and brother, glided across the worn, cracked floor, and slipped outside into the night. He was waiting by the chicken shed. Calvin, the boy she had barely noticed until suddenly she saw no one else but him, thought of nothing else but him day and night. They huddled behind the shed, out of sight.

Calvin took Angelina's hand in his own shy, hot hand. A moment of awkward, embarrassed giggling. Then quiet.

"Did anybody see you?" she whispered.

"You know I'm too slick t' get caught."

Her brow crinkled. "I hate sneakin around. We shouldn't have to."

A sliver of moon pulsed in the sky. Crickets, frogs, and peepers sang in the night.

"And I hate these Americans," she said.

He pulled her closer, smoothed her hair. "Everything be all right," he said, trying to hide the worry in his own voice.

"If we ran away, they wouldn't be able to tell us what to do." She stopped herself, lowered her voice. The chickens clucked softly in the shed behind them.

Calvin laughed. "You sound like your sister, talkin that way. Or mine."

"You think I wouldn't?"

"I told you, soon's I save some money, I'm gon' take you to a nice city. We go up north, live in a big house, maybe t' Chicago. Ever hear a' that?"

"No."

"You wouldn't run off an' leave me, would you? Find some other fella?"

She looked at him a long while. He was smiling, joking with her, but serious too. "How come your family stays here? You can leave if you want to."

"Daddy think he's some big boss here." He shook his head. "You seen what kind a' boss he is."

She held both his hands in hers and squeezed them. "That don't matter. You know I don't want no other fella."

"You stuck wi' me," Calvin told her. He leaned close and kissed her.

Even in the night she could see how bright his face shone.

Even in the night her beauty took his breath away. "You so pretty."

She smiled, blushed. "You always say that." Heat surged through her body, not the blistering daytime Delta summer heat but a vital, living heat from within.

"Calvin," she whispered. Music, the mysterious beautiful musical sound of his name. There was no other name like it.

"Angelina." He mouthed it slowly, to make it last longer.

"*Ti voglio bene*," she murmured.

"You can say that again," he told her.

✳✳✳

Isola loved teasing her sister, as did Osvaldo who also loved gears and coffee grinders because they moved, because they made sounds and did miraculous things. Isola loved Angelina's foolishness and inability to hide the fact that she was smitten by Calvin. But as much as she teased, Isola secretly wondered what this incomprehensible attraction between a man and woman was, and wondered if it would ever happen to her.

✳✳✳

It was a long, hot summer of love.

✳✳✳

How many times Amalia had lain awake beside her husband, her bruised heart aching for him, for her children, for her mother and family in Italy, for God, His Son, and the Holy Mother. As soon as she thought of the Holy Family, she chastised herself. What did she know of suffering compared to that other mother?

It was not childbirth, but what came afterwards that set the womb in torment.

She saw her babies as she held them to her breast, drinking her life-giving milk. Now they were little strangers, beyond her reach. The more she called them back, the farther she drove them.

When she tried to see ahead, her insides grew cold. Osvaldo was an odd boy, plagued by headaches and who knew what else — because of her, because she had insisted on taking him to the lake that day and then had not kept him safe. Isola was defiant, boisterous, *maschiaccio*, and only getting worse. And Angelina — defying her in a different way, sneaking around with that *'Mericano* boy Calvin.

There was no shame greater than that of a mother with no control over her own children. How could she blame Serafin for that?

What about all these Italian boys? she had asked Angelina. What about Claudio? Angelina had only scoffed at her.

"Do you want to disgrace your family?" Amalia had asked the girl.

"All you ever do is complain," Angelina answered.

"Never follow a man," she told the girl. "It only brings heartache."

"I wish you and papa liked each other," Angelina had replied.

Amalia had been taken aback by the comment. *"Like?"* she thought.

Now, in the night, the words chafed at her. There was like inside, of course there was. Like and love — and the bad, too, all mixed together. She touched her weary husband's hand. He was asleep.

***

THE weigh scales at the cotton pens and at the gin mill loved their summer emptiness as well as the anticipation of fullness and weight, the caress of human hands and cotton fibers.

***

FRED Titus' concertina loved the caress of his confident, tired fingers and called to him even after a long day of work. The night's bullfrog–croaking, insect–chirping music competed with the joyful or wistful or happy or melancholy or foot-thumping concertina music.

***

THE cotton boll loved its closed, secret darkness and loved as well its bursting into sunlight; and though the open fluff of cotton that lay nestled in its hard brown husk loved the soft touch of human fingers, it loved too the pierced flesh, throbbing with the ooze of salty blood.

***

HARLAN Gates loved his plantation, the largest in the Delta, loved it as a man loves his famous and successful business, loved the rise and fall of prices, the thrill of chance, the excitement of competition, the exhilaration of it all. He loved the prestige of his family line, the power of his name.

***

THE cottonmouth snake loved the brown water of the swamp and loved the terror it struck.

***

THE undiscerning vulture loved the stink and taste of all carcasses: rabbit, turtle, dog, mule, man.

***

THE earth at Hyner loved, in a way, the painful battering pleasure of the shovel's blade, then loved the snug relief of a rough pine box heavy with a body whose soul had left. The hole loved its own returning earth. The worm loved the earth, especially at Hyner.

***

THE ass and the horse loved each other, and both loved green grass and a bucket of oats.

***

THE creaking wooden cart loved its mule; the mule loved the end of the road. The long road loved the trouble it caused.

***

LEE Horton loved every scheme he hatched and carried out spurred on by his other love, a self–righteous sense of persecution mixed with an overblown sense of his own worth. Because he was worth more. Harlan Gates making him work with a nigger, telling him to ask Step Hall when something went wrong. And all the while Hall crossed the line, defied him, the tenants turning to Hall for help or answers. Harlan Gates didn't know the half of it. Lee Horton loved proving he was right.

***

ANGELINA Pascala loved the sound of a meadowlark outside her window at night, or chirping close by in the field or woods during the day, for this meadowlark was named Calvin Hall, and he called to her in his own secret, just–for–her call. As much as she loved meeting at night, Angelina loved sneaking away from the field into an empty shed or mule barn or under cover of the woodsy locust brush to meet with Calvin in broad daylight.

They were meeting again in the lake woods during a noon dinner break, as they had so often that summer. Angelina huddled near a locust tree, listening. Each creaking branch or rustling leaf made her turn and look.

Finally Calvin arrived, apologetic. "Pa wanted me to stay help 'im with a broke wagon wheel."

"Hmm," she said. He could see she didn't believe him.

He kicked at the ground. "All my fam'ly care 'bout any-more's who's white folks an' who's black folks," he told her.

"That again," she said. It was similar to what she heard: "Marchigian' with a Marchigian'." She held her arm out alongside Calvin's. "Hardly any difference."

"Don't matter no way," he said, running his fingers along her arm. "Ain't your skin I'm took by."

She drew him close.

"Why you shakin?" he asked, smoothing her hair.

She glanced into the woods behind them. "I don't know."

It had been a couple weeks now, with her worrying more each day, and now there was something else, too, this feeling — funny, different.

He kissed her, gently, then pulled back. "You cold."

"I wish I had my own farm," she told him.

"What you talkin 'bout, farm?" he laughed. "Thought we was gonna go up north, be city folks. You wanna be a farmer?"

This made her laugh, too. "No." She didn't know why she was saying such things. "Sometimes I could just — "

She looked beyond him again, into the woods, then lowered her voice. "Did you hear something? Did anybody see you?"

He, too, turned and looked. "Ain't nothing out there 'cept a bunch a birds." He grinned. "An' snakes."

Tears filled Angelina's eyes.

"Hey now," Calvin said.

"I'm afraid I might... Oh, Calvin. I think I might be..." *Incinta*, she thought. "Might gonna have a baby." It sounded bad either way she said it.

He came to attention, the smile drained from his face.

His reaction only made her pull farther away, and the tears fall more freely.

"I don't know," she told him, wrapping her arms around herself. "Maybe I'm not. *Dio santo.*"

"God A'mighty," he said.

"They'll kill us," she moaned. "My God, when my mother finds out..."

His own parents, he thought, after his father had just given him hell besides.

"A baby?" he murmured. "I never thought 'bout havin no baby." And it was true, no matter all his father's warnings.

She shook her head, trying to make it go away. "We should have never..."

"A baby," he said.

"Stop! Will you stop saying that?" She thrust her face into her hands.

It gave him the strangest feeling to see her like that, with the sun glinting off her dark hair while the birds called softly to each other and the ducks floated beyond them in the dark water. He touched her hair gently, his insides all stirred up.

"We can git married," he told her, surprised at his own words.

Her head shot up, and she searched his face to see if he was joking. "They're hollering if we go near each other in a cotton field," she told him. "You think they'll let us marry?"

"Maybe that preacher a' yours could —" He shook his head. "I can jes' see that." Suddenly he understood what others were talking about. But he loved her.

"Maybe Lecie can help me," Angelina said. "Get me some root tea."

"No!" he answered, aghast. "You can't do that."

She knew she would never do such a thing, not really. But how could she live like this?

"It's mine," he told her. "Ours."

"But I don't know if I really am," she said, even though another part of her knew the truth.

He leaned back against the tree again and looked at her so long that she blushed. "Stop," she told him.

"Lissen," he said. "We gonna name it Angel, after you. If it's a boy, we still gonna name 'im Angel. Okay?"

She lowered her head, afraid of it being real.

"Okay?" he insisted.

"Angel," she murmured.

He wrapped his arms around her, pulled her close, his face warm against her neck. She thought she would die. He thought he would die.

***

LEE Horton thought he would die from his delirious scandalous unspeakable discovery where he stood hidden, watching from a distance after following them. Step Hall's oldest son. Son of his nemesis, by God, caught red-handed — with the very girl he had had his eye on himself, the shiny-haired, olive-skinned Dago. He knew it. He knew something had been going on. Don't that beat all? he thought.

He was infuriated.

Exultant.

"Kiss me," Angelina told Calvin, desperate to shake the worry.

His hot mouth on hers, his strong arms holding her.

"We gonna be awright," Calvin murmured into her neck, and she held on tighter.

While Lee Horton — disgusted, furious, ecstatic, hidden — inched his own hand down his own pants, watching, moving his hand, until...

***

ANGELINA sat up breathless. "We can't," she told Calvin. "Not now. Oh God." Wasn't that what had caused the whole trouble to begin with? But she was torn, she wanted to be with him now, always. If they could just be alone together, the two of them, without everybody else thinking they had something to say about it.

"I have to go back to work, my pa — "

Sweaty, breathless, not from work but from love and from the secret she had dared to speak.

"I want ya so bad."

"We have to figure out what we're going to do," she told him.

***

LEE Horton loved the vile, scheming, contriving, self-righteous vindication beginning to take hold in his mind. All those years of humiliation, Step Hall and the Dagoes, daring to challenge him, refusing to see his worth. These two kids now, on each other like dogs in heat, the two families tied in a knot tighter than any he could have imagined.

"Too good," Lee Horton thought to himself. "Kill two birds with one stone." He stifled a laugh at his wittiness. "Bout time, too." God finally paying him back for all the humiliation and injustice he had suffered.

***

THE whip loved the tender flesh of the back.

***

BLOOD loved the thirsty soil.

CHAPTER 19

Jumping Contract

July 1906

No one rejoiced as Lecie Titus' belly grew bigger. Throughout the months of her ordeal, Lecie remained frightened, closed–up, and silent. No matter how much Lud harangued her daughter, the girl would not name the culprit.

When the fair–skinned, red–haired baby was born that spring, Fancy and Lud exchanged disturbed and knowing glances. They placed the infant in Lecie's arms, and she looked down at him with surprise and tenderness and repulsion.

Family members had taken to calling him "Boy," or sometimes "Baby," as if naming him would mean acknowledging some awful truth. Every now and then Lud or Fred would feel the questions or the rage build up and spill over and once again would try to get Lecie to name the evildoer.

The baby was a few months old when the hot weather and hard life caused another spell of outrage in Lud. This time she called for Reverend Monroe and Miss Betty, and asked the Halls to come help and bear witness. Calvin and Tobe were sent outside, although they made Birdie stay and listen "less somethin like this ever happen to you."

Reverend Monroe folded his coffee–colored hands over his stomach and smiled kindly at Lecie while Miss Betty patted Lecie's hand and tried to coax her into talking. Lecie bowed her head, trembling from the attention.

"It happen, I don't know how."

"Don't know how!" Lud spat. "Why you so dedicated to protectin the scoundrel that done this to you? We all know that man Horton done it."

Lecie's head dropped lower.

"Take one look at that poor baby an' you know." She told the others: "I like to cut his business right outta him. Thinkin he can get away w' this." Then she softened, as she had many times to no avail: "Honey, we know it wasn't no fault a' yours."

Lecie bit her lip and looked away.

Reverend Monroe cleared his throat. Miss Betty put a hand on Lecie's head. "We're just tormentin this girl. She been through enough." She raised her face to the ceiling, and the others followed as she began to entreat God to lead them down the right path.

Miss Betty's voice grew louder as the minutes passed. Birdie clenched her fists at her side and let out a sigh.

Outside, Calvin and Tobe kicked around in the dirt. "Don't know why they makin such a fuss 'bout a darn baby," Tobe said.

The words sent a shiver through Calvin. He looked his younger brother up and down. "You don't?"

"Jes' another squallin baby," Tobe said.

Calvin was torn in two, part of him wanting to educate Tobe while he showed off his own learning; the other part of him sweating over the whole idea. "It's the way the baby come is the problem," he told his brother.

"Huh?

"Somebody force himself on Lecie."

Tobe understood birds and bees, but this was something else. He had a fair idea what it was, though.

"Ain't like when two people like each other," Calvin pointed out, and as soon as he said the words his face went hot.

Tobe grinned. "You should know, huh?"

"What?" Calvin said, suddenly panicking. But you couldn't tell a thing yet by looking at Angelina's stomach.

Tobe pointed to his brother's neck.

Calvin looked down, slapped his hand over the religious medal, then tucked it under his shirt. His father had already asked him about the "charm" he'd been wearing, but Calvin insisted it was nothing, just something he'd found outside the lumber mill.

"Mm–hmm, found it," Step had said. "Must be some Italian lost it, 'cause they the only ones I see wearin such things." He narrowed his eyes and gave his son a warning: "I better not be hearin 'bout no girl trouble."

Calvin had swallowed hard, barely able to get out a feeble "Yessir."

Now he struggled to get back on the subject with Tobe, wondering if by some strange power Tobe knew they were planning to meet outside Angelina's chicken shed that night.

Perspiration was breaking out on his face as his father's warning came back to him: a black man can't love a white woman, 'cause white people gonna call it rape. And then Step had gone on to describe what the white men would do to any black man who committed such an act. Calvin shuddered as he tried to get hold of his thoughts. His father was wrong. They loved each other, and both wanted to be with each other. But a baby? He didn't want to think what his parents would do when they found out. He stared hard at Tobe. "See what I'm sayin?"

Tobe tried to keep himself from grinning even wider. "Nuh–uh," he said. "Tell me over 'gain."

***

THE Pascalas were making another sweep through their field, weeding the knee–high cotton. Osvaldo worked with a tattered rag tied around his head as he dreamed about gears and snares and flying machines and Tobe's new find that he said he wanted to show them. Isola was hoping to catch a glimpse of Birdie or Tobe, maybe sneak off to play with them. Angelina worked as far away from the two as she could, while burning with the secret that was growing inside her. Tonight, she thought, she would see her American boy who was not at all like the one she had long imagined.

He could do anything, be anything, he told her. They were standing at the lake, gazing at the village on the other side. "There's all kinds a places out there," Calvin told her. "Cities big as heaven up north. They got fact'ries to work in bigger'n this whole plantation." His father was old–fashioned, afraid to try anything new. "But not me."

"Like mine," she'd said, but it wasn't true. He'd come to America, hadn't he? But now — this would kill him.

"Okay," she'd told Calvin. "But shouldn't we wait until after he's born before we leave? Or should we go now?" Now was too soon. Everything was happening too fast. He'd laughed, and kissed her.

***

EVERY now and then Amalia glanced at her children, disturbed by the hidden lives she saw written on their faces in a language she could not read.

She was aching inside for another reason, too. It had been barely two weeks, but now, even something as simple as the wind turning a leaf in the field, or the shadow of a bird passing by made her look twice, as if La Vecchia were right there among them as always.

The old lady had turned into a sack of bones by summer, phlegmy and barely eating. When she walked along the dusty road, she looked like a bodiless dress flapping in the breeze.

Even her head seemed to have sunk into the folds of the cloth. But what could you say to Fiorenza about it? And what could anyone have done, anyway?

That Sunday at Fiorenza's, her whole family was there. The old lady coughed and played with her yarn while the others sat playing *briscola*; even the children crowded around the table watching them throw their cards down. La Vecchia began circling the table, winding long strands of yarn around the backs of their chairs. Fiorenza merely sighed at the woman.

Amalia could take it no more. "*Basta*," she'd said. She stood and pulled the yarn from her back while Fiorenza tried to quiet her mother and steer her to the bedroom.

"She's just an old woman," Serafin said, embarrassed. "Amalia, what's wrong with you?"

When Fiorenza returned, Amalia apologized. "The heat, maybe a touch of fever myself." She couldn't say why the old woman was irritating her so.

"It's all right."

They resumed playing cards.

Soon they heard a thump and scrape, like the sound of someone bumping into a piece of furniture. Minutes passed. Serafin laid a card on the table. "Well, this is no good," he said. "I'm sunk."

Claudio looked up, cocked his head. After a minute, he started toward the bedroom.

"God, no," Fiorenza cried, and she rushed past Claudio.

"Oh, Jesus," Lazzaro murmured as he went after his wife.

Amalia played it over and over in her mind. Just like that: here one minute, gone the next.

"We all have to go sometime," Serafin had told her afterwards.

"I yelled. I was mean to her," Amalia answered. "Five minutes later she was dead."

He put a hand on hers, trying to comfort her. He knew all about death and guilt, after all.

***

SERAFIN let his hoe drop, scraped up a weed, calculated the size of his plants, their vitality. Things had been rough lately, yet he felt strong in spite of everything. It gave him some satisfaction to know it wasn't just the farmers who had suffered from the flood. Sweet Hope Company itself — owner Harlan Gates and his banking associates — had made no profit for the first time ever, and even the managers were grumbling that their wages were being cut. Of course, they blamed the farmers.

But there were things to be thankful for. The Pascalas' chickens were alive and had quickly returned to laying. They'd been able to trade a few of the eggs and some of Amalia's sewing on the plantation for food or goods. The children were actually learning to read and write, piecemeal as it was, with Miss Betty's school, their own priest be damned. And now, this morning, two chicks hatched. Life goes on, he thought. Like the rains and flood waters giving birth to all that lush vegetation. Everything grew, even some of what they had planted.

And just a couple days ago he and Lazzaro had found a new, thick stand of grape vines in the woods, while cutting firewood. It was astonishing how many vines grew, and when they looked closely they saw that the vines were loaded with hundreds of tiny green clusters just forming from the flowers. They pulled weeds and cultivated around the roots to give the grapes an extra boost. "In the fall we'll have barrels of wine," Lazzaro said. "Grapes to eat, grapes to drink." They could not believe their good luck.

"Let's just pray no one else tries to claim them," Serafin said.

Lazzaro found a long bare branch and drove it into the earth, then ripped a strip of cloth from the bottom of his shirt and tied it to the stake. "There, in the name of Lazzaro *e* Serafino, *paesani di Montignano*, I claim this land." They stood with their arms around each other, laughing, their hearts full.

"*Senti*," Serafin called to Amalia. "The cotton's growing good, no? It'll be a good crop this year." She wiped the sweat from her brow. "Maybe. We'll see." She was thin, all bone and muscle. He was always surprised by how strong she was, inside and out.

"Why don't you go in?" he told her.

The children looked up hopefully.

"I'll finish up here with the kids."

She took a few more hacks at the earth, then headed in. "I'll see what I can find for supper."

Isola offered to go fishing. "Me too," Osvaldo said.

"Keep weeding," he told them.

"There's hardly any weeds left," Isola said.

"If you look hard enough you'll find some. Angelina, watch what you're doing." She was chopping without paying attention, almost digging up some of the cotton.

"I'm sorry, papa, I guess I'm just not a farmer."

***

THEIR work was almost done when Lazzaro and Claudio approached, each man carrying a small pack over his shoulder.

"What's with the sacks?" Serafin asked.

The men looked tired, but happy, too. "We're on our way out of here," Lazzaro told him, patting the bundle he carried. "Just for a few months." Claudio nodded in agreement.

Serafin was stunned. He looked around to see if anyone was close enough to hear. The children had scattered a little distance away. "Jumping contract?" Serafin whispered. "Are you crazy?"

"No, no, it's not like that at all," Lazzaro told him.

"The company knows," Claudio said. "They gave permission."

"That's impossible," Serafin said. "They'd never do such a thing."

"Things are changing, my friend," Lazzaro said. "After that damn flood nearly wiped us out — " He paused. It was easy to see he was thinking of the old lady. He cleared his throat, stood tall. "Hell, the company has to make some money — they know we're not running away." Another pause. "Sant'Angelo is coming with us."

"Sant'Angelo?" Serafin nearly choked. So, he had been right about the crazy look in the man's eyes. "What the hell are you doing with that idiot?" he blustered. "He didn't learn the first time? You'll end up in jail, just like him."

"No, he knows his way around," Lazzaro said in a wounded tone. "He wants to go again, and he can show us the ropes."

"The new manager, Garlock, he said it was okay," Claudio added.

Serafin shook his head in disbelief. Of all people at Sweet Hope to try such a crazy scheme, not his good friend Lazzaro.

The sun was beginning to sink in the sky. In a couple hours it would be nightfall. "Your wife, your son," he said to Lazzaro. "How can you think of leaving them at a time like this?"

"You're right," Lazzaro answered. "Fiorenza's all broken up, me too. But it's the best time for the crops, so I have to jump at the chance."

Serafin pointed to the sky. "The sun's setting. Where the hell do you think you're going at night?"

Lazzaro tried to explain their plan. With the company's permission they would leave at night, walk north out of the plantation around the lake and into the village from that direction. They'd go as far as they could before it got too dark to see, then wait for the moon to come out to light the way.

"If the company says it's okay for you to leave, then why do you have to sneak out in the night?" Serafin demanded.

"Hey, can you see us trying to walk all that way in the daytime, with the blistering heat and humidity, and a thousand eyes watching us?" Lazzaro said. There was an early morning train they'd take down into Louisiana. They had names of a turpentine mill and a cotton mill that they'd heard took hard workers. "Now, with the old lady gone — " His face folded. For all his bravado, he was just as shaken as his wife over the old lady's death. "What can I do?" Lazzaro said, shrugging his shoulders, a catch in his voice. "We have to go when we have the chance. You know, I never could have gone while Fiorenza's mother was alive."

"What the devil are you thinking?" Serafin insisted. "You know these farms are too much for a woman alone with a child."

"We've worked like dogs the last few days to get our land weeded. In another month the cotton will be too high to weed. They can slow down a little, and we'll be back in time to pick."

Serafin's stomach sank. They must have been planning their departure for some time, yet Lazzaro hadn't spoken a word of it to him. Planning it with an outsider, that Sicilian Sant'Angelo. And the other day, finding the grapes, what was that all about? Lying the whole time?

Serafin could see nothing but trouble ahead for the men, and things breaking down on the plantation for the women, help needed with the weeding, and who would they turn to then? He had learned his lesson with the Sant'Angelos, trying to bail them out. He grabbed Lazzaro's arm. "You fool. You can't trust this damn company. They'll throw you on a chain gang somewhere. What's to become of your family then?"

His children turned in the direction of the rising voices. Lazzaro pulled away, his own anger rising.

"You should be happy for me," he said. "*Pah*! That's why I didn't tell you in the first place. People are right, what they say about you — what you're turning into. You act more like a black American than an Italian."

"Hey," Claudio said. "*Cugino.*"

"What the hell are you talking about?" Serafin said, the blood rising in his chest.

"You. All the time you spend with *i neri*, and now your own daughter –" He glanced over at Angelina who was watching him now. "God knows what she's doing with one of them. How do you think that makes the rest of us look?"

"You no good son–of–a–bitch," Serafin said, raising his fist.

Claudio stepped between the two men as Serafin's children inched closer.

"These damn managers have been treating us like *i neri* too long," Lazzaro shouted. "Don't you know we should stay with our own kind, prove to the *bianchi* that we're not the same as the black ones? Maybe things would be a little different for us."

"You're blaming me? Blaming me and the black ones for the way the company treats us?" He felt the blood rush up through his neck. "Who the hell do you think it was who taught us how to get by in this hell of a land?"

"Maybe if there was nobody like your friend Step Hall, the company would have wised up and stopped shipping in Italians, and we wouldn't be in this mess," Lazzaro insisted. "Look, don't you understand? We have to make the Americans see we're *bianchi*, like them."

"I don't even know who you are," Serafin said, waving his hand in disgust. "I thought you were my *pad'in*." He shook his head, spit out something bitter, started to stomp away, then turned and came back.

"I'll tell you something. It's that Horton, all the managers, and the owner with all their lies and rottenness — they're the ones making problems at Sweet Hope, not Step Hall. We were niggers to the *americani* before we came here. We were just too ignorant to see it. Remember, they hired our own *paesani* agents to lie to us so we'd come over. How soon you forget."

The children stood frozen in fear as Lazzaro glared back at their father with a look of hatred.

"Why are you fighting?" Osvaldo yelled.

"It's nothing," Claudio told the boy. "Just a couple of hot heads."

"Well, stop. Let your heads cool off."

"Maybe we better get going, eh?" Claudio asked Lazzaro, and he tugged at his arm.

Lazzaro pushed his hand aside. "Yeah, leave him, *il negro italiano.*"

The two men readjusted their packs and left without looking back.

"Get to work," Serafin ordered his children with a wave of his hand. His face burned with shame over what the children had just witnessed. He dug his hoe viciously into the earth.

Isola nudged her sister. "See what you've done," she whispered.

Angelina held her tongue, praying her father had not heard as she, too, went back to hoeing. She moved the blade slowly, as if afraid to disturb the earth.

Finally Serafin could contain himself no longer. "That's what you get for being a friend," he sputtered to his children. "Don't trust anybody. The more you help somebody, the more they'll turn on you." He hacked at the earth.

Negro italiano. "The bastard," he said out loud. Then to his children, he pointed to a row: "Here, clean over here. Osvaldo, you clean over there." He moved away from them so they would not see what a state he was in. Tears seeped from his eyes and he cursed himself for being so weak.

He would have a long talk with his wife when he went home, tell her — what? "The thing is — " But his mind was reeling; he could not sort out what he wanted to say.

Of course they knew Angelina was sneaking around with Calvin and had warned her against it. But what was this *merda* about people talking? What business was it of anyone's? Angelina was too young, that's what he and Amalia were concerned about, that was the simple truth, wasn't it? And weren't they all in Sweet Hope together, after all? "Damn, damn," he found himself muttering aloud. When he looked up, his children were watching him.

"Daddy, why don't you go in?" Isola said. "We'll finish weeding."

"Will the company really let them leave the plantation?" Osvaldo asked.

"*Dio santo,*" he said. "Go home. Let's all go home."

Instead of cutting through their field back to the house, he led them onto the road and around that way to see if there was anything going on that he should know about. The other fields were scattered with workers. Serafin looked down the road in the direction Lazzaro and Claudio had gone. Empty. All was quiet, save for the calling birds and droning insects. "They won't even make it past Hyner," he said. "Where the hell do they think they're going to sleep tonight, in a ditch?"

The children dared not answer.

"Have the Hall kids said anything to you?" he asked. "Did Step tell his kids anything about us?"

The children shook their heads silently.

"Better stay away from the Halls for now," he told them. "Just for a few days." He didn't know why he was saying it. Lazzaro, the son-of-a-bitch. "You hear me?"

They answered with guilty, worried expressions.

"But —" Osvaldo started. He held his tongue.

Above them, a bird sailed in graceful, widening circles that carried it slowly away from Sweet Hope.

CHAPTER 20

Showdown

July 1906

Tobe showed off his find: a pulley he'd snagged from outside the lumber mill. A metal hook stuck out of the top, with the round, grooved metal encased in a cage. A few inches of frayed rope dangled below.

"Why'd they throw it out?" Osvaldo asked, reaching for it.

"Rope jumped its track. Metal look bent."

Osvaldo poked his finger in at the edge. "Needs a new rope. Ain't broke enough to throw out."

"You stole it," Isola said.

"What you know? Was in the junk heap."

"Huh!" she told him.

"It's ours now. Be a good way to fly, with a pulley."

Osvaldo peered up into a tree. "You think we could hook it up there and test it?" His mind raced with possibilities. Maybe this was the way to launch their flying machine: hoist it high up in a tree, then push off into air, like a bird. But so far they'd only built a wooden box big enough for one of them to squat in, and a rickety frame for one wing.

They began tugging at some of the hanging vines, but they were too thick to fit the pulley track. The thinner vines wouldn't be strong enough to hold any weight.

The ground at the marshy end of the lake was soggy, and swarms of mosquitoes attacked their arms and faces. The air was ripe with the smell of rotting plants and muck, mixed with the sharp odor of marsh grass and wildflowers.

"We don't even know how to build this machine," Isola said, exasperated now from the heat and mosquitoes. "How we gonna put all this junk together?"

They stared at the odds and ends they'd hidden beneath the drooping branches of a locust bush: the wooden box surrounded by pieces of wire, scraps of wood and tin, a discarded cog wheel, empty tin cans.

First Osvaldo had imagined some kind of cart or wagon with wings, driven by a steam engine, much like a train or gin mill or steam boat. But finally, after debating with Tobe, they decided that a set of wings might work better. They could attach them to their arms and fly the way birds flew. But they wondered how those brothers Fred Titus told them about had flown — riding together in a cart, or each with his own set of wings? Mr. Titus had called it a flying machine, not just wings. But maybe he was just making up a story. After all, Osvaldo reasoned, if you could really fly a machine through the sky, then wouldn't everyone be doing it? Wouldn't people leave Sweet Hope and fly away wherever they wanted if it was true?

"If we gather 'nough junk, we'll be able to figure out somethin that'll work," Tobe said.

Even Isola, who would rather swim with the fishes in the lake than hunker over broken cogs and gears, started to believe in a machine that could fly. Birdie thought she was crazy. "You always playin with them boys now," she'd told Isola. But Birdie was the crazy one. Liking a boy, a boy named Shake. She couldn't believe it was happening to Birdie, too. Isola looked at her brother, then at Tobe. She couldn't see it, couldn't understand what it was about boys that made girls crazy.

A branch cracked, and the children froze. Isola motioned the two boys away from the hiding place.

A baby whimpered, and in a moment, Lecie Titus approached. She carried a burlap sack and a knife in one hand, her baby in a sling across her chest.

Lecie put an arm around the baby and stared into the bushes, listening, then moved quietly on. Every now and then she stopped and listened. Tobe nudged Isola. Lecie paused for a long time at the swampy edge of the water before dropping the sack. She leaned over the edge of the water, holding the baby with one hand while she jabbed with the knife at the root of a tree. When she straightened up, a green plant with dangling, thin brown roots dripped from her hand.

"Hey, Lecie," Tobe called.

The girl swung around, the baby clutched to her breast. She let the plant fall as she held the knife in front of her.

When she saw who it was, she dropped her hand.

Tobe laughed. "You seen a hent?" he asked as the three of them came forward.

Lecie rolled her eyes up at the trees, then around at the bushes. "Why you here?" she said.

Isola stared at the lump that was the wrapped–up child. She hadn't yet seen this baby that everybody was talking about, even though it was a few months old.

"We playin, what's it to ya?" Tobe said.

"You don't gotta be mean," Isola told Tobe.

Lecie lowered her head and mumbled, "Swamp ain't a playin place."

"You diggin roots?" Osvaldo asked her. When she didn't answer, he picked up the sack and handed it to her. "We got a secret," he said.

"*Asino!*" Isola yelled.

"Damn big–mouth!" shouted Tobe.

Lecie smoothed her hand over her baby's covered head as if she hadn't heard a word, and stood swaying.

"She don't even care, no way," Tobe said. He was thinking of what Calvin had told him had been done to Lecie.

"Can you keep a secret?" Osvaldo asked her.

"You're not s'posed to tell anybody," Isola protested.

"If she's root diggin here, she's gonna find out," Osvaldo insisted. "She won't tell nobody, will you, Lecie?"

The girl said nothing.

"See?" Osvaldo said.

Reluctantly, Isola and Tobe watched Osvaldo push aside the hanging branches to show Lecie their collection of junk. Lecie peered in as her baby whimpered and kicked an arm out of the blanket. The children stared at the flailing arm. It was pale, all right, but too small to tell much.

Lecie blinked at the pile. In a minute she was back at the water's edge, digging roots again.

Tobe shook his head at the others, motioning with his finger to the side of his head that Lecie's mind wasn't right.

"Be careful where you walk, Lecie," Osvaldo warned her. He went over to show her the snare he'd set for the swamp rat man. He lowered his voice and glanced at the surrounding woods. "If the swamp rat man comes snoopin around our flying machine, we gonna catch him."

She studied the loop of thin rope barely visible on the ground, and followed it with her eyes to the edge of the swamp, then looked back at him. Osvaldo pointed beyond the mucky, weedy water to where the rope crept up the side of the cypress tree that grew several yards away, out of the swamp. The rope disappeared into its branches. "See?" Osvaldo said.

Lecie held the baby close as she peered into the high branches. "How you put it there?" she asked.

Osvaldo smiled proudly.

"He wanna be a bird," Tobe said.

"We used a long branch for a bridge across," Isola told her. "Then we sunk it there in the swamp."

Osvaldo lowered his voice as he pointed up the tree. "You know 'bout the swamp rat man?" he asked Lecie. "Uncle Blue told us. Catch him and you'll have good luck, and lots a' money."

Isola stared hard at the baby, trying to see its face, but Lecie kept it covered.

"Ain't no such thing anyways," Tobe said.

"Is too," Osvaldo insisted.

"I know," Lecie said.

***

They left Lecie to her digging and went farther up the lake where the land was drier. When the bayou widened and turned into the lake, Isola caught a glimpse of movement in the woods and motioned to the others to stop. Two shadowy figures ducked out of sight.

"That my brother, with Angelina?" Tobe said.

"Thinkin nobody know," Tobe said. "Who they foolin?"

Osvaldo raised his face to the sky and extended his arms at his sides, then called out like a crow.

The three of them sprawled on the grassy shore. The water was full of birds; ducks and geese and egrets and herons moved about. A scruffy vulture surveyed them from high in a bare, dead cypress tree.

"Wish I could see what those men made their wings from," Osvaldo said.

"We need more boards for a frame," Tobe said. "Then we cut some tin for feathers. Or maybe use real bird feathers."

"Wish I coulda seen that baby," Isola said.

"Say it's white as a biscuit," Tobe told them.

"She's always sad," Osvaldo said.

"Know why they makin all that fuss 'bout Lecie?" Tobe asked his friends.

He sat forward and whispered the word. "*Rape*. Lecie been rape. M' brother told me. Know what that means?"

Isola's skin prickled. She had never heard the word, but she knew instantly. "Why you talking 'bout that?" she asked. She'd never told anyone what she and Birdie had seen Horton do. Now she, too, sat up and looked behind her, spooked because they weren't far from where it had happened. If somebody rapes you, she thought, your baby turns white?

"Dog shit," Osvaldo said, repeating what the adults so often said. *'Mericani. Merda, cani.*

***

THE children had nearly reached the road on their way back to their farms when the sound of voices stopped them. Visible over the tops of the cotton plants ahead of them, a number of Italians lined the road, watching two horsemen approach. The children stepped forward to see what was going on.

Lee Horton and Garlock urged their horses on. Between them staggered two filthy, exhausted men, their hands bound in front at their waists, a rope tied around each one's neck. Horton and Garlock held the other end of the ropes. A small crowd of Italians followed behind them, with the onlookers staring in terrified silence. One of the women cried out, and Garlock swung around in his saddle, pointing a rifle that silenced her.

The bound men's clothes were tattered and covered in dust. Beneath the dirt and sweat, their bruised faces were unrecognizable. A shoe flopped on one of the men, threatening to fall off.

Isola clutched Osvaldo's arm. They could see that the bound men were Italian. "Who are they?" she whispered. "What'd they do?"

"God a'mighty," Tobe hissed. "They gonna string 'em up?"

The procession passed, and some of the tenants fell in behind, keeping a distance, while others gaped at the sight from the edge of the road.

The children followed, even though their homes were in the opposite direction. Osvaldo took Isola's hand, his face puckered and serious.

The road to Sweet Hope landing was filling with frightened workers trying to see. "Makin a parade through all a' Sweet Hope," Tobe said.

"We should go home," Isola said. She searched the crowd for her parents, fear gnawing inside her. She remembered the story her father had told of seeing a man shot to death right in front of everybody.

The horsemen stopped at the company store and turned to face the growing crowd. It seemed that half of Sweet Hope was there. Barretto the translator emerged from the store. The bound men staggered, and Horton yanked on his rope, making one of the men fall to his knees. The crowd let out a gasp.

A sobbing woman ran forward: Fiorenza. "*Mio marito.* Lazzaro," she cried, and Horton pushed her away. Getulio cried as he clutched his mother's skirt.

"Oh my God," Isola said, the recognition hitting her.

"*Acqua,*" the fallen man begged in a feeble, raspy voice. "*Per favore*, please, water." Lazzaro. It was his voice, and now, through the dust and filth they began to see him. The other was Claudio.

"We have to get papa," Isola said. The children frantically searched the crowd for anyone they might know.

Horton yanked the rope again, to no avail. "Stand up, you bastard."

Several people cried out. "They're going to kill them," Osvaldo said.

Garlock raised up in his saddle to address the crowd. "These men were caught on a train, fleeing Sweet Hope." He eyed Barretto, waiting for him to translate.

"They jumped their contract," Garlock continued. "This is what happens when you jump your contract." Reluctantly, Barretto repeated the words in Italian.

"You told us we could go," Lazzaro gasped. "You gave permission."

Claudio was silent, dazed and frightened.

Horton dismounted and yanked the kneeling Lazzaro to his feet, then cuffed him across the face. More cries, protests. Fiorenza screamed and tried to run forward, but the crowd held her back.

"Anyone else here try to jump contract," Garlock shouted, "and your family will never hear from you again."

A haggard Mrs. Sant'Angelo came forward with her three sickly children, desperately eyeing Lazzaro. "Cesare? *Mio marito*," she begged. Lazzaro shook his head to quiet her.

"Go home," Horton ordered the woman. "Your husband's not here."

"What? What?" she said. "You killed him?"

"Got away," Lazzaro managed to say.

"He won't dare show his face around here again," Horton growled. "Good riddance."

As Barretto translated, Mrs. Sant'Angelo shrieked in despair.

"Killed?" someone said.

"No, he got away," Lazzaro croaked. "Alive."

"Shut the hell up," Horton yelled at him.

The murmuring crowd parted to let a thin, aging black man limp through. He stopped in front of the horsemen.

"Daddy," Tobe called. "No."

Step eyed the boy, then turned back to Garlock and Horton, his face grim.

"Mr. Gates order this?" he asked.

Horton glowered at him. "You stay out of this, Hall. This ain't your business."

Step paused a moment, then answered in a quiet, even voice. "You know this my business, Mr. Horton. Mr. Gates don't want no harm come to his tenants."

"It's my job to keep things runnin while he's gone, and that's what I'm doin," Horton shot back.

"Not like this," Step answered.

Horton recoiled at the audacity of Step Hall answering back, in front of people no less.

"Daddy," Tobe whispered.

"If you'd been doin your job, you black son–of–a–bitch, they wouldna jumped contract and run." It was as if the open air and the crowd had finally loosened his tongue, freeing him to say words Step was well aware the man had felt for years.

Step looked at his son again, then back at the beaten men, and he felt himself teetering on the edge of a deep chasm. He had not forgotten what Lazzaro had told Serafin the day they buried old Ceravone, when their wives exchanged heated words: "See why the Americans say watch out for the niggers."

"I think you best untie these men," Step heard himself telling Horton. "Best they get a drink a' water."

The two managers bristled. A few murmurs went up among the Italians.

"Who the hell you think you talkin to?" Horton shouted. "I'll throw you on a chain gang, I told you, leave you there till you rot."

Garlock's hand went to his rifle; at the same time Isola's fingers sank into Tobe's arm, and she let out a whimper.

Step teetered on the edge of the chasm, dust and heat swirling up into his face, his own rage against Horton threatening to topple him. The two men locked eyes while Step stood with clenched fists at his sides, waiting to see what his own next move would be. He was no longer aware of his body. He saw a rounded, horned back climbing up out of the earth from the depths of hell. Its little beady eyes stared straight at him. He felt the spiny points of the cactus closing in on him.

I been waitin for you, the animal said.

I been waitin for you, he replied. He swallowed back the dust and stepped forward, motioning to some of the women to bring water. "*Acqua*," he told them.

"You damn fool," Horton shouted. "I'm warning you, Hall. You don't wanna cross me."

The women with the water held back; the bound men looked on silently.

Isola and Osvaldo jumped when someone grabbed their shoulders. It was Serafin. "Are you kids all right?" he whispered.

"My daddy — help him," Tobe pleaded.

Serafin had seen, but he still could not believe his eyes.

"Are they going to kill him?" Isola asked. "Where's mamma?"

"Shh," he said, gripping them. "What the hell are you kids doing here?" He was afraid to call out, lest he startle the managers into shooting.

He and Step exchanged a barely perceptible movement of their eyes. Serafin tried to warn him off with a shake of his head, but Step looked back at him defiantly. Then he moved toward the bound men while the hot dust rattled around him. A hush fell over the crowd. Tobe closed his eyes for a moment, afraid of what he might see, then opened them again. Serafin's hand was on the boy's shoulder.

"Man's gotta be treated like a man," Step mumbled as he worked to untie the ropes at the men's necks. Lazzaro averted his eyes.

Horton raised his gun. "I'll shoot you right here, you defy me."

A cold breeze descended on Step, although nothing stirred in the hot air. He kept his voice calm. "You gonna shoot me in front a' all these people? What you think Mr. Gates gonna do when he find out you kilt me?"

In that moment, he saw something he'd never seen before: the look of pure hatred in another's eye. That look said, "You are nothing; I am only a little better than nothing, but I will do everything in my power to show you how much that little bit of difference means."

With trembling hands, Step freed the bound men, let the ropes fall.

"*Dio Padre*," Serafin murmured. The two Italians did not move.

Horton scanned the crowd. Slowly, here and there, a frightened face began to show indignation, defiance. Fiorenza stepped forward with a cup of water. When Horton made no move to stop her, she gave it to Lazzaro. He drank cautiously, then eagerly. Another woman came forward with water, and Fiorenza gave the cup to Claudio. He, too, drank while Lee Horton watched bitterly, his rifle at his side.

"They're afraid to really hurt us," Serafin said, almost to himself.

"What?"

"Throwing their weight around, trying to scare us, but see —" Only a few nearby him heard.

Lazzaro wiped the water from his chin, then told the others, "We no jump contract. We tell Mr. Garlock and Mr. Horton we go find work, leave our family here to run the farm."

"You lying bastard," Horton said.

"Is true, is true. We walk around lake to train, take train."

"It's true," Fiorenza cried. "I told him not to believe these *maledetti bastardi*. Ask Serafin, he knows."

At mention of Serafin's name, an imperceptible ripple disturbed the air at the back of the crowd. It came from the recently arrived Angelina as she stiffened in fear and guilt. Unconsciously, she moved away from Calvin who had been craning his neck to see if that was really his father at the center of attention. Now he, too, recoiled, lest their parents catch them together.

Serafin raised his hands, gesturing for the group to go slowly, be careful. It was true, of course. The men wouldn't have lied to him yesterday about Garlock saying they could go. All a set-up, but for what?

"You got money for a train ticket, but no money to pay your debt?" Horton shot back at Lazzaro.

"We save, work like animals and save just enough to buy ticket to work some more."

Horton laughed at him.

Mrs. Sant'Angelo burst forward. She pointed a finger at Horton as she threw a curse: "May your outsides rot to match your insides! May you disappear from the face of the earth!"

Those who understood stepped away from her, while Horton merely tossed his head in scorn.

"*Calmati*," Serafin insisted. "Enough."

Another man was pushing through the crowd — manager Wade.

"What the good God Almighty's going on here?" he yelled. He saw the two filthy, beaten men, the ropes at their feet, the crowd, Step Hall right there in the midst of things.

"Jumped contract," Horton said. "Caught 'em on the train to Shreveport." Garlock put his rifle back in its sling.

The Italian men and their wives tried to explain to Wade: bound hands, a long march, ropes around necks. Step let them talk.

Wade glanced up at Garlock, then back at Horton. "Horton?"

"Just walked 'em from across the lake," he answered, trying to suppress a smile.

"That's nigh on ten miles, round the lake road," Wade said in disbelief. "You damn idiots."

Step glanced at Horton, his face grim.

"What you care, Wade?" Horton said. "You hate these Dagoes much as we do."

Wade ignored him. "You men all right?" he asked. Then to Step: "They all right?"

Step nodded.

"Why this kinda trouble only happen when Mr. Gates away on business?" Wade said to Horton.

A clamor of voices rose up: complaints, explanations. A number of bystanders offered their view of what had happened.

Horton shouted to Wade over the voices. "We stand together or you stand agin' us."

"Where you think you are?" Wade said. "This ain't no convict farm. These're Mr. Gates' tenants. We got a damn plantation to run. Don't matter if you like his tenants or no."

"Plantation's in trouble. You got subversion goin on here," Horton yelled. "Niggers and Dagoes sidin 'gainst the planters. Need to make an example to keep 'em all in line. I tell you, troubles comin, it's comin, you gonna be sorry."

"Ain't nobody sidin with nobody," Wade told him. "You got a problem, you tell Mr. Gates when he comes back."

"You think I ain't already talked to him about it?"

The comment gave Wade pause. There was no telling what had transpired between Gates and Horton. For all he knew, Mr. Gates might have known about the march, since the man wasn't above a little rough handling to make a point. But this was pushing things too far.

"Why'nt you go on home now, just lay low the rest of the day," he told Horton. "You too, Garlock."

"Who died and left you in charge?" Horton said.

Wade faced him off. "You goin, Horton?"

Horton hesitated a moment, then spit a gob of tobacco juice that landed just short of Wade's feet. He mounted his horse and gazed out at the crowd, saw Tobe, saw Isola and Osvaldo. And then, in the back he saw the olive–skinned girl he'd had his eyes on, the one that belonged to Serafin. She saw him watching her and moved farther away from Calvin in a way that made Horton take note. His eyes remained on the girl a moment. The boy, too, shuffled back a step and turned away.

Horton squinted over at Step Hall with a vile look that turned into a smirk. "You ain't seen the end a' this," he told Step. "You gonna wish you never crossed me."

He reined his horse around and galloped off, Garlock behind him.

Once the sound of the galloping hooves receded, the crowd turned back to the beaten men.

"Rest, then we'll go home," Fiorenza told Lazzaro and Claudio.

Lazzaro gingerly touched his bruised face as he gazed beyond the group, west, across the plantation. "I hope Sant'Angelo gets away for good," he murmured. "Damn them all."

Mrs. Sant'Angelo huddled, sobbing, with her children.

"He'll make it this time," Claudio told her. "Don't you worry."

"Is it true?" a woman asked, her face brightening a little. "Is there really a palace in the village?"

Lazzaro spat on the ground. These peasants and their fairy tales. "Shit. A dung heap," he said, and the woman gasped.

"They keep the black ones living all on one side of town," Lazzaro told them. "In broken-down little shacks worse than here. We hid out near them until the train came." He shook his head, as if seeing it again. "But they grabbed us off."

"Shh," Fiorenza said. "Don't think of it." She took the scarf from her neck, dipped it in water, and washed the men's faces while Getulio hung back, staring at the strange-looking man who was his father. Lazzaro winced at the touch of the cloth. "They beat you," she said, but he gave no answer.

"Are we going to let the bastards get away with this?" a man called out.

"You see how many of us there are," another said. "You saw how scared the *Americani* were. Just wait till word of this spreads."

"That's what I've been trying to say," Serafin said. But when he saw Isola and Osvaldo, he held his tongue.

"Who's got a wagon?" a man called out. "We need to take these men home."

A small group clustered, offering their bold ideas for revenge and justice.

"You okay?" Serafin asked Step.

Shaken, Step nodded. He put a hand on Tobe's shoulder. "I'm okay."

"Why'd you go an' do that, Daddy?" Tobe said, his voice shaking.

Lazzaro was watching them from among the crowd. If Lazzaro's face hadn't been already bruised, Serafin thought, he might throttle the man himself for being such an idiot.

"That man — you gotta be careful, Step," Serafin told him. Step could only nod in response.

Someone came forward with a wagon, and the onlookers helped the two men and Fiorenza and the boy in back.

"Serafin, you coming with us?" Fiorenza called.

He waved them on. Lazzaro watched guiltily from the back of the wagon. But Serafin kept his distance.

Finally, just as the wagon passed by him, Serafin said quietly, "Remember who saved your neck, eh?"

He turned away before Lazzaro had a chance to respond.

✳✳✳

AMALIA watched the few slivers of onion turn glassy, then begin to brown in the hot lard. She moved the pot to the side of the stove a minute, stirred in a lump of tomato paste, then carefully poured in water and stepped back as the lard sizzled and spat. She slid the pot back over the heat and stirred the sauce.

Serafin was at the table, trying to understand what he had just witnessed. "Couldn't tell who it was at first. Who even knew it was them, right, Isola? Beaten and filthy."

"You let the children see such a thing?" she said angrily, not turning around. The sauce was like blood in the pot. In all this time, Serafin had not found out about her and Isola going to the village with Fancy and Birdie. In all this time Isola had kept their secret. But she hadn't gone back across the lake since then. Two American dollars in their tobacco tin. Fancy had bought two more bushels of tomatoes for them the previous summer, and Amalia had paid her by making a dress for Birdie. She cringed now to think of the awful fate that might have befallen them if they had been found out. Her children — to think she might have put them in jeopardy for a few American coins.

"... threatening to shoot Step in front of us all," Serafin was saying. "You should have seen it. And then everybody getting mad at Horton and Garlock. Even Wade was mad at them, you could tell. Standing up to those two. It was like — what my father and his *pad'in* used to talk about, the people rising up, standing together. It's about time."

She turned and looked at her children.

Isola was nodding her head as Serafin spoke. Osvaldo fidgeted with a bandanna, winding it around one wrist and then unwinding it.

"Were Fancy and the children there?" Amalia asked. "Did they see?"

"Only Tobe," Isola said. "He was afraid they were going to kill his father, the poor boy."

"Calvin was there," Osvaldo said.

"No he wasn't," Isola told him, making a face. "Why are you saying that?"

"Well — " He hung his head as he wound the bandanna around his wrist.

Amalia narrowed her eyes at Angelina. She sat near the open door, crocheting a doily. "What are you doing?" Amalia demanded.

Angelina's hands stopped a moment, then resumed. "Crocheting."

Amalia looked at her a long, hard minute. "You weren't with your father?"

"I told you. I was chopping cotton." Isola and Osvaldo avoided each other's eyes.

"Chopping cotton," Amalia repeated. They had all been out in the field working, but then she had come in the house without giving the children much thought.

She told Serafin: "We should go to Lazzaro and Fiorenza's tonight, see if they're okay."

Serafin stopped, thrown off track in his story. "The bastard," he said. "Let him rot."

"I'll go without you then. She's still my friend."

She brushed past Angelina, and went outside to the pump to fill the *maccheroni* pot with water. The rusty clanging of the pump jarred her. The men had been marched along the edge of Sweet Hope, near the woods, and then down the lane to the landing. She peered across the cotton. There was no way she would have seen or heard the commotion from their house. And yet a crowd had formed, many had seen. Her own children. Maybe Angelina had been telling the truth. Maybe she had remained working here in the field.

A bird jeered at her from the roof of the house, a large jay. She looked up briefly, then carried the pot inside to the stove.

"I'm telling you, Amalia," Serafin said. "At first I thought Step was a goner. Then one by one, the other farmers were ready to stand up to Horton, fight him. And he backed right down."

The bird screeched outside, a harsh, grating sound.

"What are you saying?" she said to Serafin.

"Just... I don't know. There's a lot of us here. Together, we've got more clout than we think."

She studied him a moment. "Don't go getting any foolish ideas," she told him. She took the doily from Angelina. The edges were loose and rippled so that it could be starched into another useless decoration.

"We don't need any more of these," Amalia told her. "Save the thread."

Angelina hunched forward and folded her hands across her lap. Amalia looked hard at her.

"I hope it's only a doily you need to be making."

The girl blushed.

"Amalia, sit," Serafin told her.

She checked the pot of water, stirred the sauce again, then sat. "What?" Her eyes were on Angelina.

"I've been thinking about this all wrong," he said. "That Horton, he doesn't have it in him."

She turned to him. "No, not in front of a crowd."

"He wanted the crowd. He marched Lazzaro and Claudio through the plantation on purpose so people would see. But he wasn't counting on what happened. He's a coward." He opened his palms, motioned with them in the air, trying to find the words.

The bird screeched again, and Amalia snatched up a spoon from the table and went out the door. The bird eyed her from its perch on the roof, almost defiantly, it seemed. It let out another screech, as if it had called her out just to taunt her. "Get away from us, shoo!" she yelled. She flung the spoon and it clattered on the roof. The bird gave an angry cry and launched itself heavily into the air. She watched the wings pump slowly, almost lazily, as the bird grew smaller in the pale sky.

CHAPTER 21

In The Woods

July 1906

CALVIN Hall heard the trill of a meadowlark as he walked the lane near the lake woods. *See–ya, see–ya*, it called. Wound around a slat of wood in his pocket was a fishing line with a bolt for a sinker, the hook embedded in the roll of line. He planned to surprise his family with a stringer of catfish for supper, and then when they were finished eating he was going to break the news to them: he and Angelina were going to get married. He wouldn't tell them the whole truth, though. Not yet. Break it to them gently, one piece at a time.

Everything looked different to him. The lush cotton and the green trees were more lush and green than ever before. The yellow earth beneath his feet softer and warmer; the air itself soft, enveloping; the birdsong sweeter; the sky bluer. Even the sound of the lazy droning insects filled him with comfort. At the same time, a part of him twitched with apprehension. He squinted down the narrow footpath that led into the woods, then quickly looked away lest Lally Mo catch him spying. He knew she was there even though he couldn't see her. But that wasn't what caused the apprehension.

Everything was all jumbled inside him. *A father.* He was going to be a father. He could barely imagine himself holding a baby, raising it, making a home with Angelina, becoming a family.

You like a white girl, Tobe had teased. And his parents, always there with their worrying eyes, telling him *Watch your step*. Telling him. *Not that. Not here.*

She was as dark as some Negroes; some Negroes were as light as some Italians. He had never even thought about white girls before. Besides, nobody was sure she was white, anyway, not even the white folks.

He put his hand to his throat; touched the medal Angelina had given him. She was just barely beginning to show — if you knew enough to notice. Pretty soon everyone would know. She had looked so mournful when she told him, it was almost sweet. If he thought about it one way, he could almost feel happy, a bird in the sky. Think about it another way, though, and a knot of fear choked his breath.

His mother and father might kick him out of the house. If so, he'd have to figure out some place to live, and what to do for full-time work. Maybe Uncle Fred would give him enough steady work at the lumber mill for their own place. If not, they'd have to leave the plantation, find work on one of the farms outside the village. But maybe his parents would have them after all — or maybe they could move in with her family (God, what was he thinking?). But only until the baby was born. The baby! After that, they were leaving Sweet Hope. He knew that for sure.

He was seventeen years old, a man, old enough to live his life the way he wanted, where he wanted. If she didn't want to go as far as Chicago, they could go up near Memphis. There were Italians living in and around Memphis, doing all kinds of work, so she wouldn't feel so alone. He knew he'd find work for himself in a minute, a lot better than here at Sweet Hope. If they were married, the company would have to let her go with him, wouldn't they?

Married. He wondered if it was true, what some people said, that the Italians were considered white people by the rest of the country. If so, he'd be in big trouble, no matter what she said about it. Forget marrying; there were laws against that. But she loved him. A light–skinned Negro, that's what they would say if anybody said anything. But when she opened her mouth to speak, the truth would come out with her accent.

Another bird called, a little way into the trees. "See ya," he answered, saluting the air.

He turned when he heard horses approaching, and the bright day clouded over. It was Lee Horton and his sidekick Garlock. Instinctively, Calvin glanced at the guns in their saddle slings, the memory of the two men marching the Italians in ropes fresh in his mind. But maybe they were only on their way duck hunting, he tried to tell himself. If not that, then fishing, since there were no tenant shacks over this way.

As inconspicuously as possible, he moved to the side of the road to let them pass. The horses slowed to a walk and stayed behind him. He kept moving, telling himself now that maybe they were scouting a new place to build tenant housing, even though there hadn't been any new cabins going up in a while. Or maybe they were out to intimidate and harass anybody they came upon, just for something to do.

To hell with them, he thought. He turned into the woods to cut through to the lake. He was only a few yards in when he heard the horses stop, the men dismount. Then the cracking of twigs behind him.

"Hey, boy," Horton called to him.

Calvin hesitated a moment before he stopped and turned. The two men were lumbering into the woods, just yards away from him. The skin at the back of his neck prickled, and he felt the woods loom about him, big and quiet and deserted. He cursed himself for turning into the woods. What was he thinking, with these two on his tail?

"Yessir?" He looked meekly from one man to the other.

"Goin to the lake, boy?" Horton asked. The men stopped close to him. Calvin could see the two horses through the branches behind them, nibbling at the edge of the woods.

"Goin fishin, Mr. Horton. Catchin supper."

Horton looked up at the tree cover, as if there was something to see. Garlock waited patiently by his side, his expression stuck halfway between a sneer and indigestion. "Hot time a' day for fishin," Horton said. "Don't think you gonna catch anything this time a' day."

With relief, Calvin noticed their hands were empty. The guns were behind with the horses.

"Gotta try anyway, Mr. Horton," Calvin said, trying his best to sound pleasant. "Fam'ly gotta eat." His mind raced, trying to figure what the men were after, and he kept coming back to that scene of his father untying the Italians, and Horton's cold look, and his threat before riding away. He tried to calculate how close the nearest farm was. The lake was still a good 300 yards into the woods, and he doubted anyone was there this time of day. The closest shack was Lally Mo's, back in the brambles, too thick to run through. He hadn't even paid attention when he'd passed the lane to her shack. Even if he made it there, what could a small old woman do to help him?

He glanced at the grazing horses again, wondering if anyone would have reason to be passing on the road. If they saw the horses they might stop to investigate.

As if Horton could read Calvin's mind, he told his partner: "Garlock, bring them horses in here." And then, as if to ease Calvin's fears, he told him, "Best to give 'em a bit a' shade."

Calvin nodded, forced a friendly half–smile as his concern rose. "Guess I better git goin now," he told Horton. He held his breath as he slowly turned away. He could feel the two men behind, watching him. The horses nickered, tore at grass. He listened to the chewing as he walked. And then the men began to follow him through the woods.

"Funny, we was goin fishin ourselves," Horton said behind him.

Sweat trickled down Calvin's neck. He thought of taking off, running as fast as he could, but he knew the men would leave the horses and chase him. And then what? He wasn't sure he could outrun them. Even if he made it to the lake, they'd be on him. And they had the horses now, with the guns. Each step he took increased his fear and his uncertainty. He was on the verge of bolting when Horton called to him again.

"Hey, Hall, wait up. Gotta ask you something." His voice was friendly, which only worried Calvin more. He stopped.

"How long you been stickin it to that Dago girl?" Calvin froze. Garlock stifled a laugh.

Calvin tried to keep his voice steady, innocent, tried to manage a slight smile. "Don't know what you talkin 'bout, Mr. Horton."

Horton laughed and patted Calvin on the shoulder, making him cringe.

"That's okay," Horton said. "We're only playin wi' you. How's 'bout you show us your fishin line, show us what you use to catch fish in the middle of the day?" When the boy looked doubtfully at each of them, Horton gave Calvin an encouraging smile.

"Ain't got no pole," Garlock said, snickering. "Maybe uses that other pole a' his."

Horton turned to Garlock to admonish him. "Why you talkin nasty like that, Garlock?"

In the next instant, he swung back towards Calvin and caught him square in the stomach with his fist. Calvin clutched his stomach and staggered backwards. Horton punched him in the face, and when Calvin raised his hands to shield his face, Horton pummeled his stomach again. The boy was doubled over, spitting blood. "What I do?" Calvin cried in panic. "What I do, Mr. Horton?"

"Let me have a turn at him," Garlock said, and he slammed his fist into Calvin's jaw.

Calvin fell to the ground and crawled away, trying to regain his feet so he could run. His mind raced frantically for a way to save himself. Horton tackled him and kicked at his ribs and kidneys as the boy rolled from side to side. "That one's for sneakin 'round with that Italian girl," Horton said, slamming his boot into Calvin's ribs. "And that one's for your old man steppin outta line." He rammed the boot into Calvin's kidneys. "Thinkin he can do any damn thing he please and get away wi' it. I warned him."

The horses whinnied and anxiously lifted their feet. Every now and then a dog barked in the distance.

Garlock laughed as Calvin rolled on the ground. "Like a pig on a spit. Get 'im good both sides, make sure he's cooked even."

Horton pulled Calvin to his feet, cursing him and Step Hall and the Pascalas all at the same time. "Stand up like a man," Horton said as the boy staggered, blood dripping from his face.

"That ain't no man, that's a nigger," Garlock laughed. When Calvin tried to stumble away, Horton grabbed him from behind, pinning his arms while Garlock attacked him with his fists.

"You tell your father he better mind his manners," Horton said, cinching the arms tighter behind Calvin's back until there was a crack and the boy let out a scream. "He don't straighten up, we gonna do worse to your mother and sister. Gonna get that Dago bitch, too, for good measure."

"Maybe you'd like to watch that, huh?" Garlock said. "Like to watch us take a turn with that girl, show you how it's s'pose to be done?"

Outraged, Calvin raised his feet and kicked violently at Garlock, sending the man sprawling in the dirt. At the same time, he wrenched sideways from Horton, and slipped from his grasp. "Nigger's fightin back," Garlock sputtered. "Get him, damn it." But Horton was already on him, before the boy could take two steps.

The men attacked Calvin with their fists and boots, and he fought back fiercely, even as he felt his strength slipping away. When he would not stop struggling, Horton grabbed him from behind and held him in a chokehold while Garlock punched and kicked wherever he could. Blood mingled with spit drooled from Calvin's mouth and down his chin. He clawed desperately at Horton's arm, fighting for air as his knees buckled and he sagged against the man. Frantically, he tried to speak, get the words out, hoping they might show mercy if they knew he was going to be a father. "Daddy," was all Calvin managed to say.

"Your daddy can't help you now," Horton sneered. He tightened his grip.

Calvin reached for the air, at the small figure passing him. It astonished him to see the child, for he knew instantly who it was. "Baby," he whispered before everything went dark.

"Callin for his gal, too," Garlock scoffed. "Pitiful."

Horton let the limp body fall to the ground in a heap. Panting, he shook his arm through the air, flinging the blood and mucous from it. "Looka this shit he got all over me," he said.

Garlock was bent over, hands on his knees, trying to catch his breath. He straightened to massage his knuckles. "Bony som' bitch."

The dog's barking was closer, and the two men peered through the woods in the direction of the road. The horses stood quietly grazing a short distance from them.

"What the hell dog is that?" Horton said.

"He ain't movin none," Garlock said. They looked back at Calvin.

Horton nudged his toe against Calvin's chest, but the boy didn't stir.

"Is he breathin?" Garlock said.

Horton crouched down on one knee and bent close to listen. "Jesus," he said, "I don't know."

"You kill him, Lee?" Garlock said, a smile tugging at his lips.

"Let's go," Horton told him. They went for the horses.

"You gon' leave 'im?"

The dog was close, so they decided to head for the lake and follow the shore for a while before going back out onto the road, up near the Modena section. "Just don't say nothin to nobody," Horton told Garlock. "You got that?"

He mounted his horse and looked again toward the barking, but could see nothing. The two men rode for the lake, ducking to avoid low branches and bushes. Horton gave a final backward glance at the still body, his face tight with worry.

"You done it now, all right," Garlock said.

"Damn it to hell," Horton answered. "Just shut up about it."

***

THE dog began barking wildly when it came upon the body. Then it quieted as it sniffed the bloody face and torso before starting up again. "Bruno," the voice called. "Bruno, *vieni qui.*"

This is what Father Odetti remembered: stepping into the small clearing within the woods and seeing first the wiggling behind and wagging tail of his dog Bruno as he paced around a heap on the ground and ran his nose here and there at his discovery; and then the shafts of light filtering through the tree tops, the mottled shadows on the ground; then the impressions of horse shoes in the soft earth, the matted grass and broken shrubbery and kicked up earth; and finally the crumpled heap of a body, and the dark, bloody face, its eyes half–closed as if in a dream. For a long time he couldn't move, even as he became aware of what had happened. The whimpering dog looked up at him. Father Odetti bent over to get a closer look: the bloody shirt, the chest, the battered face. He knew who the boy was. Everyone knew Step Hall's son.

***

It was dinner time. Chickens clucked in the yard, mules brayed, a baby cried. The two families, Hall and Titus, called to each other — *fetch some water, get away from that bushel, what you done now?* — while some of the children argued over a green cypress switch and a tin can they were batting past the chickens, two of the children that lived there, Step Hall's boy and girl, and two that belonged to Serafin Pascala.

The children stopped and watched him as he led his horse with its grim load past them, the dog dancing around the animal's feet. Father Odetti had slung the body face–down over his saddle, then tried to cover it partially with his shirt. He was aware now that he was dressed in trousers and a sweaty undershirt stained with blood. He kept moving, and heard the children close in behind him after he passed.

Step Hall was at the trough pumping water for a mule whose dusty sides heaved in and out as it drank. Father Odetti stopped short in front of the man, startling himself with the fact that he had walked that far with no thought and no feeling other than an urgency to get somewhere he had never been before.

Step Hall stared at the priest, at his bloody shirt. Then at the horse, and at its burden, and his face turned ashen.

The priest's words choked in this throat. At last he raised his hand and pointed in the direction he had come. "In the woods. My dog was chasing rabbits."

Fancy raised her hand toward her husband, barely moving her head from side to side. "No," she said, and Step took her hands in his.

Father Odetti told them again: "I was looking for my dog."

Fancy let out a mournful wail.

"Don't tell me — " she finally said.

But the children were there, terrified, somber.

Fancy clutched at Step as if to tear his shirt from him, and his face was hard, impenetrable. Lecie picked up her baby and laid a hand over the boy's eyes.

Step moved stiffly from Fancy's side and pulled the body from the horse, and the shirt fell away. He staggered for a moment, holding the body close to his chest in a gruesome dance before bending to lay it on the ground. The weight was too much. The body slipped and fell the last foot, landing with a thud, and sending up small puffs of dirt. The bloody face looked up for all to see. Fancy howled when she saw the face, an unearthly sound that sent shivers through Father Odetti.

Fred stared in stricken disbelief. "God A'mighty," was all he could say.

The children huddled mutely. Lecie clutched her baby so tightly the child cried. They could see, even from the short distance, that death was there.

Step opened his mouth to shout, but his throat was an old well, filled in with rocks and dirt. The hole went deeper than any well he'd ever seen.

Fancy threw herself on the ground alongside the body, sobbing. She touched the boy's battered face, his hands, his shoulders, trying to embrace him while her other two children hung back, watching. A stabbing icy fear of knowledge hit Tobe and Birdie. Brother, their brother. It couldn't be real.

Step tried to ease Fancy away, but she shrieked when he touched her.

Father Odetti was shaken to the core. He had seen death many times since coming to Sweet Hope, but this — murder. There was no other way to look at what he had come upon. The word caught inside him so that he actually gasped for air. He was too stunned to even think of praying. He could feel the startled heaviness from the children, and from Lud Titus beside him. Now and then Fancy cried out: "Why? What he done? I tried to tell him." Then she would be quiet for a few moments.

They did not even ask who had done it. They knew.

Father Odetti thought he should round up the children, shield them from the sight, but it was too late. The Italian children huddled close to the Halls' two children, all of them eyeing the body with the same startled faces.

Finally, a man's anguished cry shattered the air, chilling Father Odetti. He had never heard anything like it: a deep, roaring bellow as if from some great, mortally wounded animal. It came from Step. Fancy let out a responding, higher-pitched cry. Lud knelt to embrace her friend.

"Children," Father Odetti called to the Pascalas, the word coming out in a hoarse whisper. They ignored him, held back with their frightened eyes on Step Hall.

Fancy stared up at her husband, her own face mimicking his, as if both faces were collapsing into each other. She let out a long chilling wail as she tried to claw her way up, toward Step. Lud fumbled to hold her back.

Father Odetti kept his eyes on the Pascala children — the girl who had carried the cypress switch from the yard and her younger brother, who acted strange at times, gazing into space with an inscrutable expression.

He began to think now about all those who must have seen him leading the horse and dead boy along the woods road, then through the plantation straight to Step's place. A number of farmers had looked up from where they worked in the fields, and twice he had passed black workers on the road who stared and moved aside, giving him more room than was needed. Only now was he aware of how many people he had passed in his sleepwalking journey to the Hall house. Word would spread quickly. It was important that Father Odetti keep a neutral position, he had told himself numerous times, not appear to fraternize with any one group, given the confidence in which Mr. Gates had hired him, and the special considerations extended to him. How had he been so oblivious?

Far off in a field a black family was gathering their tools. An old black couple shuffled past the house on foot. They glanced at the gathering, then back down at the ground as they walked by, confirming Father Odetti's fears that many had seen, and word was already spreading.

The Italian children stood far down the lane outside the yard, the boy quiet now.

A thin, older Italian girl was approaching, her body hunched forward as she hurried across the fields. She raised an arm and waved to the other two, then called in Italian for them to come home to supper. When the two did not budge, the girl quickened her pace, as if angered by their defiance. She began to yell again, but when she saw where they were looking, she slowed, stared at the gathering in the Hall yard, and then brushed past her siblings.

Father Odetti tried to stop her, but it was too late. She was there, among them.

"You," Fancy cried at the girl, pointing a finger, suddenly alert. But then her head lolled, as if she were drugged, and the wailing started again. Her legs buckled, and Step struggled to support her.

Angelina balked, looking from one face to another. Then she stared down at the body that had at first lain hidden from her view by all of them. Her face collapsed, the blood draining from it. A strangled cry escaped her, a gasp for air. Her body teetered for a moment, as if it could not decide if it would fall forward or stumble backwards and run. She fell to her knees, her arms outstretched toward the lifeless Calvin, and let out a long wail.

"Go," Step commanded, and Father Odetti pulled her to her feet.

Fancy raised her head to the girl, cried out, "You killed him."

Angelina's stunned mouth tried to form words even as she began backing away.

"I'll track him down an' kill him," Step hissed.

"Doin this to a boy," Fred Titus said. "Here at Sweet Hope." His eyes slid sideways at the retreating Angelina as he spoke.

"I'll kill him with my bare hands," Step said.

Angelina stumbled against a bucket as she backed away. Then she turned and began running across the field, past her brother and sister, toward home. The levee was bursting; the plantation was flooding; she was drowning; there was no air, never again. The picture of Calvin's bloody face, his broken body, hovered before her eyes as she ran.

Step grabbed the priest's arm. "You tell me what you saw. Everything." Father Odetti stammered and tried to free himself from the hand clutching his shirt, shaking him. "Please," he cried.

Finally Step let go.

Birdie inched near her mother and finally, awkwardly, took Fancy's hand.

Shaken, Father Odetti moved toward the road. The two Pascala children had already reached the edge of the Hall property. The girl still carried the cypress switch she had retrieved from Tobe Hall. Osvaldo walked in circles, his arms outstretched, looking up at the sky.

The light was dimming, the air taking on its pale orange cast in the long dusk before sunset. There was something sickeningly pretty about the fields and sky.

These children, Father Odetti thought — they might as well be dead, too.

CHAPTER 22

The Wedge Is Driven

July 1906

WORD trickled down and out and throughout Sweet Hope plantation like water seeping through a flood–battered levee, spreading across the land. The wind agitated the water.

From the Pascalas to Lazzaro to Barretto the translator to Uncle Blue and Lally Mo, to all the sections of Sweet Hope, bottom land and prime land, Bolognese, Veneto, Senigallia, Modena sections, to Vaucluese and Hyner and then beyond to the postmaster and blacksmith and hotel owner across the lake and the workers at nearby Three Point plantation and even to all the little farms and plantations throughout the county word spread: a black boy had been murdered at Sweet Hope.

Reverend Monroe and his wife Miss Betty looked out from the small Baptist church across the troubled water that separated them from Sweet Hope plantation, and they too heard the word, and the word spread throughout the ram-shackle hovels on that side of town in the village, the little well–kept and broken–down shacks along the worn dirt lanes.

The trickle that became the stream or puddle or pond or lake added: One a' his friends killed him over a gal.

No, others said, some Italian killed the boy for courtin one a' theirs on the sly.

Or: One of the managers did it; wanted the Dago girl for himself.

Some of the poor white farmers added their conjectures: Blacks getting out of hand, Italians getting out of hand, somebody had to put a stop to it before the whole Delta's ruined.

The wind carried the whispered rumors mixed with accidental truths. People looked at the sky, then back at the troubled water, with only one thing on their minds: storm coming.

Owner Harlan Gates fretted over the current turn of events. What to do now, at this delicate time? His rising political aspirations, his expanding business — all hung in precarious balance with the eyes of the Delta upon him. Horton had as much as confessed privately to him his hand in the boy's demise — an accident, Horton had insisted. Gates understood completely how matters could get out of hand with unruly Negroes, especially the young, hot–tempered ones. And he understood as well Horton's penchant for using a heavy hand, and his inclination toward public acts of intimidation.

Gates himself was not above resorting to extreme measures when necessary, but murder? It was abominable, horrific, absolutely unacceptable. *But wasn't there that time five or six years ago,* a little voice in the back of his mind whispered, *the black man inciting others as they worked to clear the swamps, complaining of wages, work conditions?* Horton's doing again, but at Gates' decree that time. No, he would not allow those thoughts. A completely different time, a completely different set of circumstances, laid to rest once and for all, as was the unfortunate perpetrator.

It was as if the Fates were conspiring against him just as he was about to — if all went as planned — move into a position that would open the door to his becoming senator. Thank God for his impeccable reputation, his good family name, his many acts of generosity toward the less fortunate. The Italian Colony experiment itself had earned him praise, even from some of his earlier detractors, for replacing the recalcitrant and diminishing Negro labor supply with eager, industrious Italians.

Now this. Something, he would have to do something.

***

STEP Hall had it from the wind, had it from what he suspected in his own tormented heart, had it from his own various and unpleasant interactions: Lee Horton was the evildoer. The man's words haunted him: *You ain't seen the end a' this — gonna wish you never crossed me.* But going after his son? And right after threatening him in front of so many witnessing tenants? Lee Horton had an evil heart, but was it possible someone else had killed Calvin? Serafin Pascala had a daughter to protect. Still, Step couldn't fathom Serafin hurting his boy, much less killing him, just for courting his daughter. Step accused first one, then the other. For a moment he even imagined the two of them conspiring on the deed. And if Harlan Gates had hired Horton, had kept him on his payroll for so long, what did that say about the man Step had looked up to for all these years? Could Mr. Gates himself have had a hand in the murder?

He had to see for himself. He followed the plantation farms along the tree line, the same path Calvin would have taken down toward the bayou, past Lally Mo's lane; then he dipped into the woods at about the same spot Calvin must have. It didn't take long to find the place the priest had described. Two different sets of horses' hoofprints led him there. Broken tree branches and bushes, and the ground torn up with scuffling and fighting, and the hoofprints in the soft, dug-up earth, mingled with man-sized shoe and boot prints, and the barefoot boy's; then the hoofprints heading deeper into the woods toward the lake. No Italian had a horse, let alone two horses, least of all Pascala.

He knelt and laid a hand over Calvin's footprint and closed his eyes. The boy breathed in his hand; he could feel him, the hand growing warmer with the touch. Slowly, he looked about. Drops of dark, dried blood were sprinkled on the ground, on green leaves, the sight making his body go weak. He put his fingers to his lips, tasted the bloodied earth, swallowed. A sharp taste of dirt, that was all. After the first rain, nothing would be left of Calvin. His eyes stung; his throat tightened. He laid his hands on the blood–speckled leaves, the earth, then scooped the earth. He placed his hand inside his shirt and rubbed the bloodied earth into his chest. *Blood of my heart.* He let himself cry.

He thought of his childhood on Sweet Hope, and hearing his Auntie T's slave stories. Thought of the many places he had lived and worked afterwards. Thought of that time just after glory days when he was young and hot–tempered, fool enough to pass words with a white man who swung an axe at him, nearly lopping off his foot. Thought of his first wife and her dark bloated pleading face as she lay dying from snake bite that no white doctor would take the time to treat. Thought of walking down a dusty Sweet Hope road years later and coming upon a tall strong woman and falling in love when he thought love had left him for good. Thought of the birth of their children, the flutter in his heart when he first laid eyes on his first sweet baby, Calvin. Thought of every secret dream he'd dared to dream for his children.

My day is gone, your day comin, he would tell them.

But Calvin's day was come and gone, just like Step's father's and his grandfather's and the ones before them. His life was worth nothing.

And he thought of Pascala and his family — the man who had become his friend, the man who had saved his son Tobe from drowning, the man who was now tied to the death of another son. Innocent or not, tied just the same.

And he thought how in his secret mind he had gone back and forth with his allegiances, for Mr. Gates had trusted him, put him in charge, singled him out to oversee the running of more and more of the plantation; and Step had been proud to work for him, proud to work for a man like that. Yet wasn't there that tiny kernel deep inside him that knew the truth that could not be dreamed away? The injustices, the harsh treatment of blacks and Italians alike, the unending suffering for the sake of a bank roll the tenants and day laborers could never imagine touching. Harlan Gates decided how his plantation would be run, and hired Horton and his ilk, and kept them on the payroll — it was hard to think it even now — no matter how the farmers were treated. Hadn't Step seen dozens of blacks leave Sweet Hope for a better life? Hadn't his own family talked of leaving? Hadn't he been the one who insisted they stay? The truth deep inside him was a throbbing ache. And didn't that truth put the blood of his own son on his hands?

Back and forth his mind went.

He had dared dream of his own days ahead, his place on earth, running a plantation, owning one someday, when everything around him pointed to the impossibility of such a thing. Trusting a white man, Gates. Then trusting a Dago, Pascala.

Fool, he told himself.

As he rose to go, a metallic glint caught his eye, and he bent at a jewelweed bush and retrieved it: a small triangular medal hanging from a dirty string. It was like ice in his hand. He squinted to make out the shape of a woman in a long cone–shaped robe, holding a baby near her shoulder; stars and little squiggles of writing adorned the other side. He closed his fist around it and squeezed. Vaguely, he heard the muted birds above him, felt the humid air move around him, saw the earth at his feet, torn and beaten. He stuffed the medal in his pocket and left.

He could barely remember what happened after the Italian priest brought Calvin to them. There were people in and out, carrying food, sitting to pray and sing, and then talking in hushed voices, and then in louder, angry voices. Where was his wife Fancy in that day? Had he comforted her, spoken with her? And Tobe and Birdie. They were all there, but he could see none of it. He could remember no bed at night; could not remember sleeping, but could not remember not sleeping either. Except he remembered Serafin Pascala coming to his door, the priest Father Odetti with him, and everyone standing in awkward silence until Step shouted at them: "Get out!" He was yelling and grabbing for whatever was at hand, there at the door. A basin. A tin washbasin, raising it in the air to hurl at them. Someone — Fred? — prying the basin from his hand, walking him outside, around and around the yard.

He left the house in the early morning, stepping outside to the dark and humid earth–smelling haze, the air thick and damp about him.

Sweet Hope was a dream. It was a layer of billowy fog rising from the swamps on a still cool summer morning and stretching its smoky fingers across the flat and mournful land.

And he was walking in the light before light, before the rays of sun broke over the horizon and changed everything once again.

For his eyes could see, even without the light. And his mind could count.

We were five, and now we are four. The ciphering seemed impossible, the number four incomprehensible.

It could have been an ordinary day, like any other at Sweet Hope. He could have been walking in early morning to the mule yard to oversee the hitching and plowing, although it was months past plowing time. Or going to gather a work crew to clear swamp or build new settlement houses, although it was not time for such work either.

In truth, he was headed for the lumber mill, walking instead of taking the mule cart because his legs needed to walk.

Fred Titus was waiting for him, nodded a silent hello. They went inside the mill. Fred left the doors open, to let in what morning was just beginning to rise. He struck a match to the lantern, throwing a circle of weak light around them.

Step fingered some planks stacked inside the door.

"I'm almost done w' it," Fred told him.

"You make it long as me?" Step asked. "He was tall as me, you know." He shook his head, his hand still resting on the plank.

"I know," Fred told him. "I used good wood." The words came out like bubbles under bayou water and drifted up into the dark rafters where they disappeared. Fred put his hands in his pockets, looked around at nothing. A mule from the nearby yard brayed.

Step stared down at the pile of planks. He looked down at his feet that he could barely see for the dark. Then the feet started moving and he was outside the mill, back in the morning light. A wheelbarrow was tipped upside down against a pile of sawdust. On its rusted wheel a gray catbird perched, eyeing him with cold, accusing eyes.

Fred followed. "I'll bring it 'round later." A long pause. "Step? You okay?"

"You sure you makin it long 'nough?" Step answered.

Instead of heading home where his wife and two children not three needed him, he continued north of the mill, past the building the Italians used for their church services, on to the small cotton pens and deserted storage shacks where there were fewer farms. No one was up this way so early in the morning, on the low levee road that passed the idle lumber mill and church building. Hulking company cows grazed along the levee.

The fog was clearing now as the rising sun warmed the earth; and birds called in the trees between him and the great levee–hidden river beyond. He felt the river, felt his boy Tobe slipping away that time long ago. But not Tobe. Tobe was saved.

In the light of the empty road, and clear of the closed up bare earth and sawdust–smelling building, he could think it now: *That very mill I didn't want him workin in 'cause it was too dangerous. When all along the danger weren't with saw blades or fallin timber or breakin machines, but with a two–legged animal that's still roamin free.* Was that it, God wanting a son from him, one way or another, for whatever reason he could not discern? And underneath it all, he knew Horton had done it out of hatred for him, and the blame he heaped upon himself was unbearable.

His feet moved forward, but part of him stayed back at the lumber mill, feeling the roughness beneath his hand, knowing what the planks would hold within a couple hours. We were five, and now we are four.

He turned abruptly and started back. A few people were leading their mules from the mule barn, hitched for wood chopping or ditch digging. Others were beginning work in the fields, cleaning weeds, though the cotton was too high to really need it. All Italians. Not a single Negro anywhere. There were scarcely two dozen of them left at Sweet Hope.

His mind was cranking like a ready–to–bust gin mill, though he could not tell through all the noise exactly what his mind was trying to tell him.

He passed the lumber mill again and then the hay barns and mule barns and blacksmith shop and soon the idle gin mill. Next to it, the company office and commissary. A few Italians were there at the store, and he could see that the office was open already. He stopped and watched from a short distance, the trembling inside him refusing to be still. The office door opened, and Mr. Wade stepped onto the porch. When he turned, his eyes met Step's, and the man stopped, his hand still on the door behind him. And then, as if he had forgotten something, he went back inside the office. Step could see him at the window. Guilty, the shadow behind the window said, as if the guilt of one manager was visited upon them all.

***

INSIDE Step's house, Lud and the preacher and some of the other women were trying to comfort Fancy and the children. Step joined them now, sitting vigil. Miss Betty led them in mournful hymns that could barely scratch the surface of telling their sorrow.

Before noon, Fred's wagon creaked into the yard. The wailing started the second the men carried the box inside.

It took Fred and Lud and both Birdie and Lecie to hold Fancy back while Step lifted Calvin's body from the boards and laid him in the coffin. Tobe hung back near the door, shuddering as he watched.

Through all the shrieking and the prying loose, Step talked to Fancy in a quiet, even, troubled voice, and Reverend Monroe let the husband tend his wife. "You got to let go now. Time for him to go. Got to let him rest." The words rang hollow even as he said them. How was it possible that his strong, beautiful seventeen–year–old son was gone forever?

Over and over he murmured to Fancy, with Fred and Lud repeating some of the words, and Birdie and Tobe hanging in the shadows now, watching, trembling at the thing that had walked right into their house and taken over.

"I told you make him stay 'way from them," Fancy wailed.

"Hush up, now," Lud told her, smoothing Fancy's hair. "That just the hurt talkin."

Fancy slapped her friend's hand away.

"You might's well killed him yourself," Fancy cried at Step.

Inside him, that gin mill clanged, spat steam.

Fancy clawed at the coffin as Step closed it and blinked against his final image of the bruised, sleeping face. She dragged her feet in the dust as he and Fred carried the coffin to the wagon. Then she refused to ride in the wagon. He nudged the mule forward slowly, letting her walk behind crying as they headed for Hyner. Just outside their lane, he stopped the wagon, got down and went to her. She collapsed in his arms. "It hurt all the way inside my bones," she sobbed.

He lifted Fancy and sat cradling her in back while Fred drove them the rest of the way, with their friends and family walking behind — but no Italians; no Pascalas; no Father Odetti. He had banished them, he reminded himself. And Reverend Monroe and Miss Betty walking with them to the low and mournful cadence of coming home to glory land.

They stared uncomprehending at the dark hole, the hole that finally opened the abyss inside Birdie and Tobe. She was the first to begin crying, then Tobe, then the others, and the wailing became a prayer.

Reverend Monroe raised his hands to heaven and called out for God's strength and understanding, and then he called out for justice and the power to carry it through.

No tambourine punctuated his words, only the fury of the human heart given human voice.

Step and Fancy clutched each other, each one's free arm hugging Tobe and Birdie close to them.

And so they buried Calvin at Hyner in the little grave-yard mound next to the Italians' burying place — and left him to the sounds of crickets and bullfrogs and complaining mockingbirds.

But even as Step's confused mind raged with plans for revenge, he knew when he looked at his grieving wife and children that he could not lift a hand against another lest they lose him, too.

✷✷✷

EARLY next morning he called Tobe and Birdie from the yard. "Today is the wake-up day," he told them. "Ain't no more children live in the house a' Step Hall."

He took them with him to the Pascala house, "Otherwise we won't never be able to look each other in the eye. We still gotta work together."

Serafin was outside, stoking a fire in the *forno*, and he straightened when Step approached.

"What I got to say is for your whole fam'ly to hear."

Serafin led him into the house where the children huddled behind their mother. Angelina had gone into the bedroom, afraid to show herself.

The room was warm, and smelled of yeast. Half a dozen loaves of bread dough were scattered about the room, covered with cloths to help them rise. Step eyed the cloth-covered humps.

"Come inside," Amalia told him and his children.

"It the most terrible," Serafin said, language slipping from him and knotting his tongue while his hands fidgeted in his holey pockets. "So much sorry for the terrible terrible..."

His face was sleepless, anguished, as was his wife's, so that Step felt a pang of doubt at keeping them away. He squeezed the medal in his fist inside his pocket, then turned his eyes to the statue on the kitchen table: their holy lady, her outstretched arms ending with broken-off hands, an unlit candle at her feet.

"The most terrible since we come here," Amalia told Step. "Who ever think this kinda thing?"

Finally the eyes met.

"Where is she?" Step said.

"Please, Mr. Step," Amalia said.

"Bring her out here. I got to see."

The children waited nervously. Amalia rose from the table, gave Serafin a pained, resigned look, and went to the bedroom.

All eyes stayed on the doorway until Amalia emerged with Angelina, her face bowed.

The sight of the girl sent a new stab of pain through Step.

"You crossed the line," he said, but he was talking to the parents, not to the girl. "We all did. Now my fam'ly got to pay."

Angelina began to cry.

Amalia put her arm around her daughter. "She no try to make trouble, Mr. Step," Amalia told him. "She just a girl who like your boy. They both good kids."

"My Calvin good 'n dead."

Angelina sobbed. "Sorry, sorry. I loved him, that's all."

The air trembled with her admission. The word *love*, the idea of love trembled in the fragile, mute, stifling air.

When she saw the rage building in Step's face, Amalia broke the silence. "She no do this bad thing to him." She was protective now, turning angry.

Step stared hard at the girl.

"I ain't blamin you," he said, but he wasn't so sure. Finally he let his eyes travel to Serafin. "I tryin to let you know the way things are here."

Again the doubt, the uncertainty. He looked at his son Tobe, and a brooding expression came over his face.

Then back at the Pascalas: "Best we stay away from each other. You children hear me? Best we stay with our own kind."

Again, the air trembled at the words.

"That not right," Serafin said.

"That just the way it is here," Step told him, trying to hold back his rage. "Best you learn that."

He steered his children toward the door. "This how it be at Sweet Hope," he mumbled. "Ain't nothin gonna change it."

"No!" Angelina cried.

They turned; all eyes were on her.

She hung her head, tried to stammer the words out. "There's something... got to tell you something."

They waited as she fidgeted with her dress buttons, looked up pleadingly. "It wasn't supposed to happen — it was an accident..."

"Murder no accident," Step snapped.

"I... I don't mean that," Angelina pleaded. "I mean..." She paused, gathered strength. "I'm going to have a baby."

Their bodies, the room, the very air — all turned to stone. And then the stone shattered.

Step felt his legs begin to buckle, but he held himself steady.

"*Santa Madonna* in heaven, you're what?" Amalia cried.

"Mama, I'm sorry," Angelina pleaded. She steeled herself, ready for the furious hand across the face. But it did not come.

Step Hall's eyes went to her stomach, as if looking for proof. He ran a hand through his short hair, his two children silent behind him. "What you say?"

Angelina lowered her head, tears brimming in her eyes. "We wanted to get married," she told them.

"No," Step said. His throat wanted to scream the word. It came out as a sharp command instead, so that the others jumped.

Amalia searched her daughter's face for the lie. "Impossible! *Che peccato! Che vergogna!*"

Angelina shook her head forlornly.

"You don't say things like this," Amalia scolded. "Are you sure?"

"You think I'd make this up?" Angelina cried. She took a deep breath. "Yes. I'm sure." She moved her hands to her stomach. "Over two months."

Tobe furrowed his brow, trying to make his mind go somewhere else.

"Can't be," Step said, his hand moving to his own stomach, as if he were sick.

"He was glad," Angelina told them. "We were going to tell you. We were going to get married."

"*Married*!" Step said.

Amalia took the girl's face roughly in her hands, searching for something while Angelina cringed. "You — " Amalia said, almost a sound of pity in her voice now. "My girl, my little girl."

Step's mind was reeling. He looked Serafin in the eye, trying to detect how much the man knew. But nothing. He couldn't tell anything anymore.

Yet he could not staunch the words that spilled from him. "This why you done it?" he shouted at Serafin.

"Done it?"

"This why you killed my boy?"

Serafin recoiled. "Me? You think I — some animal you think I am?"

Step grabbed Serafin's shirt with both his hands and began shaking him.

"Everybody know the manager do this," Serafin shouted as he tried to free himself. "You hear what the priest say — "

Step threw a punch at Serafin's face that sent him stumbling against the wall. Amalia let out a cry. He put his hand to his bleeding nose in disbelief while Step stared in shock at what he had done.

"It wasn't him," Isola yelled as she ran to her father. She looked to Birdie for help. "Tell him, Birdie," she pleaded.

All eyes went from one girl to the other.

When Birdie looked on gloomily, Isola told them: "Horton's bad, always watching us. We saw him... what he did to Lecie."

Birdie nodded sheepishly.

"Lecie?" Step said, caught off guard. "Who talkin 'bout Lecie?"

"He's bad," Isola repeated. "He didn't like Calvin."

Step's eyes narrowed. "What you sayin?"

Isola cast an accusatory glance at Angelina. "He was gonna do to Angelina —"

"No," Angelina said. "No."

"Why you ain't said nothin all this time?" Step demanded. "All the trouble we got over this."

"Said he'd kill Lecie's fam'ly if she told," Birdie stammered. She barely got the words out before the tears started. "But he killed Calvin."

Step straightened up, and for a minute seemed as if he would relent. But then he closed his fist. "That 'bout Lecie. Got nothin t' do with Calvin." He glared hard at Serafin. "Stay away from each other, you hear?" he said. "Childrens, everybody."

Serafin's own fists were clenched; blood trickled down his face. "Go, you. Go outta my house. I don't know you no more."

CHAPTER 23

Sciopero

August 1906

SERAFIN pulled a cloth from one of the loaves of bread on the table and stuffed it against his bleeding nose. "You saw that?" he said to his wife. "You heard him accuse me, the son–of–a–bitch? First keeping us from the burial, now this — "

But Amalia's eyes were on Angelina. She pointed to the bedroom. "Off," she told the girl. "Everything, so I can see."

Angelina backed away from the table. "Mama, what are you talking about?"

"Take off your dress. I want to see."

"Daddy," Angelina pleaded as she moved away from her mother. She told Amalia, "You can't see anything."

"You want me to rip those clothes from you myself?" She started for the girl, and they began a dance around the table.

"Amalia, what the hell's wrong with you?" Serafin shouted. He pulled the rag from his face, looked at the blood, then pushed it back against his nose.

Isola and Osvaldo jumped out of the way as Amalia and Angelina stalked each other. When Serafin reached for Amalia's arm, she pulled back and turned in the other direction. She pounced on Angelina, and the girl let out a shriek. Amalia yanked at the clothes with one hand while she pushed the girl toward the bedroom with the other.

"Daddy, stop her," Angelina cried.

He reached Amalia just as the dress gave way with a loud ripping sound. One sleeve hung from Angelina's shoulder while the rest dangled at her waist.

"Are you happy now?" she sobbed.

"No, I'm not happy." Amalia yanked on the sleeve, ripping the dress the rest of the way, and letting it fall to the floor.

"Jesus," Serafin said. The girl stood naked before them. Isola and Osvaldo pressed themselves against the wall, afraid to move.

Amalia turned Angelina around to face her. She was small and thin, but now Amalia saw. The breasts were just beginning to swell; the belly had the slightest roundness to it.

She stared at the stomach. "You let that boy touch you in sin," she said.

Angelina bent to retrieve the torn dress and held it in front of herself. Her crying had stopped. "I touched him too," she answered defiantly.

A slap resounded in the room. Angelina clutched the dress and held her head steady, as if she had not even felt the blow. "It's done, mama, there's nothing you can do about it."

"I want you to pray," Amalia said. She pointed to the statue on the table.

"Praying won't change anything."

Amalia raised her hand again, but then stopped herself. Her face contorted, and she struggled to maintain control. "You're just a baby," she said. "Just a girl yourself." Her jaw tightened as she tried to keep her voice from shaking.

"Mama, please," Angelina said.

Serafin went for one of his shirts, and now he put it around Angelina's shoulders.

The gesture seemed to awaken Amalia to what she had done. She flushed. "Where's my needle and thread?" she said, searching the table, the shelves.

"No," Angelina answered. "I'll fix it myself." Sniffling, she disappeared into the bedroom.

Amalia fell into a chair and said nothing.

Serafin threw the rag on the table. "That damn boy. I could throttle him for what he's done." As soon as the words were out, he looked at her in despair. "God no, no, I don't mean that."

They sat together in silence a long time. Amalia folded her hands on the table; Serafin's own hands played with the edge of the rag. It was as if the hands spoke to each other, of all they knew, and all they had endured, and all they would continue to endure. The lines and gouges in their hands were as familiar to them as those in each other's faces, as familiar as a furrow plowed across their land, as familiar as a loaf of bread.

We thought our life was one thing, the hands said.

And now it is something else entirely.

Are you afraid?

Of course.

Then we will be afraid together.

"People will talk, you know," Amalia said finally. "The priest — "

Serafin turned the cloth this way and that. "To hell with all of them."

She gazed at the door and thought of Valerio's death and how she had almost walked through the door that time a few years after the death. No, she had decided to stay.

Serafin was at the stove, moving pots, boiling water, and she watched him. "If you want to do something, you should put this bread in the *forno* to bake," she told him.

He placed a cup in front of her, and she looked down at it. "Tea? What do I want with tea?"

"Drink. Tea is good. Isola, Osvaldo, tea for you, too." They looked suspiciously at the cups he handed them, then carried them out to the stoop.

He sat across from her again. "I have to go check our wagon, and then the cotton pens, the weigh scale. I want to make sure everything's working right before we start picking."

"Picking?" She turned the cup in her hands without tasting. There was that thing inside her daughter, and every time she felt she was getting close to looking at it, she squeezed her eyes shut and turned away.

"Before you know it, the cotton will be ready." He knew he shouldn't be talking about work, but it was the only thing he could think to say.

Angelina was in the doorway again, wearing an old dress with holes in it. She eyed the cups of tea. "We were going to leave Sweet Hope," she said dryly. "We were going to get married and go away from here."

Amalia raised her head at this. The eyes flared for a moment.

"He wanted to." She touched her neck, as if thinking. "Mama, he was sweet."

"Stop," her mother said. "I don't want to hear it."

"You don't know what it's like to love somebody," Angelina said. "To plan a life together — "

Serafin sat rigidly, looking at his wife and daughter. Amalia returned his gaze.

"All you care about is your plaster statue and your prayers — "

"Love," Amalia said to the girl, "is not what you think it is."

Serafin looked at the bloody rag, and a stab of pain went through him.

***

THE day's work would wait for no one. Serafin went off to the wagon, the cotton pen, the weigh scales. While the bread was baking, Amalia sent Isola and Osvaldo to feed the chickens and then to the lake to fish, instructing them as usual to carry back firewood. She took the bread from the outdoor oven and set it on a plank to cool while Angelina watched. "Wash the bread pans and straighten the house," she told the girl, leading her back inside. It felt strange being alone in the house with her daughter. "There's work to do, baby or no baby. You'll learn that fast enough." *Baby.* She looked at the door, then the stove, as if someone had entered the room.

"Mama, I've been working right along. Why are you saying that?" She gathered the mixing pans to take outside to scrub, just to show her.

"When you're done, you can go to the bushes along the levee, see if you can find any berries. Make sure you cover up." She eyed the girl's stomach for emphasis.

Angelina shook her head in dismay. But berry picking was easy work. She knew her mother was trying to be kind, no matter what she said.

Once she was alone, Amalia carried the loaves inside, gathering all six to her breast at once. The loaves were warm and fragrant against her. She stood for a few moments, feeling their warmth before dropping them on the table. Then she sat staring at the bread.

She knew what it was like to say things in grief you might regret later. Serafin should know, too, the way he had acted those years. People had been afraid to come visit them after Valerio died, and it hurt her almost as much as the death itself. It was hard to separate the grief and pain from a person's real feelings, though. She thought of the Halls getting up each morning, trying to go on with their lives. It was as if

Calvin was away working, though, and Amalia had the funny thought that she might see him again, maybe tomorrow or the next day, walking back from William's livery stable.

She lay a hand on a loaf of bread, then eyed Serafin's bloody towel. Why is it, she wondered, that we don't even really see our children until they're gone? She remembered her bloodstained dress, her sickness after the lost child. And there it was again, that fear for all her daughter would have to endure now, in body and in mind. *Nanna-ó, Nanna-ó.*

It was mid-morning already. Before long, Serafin and the children would be coming in, expecting their dinner. She would fry some fish if Isola and Osvaldo caught anything. If not, they'd eat bread and greens again. At least the bread was fresh.

She found a basket, placed a clean cloth inside, then laid two loaves on the cloth and covered them. She gave a quick glance around the kitchen, and started for the Hall house.

Birdie came to the door, her hair loosely tied in braids, her dress faded and hanging on her. She stared at Amalia in surprise.

"Can I see your mother?" Amalia asked.

"Ma's in bed. Don't wanna see nobody."

Amalia touched the girl's cheek, then drew her hand back. "Everybody, we all hurt too much, you know?" Birdie's lip trembled.

Amalia walked in and set the basket on the table. Birdie followed. "Ma won't see you," she said. "Pa told you don't come."

The kitchen was bare. "Is she eating?" Amalia asked, glancing toward the bedroom door.

Birdie shook her head. "Won't hardly drink nothin neither." The girl's eyes were dark, her face hollow.

"Birdie Hall," a weak voice called from bedroom.

"It's Miz 'Malia," Birdie said.

No reply.

"Told ya," the girl whispered.

Amalia faced the bedroom door. "It's me, Fancy. Okay I come see you?"

Again, silence.

Amalia touched the basket. "I bring bread," she told Birdie.

Birdie glanced at the door. "Issy didn't come w' you?"

"I come alone."

Birdie nodded.

A coffee pot sat on the stove. Amalia went over and touched the cold stove, lifted the pot. It felt heavy. "I make a fire?" she asked. They spoke in low voices, as if not to disturb Fancy in the next room.

"Ain't nothin t' cook. People's bringin us food. She won't eat no ways."

Amalia knelt and started a small fire. "C'è milk?" she asked Birdie.

Birdie nodded toward a jar on the sideboard. "From this mornin. Ain't much."

Amalia heated the milk in a pan. When it was hot, she filled a cup.

"She like it w' sugar," Birdie said, handing Amalia the bowl. Amalia tore a piece of bread from a loaf and carried the sweetened milk and bread into the bedroom.

Fancy was sitting up, an icy scowl on her face. "Why you here?" she asked Amalia.

Amalia set the cup and bread down on an upturned peach crate next to the bed.

"I come pay my respects."

Fancy turned her head away.

"I told her don't come in, Ma," Birdie said.

Amalia took a breath. "Me, my family, we all sorry such a terrible thing happen. It's no good, so bad." She touched her breast.

"You don't know nothin 'bout it," Fancy said. Her face was hard as she stared at the door frame behind Amalia.

"We like your boy," Amalia said. "He's a good boy."

A whimper escaped Fancy's lips.

"I know Mr. Step don't want us here," Amalia said. "But we all hurt, everybody hurt."

"Birdie, take her outta here," Fancy said.

"Miz ''Malia," Birdie pleaded. "Mama."

Amalia held out her hand. "We gonna be *le nonne*," she told Fancy. Their eyes met, dark and liquid, eyes that went deep. In that instant, Amalia saw again the eyes of her own newborn infants looking up at her.

What did they see? she wondered. "We the grandmas," she said. "That baby come to all us, together."

"No," Fancy whimpered. "No."

Amalia sat in the chair next to the bed. She placed a hand on Fancy's, and Fancy did not remove it. "We gotta be good for the baby."

She lifted the cup for Fancy to drink, but Fancy shook her head. "Just you taste, just a little bit."

Fancy tried the milk, shook her head again.

"Here," Amalia said. She broke off a piece of bread and dunked it in the cup of warm milk. She shook drops of milk from the bread and lifted it to Fancy's mouth. "See? Good. You gotta eat so you get strong," she said as Fancy closed her eyes and tasted the bread.

***

Isola and Osvaldo walked glumly toward the lake, their fishing lines wound around a stick, and old feed sacks for carrying firewood slung over their shoulders.

"We could fish down near the bayou," Osvaldo said. "Near the swamp woods."

"You just want to check your swamp rat snare."

"So?" He kicked at the dirt. "Everybody's always fighting," he said. "I thought they liked babies."

"Only some babies," Isola answered. "Daddy should have hit him back."

"Now we don't have any friends," Osvaldo said. "I wonder if Tobe's been working on our flying machine."

He scanned the trees as they neared the lake. Everything seemed still and quiet in the hot morning. Few people were in the fields, since they were in what farmers called the "waitin time," the week or two before the bolls burst open and picking began.

"He's up at Hyner, you know," Isola said.

Osvaldo turned south along the tree line.

"Where you going?"

"I want to see."

"That ain't the way to the cemetery."

"I don't mean that," he said.

She followed her brother along the line of trees toward the bayou. They had walked this way many times, on their way to the lake or farther down to the swamp woods where they'd hidden the junk for the flying machine. But now they walked in silence, the thick growth of locust and pine and scrub oak on one side, the high lush cotton on the other, closing in on the narrow yellow road. Calvin was a boy just like any other boy, only a little bit older. The company beat grown men, like Sant'Angelo and Lazzaro and Claudio, but they'd never heard of the company beating one of the children. Killing him. A frog hopped across the dirt ahead of them and disappeared into the trees. Birds and insects filled the woods with chatter.

They slowed when they reached a narrow path into the woods, and both looked down it out of habit. They were too far away to see the small cabin tucked deep within the trees. Osvaldo raised his hand and waved down the path.

"You see her?" Isola asked. Her two middle fingers automatically folded down in the sign of *il corno*, to ward off the evil eye, and she held it ready against her leg.

"No."

"Priest said it happened just past here."

They crept along, inspecting the trees and shrubs a short distance beyond Lally Mo's lane for signs of entry. When they saw broken branches and bent grass they stopped. "You think a horse could go through here?" Isola asked. "Two horses?"

Osvaldo squatted and touched the broken branches close to the ground, then squinted into the woods.

Isola looked behind them at the tall cotton plants, then back at the woods. "It's too spooky," she said.

He stood and brushed his hands down the sides of his pants. "Don't tell anybody."

"We better not," Isola said, but Osvaldo was already stepping into the woods. He stopped a few feet in, and she followed. She took hold of his shirt to keep him back. They could tell by the light ahead that there was a clearing about a hundred feet in. "There," Osvaldo said, pointing in the direction of the light. "I bet that's where it happened."

"I don't want to see," she said, shivering.

An owl's screech startled them; Isola clutched Osvaldo's shirt more tightly. "*Merda*! What's a hoot owl doing out in the daytime?"

"Lally Mo," Osvaldo whispered.

The children flew out of the woods and down the road towards the bayou. When they rounded a curve in the road, they stopped to catch their breath.

"Did you see her?" Osvaldo asked, bent over.

"Nobody ever sees her."

"Lecie sees her," Osvaldo said. "I've seen her."

"You have not."

"Not her face, but the rest of her," Osvaldo said.

"What?"

Panting, he lifted his head just in time to see Bruno, the priest's dog, waddling toward them. "Oh–oh." In a minute, Father Odetti rounded the curve.

"What are you children doing way down here?"

"Going fishing, Father," Isola said, holding up the line to show him.

"Fishing in the bayou? So far from home?"

"We wanted to see where it happened," Osvaldo told him. "Is that why you came, too?"

Father Odetti glanced behind him. "I went to visit Mrs. Sant'Angelo and her children," he said. "And the others down in the bottom land."

Osvaldo smiled knowingly at the priest. The quickest way back home from the bottom land was back toward the landing, not up along this stretch of road.

"I guess you're too smart for me," he told Osvaldo. He sounded weary. "But you shouldn't be out here alone. It's dangerous, you should know that by now."

"We heard a hoot owl, but it was really Lally Mo," Isola said.

"Lally Mo won't hurt us," Osvaldo told his sister.

"That why you ran so fast?"

"What are you kids talking about? Come, I'll walk you to the lake where you can fish."

"But we have to go to the swamp woods," Osvaldo said.

"Swamp woods?"

Father Odetti was already turning them around and nudging them back in the direction they had come.

"Our machine," Osvaldo said.

"*Idiota*," Isola told Osvaldo. "He thinks he can fly, Father."

Father Odetti looked around nervously at the trees. "You'd better leave flying to birds and angels," he said. His eyes settled on Isola. "You should watch out for your little brother."

"I try," she said. "But he has a hard head."

The dog waddled beside them as they neared the place.

Osvaldo pointed to the broken branches. "Is that where you found him, Father? In there?"

Father Odetti put an arm on each of their shoulders and tried to hurry them past. "Let's not think about it."

"Angelina said they were going to get married."

"Married?" the priest said.

"Shh," Isola told Osvaldo.

"Do you think that's why they killed Calvin?"

"Nobody knows what happened," the priest told them, more tersely now.

"I bet Lally Mo knows," Osvaldo said, pointing to the path into the woods that they were just passing.

Father Odetti peered down the path. It was narrow and nearly overgrown with shrubs. Of course he had heard of the woman.

"She knows everything," Osvaldo said. "That's why people are afraid of her. But I'm not."

"You are too. You ran when we heard the hoot owl."

The priest gazed down the path. "That's where she lives?" It might not be a bad idea to try to talk to her, he thought, and the thought startled him.

"I hope they catch him, Father," Isola said. "Do you think they'll hang him?"

"Enough of this talk," Father Odetti told them. "Children shouldn't be thinking such bad things." He hurried them forward, but not before casting one more glance at the narrow path that led into the woods.

***

Serafin followed the farm road just north of the lumber mill, his mind on fire. When he reached the church he stopped a moment and looked at it. It was a cotton shed, a shack. Nothing. He kept walking.

Minutes later he left the farm road and climbed the levee, remembering with surprise that he'd been up here haying a few years back, before they'd planted their first crop. He went down the other side of the levee, fighting the thoughts that crowded his mind. Someone had set up beehives at the edge of the woods between the levee and the river, and he stopped, wondering if he should turn back lest they think he was out to steal their honey.

A few bees hovered above the boxes. The weeds grew waist-high. He noticed now that some of the trees near the beehives had been cut. A few old stumps, half buried in the tall grass, stuck up here and there. He stomped the grass around one of the stumps to chase away snakes and sat down.

The sun was hot. Bees floated in the air around the hives. A few wild flowers swayed in the grass.

In his mind he saw the weigh scales at the cotton warehouse, and on the hook he saw himself hanging a sack, and in the sack lay the weight of his family. Together, they did not equal one bale of cotton. Even when he added his own body to the sack they did not add up to the weight of one bale. He took himself out again, watched the needle on the scale dip.

He had been planning it for longer than he could remember, without even realizing it. But now he looked it straight in the eye, and what he saw chilled him. If his plan worked, they would be free. If it failed, there was no telling what would become of them. In that case, he would throw himself at the company's mercy, offer himself as bond, if only his family were allowed to leave. He saw them on the boat now, departing for Italy, while he stood on Sweet Hope's shore indentured for the rest of his life. His throat tightened. Yes, if that's what it took.

He let out a sigh, touched his throbbing nose, and everything came rushing back: Angelina running home sobbing, unable to speak, then the priest coming with the other two children, telling what he had seen, the hoofprints, the men's shoe prints, the body.

And then Step Hall, his one American friend, hitting him, accusing him. Goddamn *il nero*.

His breath caught in his throat.

The boy was dead. Murdered. He had been holding everything in since it happened. All he could feel was fear, then numbness. He couldn't say it although he thought it: if not for his daughter, Calvin would be alive. Angelina, his flower...

He fell to his knees with the waving green grass just above him. He looked up at the blue sky, waiting. Valerio, are you there?

For a moment it seemed that he really was hearing the old familiar voice calling from a distance, the younger brother admonishing the older: *Be a man. Stop this nonsense.* But the voice was the simple pounding of his own thoughts inside his head. And his mind could not halt the infernal noise of waves against rocks in an invisible storm.

A wisp of cloud came into view, and he studied it, waiting for something as it moved across the sky. "*Fratello*," he cried out. "Brother." Pieces of himself were breaking off, floating away.

Nothing. No answer. No voice from the other side. The faces of his children, his wife fluttered behind a veil, moved on without him. "Valerio, answer me!" he said. Not even the sound of a bird for response.

His knees began to hurt. He shifted his legs, blinking his eyes in the sun. So be it. At last he stood, clumsily, shook his head to clear it. Then he turned and started walking.

***

LAZZARO was spading his garden, digging out some of the old bean and tomato plants and chopping them into smaller pieces with the point of the shovel. When he saw Serafin approaching, he dug the shovel into the earth and waited. Getulio sat nearby, building mounds of dirt with an old macaroni box.

Serafin stopped a few feet from them. "You're feeling okay now?" he asked clumsily.

Lazzaro narrowed his eyes. It had been two weeks since that march back from across the lake. A lot had happened since then, all without his seeing a hair on Serafin's head. The two women had talked a few times, but that was all.

"What about you?" Lazzaro asked. "What happened to your face?"

Serafin touched his nose. "Nothing. The damn barn door at the mule yard got me."

Lazzaro nodded. No one was using the mules lately. But what could he say? There was nothing at all to talk about. "A hell of a thing about that boy," Lazzaro said. "Your girl must be upset."

"*Eh*." So, everybody knew everything at Sweet Hope.

Serafin motioned him to the water trough. They sat on the edge of it, watching Getulio push scraps of wood, his horse and wagon, up the mounds he had built.

"*Allora*," Serafin said. He paused, uncertain how to begin. "Maybe you were right, Lazzaro. About leaving Sweet Hope. Who knows."

Lazzaro cast a sideways glance at Serafin. "*Davvero?*" There was a note of sarcasm in his voice. "What brings this on?"

Serafin waved his hand through the air. "I've been thinking about it for awhile."

"You could have fooled me. So now you want to jump contract? That's a good one, *pad'ine.*"

"Not jump contract exactly," Serafin said. "Maybe it's time to try something else."

Lazzaro snorted.

"What would you say—" Serafin began. "I'm thinking—if all the farmers stood together, stopped working. If we called for a strike. *Uno sciopero.*"

Lazzaro turned to look at his friend.

"They'd have to give in to our demands," Serafin continued. "The company's afraid of us. They know they can't run the plantation without us." It was a long shot, he knew that. The plan needed others in order to work. Even then, who knew?

"A strike, just like that?" Lazzaro said. "Stop working right now during picking season? They'd line us up like ducks and shoot us without blinking an eye."

"I don't think so," Serafin said.

Fiorenza opened the door and looked out. When she saw Serafin, she hesitated, then raised her hand in greeting. He nodded to her. "Getulio," she said. "Don't bother your father."

The boy looked up a moment before returning to his dirt piles. "I'm not."

Quietly, as if not to disturb the men, Fiorenza closed the door and went back inside.

Lazzaro took his hat off, inspected the brim. "I could have used a little encouragement when Claudio and I left Sweet Hope."

"I know. But you found out—it was all a set-up, just like I said. A pat on the back from me wouldn't have meant anything."

Lazzaro's eyes flared.

Serafin saw his mistake immediately. "You're right," he said, backing down. "What's the use of thinking about what's done?"

"The tables are turned now, eh?" Lazzaro said.

Serafin tried to keep his voice calm. "I'm talking about something that's going to help every one of us. We all have to be in this together."

"*I neri* too?"

Serafin looked down at his shoes a moment. "What the hell do I care what *i neri* do?"

"That's a new one," Lazzaro answered. He waited for an explanation, but none came. "To call for a strike now, just when people are ready to pick their crops?" he said. "That's suicide."

"What better time?" Serafin asked him. "With their precious cotton sitting out in the fields, the company will have to give in. Don't you see?"

"They'll just hire day laborers and bill us for it on top of everything. We'll end up in a shit hole in hell — if they don't kill us first."

"They won't be able to find enough day laborers in all the Delta to pick the crops, not on such short notice," Serafin said. "Everybody's got their own fields to pick."

Lazzaro moved to the edge of the yard where the cotton grew as high as his chest. Serafin followed. Lazzaro fingered a handful of leaves and bolls. "See?" Some of the bolls were just beginning to crack open. The plants were heavy with them.

Serafin, too, touched the plants. In spite of everything, it was good to see such a crop, to feel the strong bolls in his hands. It would be hard for any of them to leave the crops they'd raised with their blood and sweat and tears.

"I've got a wife and kid to worry about," Lazzaro said, nodding toward Getulio. "So do you. What happens to Amalia and your kids if this thing fails?"

"I've thought about it, all of it," Serafin answered. "I'll buy their freedom with my life if it comes to it." Even as he spoke, his face clouded over.

Lazzaro smirked. "As if anyone's freedom is for sale here. The company doesn't want our money. They want our bodies. Let me know if you find anyone willing to go along with your big idea."

"We used to be like one," Serafin said. He crossed his fingers to show Lazzaro. "The same mind. Everything together."

Lazzaro gave him a long, meaningful look. "Well? I came here with you, didn't I? A man has to get smart sometime."

The remark cut him to the core, but he tried to ignore it. "It can work, Lazzaro. If we talk to as many people as possible and get them behind us."

"*Us*," Lazzaro said. He was cool, detached. Serafin could see he was losing him. "When your strike doesn't work, they'll destroy us once and for all."

Serafin was silent a moment. "They won't hurt us," he told Lazzaro.

"They beat the hell out of me," Lazzaro said. "What do you call that?"

"That's as far as they'll go," Serafin insisted. "Intimidation, that's all."

"They killed Step Hall's boy."

The words stopped Serafin.

Lazzaro motioned to the surrounding cotton plants. "Just leave it standing in the fields, that's what you're saying, eh? How many people have agreed so far?

"I came to you first," Serafin answered.

"You haven't talked to anybody? What the hell's wrong with you?"

"I'm talking now. No one's ever getting out of debt at Sweet Hope the way things are," Serafin told him. "Wake up. Who are we fooling?"

"*Uno sciopero*?" Lazzaro said in an almost mocking tone.

"If each one of us convinces one other man, within a few days we'll have all of Sweet Hope behind us," Serafin said. "Are you with me?"

"I don't know," Lazzaro answered. "I don't know anymore if I'm with you or not."

CHAPTER 24

Meeting

August 1906

ANYONE walking near the building that served as the black church on Sweet Hope could hear the raised voices and occasional shouts, interrupted at times by waves of plaintive singing. In that church sat most of the black farmers of Sweet Hope, and a few of their friends from surrounding plantations as well. Fancy had surprised everyone by rising from her grief bed and insisting on coming. She sat now beside her husband and two children. Even Uncle Blue was there, sitting alone in back.

Reverend Monroe was telling the gathering that he had consulted a lawyer from Jackson, and that, with the farmers' support, they would bring murder and rape charges against Lee Horton. Birdie Hall — and supposedly the Italian girl as well, he told them — had confessed to having witnessed the rape of Lecie Titus by Lee Horton. Lecie trembled both at the word becoming public and at fear of what Horton had threatened to do if she told. "All the more reason to stand behind the child," Reverend Monroe said, anger shaking his voice. "And to go after Horton. The evil hand knows only to do more evil." Miss Betty eyed him staunchly from the front row. The evidence was weak, and no one could prove what they all knew: that Horton had murdered, and his sidekick Garlock was in on it as well.

"They ain't gonna do nothin 'gainst those men," Fred Titus insisted. "What white folks gon' listen to two little plantation girls?" Lecie sank lower in her seat, clutching her pale–skinned child.

Step looked around at the gathering. His ears heard, his eyes saw, his body was there, alongside his wife and two children, but he felt like a bird in a tree on a hot, still day. Lawyer, charges, evidence. "Dead" was the one word he was trying to comprehend. All those other words were mere leaves rustling in the wind.

He watched Fred, watched him stand and open his mouth, his face determined and angry. Watched Lud put her arm around Lecie's shoulder, watched Lecie bow her head to her baby.

And Lecie was sitting there alive and whole, and she held a baby child alive and whole, but Calvin was cold in the ground.

Fancy's fingers were digging into his thigh: something Fred was saying, or somebody was saying, everybody talking and uh–huhing while he perched there, far away, the frail twig swaying slightly beneath him.

He and his wife had argued the previous night, Birdie and Tobe there at the kitchen table hearing it all. She'd finally risen from the bed, eaten a little of the supper Birdie had put to-gether. Then she'd asked him outright, "What reason you got now to stay? What excuse now? Take us far 'way from here."

His mind had already been there, weighing the idea. But no, he'd told her, not yet.

"No? You waitin t' give them the rest a' our blood? Why not git a knife an' cut our hearts out now, bleed us now till we all just one dead heap?"

Birdie looked toward the stove, then the sideboard, fear-ing anything sharp. Tobe glanced at the door, checking for a clear path if he needed a quick escape.

"Not yet," Step had said to Fancy. "Not till it's finished."

"You still dreamin," she said. "Still thinkin you somebody to Mr. Gates? You the high an' mighty one. You nobody t' Mr. Gates."

"Not 'bout that," he told her. His mind was ticking off numbers, days.

"After what they done to my baby — " Her voice caught, and she broke down once again.

He rose from the table, laid a hand on her shoulder to comfort her. But he was only going through some strange motions; he knew nothing of comforting anyone.

"The farmers' crops not all ginned and sold yet," he'd told her, as if talking in his sleep. "When all the crops is in, when everybody paid or got their debts squared 'way, then — "

He paused, wondering *What?*

"Then I done here," he said flatly. The words were unreal to him. In truth, he could not see ahead even one day, let alone months. Winter? December? Leave Sweet Hope in December? Ever?

"Farmers already leavin," Fancy said.

"Only if they paid. Not all. And not any Italians."

"Italians!" She faced him squarely. "You talkin t' me 'bout *'talians*? Those people the reason we come to this." Her face broke again as she wailed the words: "My boy."

He raised his hands in surrender while Birdie and Tobe watched silently. Empty hands. They were all he could give her.

In the church now, a hymn was ending. Reverend Monroe's voice rose above the last strains: "We talked and we talked, but we did not act. And now blood is spilled, and Calvin Hall has paid the price."

Step startled at the name, and again Fancy's fingers dug into his leg. But then he let the words float away from him, and he sat listening as if the preacher were talking about somebody else's troubles.

He would not stoop, that is what he kept telling himself. He would not become some low–life animal like the ones who had murdered his son. Fancy did not understand. He had a duty, and he would fulfill it — not to the company anymore and not to Gates anymore, but to hard working farmers, and most of all to himself. And then he would be done.

No real trial, Reverend Monroe was telling them. Without concrete evidence, they could not go to a courthouse trial. Inquiry, they called it. That would be first; then maybe a trial.

"Ain't gonna be no trial, noways," Fred Titus shouted. "Even if they had whatever kinda evidence they cryin for. Lecie's baby ain't proof enough? That poor boy's grave ain't proof enough?"

Tha's right, people said.

"If 'twas one a' them Italians Horton murdered or raped," Fred went on, "see how fast they jump."

Uh–huh.

When the door opened, all heads turned to see Father Odetti standing sheepishly, his hat in his hands.

A few murmurs went up: *Tha's him. One tha' found the boy. Mmm–hmm.*

Reverend Monroe and Miss Betty exchanged glances. He cleared his throat. "Rev'rin? You thinkin to join us?"

Father Odetti looked about, dazed. He had never set foot in the black church before, had hardly spoken more than a few words to any of them. *If Horton had attacked an Italian* — He had heard Fred say it, clear as day as he pushed the door open.

Step stood and faced him. "You don' belong here, Mr. Rev'rin. This our business."

"I think you'll want to hear what I've come to tell you," he managed to say.

Reverend Monroe and Miss Betty waited for the murmuring to die down. Step's insides were hot embers sifting and shifting inside the sack that was his body. His eyes burned him, his throat burned. For a moment it crossed his mind that he might burst into flame, an ember igniting a dry cotton shack. He moved his hands closer to his body, so as not to harm anything in the church when it happened. As from a distance, he heard a soft whimper escape his wife.

"You hear me?" Step repeated. "Go on, now."

"Just hold on a minute," Reverend Monroe told Step. He turned to Father Odetti. The priest's face was flushed. He gripped his hat as if his life depended on it. "You got something to say, Mr. Reverend?"

They watched Father Odetti walk stiffly to the front of the church. He turned, wiped his brow, and glanced at Reverend Monroe for a sign of encouragement that did not come. Reluctantly, Step took his seat.

"I'm sorry," the priest stammered. "All this — " He waved his hand, cleared his throat. A few people grumbled at the intrusion.

"I've found a witness to the murder," he told them.

The buzzing, murmuring voices skipped a beat, then rose. Step leaned forward in order to catch what the priest was saying.

"I've spoken with her briefly," Father Odetti said. "She might still need some coaxing."

"Somebody saw the murder?" Reverend Monroe said. "And hasn't spoken up?" Now he looked directly at Lecie. "Is it one of the children?"

"No, not a child," Father Odetti answered. "She's a grown woman."

Impatience was beginning to creep into Reverend Monroe's face. "Well, who is it?"

"The old woman in the woods," Father Odetti said. "She lives not far from where — where the murder happened."

More murmurs from the congregation. "Only one live that way's Lally Mo," Fred said.

"That's her name," Father Odetti answered.

A collective *ohh* went up, a puff of smoke, a breath.

Birdie and Tobe and Lecie squirmed in their seats.

He talked w' Lally Mo? Went t' see her?

Hmmph. Now that somethin, for sure.

"Now why would you go talk to Lally Mo?" the preacher asked with deliberation. The faces staring back at Father Odetti were asking the same question: How come the likes a' you gettin involved?

Father Odetti shifted nervously where he stood. "He was just a boy," he stammered. "I found him — " He held his hands out, and they stared at the hands, as if they would see the body of Calvin lying there. Father Odetti shook his head and looked back at them in renewed disbelief.

"Did she agree to testify?" Reverend Monroe asked, bringing the priest back around.

"Not exactly. If somebody could — " Father Odetti stammered. "I don't think there's anything more I can say to her."

"Lally Mo never leave the woods for nothin," somebody shouted.

Reverend Monroe waited a few moments for the noise to subside. "She understands that we're calling for murder charges against Horton and the company?" he asked. "That there will be a public hearing?"

The priest nodded yes to the questions.

"She's not daft," Lud called out.

Eyes wandered the room, falling first on Step, then on Reverend Monroe, then on his wife.

"Lecie know her," someone said.

"Not my girl," Lud told the gathering. "She been through 'nough."

The eyes wandered again, then settled back on Reverend Monroe. "She and I have different views on worshipping our

God," he told them. "I don't know that I'd be welcome on her property."

"Ever'body wrong," Lecie said.

The surprised congregation turned to look at her. She hung her head and stammered, "Lally Mo good lady."

Lud put a hand on her daughter's arm.

Reverend Monroe considered the priest again. Then he reached for the old cigar box on the front table. "In the meantime — " he said to the congregation, and he gave Miss Betty the collection box to hand over to the first row. "A conjure lady and two little plantation girls?" He shook his head, keeping a guarded eye on the priest. "The collection will go toward consulting the lawyer."

People rustled and shuffled in their seats as they dug into worn pockets. They murmured about Reverend Monroe's lawyer, and what high price he might charge, and what kind of evidence, beyond Lecie's red-haired baby, a white man's court might want to see. The cigar box passed from one gnarled hand to the next as pennies, nickels, and dimes — and even a couple of two-bit pieces — clinked against each other into the bottom.

***

SWEET Hope shimmered with activity invisible to the human eye. When people passed each other on the dusty roads to and from their fields, they briefly nodded and moved on. But in those moments of recognition the eyes spoke, the bodies moving through air spoke: *Gettin ready*, they said.

Reverend Monroe's lawyer arrived two days before the inquiry. He spent most of the time sequestered with the minister, talking, preparing notes, planning strategies. If the judge and managers found out about a black lawyer being hired, they would be sure to come up with a way to have him barred from setting foot on courthouse property. So the inhabitants of that side of town were more careful than usual with the words that escaped their lips. Father Odetti rowed across the lake and slipped into the Monroe home one evening, staying long enough to repeat in detail everything he could remember happening the day Calvin died. Then he slipped out and rowed his boat alone across the dark lake back to Sweet Hope.

Rumor traveled all through Sweet Hope and the surrounding land, too, from across the river, telling of the arrival of Harlan Gates. Him, too: *Gettin ready.* He was agitated as much by the inconvenience of having to halt his political campaigning as by the unfavorable public scrutiny an inquiry would cast on him. "A *pro forma* inquiry," he told his supporters. "We have nothing to worry about."

On the night of his arrival, Gates met privately with county Judge Garrett Lydle to discuss the matter. They were old friends. Gates told himself they were only catching up on old times. And clarifying a potentially difficult situation. He offered a box of Cuban cigars and two bottles of brandy, "From the *Charente*, a little trip I took."

"The boy didn't inflict a fatal beating on himself," Judge Lydle told Gates as he took the gifts. "You know I have to remain impartial and hear all sides."

"Of course. I'm as appalled as the next man by this turn of events," Gates assured him.

"If it was just the Negroes fighting among themselves," Lydle told him, "we wouldn't hear more than a chitter."

"It was just the Negroes fighting among themselves," Gates interrupted. "The Italian priest *found* the body. That's all." He forced a strained smile. "You know me, Garrett. You know what kind of man I am. I would never allow such an abomination on my property — " He flinched slightly. "Especially given my current position. I was hoping that we understood each other."

"I think I understand more than you give me credit for."

Gates crossed his legs, looked away for a moment. "I think I have a good shot at becoming senator. You know what a boost that could mean for the Delta planters, for the whole economy down here."

Lydle's expression did not change. "I know that."

Gates took a long time picking up a cigar and lighting it. The two men watched the smoke billow away. Finally Gates told him: "County judge doesn't have to be the end of the line for you."

Judge Lydle considered the information. He picked up a cigar and passed it under his nose. After a moment he asked, "When were you in France?"

The tension eased from Gates' face.

They talked for several hours into the evening.

✳✳✳

MOST farmers listened guardedly to Serafin, some averting their eyes as he spoke. Only Ceravone's grandson Ettore declared he was ready to take action if enough others were behind them. "You should call a meeting, though," he said. "You can't organize like this, going from farm to farm one man at a time. Everybody's afraid. If you had people meet as a group, you could get them fired up. Maybe it'd give them the courage to stand up for their rights."

Ettore's enthusiasm renewed Serafin's hopes. "The church," he said. "It's the only place big enough. And that way, if the company says anything, we'll just say we're having a Mass."

"Without the priest?"

"He's a lackey for the company, any way you look at it," Serafin said. "Best to keep him out of it. We'll just say we go there for prayers on certain nights, that's all. No priest involved."

"You better get moving," Ettore told him. "You don't have much time if you want to pull this off."

"I was hoping you'd help me," Serafin said, confused now. "I can't cover the whole plantation myself, you just said so."

"Well, yes," Ettore stammered, as if surprised to find himself in such a position. "I suppose I can talk to a couple people." He shoved his hands in his pockets and looked around at the fields. "I'm awfully busy right now. But — well, we'll see."

✳✳✳

WHEN Serafin came in from walking the plantation, Amalia was waiting for him. Something cold was settling inside her. It had been there when he first mentioned the idea to her, and it had only grown larger as the days went by.

When she saw his face, the coldness turned to fear. "I told you not to do it," she said.

"I have to try," he answered. "Others might come around yet."

"It'll be too late. It's already too late."

He paced throughout the room, picking up a pot here, a basket there, then putting it back down. The children were outside. Three chicken feathers lay on the table. He picked them up, held them to her.

"Osvaldo," she explained.

He sat, fingering the feathers.

"I can talk to some of the ladies if you want," she told him. "I still don't think it's a good idea, not without the men behind you. What did the others say today?"

He shrugged. "You know. The same. Ceravone's grandson, he's the only one really interested. If you can call it that." He spread the feathers on the table. "Who would have thought, him of all people?"

"Two families," she said. Her eyes swept around the room. "Like pissing in the sea."

"Lazzaro too, maybe. I can't tell with him."

"A little bit bigger piss, then," she said. "*Allora*. So that's the end of that idea." She almost sounded disappointed.

"Not the end yet," he said. "We won't know until we meet. The trial's tomorrow."

"*Un' inchiesta*," she reminded him. A hearing.

Isola wandered into the room; she had come up on the stoop, listening. "We've been sheep, blind sheep," she said.

Serafin drew the girl to him, pulled her up to sit on his lap. She laughed. "Daddy, I'm too big for that."

"You weigh as much as a barrel of oats. We're sheep, eh?"

"Not if we strike we're not."

"You remember your grandfather, in Italy?"

"A little bit. I remember his rabbits."

"Well, when we go back to Italy you can talk to him about the time you helped organize a strike in America." He looked over at Amalia. She was watching with an anxious expression. "Your *nonno* will be proud to find out he has such a brave granddaughter."

She lay her head on his shoulder, and she was trembling.

"What's the matter, little chicken leg?"

"It's not fair that the company has guns and we don't," she murmured into his shoulder.

✳✳✳

LAZZARO arrived early in the morning with Claudio to explain to Serafin: he'd given it a lot of thought, and he couldn't risk losing his farm. No one would go along with Serafin's idea. Lazzaro looked down for a moment at Osvaldo who had followed his father through the cotton patch, his head tied with a dirty calico rag. "It's a simple fact, most of the other farmers don't feel the way you do. We can't go fighting battles for the black ones now."

Serafin threw his hands in the air. "That again. Who the hell ever mentioned *i neri*? This battle's not for them, it's for us. Remember how brave we used to be?"

"No, I don't remember."

Serafin made a disgusted sound. "Claudio? What about you? You're the one who came to Sweet Hope ready to start a revolution. What happened to your fire?"

The young man lowered his eyes, shrugged apologetically. "I got beat to a pulp once already."

"Look," Lazzaro continued. "You should hear what they're saying about this strike down at the company store — "

Serafin exploded. "At the store? Jesus, you talk there and the managers will find out in no time. *Per Dio*, you know you can't go around shouting something like this." He started pacing while Osvaldo furrowed his brow and watched.

"Calm down," Lazzaro said. "People talk. What do you think? You yourself go around telling everybody — "

"Not right in front of the bastards I don't," Serafin said. "I'm sunk."

"Hey, *pad'in*, even if I wanted to help you, I can't risk it. Nobody's behind you on this thing, don't you see?"

"*Pad'in*, is it?"

"I'm sorry, *amico*," Lazzaro told him as he and Claudio left.

"Maybe we should just listen to Reverend Monroe's lawyer," Osvaldo told him, as they continued their walk.

"What? What lawyer?"

Osvaldo hung his head. "Tobe told me. Papa, I can't help it. Tobe's my friend."

Serafin stopped and looked at the boy. A pain went through him, a knife. He could not bear to think of living without his son, his children. Without Amalia. He imagined what it might have been like, all these years of never knowing them, if she had left him when they lived in Italy. Of course he knew she had been thinking about it. He'd been a fool, and maybe he'd lost his mind with grief, but he wasn't blind.

"What do you know of American lawyers and courts?" Serafin asked.

"Nothing," Osvaldo said. He thought a minute. "Did you ever get people to go on strike before?"

They walked along in silence. His heart was throbbing.

People looked at them strangely as they passed. Osvaldo brushed the corner of his bandana from his face.

"*Diavolo*, how word travels out here," Serafin said. "Worse than malaria."

Not far ahead, manager Wade was riding from one lane to another. Serafin steered the boy into the cotton. "Just act like you're working," he said. When the horse was gone, they went back into the road.

He shook his fist at one of the ogling farmers. "What the hell are you looking at?" The man watched a moment longer before going back to picking his cotton.

"It's all right, papa," Osvaldo told him. "I know what it's like to have good ideas nobody wants to listen to."

CHAPTER 25

Swamp Rat Man

September 1906

A small group of Negroes stood vigil across from the court-house, Step and Fred and a number of their friends among them. There were others too, mostly men from the village, or plantation and farm owners or cotton factors from the surrounding area. They were there not for Lee Horton or Garlock but for Harlan Gates, the most well–known and respected planter in the Delta.

After a mere thirty–seven minutes of closed doors, a pudgy, gray–haired man pulled open the door, surveyed the crowd, and matter–of–factly announced the word: No grounds for a trial. No charges would be filed against Lee Horton. To the farmers of Sweet Hope the word meant one thing: They let a murderer go free.

What did we expect? they asked themselves.

Thinkin they gonna listen to a black lawyer.

Or to Lally Mo.

Can't trust no white folks.

Some of the men vowed to leave Sweet Hope or the county. Some vowed worse, most of it just talk.

An old black man with a cloud of white hair was helping a woman down the courthouse steps. She was a small, bent woman wearing a dress made from a patchwork of feed sacks, a well–worn man's work hat perched on her head.

Lally Mo.

The two were followed by Father Odetti, Reverend Monroe, and the young black lawyer from Jackson, all looking disgruntled and dismayed. Reverend Monroe had not been allowed to speak, and the young lawyer was given only two minutes to state his case, then informed that, should grounds be found for a trial, he would not participate: Negro lawyers were barred from trials involving white planters — or anyone holding political office, as with Harlan Gates.

The sheriff stood on the courthouse steps, calling for his deputies to disperse the Negroes with force if necessary. "Get them outta here 'fore Gates and the others come through." Reluctantly, some left, although most scattered along the periphery to watch.

A shaken Father Odetti made his way past the gathering on the steps, slightly aware of the few murmurs of recognition. He squeezed through the crowd and began walking briskly, turning down the first street he came upon. There he stopped and leaned against the wall of a hat shop, breathing heavily.

That day when he had run into the Pascala children in the woods where Calvin had been killed, he had gone back again, thinking (if it could be called thinking, all hazy and vague and unformed in his mind) that he would somehow speak to Lally Mo about what she had seen. He had stood looking down her lane when a creaking voice at his elbow made him jump: "You finally come." She was small and shriveled and reminded him of a sinewy piece of meat. If anyone had asked him a few hours ago, he would have said he had gone out on a limb to convince the woman to testify. In truth, it seemed she had called him to her. Either way, in the white light of the courthouse, she was scoffed at and summarily dismissed ("The wind tell me t' look. When I look't, I seen the evil hands go at the boy. My eyes seen." The courtroom had erupted in snickers). When it was his turn to be questioned by the judge, he, too, spoke the truth. But the truth was not what they wanted. The black minister and lawyer had been silenced. Every one of them had been silenced. The spirit of Harlan Gates and all he stood for filled the courtroom. There was no other God, he saw that now.

And now he understood, as he could not when Serafin Pascala came to him for help, or when Pietro the shoemaker tottered before him on crutches and petitioned him. Pietro, crippled for life because of a Sweet Hope accident. Father Odetti had been asked many times over by various tenants to contact the Italian Consulate. It had meant nothing to him. He could not understand their request. Now the scales were lifted from his eyes: Pietro dead. Babies dead. Malaria and malnutrition, disease and crippling accidents, a child raped, a boy murdered. His soul was blackened. *I have tried to serve both God and mammon, and God's children have suffered at my hand.* He moaned aloud in anguish.

Calvin's bloodied, battered face loomed before him as he struggled to regain his composure. His knees felt weak; his legs could barely support him. He was reviled, hated, but it did not matter, now that his eyes were opened. The train station was a few blocks away. He'd be able to reach New Orleans within two days, and no one would question his traveling. He would tell everything he knew — no matter the consequences for him at Sweet Hope.

A commotion of voices rose from the area of the courthouse: cheers and congratulations. He lifted his head in the direction of the voices, then began walking stiffly toward the train station.

✻✻✻

WHEN Harlan Gates appeared on the courthouse steps, people flocked to the tall, handsome blond man. Gates, his face showing wear and relief, accepted the handshakes and words of support while occasionally casting a watchful eye at Lee Horton. And beyond the well–wishers and Horton stood the grumbling Negroes he would have to find some way to appease. His eyes fell upon the haunted face of Step Hall, his long–time trusted worker. Step returned the gaze with pained recognition.

The priest had sweated over his testimony, stopping short of accusing Horton and Garlock outright. In truth, though, there was no evidence. The priest had seen no one, had seen only the hoofprints and footprints. It was Lally Mo, the old black conjure lady, who insisted she had seen the men go after the boy. "And why didn't you speak up right then, if you thought you'd witnessed a murder?" the judge asked her. "Time weren't right. I's speaking now."

They wouldn't accept any of her testimony, of course — a crazy old niggra lady. Yet he couldn't shake the uneasy feeling the woman gave him. He knew — as did the others, most likely — that she had been telling the truth.

Someone uncorked a bottle of champagne, breaking Gates' brief reverie, while the *Gazette* editor took notes.

"Now what, Senator?" one of the cotton factors asked good–naturedly.

The crowd laughed.

"Don't jump your guns," Gates answered with his confident, yet tight smile. "I'm not in the Capitol chambers yet."

He postponed an interview with the *Gazette* saying he had urgent business to attend to first, and told his managers to meet him back at the Sweet Hope office. Everyone, including the villagers who heard him, expected a congratulatory drink, perhaps even an appreciative bonus.

Instead, Gates chastised every one of the managers for the disparaging attention they had brought to Sweet Hope and for putting his political and social standing under such embarrassing scrutiny. Then he quickly outlined for them a new code of behavior he had thought long and hard over in the trying last two weeks: "You are here to see to the welfare of the tenants. We want them as productive and cooperative as possible, but not at the expense of their physical and mental well-being. And not at the expense of our profits — or my reputation."

He outlined the changes he was calling for: filters installed on the wells, to improve the drinking water. Each household would get free mosquito netting, and the cost of quinine tablets would be reduced.

"It's the high store prices and taxes they're hot about," Wade said. "And they want to be able to sell their cotton off Sweet Hope."

"I'll cross that bridge when I come to it — if I have to. Let's see if we can't pacify them with a little sugar water first." His pat smile was almost a grimace. "It costs a lot less."

"You cavin under the pressure?" Wright asked.

"Under the circumstances..." Gates paused. "Let's just say it would be best that no more negative attention be visited upon Sweet Hope."

"You ain't thinkin to take the cost outta our pockets?" Horton asked.

Gates eyed him coolly, then turned back to the others. "These changes should make your jobs a little easier, without taking much of a bite out of company profits."

"When they takin effect?" Wade asked.

"Right now."

"Troubles go deeper than store prices and well filters," Horton grumbled. "Them Dagoes always gripin about something."

"There's one more matter to address," Gates told the men. "Concerning Mr. Horton here. And Mr. Garlock."

The smile faded from Horton's lips. Garlock looked nervously toward the door.

"I want both of you off Sweet Hope by noon tomorrow. You have twenty-four hours to gather your belongings and make arrangements to leave. The other managers here will see to it that you abide by my decision."

Garlock kept his eye on the door, and nodded stiffly, as if he'd been listening to some hard news about someone else. His only clear thought was to get as far away from Lee Horton as soon as possible before he found himself in real trouble.

In those few moments, Horton's face went from amused uncertainty to disbelief to rage. "After all I giv'n you, all the time I put in..." he sputtered at Gates. "I'm innocent, you heard what the judge said." When Gates did not respond, he added, "You gonna sink without me."

"I think you'd better stop before you make things worse for yourself," Gates told him evenly. "The only thing you've done for Sweet Hope is create a scandal."

"*Scandal*," Horton spat. "I didn't do nothin, and the law says so." He shot a look at Garlock, but the man remained silent.

"You can walk, or take the ferry out when you go," Gates told them. "But make sure you leave your horses at the stables."

"My horse?" Horton said.

"My horse," Gates corrected him. "You were outfitted with those horses when I hired you on."

Horton fumed: "Takin a man's horse is like takin his legs away. People get hung for less than that."

Gates merely stared at the man who had done his dirty work up until now. "Everyone is expendable, Mr. Horton," Gates said. "You of all people should know that."

Garlock kept his eyes averted, sweat prickling his neck. The other managers shifted uneasily, afraid Gates would fire them next.

And all the while, Gates was mulling over his next decision, the action he would have to take within the next few days to restore Sweet Hope to order as quickly as possible. In the end, he hoped to be seen as benevolent and long–suffering in the way he dealt with the disgruntled Italians. In truth, he had to stop the instigators.

"Looka the other tomfools you got workin this place," Horton blustered. "What 'bout them? You can't get rid of me."

"I just did," Harlan Gates said.

❋❋❋

A pall of death hung over the plantation. The closer he got to Step Hall's place, the more unsettled he became. Wary eyes watched from the fields as he passed, or tenants paused along the dusty roads, their eyes lowered, stealing glances nonetheless. What in God's name have I done, he wondered.

There were hardly any Negroes left on Sweet Hope, and it surprised him to see how much things had changed since he'd last taken these roads.

Step's yard was empty. But as soon as Gates pulled his horse to a stop, Step came outside, his two children behind him in the doorway.

Gates gazed at Step an awkward moment before dismounting and retrieving a package wrapped in a checkered cloth from the saddlebag. "We have to give them something, after all," his wife had told him before he left.

"I'm sorry, Step," Gates finally said, glancing a moment at the children. "I've come to tell you how sorry I am about this unfortunate accident."

Step's eyes flared at the word "accident," but he held his tongue.

Gates handed over the cloth, and Step took it, dumbly. "From my wife," Gates said. "She sends her condolences."

Step looked at the cloth in his hand, unwrapped it, stared: a jar of orange marmalade. The world stopped for a long, hard moment.

"Your children might like it," Gates said, and then paused, ashamed at having said the one word that would bring the man pain: *children.*

Step kept his eyes on the jar, the rage building inside him. Finally he said the only words that would come out: "Why you let them murder my boy, Mr. Gates?" Anger rattled his voice. He looked directly at Gates now with pained, accusing eyes.

Sweat trickled down his back, his chest. His shirt collar was tight as a noose. He could feel the two children watching him from the doorway.

"I'm truly sorry for your loss," Gates said, struggling to maintain his composure.

Tobe turned his face into the doorjamb, seeming to hug it.

"I will pay for the coffin, of course," Gates told Step.

"Already been paid for, Mr. Gates," Step replied.

"Shall I talk to your wife?" Gates said. He prayed the answer was no.

"Talk? What talk gonna do? That was her baby, her first born."

"Yes, I know," Mr. Gates said, trying to ease his neck away from the constricting collar.

The man in front of him was haggard, beaten; yet strong, dignified. It was easy to tell just at a glance how Step Hall stood out from the other workers, why Gates had chosen him years ago to help work the plantation. And so he thought, for a moment, that perhaps they could address each other as men, one to another. Gates motioned Step away from the door. "Could we talk a moment, in private?"

The request took Step by surprise.

They made their way to the side vegetable garden while Tobe and Birdie kept watchful eyes on them.

"I know there have been rumors," Gates began. "This morning the court found there were no grounds for bringing charges."

"Yessir, that's what they say."

Gates gave an understanding nod. It pained him to think one of his own men was responsible for the boy's death. "I want you to know I let Horton and Garlock go."

Step barely registered any reaction.

"So," Gates said. "Perhaps you can spread the word about their firing. I think people will want to know. There will be no more trouble from those two on Sweet Hope."

"*Trouble*," Step said.

Gates hesitated a moment. "I've ordered some changes on Sweet Hope that you should know about." He began to outline his improvements, never thinking for a moment that Step — or Fred or any of the others — might be thinking of leaving Sweet Hope. Calvin's death was already an abstraction for him.

It was as if a shade was pulled down over Step's face. His eyes moved slowly just to the side of Gates and fixed themselves vaguely somewhere in the distance. Gates breathed deeply before continuing, his eyes falling on a tarnished medal that hung from a nail on the back of the chicken shed.

"There's another thing," he began, turning back to Step. "This rumor of a work strike... the Italians." Step looked up. Rumors traveled both ways on Sweet Hope. "Your friend was behind it, no?"

Step made no answer.

"Step, you know I cannot abide such insurrection."

"Yessir. Wasn't no strike I know of," he answered.

"I can't run a plantation if there's upheaval the way there's been."

"You firin me, too?" Step asked simply.

Gates hesitated again, as if trying to understand. "That's not what I'm getting at." He looked deeply into the wounded eyes. At last, he dug his hand into his pocket. "Here," he said, pressing a folded bill into Step's hand.

Step looked at the money in his palm. "Ten dollar?" he said.

"I hope this helps a little."

Step stared at the money.

"If you need anything, Step, if there's anything I can do, you let me know, you hear?"

Harlan Gates climbed onto his horse and rode away, letting the warm Delta air cool his shirt, his neck, his burning face.

Step watched the cloud of dust grow smaller, then turned to Tobe and Birdie. He called them both down to him.

"Daddy?" Tobe said.

Step held his hands out toward his children.

"Ten dollars and a jar of marmalade," he told them. "I want you two t' remember this the rest a' your lives."

***

Lee Horton had never been let go from any job before, and it gnawed at him as much as losing his horse. By the time he'd reached the bottom of the office steps, he was envisioning hand-to-hand combat with the pompous owner of Sweet Hope, himself coming out the undisputed winner. He mounted the horse that only belonged to him for another twenty-four hours, and by the time he passed the gin mill, he had done battle with Step Hall and all the niggers of Sweet Hope. By the time he'd reached the levee road that led past the mule barn and stable to his shack, he had wiped out a couple dozen Dagoes and most of the other plantation managers for good measure, becoming a legend. He glanced down at the rifle in its sling, touched the stock. Let Gates try to take his rifle away, and see how far he got. To hell with the lot of them, he thought. His shack was sparse. He'd never given much thought to owning possessions. He pulled out a rucksack and stuffed in a few clothes, a couple pans, a knife, a couple tins of sardines, a tin of coffee, some cartridges. Then he found half a bottle of whiskey and sat at the table drinking it. The horse? Maybe he should take the horse, ride away right then. But then he remembered what he'd told Gates — out of his own mouth, damn it — about horse thieves being hung, and he cursed his bad luck, and cursed Gates and the whole damn place all over again. Damn those other managers, too, ready to denounce him now. It took all the strength he could muster to put the bottle down, lead the horse into the stable and unsaddle, feed and water him. He'd leave in the morning, damn it. Let that bastard Gates try to change his mind and take him back, but it would be too late.

He fumed all night, especially after the bottle ran out. It was past ten o'clock when he let himself into the commissary, lit a coal oil lamp turned low, and helped himself to a couple more bottles of liquor, a new shirt and hat, a couple plugs of tobacco, a box of slugs for his rifle, a tin of crackers, and a slab of salt pork — his due. Too bad he didn't know the combination to the safe. Before he left, he spat a gob of tobacco juice at the wall near the door, watched it dribble down. "There's your I.O.U.," he said.

He finished half of another bottle before he slept.

The sun had been up some time when the heat awakened him. He opened his eyes, startled at the bright light and how late it was.

He scanned the room, saw the whiskey bottles, the stuffed rucksack and bulging burlap sack, and the memory of the previous day hit him. He sat up slowly, only to discover he was fully clothed, and wearing his boots. Twenty–four hours, Gates had said.

He went to the door and peered out at the row of managers' shacks: no one there, but they'd be watching him.

He took his time lighting a fire, frying the salt pork with a can of beans. He ate from the pan, slowly, sitting on the stoop of his open door as he looked out over the fields at the toiling farmers. The fields were just at first picking. The clanging gin mill made his head throb. He dumped the pan on the ground and went to get his things.

Everyone was out picking or hauling loads. A few of the Italians looked at him askance, so that he wondered if word of his firing had gotten out already. As for Wade and Wright and the other managers, he could feel them out there somewhere in the fields, waiting for him to make an appearance. Probably just itching to make a big show of escorting him off the plantation if he wasn't gone by noon. He still had a couple hours.

He was nearing the Titus fields, and when he saw her — the one who'd caused half his trouble — he tried to catch her eye. She kept her head bowed as she picked, but he knew she'd seen him. He wanted to call out to her, taunt her — wring her neck, really — but the others were too close. He debated going after her right there with her family in the field, then dismissed the idea. A few of them sang a slow, thrumming work song that set him on edge, he couldn't say why. Far ahead, a horse emerged from the high cotton, and Horton ducked into the field and crouched under the plants before waiting to see which manager it was, or if he was headed his way. Keep the bastards on their toes, he figured, if they wanted to treat him like dirt.

He crouched in the cotton, one hand on the ground, listening to the sound of his own breathing against the droning work song. A movement caught his eye, and he drew his hand back as a small lizard skittered away. He couldn't think of a damn thing he'd miss about this place. While he waited for the road to clear, the idea struck him. He would take a shortcut through the bayou woods to avoid being seen, even though it meant he'd have to loop back up the way he'd already been heading. But it was a long way around the lake, and then into the village, and he didn't fancy the idea of hoofing it in the middle of a hot day. The Dago priest had a rowboat he almost never used, and with picking started, no one would be over at the lake. He'd take the boat and row across, then ditch it, let them think what they wanted.

He brushed off his pants and backtracked, keeping to the edge of the fields. The sun was hot and dust parched his throat, reminding him of his night of drinking. Good riddance to Sweet Hope, he thought.

He was a few hundred yards into the woods when he saw Lecie at the swamp's edge, the baby in a sling, like a sack of flour against her chest. "What the hell?" he said. Lecie stiffened before she turned around. "What you doin here? I just seen you out pickin, five minutes ago."

When she didn't answer, he grinned. "Don't tell me you come looking for me?" He ran his eyes up and down her body, considering.

"I always known you was a little whore," he told her. "Bringin your baby along, besides, now that's low." He paused. "Well — ain't you gonna let me see that baby everybody's raisin such hell over?" He squinted at the fine red hair on the back of the baby's head while the boy squirmed and tried to turn in the direction of his voice. Lecie drew an arm around the child as she backed away. Horton followed. "Hey. Where you think you're goin? Thought you wanted somethin from me."

She looked down at the ground, as if picking her way over stones, then climbed onto a bulging cypress root that protruded from the water a foot from shore. She hefted the baby in its sling to readjust its weight and steady herself.

Horton was in no mood for games. His head hurt and the day was growing hotter. "Crazy nigger. You gonna jump in th' swamp wi' your baby?"

For answer, Lecie inched farther around the cypress tree, carefully inching herself over the mucky water.

"I ain't got all day." He cocked his head, trying to figure out what she was up to. "You don't wanna make me mad now."

Every time he took a step forward she retreated farther behind the tree. He tried to keep his anger at bay, so as to coax her out. "You gonna drop that baby in the swamp," he said. "You tryin t' get your baby killed on purpose?" Then he laughed, trying to cajole her. "Come on out, honey, afore you get hurt. I ain't mad 'bout what happened. Just let me give you a little goodbye present."

She was completely out of sight behind the big tree now. He knew he would hurt her when he got his hands on her, and he could barely control the anger in his voice. "What the damn hell's wrong w' you? I gotta come drag you outta there?" He stepped to the edge of the swamp and the air cracked loudly. His rifle and sack of belongings flew out across the swamp and landed with splats on the fetid surface. In the same instant, a shadow shot across the water, accompanied by a scream, as Lee Horton himself was yanked into the air.

Lecie made her way around the other side of the tree and back onto land. Horton was swinging upside down over the muck, one leg caught in Osvaldo's snare, his other leg dangling, while his arms flailed helplessly. He kept trying to reach up for his ankle, to free himself, but every time he moved, the branch creaked lower, moving his head closer to the swamp water. Lecie backed away, holding the baby. It babbled and waved its arms.

"Help me," Horton cried. "Hurry up, gal." When she didn't move, he cursed louder. "You daft, you damn crazy nigger? Go get help, hurry up." With each shout and wave of his arms, his body dipped closer to the swamp.

His hands splashed the mucky water. "God a'mighty," he cried.

Lecie stood watching, her face expressionless.

Horton lunged for the rope that held him, making the bough bend closer to the swamp. Lecie hitched her baby up in her arms, turned the child to face the swamp, and the boy's big eyes looked this way and that and his arm reached out at the air.

"Lecie, run git help quick, you tryin t' kill me? Ain't you a Christian? You gon' burn in hell, girl." Horton's body contorted like some giant, writhing snake, trying to twist back and climb up itself. Finally, exhausted, he let himself dangle while he gathered his strength again. He felt his pockets for the knife he carried, but the pockets were empty. After a few moments he screamed for help, in spite of their distance from the cotton fields. His arms sank into the swamp, and when he brought them up oozing yellow mud he cried out in horror. "God, help me!"

When his red hair finally touched the water, he let out a wrenching scream. "Lecie, God a'mighty, girl, do something."

Lecie watched dispassionately.

The bough creaked. Horton choked and sputtered and arched his neck in an attempt to raise his heavy, exhausted body at the waist. When that failed, he patted at the water, as if he would finally find some solid surface to push off from. He cried out again for help.

Then another creak, and the bough dropped lower, and Lee Horton's face went under.

He flailed at the swamp, churning the thick ooze and mud and stinking water. One hand emerged and groped for his leg and the rope that held him, while his body bucked and twisted. Finally, the flailing slowed, and then all movement stopped. The water rippled slowly about his chest.

Lecie bent to pick up her root sack before sliding out of the woods. She did not look back. Behind her came the loud crack of the bough breaking, and then the heavy splat of the branch falling into the muck. Then silence.

CHAPTER 26

Taking Leave

September 1906

THE September air was soft against Serafin's skin, the air muted in the slanted golden light near end of day, as if something living were suspended among the motes of dust.

Some farmers had already started picking. Life would go on as it had, in spite of all that had happened. Lazzaro would become his *pad'in* again. Step Hall's pain would subside. But only God knew if they would ever be able to face each other as friends again. It seemed hopeless. He counted the months on his fingers. By spring they would have a baby. People would talk, as they were already. And they would recover from that, too. They would pick their cotton, and gin and sell it, and maybe get a little closer to coming out of debt. Maybe not.

And Italy? They might never see their homeland again. They might never leave Sweet Hope. And the pain of that would subside, too, and they would endure. Life would go on.

When managers Wade and Wright came galloping through his cotton, he was not alarmed. Even with their shouting "Home, get home, now," it took him moments to come back to the world of hard edges. And even then, he was calm inside as he moved — trotted — in the direction they prodded him.

His family came out when they heard the shouting.

Wade gave them the news. The Pascalas would spend the night under guard in the church at the levee; at first light they'd be taken by ferry across the river and put on a train for Memphis. Once off the train, they were free to find work and living quarters where they could. The company was confiscating their cotton, their chickens and vegetable gardens, household goods, anything of value as partial repayment of their debts. Once they found work, they would still owe the rest.

He had felt it coming. Not this, but something.

His wife and children were like a flock of startled birds rising from the water after gunshot. "What are you talking about?" Amalia kept demanding. "What do you mean?"

Serafin faced the managers. "Why are you tormenting us?"

"Get moving. One small sack for each adult," Wade told them.

"They're not lying?" Amalia motioned the frightened children behind her, away from the managers. "You can't take everything away, just like that."

"Mr. Gates can do whatever he wants," Wade answered wearily.

"You can't just kick us out on a minute's notice," Serafin told the men. His mind was racing: Where were they going? Would they be harmed? What was the company up to now? "Look, we need more time."

"You've been grousing about wanting to leave since you came here," Wright said. "Now you're grousing that Mr. Gates says you can go?"

Of course they wanted to leave, start fresh somewhere where they had half a chance — but not like this, with no warning, like rats beaten out of an empty larder.

Serafin turned toward the road. "I'll find out what these *merda cani* are up to," he told his family.

Wade stopped him. "I told you, get packing, we'll be back in an hour."

"I go see Lazzaro, my *pad'in*, " Serafin answered. The word was like gall on his tongue.

"You'll see plenty of him tonight," Wade said. "He's leaving with you."

"Everybody leaving? No more Sweet Hope?"

Wright grunted.

"Just you two families," Wade told him.

"Just the troublemakers," Wright said as they turned to go.

Troublemakers, Serafin thought. It had to be about the strike. He thought of Ettore and his family, and the others who had expressed even halfhearted interest in striking. But he dared not mention their names.

Angelina's hands went to her stomach, and her face clouded over.

"What about my flying machine?" Osvaldo fretted.

"Serafin, what have you done to us?" Amalia cried. She looked at their yard, as if seeing the house and chicken shed and cotton for the first time. The outhouse, a washtub and bucket outside the door, *the forno,* the watering trough. "This is what comes of your big plans? Your big strike? My God, just when I started to believe in you — "

He was trembling as he held his arm out to calm them. "Everything's okay, don't worry."

"Jackasses!" Isola said. "We signed a contract. We should have gone on strike."

"Start packing," Serafin told them. "In case it's true." He felt hot, dazed.

"Who's going to pick our cotton?" Osvaldo asked.

He brushed them aside. "Doing this in the night, in the dark." He thought of going to see Step, but there was no time, and besides, what could Step Hall do for them now — even if he would see them?

"Listen, Amalia, if we think this through, if we just stay calm — "

"Calm? I'm calm. There's nothing left inside me. Let the wind blow me — here, there, what does it matter?" She herded the children inside to begin packing.

He walked around the yard in the dying light. No matter what the company had in mind, he vowed that not a hair on his family's heads would be touched. He saw himself fighting off the managers, then saw Step's fist coming at him. "God," he moaned.

He stopped outside the chicken shed. They had six chickens now, red and black hens, and two white bantams. The first one, Old Shoe, was hardly laying anymore, but he had refused to kill her. It crossed his mind to kill the bird then, but he shook the thought away. No time to clean and cook a chicken. That bird would not end up on his plate, no matter what.

It pained him, though, to think what the company would do with their belongings. Give them away, to the stinking managers? To the no-good priest? He wondered if the priest even knew what was happening. Maybe he was in on it. Serafin passed the *forno*. He had pried every stone, carried every rock and grain of sand himself to build it. What did it matter? The world was full of rocks and sand.

He went into the house. The table was strewn with cooking utensils, Amalia's sewing basket, a jacket, a pair of boots; a pot of beans cooked on the stove. In the bedroom, Amalia was directing the children to separate their few clothes into piles: the ones they needed most; those they could do without.

"This is awful," he said.

She held up a pair of his pants, torn at the thigh. "I was going to mend these." The statue of the Blessed Virgin lay on the bed next to a folded blanket.

"Yes, yes, don't throw them out," he told her.

"Mama, I want all my clothes," Osvaldo said.

"Put them on," she told the children. "Two shirts, two pairs of pants, everything."

"It's too hot," Osvaldo said.

"The more you wear, the more room in the sacks for other things."

Isola pulled a second dress over her first.

Serafin lifted the corner of his mattress and pulled out the tobacco tin while Amalia eyed him silently.

"What is it, Daddy?" Angelina asked.

He opened the tin, relieved to see the two American dollars.

"Money?" the children asked.

"You carry it," Amalia told him. "At least we'll have that."

He closed his fist around the tin and put it in his pocket.

***

Dusk fell quickly. When the wagon arrived with Lazzaro's family and Claudio hunched in back, the Pascalas went out to meet it. Lazzaro turned his open palms up as if to say — what? It's not my fault, who could have imagined?

The managers carried lanterns inside to make a quick search of the house, then came out and began nosing through their sacks. Wright pulled out the coffee grinder and tossed it in the dirt, and Osvaldo ran to retrieve it.

"We have to grind our coffee," Serafin told the man.

"Drink water," Wright answered. He took the grinder from the protesting boy and tossed it farther away into the darkness. When he found a couple of girls' dresses and a sweater that weren't tattered, he set them aside too.

"Our clothes," Amalia protested. Some were clothes they hadn't worn since their first Christmas, when the American priest never showed up. She didn't know why she had held onto them all this time.

"It's okay, Amalia," Serafin said. "If the company can sell them, take it off our debt, better for us, no?"

Wade inspected the large, flat sieve, and held it up to show Wright. Wright shook his head. "Maybe if we were panning for gold." They threw the sieve and the sacks in the wagon, and the Pascalas started to climb in. Isola carried the pot of nearly-cooked beans that was to have been their supper.

"I'm not going," Angelina said.

Her mother pushed her ahead. "*Pazza*, get in."

Wright stopped Amalia. "What's that?" he said, indicating the bundle in her arms.

She pulled back, furious with the man for touching their personal belongings. "Holy lady," she said.

Wright and Wade exchanged looks. Wright moved the cloth aside to investigate. "Leave it here," he told her.

Amalia clutched the statue. "Mine, I bring from Italy."

"Maybe worth a dollar," Wade said. He moved to take the statue from Amalia, and she fought him off.

"Hey, don't touch my wife," Serafin yelled at the men, and they stopped in surprise.

Serafin tried to explain, but Wright interrupted him. "When you owe the company, nothing belongs to you." He wrestled the statue from Amalia as she cursed and slapped at him, and he stepped back nervously.

"Never mind, don't cry," Serafin told her. "It's only a statue."

"My mother's — it's always been in our house."

"Broken besides," Wright said. He tossed it gently into the dirt. "Better than nothing."

Amalia pushed past her husband and ran to retrieve the statue.

"Amalia!" Serafin called.

She turned on the manager as she clutched the statue. "*Basta*," she yelled at him. "She's mine, I keep her. You want her, you shoot me."

"Mama," her children cried.

"*Oh santo cielo*," Fiorenza murmured from the wagon, and she drew her frightened son close.

"Please," Serafin begged his wife.

She shook a fist at the men. "I rip you with my hands," she threatened them.

Wright shook his head, keeping his distance. "What's with these crazy Dagoes? Want I should go after her?"

"To hell with it," Wade answered. "It's no good anyway." He motioned Amalia into the wagon.

The Pascalas settled stiffly beside the Lazzaros. Claudio moved aside to make room for Angelina, but she ignored him. Amalia hugged the statue and glared out at their yard. A small white hump caught her eye: a broken white doily bowl that lay amid the pile of their belongings. And then Wade slapped the mules forward.

Serafin eyed Lazzaro. They'd barely spoken to each other lately. "It's one thing if you don't agree with me," he said. "But to go shouting my plans where all these bastards can hear — "

"It wasn't like that. I didn't."

"Eh, now you get what you deserve," Serafin told him.

Fiorenza raised a warning hand to quiet the men.

"Quit your jabbering," Wright yelled at them from his horse.

They watched the shadowy yard — the chickens ruffling in the dirt, the few tomatoes growing at the edge of the house, the *forno* almost hidden by the high cotton — disappear into darkness. The cotton rustled slightly as a faint breeze stirred it.

And something stirred in Serafin, too, as if a cool breeze were coming through and clearing out the dust. He sat forward, studying the shadowy fields as the breeze passed through. He glanced over at Wade where he sat driving the wagon, then at Wright who rode his horse alongside the mules, leading Wade's empty horse by the reins, then at Amalia holding her statue. So this is what it came to: no beatings or chain gang or jail, no murder. Just the managers driving them to the levee, sending them off somewhere in America. He nodded to Amalia. "You see? *Hanno paura di noi.*"

"Afraid of us?" her eyes said. "I don't think so."

The land was dark, the fields empty, although the gin mill sounded at the levee. Lazzaro held one dim lantern for them in back, and it threw a feeble light on them. He narrowed his eyes, fuming, conflicted, and said nothing.

As the wagon lurched onto the levee road and headed north, Fiorenza let out a sob. "Mama," she cried, straining to see beyond the darkened fields all the way to Hyner cemetery. "What have I done to her, leaving her in this cursed place?"

Angelina stiffened. She stared coldly at the woman as Amalia patted her friend's arm.

***

Wade and Wright herded them into the church, and hung a couple lanterns for light. Two sleeping pallets had been laid down just inside the door, for the managers. The others would have to sleep on the bare floor.

"We damn well better get paid extra," Wright said, looking disdainfully at the pallets.

The air was closed-up and dusty; the building held nothing but a table and benches.

"What's wrong?" Wright said to them. "You don't like your hotel?"

The Italians dropped their bundles and sat on the benches. Satisfied, the managers went outside.

Getulio saw a frog hop into the shadows under the short altar table and called for Osvaldo to help him catch it, but Osvaldo merely squinted into the shadows.

Fiorenza turned to Amalia. "This isn't Lazzaro's fault. He's not the only one Serafin talked to."

"I know," Amalia said "He knows too."

She shooed Osvaldo away as they began moving benches aside to make a place for their families to rest. Getulio crawled under the rickety table Father Odetti used as an altar and hunched there, watching the adults.

Serafin paced the room.

"Where are we going?" Isola asked.

"We'll find out soon enough," he answered.

"Pulling us out at a time like this," Lazzaro said. "Well, you got what you wanted, *pad'in*. And dragged us into this besides."

"*Eh, merda*," Serafin said.

Claudio shrugged. "We don't know. Maybe they're just trying to scare us like they do."

Serafin gazed at the dark window.

"Maybe if we went to the village," Isola whispered to her mother. "Maybe the Halls' friend William can help us. Or Reverend Monroe."

"Hush," Amalia said, checking to make sure Serafin hadn't heard. "Don't say those names."

"But they're nice people."

"It's too late for nice people," Amalia said. "Never mind the village."

Angelina miserably eyed Getulio. She tried to imagine the thing inside her as real, living, a baby that would turn into a boy like him. But the boy had nothing to do with her. She hugged herself as it hit her, worse than ever: Calvin — gone. She could not believe he was dead. His bruised and bloody face haunted her, the last image she'd had of him. She could not imagine what he had suffered. If she'd only agreed to leave with him right away, maybe they would have gotten out in time to save him.

Osvaldo had dragged a bench to the window and was peering out, up into the black branches of the giant oak. They had chosen a tall loblolly pine in the woods, and it was all his idea. They were going to use Tobe's pulley to hoist him up to a high branch, then they would attach the wings to his arms, and then he would jump, and fly. The wings were made from thin scraps of wood and tin. Isola made them fix a harness with a rope, to keep him from falling to the ground in case the wings didn't work. But he didn't need a harness to keep him safe.

Smoke drifted toward the boy, from the smudge fire the managers had lit to keep the mosquitoes away. Bats swooped through the dark air near the tree. "Mama," Osvaldo asked, "is it true we have guardian angels?"

Amalia stopped in the middle of laying down a blanket. "Does it look like we do?" she answered.

Serafin went to the window, ignoring her comment. The managers were sitting on tree stumps near the fire, their rifles propped against the building, spitting tobacco juice and talking. Their unsaddled horses were tied under a tree; they'd already walked the mules down to the mule yard for the night.

"Look at those bastards," Serafin said to no one in particular. "We may as well be under arrest."

Lazzaro moved in to get a look. "Maybe we should jump them, you know?"

"You're a fine one to come up with that now," Serafin said. "And then what? They'll drive us out one way or another, if that's what they want. We should be glad we're leaving this shit hole."

"That's right," Amalia said. Her words stopped him, and he wondered anxiously if she was trying to tell him that she was with him after all — or something else.

"Are we going back to Italy?" Isola asked. She sat a couple rows down from Angelina, following her father with her eyes as he started pacing the room again.

"They mentioned Memphis," Serafin told them. Step and Fred Titus had talked of Italian farmers living outside Memphis, doing all right. Sant'Angelo, too, had talked of it. He slid his hand into his pocket, feeling for the tobacco tin.

Claudio sidled closer to Angelina. All this time he had been wanting to say something, let her know he wasn't like the others, even though her softly rounding belly frightened him a little. She scowled, to warn him away.

"It's okay," he told her anyway. "Everything will work out."

"Why are you talking to me?"

He stammered. "It's just... I thought you looked worried. Trying to be friendly, that's all."

She stiffened. All she could think of was Calvin. All she cared about was Calvin. Claudio was a fool. She dismissed him with a wave of her hand. "Go play with the little boy over there," she told him.

Isola snickered as Claudio retreated.

The room was nearly pitch dark, except for the feeble light thrown out by the lanterns. The smell of kerosene hung in the room. "Don't you think it's odd that they dumped us in this building and they're not even checking up on us?" Serafin said to the others. "For all they know we could have slipped out the windows." The others looked over at the windows facing the woods and the river.

"And sneak away where?" Fiorenza said. "Back to our farms they just kicked us off of?"

"I tell you," he said. "We have more power than we think."

"That's why they have guns?" Lazzaro said sarcastically. "When we have none — we're that powerful?"

"Maybe the idea of a strike shook them up," Serafin said. "See? It could have worked." He shot Lazzaro an accusing look.

"I think you're dreaming."

"Sending us off in the night, so no one will know," Serafin said. "If we were nothing to them, they'd just slap more charges on us and leave us to rot in debt as always."

"I don't know," Claudio said. "Maybe they don't want to kill us in front of everyone, make a scene."

Fiorenza covered her boy's ears. "Enough," she scolded. "That's a fine way to talk in front of the children."

Serafin considered the young man. "I think they want to get rid of us before anybody else has a chance to speak up." Even in the dim light, the anger was evident on his face. "The whole plantation would want to leave with us if they knew."

"Even if you're right," Lazzaro said, "what about when we get to wherever the hell they're sending us? We can cause trouble for big shot Gates if we tell people what's going on here."

"Eh, if people believe us," Fiorenza said. "Maybe that's what they're counting on, that nobody believes a bunch of crazy Dagoes."

***

When the children complained of hunger, Amalia pulled out the stale loaf of bread, and they dipped it into the pot of beans. She had to put a lantern down beside the food so they could see what they were eating.

"What will we eat tomorrow?" Isola asked.

It was the same thing she had been wondering. "Let tomorrow take care of itself," she told the girl.

Again, Serafin went to the window that faced the road, hoping to catch a glimpse of someone, something, even in the dark. The fire threw out only a small circle of light. Beyond the dirt road lay fields belonging to farmers he didn't know. Hardly anyone ever came up here, north of the landing, unless they were going to church on Sunday or heading for one of the few farms up this way. No one would be coming here in the night.

"I wonder if he knows," Serafin said, although they'd hardly been able to face each other and speak in the last week or so. "He'd come if he knew."

Amalia, too, glanced at the window. "Maybe he can't."

The door was closed, the managers just a few yards beyond it. "No," Serafin said. The company wouldn't lay a hand on the Halls, not after they'd lost their boy.

Angelina paced along one wall, her hands clasped over her belly, as she tried to ignore the adults' murmurings. Something was tugging at her, dividing her in half, and it chilled her, even in the warm night. Each time she passed the window, another shade of darkness seemed to descend. She leaned against the wall, folded her arms across her chest, and let out a wretched sigh.

She thought of Lecie's baby, and pale, red–haired Horton. But her own skin was dark, and her hair almost as dark and curly as Calvin's. Her hand went to her hair, and she ran her fingers through, separating long strands and twining them around her fingers. She tried to imagine holding a baby in her arms, seeing his face in the infant's. But no, she was alone. It was impossible.

"Mama, I'm not leaving," she said. "I'm sorry. I can't go. I won't."

"What?" Amalia said. She stared at the girl. "What did you do with your hair?" Half of it hung loose while the other half was fixed into long, thin braids.

Isola laughed at the sight.

"I'll live here alone," Angelina said. "Or I'll stay with the Halls." Her voice was shaking. "I can't go with Calvin here." As soon as she said his name aloud, her heart started pounding. "I want him to see his baby."

Amalia threw her arms in the air and turned to Serafin. "See? She gets this from you!"

"It's just her heart talking," Fiorenza assured them. "Too much for everybody." She tried to put a comforting arm around Angelina, but the girl pulled away.

Amalia turned back to her daughter. "The Halls won't have anything to do with you — why would they want such a reminder?"

"Look," Serafin said, trying to calm the two, "the company's already decided matters for us." He gestured around the room. "We're here now."

"It's you they're mad at, not me," Angelina shouted. "What do they care about a Dago girl with a Negro baby?"

The words struck like swords.

"If the priest was here, I'd make you say confession this minute," Amalia cried. She raised her eyes to the ceiling. "In God's house, besides. *Disgrazia*." But her words rang empty in her own ears.

"What do I care about the priest?" Angelina shot back. "I'm not a Catholic anymore. I don't know what I am anymore."

"I can beat you right here in front of everyone," Amalia shouted at her daughter.

"Beat me," Angelina said. "It won't change anything."

CHAPTER 27

Morning

September 1906

A dampness they were unaccustomed to filled the night air, the water lifting off the great river, and seeping from the earth and grasses along the levee and from the trees, all so close. Frogs and peepers sang out, and a lone bird called repeatedly under the quarter moon while mosquitoes buzzed around their heads. And then there was the incessant thumping and clanging of the gin mill that finally stopped at ten. It would only start up again at five in the morning. Knots of anxiety moved among them like crawling, biting insects. Finally, they slept.

When an owl screeched, Amalia's eyes flew open. She raised herself on her elbows to look around at the dark shadows that were her children, and the knot came back. She knew she was the one to blame for Angelina's behavior, and for everything her children had suffered. Didn't a daughter learn from her mother, after all? As if in reply to her thoughts, Osvaldo groaned and turned over. Was it possible that she herself had brought damnation upon her children with her own sinful thoughts and behavior? She had failed all of them. In the name of God she promised right then, once they left Sweet Hope, if they didn't end up in a worse hell, she would be a better mother. But the vow seemed hollow. What did she know of being a mother?

"Serafin," she whispered. "Are you awake?"

He stirred beside her. "What is it?"

Words failed her. "I don't know."

"It's okay," he mumbled. "Once we get settled. You'll see." He wanted to sleep, so he could forget, that was all. There would be time for worry and regret when they were awake. But the peace and stillness he had felt earlier while walking his field eluded him.

Amalia sighed, brushed an insect from her face, and stared into the blackness above.

Serafin muttered something unintelligible. She tried to search her heart, to find a little room that belonged to him. All she found was a wall of doors shrouded in mist, each one shut. She reached out and clasped Serafin's hand, wishing she could take back all her hateful words and actions. We each become two people here, she thought, the rind and the fruit. One bite bitter, one bite sweet.

✳✳✳

THE clang of the company work bell woke them. Soon the gin mill boilers were being fired up, and the managers rose and went outside to the foggy, pre-dawn light. Amalia lit a lamp and went to the stove to build a fire. A rusty pan sat on the stove, and she thought she would at least boil some water, even if there was nothing to cook. Serafin came to her, bleary-eyed. "Get the children up," she told him. "We have to be ready."

But Angelina was missing.

"She's probably in the outhouse," Serafin said.

"I knew something was going to happen," Amalia told him.

Wright came back from checking the privy, shaking his head, his worried expression alarming the others. "She must've snuck off in the night while we was sleepin."

"She said she didn't want to leave," Fiorenza reminded them.

"How the hell'd she get past without wakin us up?" Wade said, glancing at the windows, then the door. "Damn it to hell."

They spread out into the bushes and trees behind the church, calling for her. Amalia ventured into the overgrowth, startled at all the dangers out there if you couldn't see where you were going: brambles, fallen logs, the river.

"What if we don't find her?" Isola asked.

"Keep moving," Amalia commanded.

They lit a lamp and searched the closed lumber mill and an empty cotton pen while Lazzaro, Claudio and Serafin looked in widening circles around the church. Wade rode out to the Pascala farm, thinking she might have gone back there. "Nothing," he shouted, on his return.

"Will she die?" Osvaldo asked.

Serafin gave him a shake to quiet him, then glanced over to see if Amalia had heard.

"Maybe she went somewhere to have her baby," Osvaldo said. "Won't we ever see her again?"

Isola took her brother's hand and led him away from their mother. But now she was frightened. For all her fighting with Angelina, she didn't want to lose her.

"The damn ferry's gonna be leaving," Wright announced.

Amalia ran to the road and across, into the cotton, shouting for Angelina, and Wade had to go and bring her back.

Finally Wade called a halt to the search. "We're leaving without her."

"*Idiota. Scemo,*" Amalia shrieked. "You think I'm leaving my daughter?"

Osvaldo began turning in circles, waving his arms and shrilling strange, unintelligible sounds.

Serafin grabbed the boy. "What the hell are you doing?"

"Calling Angelina," he said.

"Into the wagon," the managers ordered them. Wright pulled his rifle from the sling and nudged his horse around the side. "I'll keep an eye on them," he said. "We don't want another one of them running off."

"Easy," Wade said, motioning the rifle back.

The gun was nothing to Serafin. "See?" he told the others, meaning: *They're bluffing; they won't shoot us.*

"She'll show up, *amico*," Lazzaro tried to reassure them.

"We can't go without her!" Amalia cried. But they climbed into the wagon as told.

Wade motioned Wright up front.

"What do we do when she turns up — afterwards?" Wright asked. "If she turns up?"

Wade glanced back at the others who were calling for Angelina from the wagon. "Mr. Gates doesn't have to know anything about this. Understand?" He slapped the mules forward.

The Italians quieted with the sudden movement. They strained to see into the fields as they rode along the foggy levee road to the landing.

Every few moments Amalia called Angelina's name, and with each passing moment her heart sank deeper.

Fiorenza held the whimpering Getulio tightly to her bosom.

"We should resist," Isola blurted. "We should stand together and strike."

Serafin pulled Isola to his side. "Shh," he told her. "That's what got us in trouble in the first place."

Osvaldo squinted into the dark, sucking in his lower lip. "I wanted to see her baby."

Only a few men were at the landing, beginning work at the gin mill. Below at the river, the ferry sat shrouded in the haze, with two ghostly Americans standing at the dock. The managers prodded the Italians down the steps.

Amalia balked on the steps. "Do something, Serafin," she cried.

He tried to explain to the managers: "Don't you understand? We can't go without our daughter." His own heart was pounding. "What kind of animals are you?"

Wade pushed them forward. "On board, go." But his voice was shaking.

"You said they were bluffing," Amalia yelled at Serafin. "You said she'd show up." She grabbed the railing and held fast. "Shoot me!" she screamed at the managers. "I don't leave without my girl."

When Wade could not pry her hands free, he ordered Serafin to make his wife move, to no avail.

"Not without our girl," Serafin repeated.

The two men on the dock watched the spectacle. "Everything okay?" one of them called.

"All under control," Wade yelled to them. Cursing, he grabbed a rope from his horse. With a nod to Wright to keep the others at bay with his rifle, he bound Serafin's hands behind his back. In the next instant, as Amalia ran at him flailing her arms, he slung her over his shoulder and carried her on board. Wright trained his rifle on the group of screaming Italians as he dragged the bound Serafin onto the deck, and they followed.

The children wailed and called for help as Wade bound the kicking and cursing Amalia with another length of rope and lashed her to the railing.

"*Animali*," Fiorenza screamed at the managers.

"You'll roast in hell for this," Serafin shouted as he struggled to break free of Wright's hold.

Yet even up to the end he believed that the managers would finally back down. They all watched the shore, expecting Angelina to appear at any minute.

Then the ferry started moving. Amalia let out a piercing wail. Osvaldo cupped his hands to his mouth and imitated her cry.

"What the hell's wrong with you?" Serafin said, struggling to free himself. "If anything happens to our girl — "

"Nothing's going to happen," Wade answered, shaken. "She's probably off chasing after some boy."

Serafin threw a kick at the man, but he jumped out of the way. "Easy, old man," Wade told him. "Don't make it worse for yourself."

Finally, a distance from shore, they untied Amalia and Serafin. Serafin swung at Wright, catching him in the jaw. Amalia spat at Wade and slapped at his face.

Before Serafin knew what was happening, Amalia had flung one leg over the railing.

"No," he cried. He caught her skirt and pulled her back. "What in God's name are you trying to do? You'll kill yourself."

"Let me go," she cried. "I'll swim back for her. I won't go without her."

Serafin turned on the managers. "I'll kill you for this, I swear. Turn this boat around."

"Impossible," Wade answered, keeping his distance. "Can't change course in the middle of the current."

Isola backed away from them. She was glad now that she had no boyfriend, and she prayed she never had one if this is what it did to people. She folded down her two middle fingers and extended the first and fourth, in the sign of *il corno*, and held her hand out at the managers.

Serafin pulled Amalia close to him, his arms encircling her thin, trembling shoulders, and finally she broke down. "She's strong," he told her. "Strong–willed, like you. She knows what she's doing. She knows how to survive."

But his wife could not be consoled.

"The priest will look out for her," Fiorenza said.

"She'd spit in that priest's face," Amalia cried against Serafin's shoulder. "You heard her."

He gave her his shirtsleeve to dry her eyes, and she took it, then shook out her own kerchief. She stared at the river in disbelief as she dabbed at her eyes.

"You'd think he'd be here now, if he cared about us," Claudio said. "It's the priest's job to look out for his people."

"The priest," Lazzaro said. "Just forget about the priest. He's a crook like the rest of them."

"She said she wanted to stay with the Halls," Fiorenza reminded them.

And there it was again for Serafin: *Abbandonato.* It was the most alone he had felt since setting foot on Sweet Hope.

Fiorenza rubbed Amalia's back to comfort her while Lazzaro held Getulio. "God will watch out for her."

"She doesn't want God either," Osvaldo said, and Serafin silenced the boy with a stern shake of the arm.

"You should be quiet," Isola told him. "You're making mama cry more."

Osvaldo pressed his hands to the sides of his head and squinted into the haze. The ferry gave a short blast of its horn, and the floor shuddered beneath them as they moved farther into the current.

Serafin watched the shore. Ghostly trees were emerging from the fog. It was all a dream, an unreal dream that was really happening to them. Was it possible that they were leaving Sweet Hope at last, but without their daughter?

"As soon as these Americans let us go, I'll come back," he told his family. "I'll find her."

The others did not say what they were thinking: How would it be possible to sneak onto Sweet Hope property?

"Somehow," he said. "I'll find her." The words were hollow in his throat.

The ferry moved slowly into the thick fog that rose from the river. Serafin held his sobbing wife; his own heart was rent. He stared at the hazy, receding shore and prayed for Angelina's safety while his mind raced ahead, imagining where she might be hiding, and what might become of her. "Keep her safe," he prayed aloud. And then he added another, silent prayer: that someday his children would forget there ever had been such a place as Sweet Hope.

Osvaldo turned back to his mother. "Don't worry, mama," he said. "She's eating bread, and she's happy."

A heron swooped out of the fog, startling them as it glided close to the ferry. "A ghost," Osvaldo said.

Serafin looked at the place the bird had been. The wisps of fog had turned the air palpable. The fog was moving, disintegrating before his eyes. Soon the sun would be rising.

He strained to see a shadow of a man standing on the levee. Step Hall? he wondered, relief and anger and pain mingling in him. It looked as if the man's hand was raised, and Serafin raised his own hand. His throat tightened. That awful feeling tore at his stomach, an emptiness that choked him. The touch — he felt it, for just one moment, then nothing, air.

***

STEP Hall stood at the top of the levee, watching the ferry depart through the early morning fog. He held his hand up, not knowing if they could see him. The heron swooped out of the mist, almost clipping the side of the boat. Then it was gone.

Inside him, something slipped, as though he'd lost his grip on a heavy sack. Below at the landing a few people went about their work. Nothing. He was empty. He watched until the ferry was just a small dark spot across the wide river. He had heard them crying and shouting as he'd stood there watching, and it had chilled him. Now they were gone. Even their voices were gone.

He turned and walked slowly a few yards along the levee to where a stand of trees grew down one side all the way to the water. He knew she was there, he had felt her the whole time, and now he waited to see if she would move. When she didn't, he called to her: "What you doin in there?"

Finally, the girl crept out, dazed and dirtied from her long restless night. She looked smaller than he'd remembered: thin and short, with her belly just starting to round out, that was clear as anything now. And her hair, done crazy, half of it twisted into thin braids, the other half hanging loose. It startled him to see her now, in the flesh, this close up, a woman, yet not much more than a child.

From where she'd crouched in the bushes, she'd have had a good view of the boat pulling away.

He said it anyway: "They're gone."

She stifled a sob.

He looked her up and down a moment, then reached a hand out to help her onto the levee. "Gotta git pickin that cotton," he said, more gruffly than he'd intended. She lowered her head, and he felt bad for sounding so harsh.

"You hungry?"

She shrugged.

"Don't even know if you're hungry?" Again, the gruff voice. His insides were turning. He couldn't have said how he felt if his life depended on it.

He started walking, but she didn't move. After a moment he said, "Come on, then."

She followed behind him along the levee and then down a narrow lane into the fields. He slowed to let her catch up.

"Fancy gonna worry what keepin us if we ain't home soon," he told her.

She nodded.

The mist was lifting. It was going to be another hot day.

AFTERWORD

In 1907, a Federal investigation brought charges of peonage and violations of alien labor laws against the owners of the Arkansas plantation that inspired *Sweet Hope*. Although acquitted, the owners agreed to make some significant changes that resulted in a number of Italians paying their debts and leaving. By 1912, flood damage, a boll weevil infestation, and new restrictions on the recruitment of Italians by the company's Italian labor agents further reduced the number of immigrant farmers. Between 1910 and 1920, African Americans once again became the plantation's main source of labor, with only a handful of Italians remaining. The plantation changed hands several times, and fire destroyed a number of buildings, including the cotton gin and company store. In 1927, the Great Flood wiped out almost all remaining traces of the once-thriving "Italian Colony Experiment."

ACKNOWLEDGEMENTS

THANK you to all those who have helped make *Sweet Hope* a reality.

PASQUINA Fratini Galavotti, Marietta (Mary) Rotondo, and Pauline Teresa Galavotti Bucci Bush.

AND Lorrraine Bruno Arsenault, Wendy Belcher, Randolph Boehm, Mary Jo Bona, David Bucci Bush, Kathryn Bucci Bush, Mary Russo Demetrick, Rachel Guido deVries, Tish DeMauro and Dean Dickinson, Sally Daniels Dike, Marilyn Elkins, Maria Famà, Montserrat Fontes, Dan Foster, Fred Gardaphè, Maria Mazziotti Gillan, Mary Ellen Kavanaugh and My Sister's Words Bookstore (Syracuse), Ellen Krout–Hasegawa, Audrey May and Meristem Bookstore (Memphis), Kathleen McHugh, Ernesto Milani, Margaret Galavotti Miller, Susan and Thomas Bucci Mockler, Harryette Mullen, Susan Murphy, Sylvia Needel, the Nodini families, cousin Patti, Patricia Pritchard, Gloria Montebruno Saller, Kenneth Scambray, Marsha Sumner, Anthony Julian Tamburri, Douglas Unger, Pasquale Verdicchio, Mary and Joseph Verro, Alice Wexler.

ALSO, AIHA (The American Italian Historical Association), California State University Los Angeles, CSULA Munitz Award, Chico County (Arkansas) records office, Hamilton College Women's Research Grant, The Millay Colony for the

Arts, The National Endowment for the Arts, Syracuse Women's Information Center.

FINALLY, the many residents of Lake Village, Arkansas and environs who opened their homes and their hearts to me.

PUBLICATIONS

THE following chapters from the novel *Sweet Hope* have been published in slightly different versions:

"Drowning" in the anthology *From the Margin: Writings in Italian Americana*, 2nd edition, eds. Tamburri, Gardaphè, Giordano. Purdue University Press, 2000.

"Drowning" in the anthology *Growing Up Ethnic in America*, eds. M. Mazziotti Gillan, J. Gillan. Penguin, 1999.

Drowning. Chapbook. Parentheses Writing Series, 1995.

"Planting" in the anthology *The Voices We Carry: Recent Italian American Women's Fiction*, ed. Mary Jo Bona. Guernica Editions, 1994 & 2000.

"Mule" in *VIA (Voices in Italian Americana)*. 1997.

"Love" in anthology *HERS 2: Brilliant New Fiction by Lesbian Writers*, eds. Terry Wolverton & Robert Drake. Faber & Faber, 1997.

www.marybuccibush.com